12776064

RAGE OF
Ares

Also by Christian Cameron

THE TYRANT SERIES

Tyrant
Tyrant: Storm of Arrows
Tyrant: Funeral Games
Tyrant: King of the Bosporus
Tyrant: Destroyer of Cities
Tyrant: Force of Kings

THE LONG WAR SERIES

Killer of Men
Marathon
Poseidon's Spear
The Great King
Salamis

THE CHIVALRY SERIES

The Ill-Made Knight
The Long Sword

OTHER NOVELS

Washington and Caesar
God of War

EBOOK EXCLUSIVES

Tom Swan and the Head of St George Parts One–Six
Tom Swan and the Siege of Belgrade Parts One–Seven

RAGE OF
Ares

CHRISTIAN CAMERON

First published in Great Britain in 2016 by Orion Books,
an imprint of The Orion Publishing Group Ltd
Carmelite House, 50 Victoria Embankment
London EC4Y 0DZ

An Hachette UK Company

1 3 5 7 9 10 8 6 4 2

A CIP catalogue record for this book
is available from the British Library.

ISBN (Hardback) 978 1 4091 1453 6

Typeset by Deltatype Ltd, Birkenhead, Merseyside

Printed in Great Britain by CPI Group (UK) Ltd,
Croydon CR0 4YY

www.orionbooks.co.uk

Giannis Kadaglou

Glossary

I am an *amateur* Greek scholar. My definitions are my own, but taken from the LSJ or Routledge's *Handbook of Greek Mythology* or Smith's *Classical Dictionary*. On some military issues I have the temerity to disagree with the received wisdom on the subject. Also check my website at www.hippeis.com for more information and some helpful pictures.

Akinakes A Scythian short sword or long knife, also sometimes carried by Medes and Persians.

Andron The 'men's room' of a proper Greek house – where men have symposia. Recent research has cast real doubt as to the sexual exclusivity of the room, but the name sticks.

Apobatai The Chariot Warriors. In many towns, towns that hadn't used chariots in warfare for centuries, the *Apobatai* were the elite three hundred or so. In Athens, they competed in special events; in Thebes, they may have been the forerunners of the Sacred Band.

Archon A city's senior official or, in some cases, one of three or four. A magnate.

Aspis The Greek hoplite's shield (which is not called a hoplon!). The *aspis* is about a yard in diameter, is deeply dished (up to six inches deep) and should weigh between eight and sixteen pounds.

Basileus An aristocratic title from a bygone era (at least in 500 BCE) that means 'king' or 'lord'.

Bireme A warship rowed by two tiers of oars, as opposed to a *trireme*, which has three tiers.

Chiton The standard tunic for most men, made by taking a single continuous piece of cloth and folding it in half, pinning the shoulders and open side. Can be made quite fitted by means of pleating. Often made of very fine quality material – usually wool, sometimes linen, especially in the upper classes. A full *chiton* was ankle length for men and women.

Chitoniskos A small *chiton*, usually just longer than modesty demanded – or not as long as modern modesty would demand! Worn by warriors and farmers, often heavily bloused and very full by warriors to pad their armour. Usually wool.

Chlamys A short cloak made from a rectangle of cloth roughly 60 by 90 inches – could also be worn as a *chiton* if folded and pinned a different way. Or slept under as a blanket.

Corslet/Thorax In 500 BCE, the best *corslets* were made of bronze, mostly of the so-called 'bell' *thorax* variety. A few muscle *corslets* appear at the end of this period, gaining popularity into the 450s. Another style is the 'white' *corslet*, seen to appear just as the Persian Wars begin – re-enactors call this the 'Tube and Yoke' *corslet*, and some people call it (erroneously) the *linothorax*. Some of them may have been made of linen – we'll never know – but the likelier material is Athenian leather, which was often tanned and finished with alum, thus being bright white. Yet another style was a tube and yoke of scale, which you can see the author wearing on his website. A scale *corslet* would have been the most expensive of all, and probably provided the best protection.

Daidala Cithaeron, the mountain that towered over Plataea, was the site of a remarkable fire-festival, the *Daidala*, which was celebrated by the Plataeans on the summit of the mountain. In the usual ceremony, as mounted by the Plataeans in every seventh year, a wooden idol (*daidalon*) would be dressed in bridal robes and dragged on an ox-cart from Plataea to the top of the mountain, where it would be burned after appropriate rituals. Or, in the *Great Daidala*, which were celebrated every forty-nine years, fourteen *daidala* from different Boeotian towns would be burned on a large wooden pyre heaped with brushwood, together with a cow and a bull that were sacrificed to Zeus and Hera. This huge pyre on the mountain top must have provided a most impressive spectacle; Pausanias remarks that he knew of no other flame that rose as high or could be seen from so far.

The cultic legend that was offered to account for the festival ran as follows. When Hera had once quarrelled with Zeus, as she often did, she had withdrawn to her childhood home of Euboea and had refused every attempt at reconciliation. So Zeus sought the advice of the wisest man on earth, Cithaeron (the eponym of the mountain), who ruled at Plataea in the earliest times. Cithaeron advised him to make a wooden image of a woman, to veil it in the manner of a bride, and then to have it drawn along in an ox-cart after spreading the rumour that he was planning to marry the nymph Plataea, a daughter of the river god Asopus. When Hera rushed to the scene and tore away the veils, she was so relieved to find a wooden effigy rather than the expected bride that she at last consented to be reconciled with Zeus. (Routledge *Handbook of Greek Mythology*, pp. 137–8)

Daimon Literally a spirit, the *daimon* of combat might be adrenaline, and the *daimon* of philosophy might simply be native intelligence. Suffice it to say that very intelligent men – like Socrates – believed that god-sent spirits could infuse a man and influence his actions.

Daktyloi Literally digits or fingers, in common talk 'inches' in the system of measurement. Systems differed from city to city. I have taken the liberty of using just the Athenian units.

Despoina Lady. A term of formal address.

Diekplous A complex naval tactic about which some debate remains. In this book, the *Diekplous*, or through stroke, is commenced with an attack by the ramming ship's bow (picture the two ships approaching bow to bow or head-on) and cathead on the enemy oars. Oars were the most vulnerable part of a fighting ship, something very difficult to imagine unless you've rowed in a big boat and understand how lethal your own oars can be – to you! After the attacker crushes the enemy's oars, he passes, flank to flank, and then turns when astern, coming up easily (the defender is almost dead in the water) and ramming the enemy under the stern or counter as desired.

Doru A spear, about ten feet long, with a bronze butt-spike.

Eleutheria Freedom.

Ephebe A young, free man of property. A young man in training to be a *hoplite*. Usually performing service to his city and, in ancient terms, at one of the two peaks of male beauty.

Eromenos The 'beloved' in a same-sex pair in ancient Greece. Usually younger, about seventeen. This is a complex, almost dangerous subject in the modern world – were these pair-bonds about sex, or chivalric love, or just a 'brotherhood' of warriors? I suspect there were elements of all three. And to write about this period without discussing the *eromenos/erastes* bond would, I fear, be like putting all the warriors in steel armour instead of bronze . . .

Erastes The 'lover' in a same-sex pair bond – the older man, a tried warrior, twenty-five to thirty years old.

Eudaimonia Literally 'well-spirited'. A feeling of extreme joy.

Exhedra The porch of the women's quarters – in some cases, any porch over a farm's central courtyard.

Helots The 'race of slaves' of Ancient Sparta – the conquered peoples who lived with the Spartiates and did all of their work so that they could concentrate entirely on making war and more Spartans.

Hetaira Literally a 'female companion'. In ancient Athens, a *hetaira* was a courtesan, a highly skilled woman who provided sexual companionship as well as fashion, political advice and music.

Himation A very large piece of rich, often embroidered wool, worn as an outer garment by wealthy citizen women or as a sole garment by older men, especially those in authority.

Hoplite A Greek upper-class warrior. Possession of a heavy spear, a helmet and an *aspis* (see above) and income above the marginal lowest free class were all required to serve as a *hoplite*. Although much is made of the 'citizen soldier' of ancient Greece, it would be fairer to compare *hoplites* to medieval knights than to Roman legionnaires or modern National Guardsmen. Poorer citizens did serve, and sometimes as *hoplites* or marines, but in general, the front ranks were the preserve of upper-class men who could afford the best training and the essential armour.

Hoplitodromos The *hoplite* race, or race in armour. Two *stades* with an *aspis* on your shoulder, a helmet and greaves in the early runs. I've run this race in armour. It is no picnic.

Hoplomachia A *hoplite* contest, or sparring match. Again, there is enormous debate as to when *hoplomachia* came into existence and how much training Greek *hoplites* received. One thing that they didn't do is drill like modern soldiers – there's no mention of it in all of Greek literature. However, they had highly evolved martial arts (see *pankration*) and it is almost certain that *hoplomachia* was a term that referred to 'the martial art of fighting when fully equipped as a *hoplite*'.

Hoplomachos A participant in *hoplomachia*.

Hypaspist Literally 'under the shield'. A squire or military servant – by the time of Arimnestos, the *hypaspist* was usually a younger man of the same class as the *hoplite*.

Kithara A stringed instrument of some complexity, with a hollow body as a soundboard.

Kline A couch.

Kopis The heavy, back-curved sabre of the Greeks. Like a longer, heavier modern kukri or Gurkha knife.

Kore A maiden or daughter.

Kylix A wide, shallow, handled bowl for drinking wine.

Logos Literally 'word'. In pre-Socratic Greek philosophy the word is everything – the power beyond the gods.

Longche A six to seven foot throwing spear, also used for hunting. A *hoplite* might carry a pair of *longchai*, or a single, longer and heavier *doru*.

Machaira A heavy sword or long knife.

Maenads The 'raving ones' – ecstatic female followers of Dionysus.

Mastos A woman's breast. A *mastos* cup is shaped like a woman's breast with a rattle in the nipple – so when you drink, you lick the nipple and the rattle shows that you emptied the cup. I'll leave the rest to imagination . . .

Medimnos A grain measure. Very roughly – 35 to 100 pounds of grain.

Megaron A style of building with a roofed porch.

Navarch An admiral.

Oikia The household – all the family and all the slaves, and sometimes the animals and the farmland itself.

Opson Whatever spread, dip or accompaniment an ancient Greek had with bread.

Pais A child.

Palaestra The exercise sands of the gymnasium.

Pankration The military martial art of the ancient Greeks – an unarmed combat system that bears more than a passing resemblance to modern MMA techniques, with a series of carefully structured blows and domination holds that is, by modern standards, very advanced. Also the basis of the Greek sword and spear-based martial arts. Kicking, punching, wrestling, grappling, on the ground and standing, were all permitted.

Peplos A short overfold of cloth that women could wear as a hood or to cover the breasts.

Phalanx The full military potential of a town; the actual, formed body of men before a battle (all of the smaller groups formed together made a *phalanx*). In this period, it would be a mistake to imagine a carefully drilled military machine.

Phylarch A file-leader – an officer commanding the four to sixteen men standing behind him in the *phalanx*.

Polemarch The war leader.

Polis The city. The basis of all Greek political thought and expression, the government that was held to be more important – a higher god – than any individual or even family. To this day, when we talk about politics, we're talking about the 'things of our city'.

Porne A prostitute.

Porpax The bronze or leather band that encloses the forearm on a Greek *aspis*.

Psiloi Light infantrymen – usually slaves or adolescent freemen who, in this period, were not organised and seldom had any weapon beyond some rocks to throw.

Pyrrhiche The 'War Dance'. A line dance in armour done by all of the warriors, often very complex. There's reason to believe that the *Pyrrhiche* was the method by which the young were trained in basic martial arts and by which 'drill' was inculcated.

Pyxis A box, often circular, turned from wood or made of metal.

Rhapsode A master-poet, often a performer who told epic works like the *Iliad* from memory.

Satrap A Persian ruler of a province of the Persian Empire.

Skeuophoros Literally a 'shield carrier', unlike the *hypaspist*, this is a slave or freed man who does camp work and carries the armour and baggage.

Sparabara The large wicker shield of the Persian and Mede elite infantry. Also the name of those soldiers.

Spolas Another name for a leather *corslet*, often used for the lion skin of Heracles.

Stade A measure of distance. An Athenian *stade* is about 185 metres.

Strategos In Athens, the commander of one of the ten military tribes. Elsewhere, any senior Greek officer – sometimes the commanding general.

Synaspismos The closest order that *hoplites* could form – so close that the shields overlap, hence 'shield on shield'.

Taxis Any group but, in military terms, a company; I use it for sixty to three hundred men.

Thetes The lowest free class – citizens with limited rights.

Thorax See *corslet*.

Thugater Daughter. Look at the word carefully and you'll see the 'daughter' in it . . .

Triakonter A small rowed galley of thirty oars.

Trierarch The captain of a ship – sometimes just the owner or builder, sometimes the fighting captain.

Zone A belt, often just rope or finely wrought cord, but could be a heavy bronze kidney belt for war.

General Note on Names and Personages

This series is set in the very dawn of the so-called Classical Era, often measured from the Battle of Marathon (490 BCE). Some, if not most, of the famous names of this era are characters in this series – and that's not happenstance. Athens of this period is as magical, in many ways, as Tolkien's Gondor, and even the quickest list of artists, poets, and soldiers of this era reads like a 'who's who' of western civilization. Nor is the author tossing them together by happenstance – these people were almost all aristocrats, men (and women) who knew each other well – and might be adversaries or friends in need. Names in bold are historical characters – yes, even Arimnestos – and you can get a glimpse into their lives by looking at Wikipedia or Britannica online. For more in-depth information, I recommend Plutarch and Herodotus, to whom I owe a great deal.

Arimnestos of Plataea may – just may – have been Herodotos's source for the events of the Persian Wars. The careful reader will note that Herodotos himself – a scribe from Halicarnassus – appears several times …

Archilogos – Ephesian, son of Hipponax the poet; a typical Ionian aristocrat, who loves Persian culture and Greek culture too, who serves his city, not some cause of 'Greece' or 'Hellas', and who finds the rule of the Great King fairer and more 'democratic' than the rule of a Greek tyrant.

Arimnestos – Child of Chalkeotechnes and Euthalia.

Aristagoras – Son of Molpagoras, nephew of Histiaeus. Aristagoras led Miletus while Histiaeus was a virtual prisoner of the Great King Darius at Susa. Aristagoras seems to have initiated the Ionian Revolt – and later to have regretted it.

Aristides – Son of Lysimachus, lived roughly 525–468 BCE, known later in life as 'The Just'. Perhaps best known as one of the commanders at Marathon. Usually sided with the Aristocratic party.

Artaphernes – Brother of Darius, Great King of Persia, and Satrap of Sardis. A senior Persian with powerful connections.

Behon – A Kelt from Alba; a fisherman and former slave.

Bion – A slave name, meaning 'life'. The most loyal family retainer of the Corvaxae.

Briseis – Daughter of Hipponax, sister of Archilogos.

Calchus – A former warrior, now the keeper of the shrine of the Plataean Hero of Troy, Leitus.

Chalkeotechnes – The Smith of Plataea; head of the family Corvaxae, who claim descent from Herakles.

Chalkidis – Brother of Arimnestos, son of Chalkeotechnes.

Cimon – Son of Miltiades, a professional soldier, sometime pirate, and Athenian aristocrat.

Cleisthenes – A noble Athenian of the Alcmaeonid family. He is credited with reforming the constitution of ancient Athens and setting it on a democratic footing in 508/7 BCE.

Collam – A Gallic lord in the Central Massif at the headwaters of the Seine.

Dano of Croton – Daughter of the philosopher and mathematician Pythagoras.

Darius – King of Kings, the lord of the Persian Empire, brother to Artaphernes.

Doola – Numidian ex-slave.

Draco – Wheelwright and wagon builder of Plataea, a leading man of the town.

Empedocles – A priest of Hephaestus, the Smith God.

Epaphroditos – A warrior, an aristocrat of Lesbos.

Eualcides – A Hero. Eualcides is typical of a class of aristocratic men – professional warriors, adventurers, occasionally pirates or merchants by turns. From Euboea.

Heraclitus – *c.*535–475 BCE. One of the ancient world's most famous philosophers. Born to an aristocratic family, he chose philosophy over political power. Perhaps most famous for his statement about time: 'You cannot step twice into the same river'. His belief that 'strife is justice' and other similar sayings which you'll find scattered through these pages made him a favourite with Nietzsche. His works, mostly now lost, probably established the later philosophy of Stoicism.

Herakleides – An Aeolian, a Greek of Asia Minor. With his brothers Nestor and Orestes, he becomes a retainer – a warrior – in service to Arimnestos. It is easy, when looking at the birth of Greek democracy, to see the whole form of modern government firmly established – but at the time of this book, democracy was less than skin-deep and most armies were formed of semi-feudal war bands following an aristocrat.

Heraklides – Aristides' helmsman, a lower-class Athenian who has made a name for himself in war.

Hermogenes – Son of Bion, Arimnestos's slave.

Hesiod – A great poet (or a great tradition of poetry) from Boeotia in Greece. Hesiod's *Works and Days* and *Theogony* were widely read in the sixth century and remain fresh today – they are the chief source we have on Greek farming, and this book owes an enormous debt to them.

Hippias – Last tyrant of Athens, overthrown around 510 BCE (that is, just around the beginning of this series). Hippias escaped into exile and became a pensioner of Darius of Persia.

Hipponax – 540–*c.*498 BCE. A Greek poet and satirist, considered the inventor of parody. He is supposed to have said, 'There are two days when a woman is a pleasure: the day one marries her and the day one buries her.'

Histiaeus – Tyrant of Miletus and ally of Darius of Persia, possible originator of the plan for the Ionian Revolt.

Homer – Another great poet, roughly Hesiod's contemporary (give or take fifty years!) and again, possibly more a poetic tradition than an individual man. Homer is reputed as the author of the *Iliad* and the *Odyssey*, two great epic poems which, between them, largely defined what heroism and aristocratic good behaviour should be in Greek society – and, you might say, to this very day.

Idomeneus – Cretan warrior, priest of Leitus.

Kylix – A boy, slave of Hipponax.

Leukas – Alban sailor, later deck master on *Lydia*. Kelt of the Dumnones of Briton.

Miltiades – Tyrant of the Thracian Chersonese. His son, Cimon rose to be a great man in Athenian politics. Probably the author of the Athenian victory of Marathon, Miltiades was a complex man, a pirate, a warlord, and a supporter of Athenian democracy.

Penelope – Daughter of Chalkeotechnes, sister of Arimnestos.

Polymarchos – ex-slave swordmaster of Syracusa.

Phrynicus – Ancient Athenian playwright and warrior.

Sappho – A Greek poetess from the island of Lesbos, born sometime around 630 BCE and died between 570 and 550 BCE. Her father was probably Lord of Eressos. Widely considered the greatest lyric poet of Ancient Greece.

Seckla – Numidian ex-slave.

Simonalkes – Head of the collateral branch of the Plataean Corvaxae, cousin to Arimnestos.

Simonides – Another great lyric poet, he lived *c.*556–468 BCE, and his nephew, Bacchylides, was as famous as he. Perhaps best known for his epigrams, one of which is:

> Ω ξεῖν', ἀγγέλλειν Λακεδαιμονίοις ὅτι τῇδε
> κείμεθα, τοῖς κείνων ῥήμασι πειθόμενοι.
> *Go tell the Spartans, thou who passest by,*
> *That here, obedient to their laws, we lie.*

Thales – *c.*624–*c.*546 BCE. The first philosopher of the Greek tradition, whose writings were still current in Arimnestos's time. Thales used geometry to solve problems such as calculating the height of the pyramids in Egypt and the distance of ships from the shore. He made at least one trip to Egypt. He is widely accepted as the founder of western mathematics.

Themistocles – Leader of the demos party in Athens, father of the Athenian Fleet. Political enemy of Aristides.

Theognis – Theognis of Megara was almost certainly not one man but a whole canon of aristocratic poetry under that name, much of it practical. There are maxims, many very wise, laments on the decline of man and the age, and the woes of old age and poverty, songs for symposia, etc. In later sections there are songs and poems about homosexual love and laments for failed romances. Despite widespread attributions, there was, at some point, a real Theognis who may have lived in the mid-6th century BCE, or just before the events of this series. His poetry would have been central to the world of Arimnestos's mother.

Vasileos – Master shipwright and helmsman.

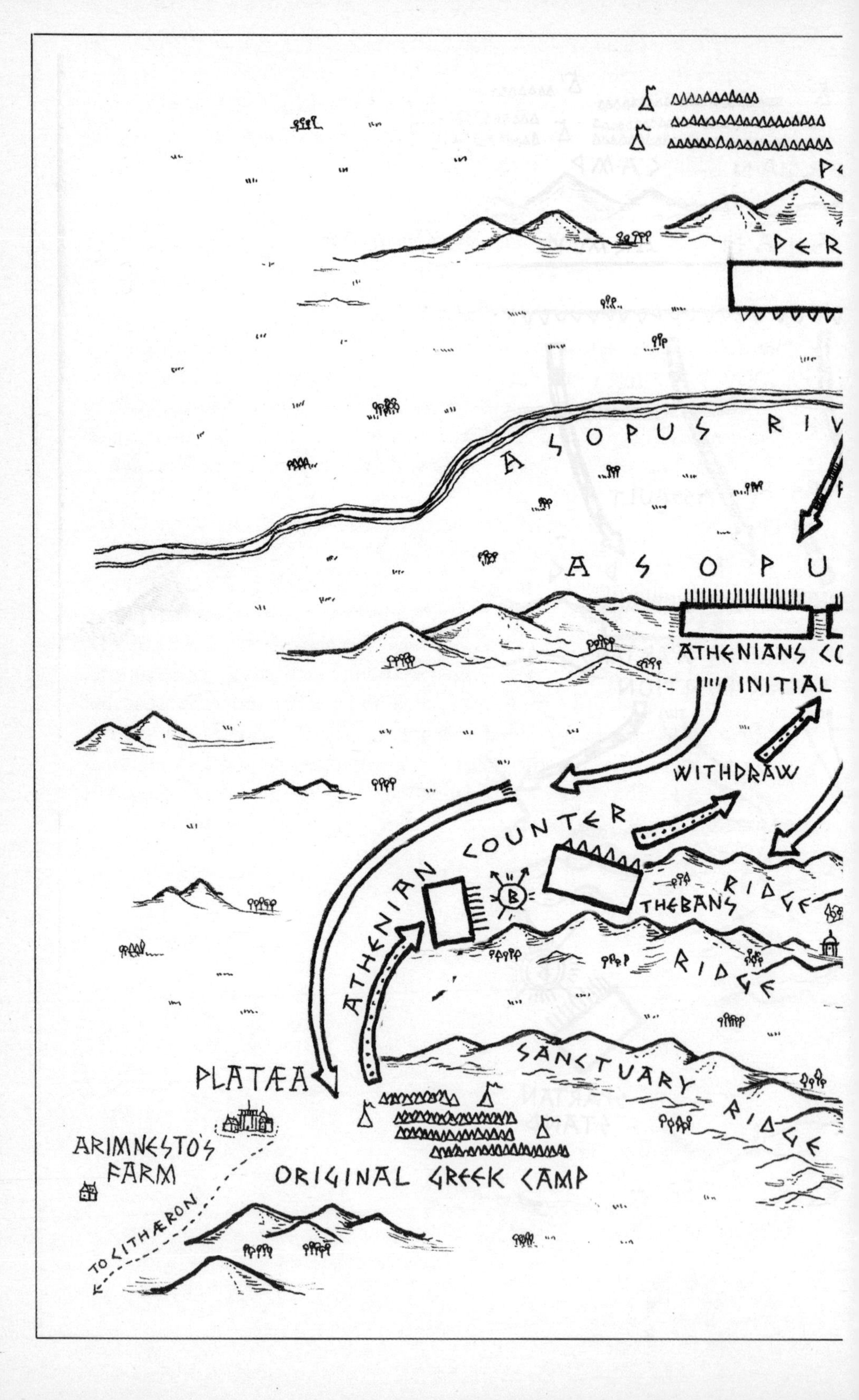

PER
ASOPUS RIV
ASOPU
ATHENIANS CO
INITIAL
WITHDRAW
ATHENIAN COUNTER
B
THEBANS
RIDGE
RIDGE
SANCTUARY RIDGE
PLATÆA
ARIMNESTO'S FARM
ORIGINAL GREEK CAMP
TO CITHÆRON

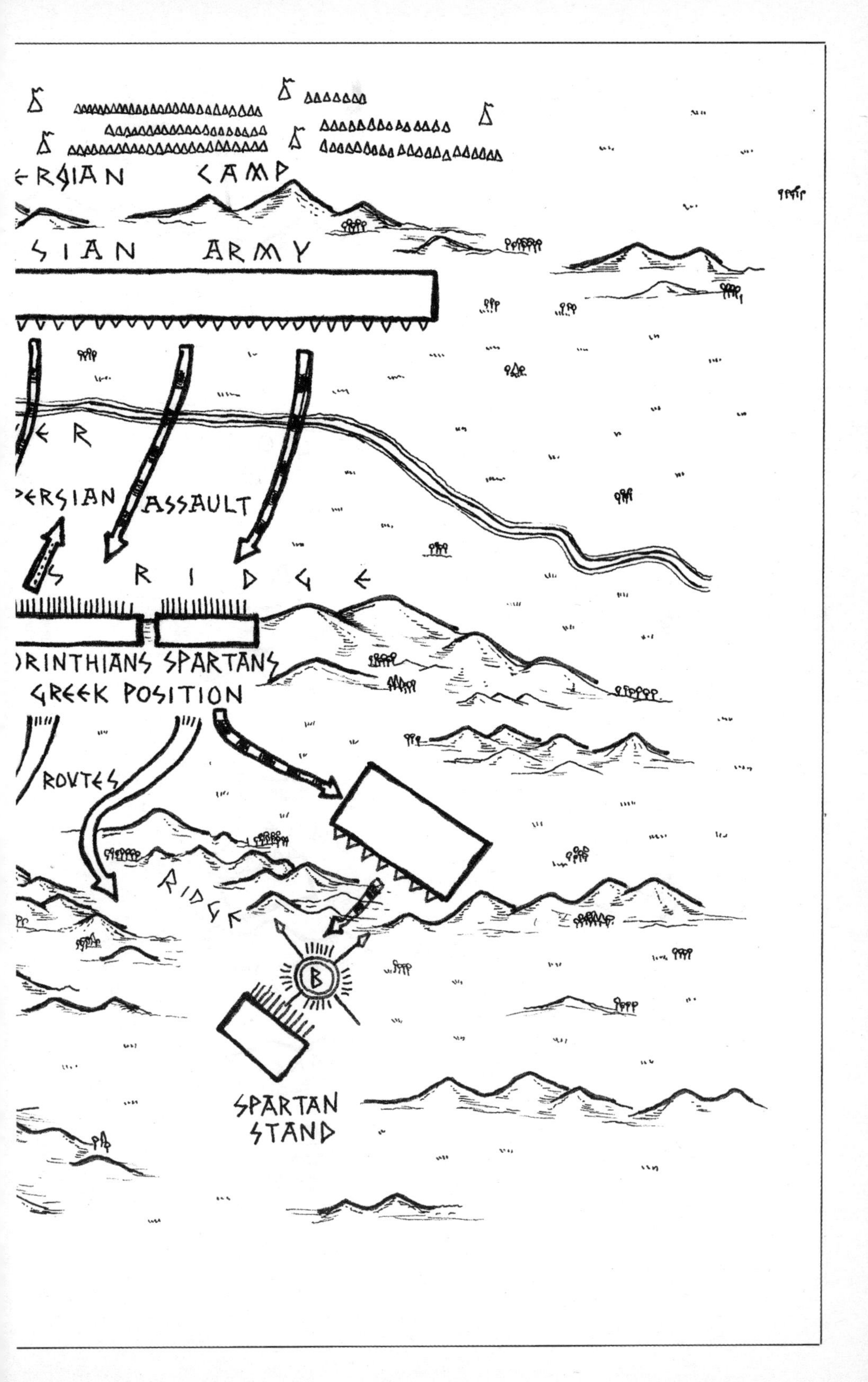

ERSIAN CAMP
SIAN ARMY
ER
ERSIAN ASSAULT
S RIDGE
ORINTHIANS SPARTANS
GREEK POSITION
ROUTES
RIDGE
B
SPARTAN STAND

Here we are again – the last night of my feast. Or is it? Perhaps I'll hold a hunt party later in the year, and tell you my other tales: how we travelled to Africa; how we brought a cargo from India; and how we conquered this fine place. You all seem to enjoy the tales, and they make me feel young and hale again. Indeed, while I tell the tales, Calchas lives, and my mother, and Paramanos and Idomeneaus. Let me send this wine to their shades, so they may know that they are still spoken of with love.

But this is the best of tales since Troy – with sorrow and joy, men and women, heroes and traitors and men, like Themistocles, who were both. May you never see such times, thugater.

The first night, I told you of my youth, and how I went to Calchas the priest to be educated as a gentleman, and instead learned to be a spear fighter. Because Calchas was no empty windbag, but a Killer of Men, who had stood his place many times in the storm of bronze. And veterans came from all over Greece to hang their shields for a time at our shrine and talk to Calchas, and he sent them away whole, or better men, at least. Except that the worst of them, the Hero called for, and the priest would kill them on the precinct walls and send their shades shrieking to feed the old Hero, or serve him in Hades.

Mind you, friends, Leithos wasn't some angry old god demanding blood sacrifice, but Plataea's hero from the Trojan War. And he was a particularly Boeotian hero, because he was no great man-slayer, no tent-sulker. His claim to fame is that he went to Troy and fought all ten years. That on the day that mighty Hector raged by the ships of the Greeks and Achilles skulked in his tent, Leithos rallied the lesser men and formed a tight shield wall and held Hector long enough for Ajax and the other Greek heroes to rally.

You might hear a different story in Thebes, or Athens, or Sparta. But that's the story of the Hero I grew to serve, and I spent years at his shrine, learning the war dances that we call the *pyrriche*. Oh, I learned to read old Theognis and Hesiod and Homer, too. But it was the spear, the sword and the *aspis* that sang to me.

When my father found that I was learning to be a warrior and not a man of letters, he came and fetched me home, and old Calchas – died. Killed himself, more like. But I've told all this – and how little Plataea, our farm town at the edge of Boeotia, sought to be free of cursed Thebes and made an alliance with distant Athens. I told you all how godlike Miltiades came to our town and treated my father, the bronze smith – and Draco the wheelwright and old Epictetus the farmer – like Athenian gentlemen; how he wooed them with fine words and paid hard silver for their products, so that he bound them to his own political ends and to the needs of Athens.

When I was still a gangly boy – tall, and well-muscled, as I remember, but too young to fight in the phalanx – Athens called for little Plataea's aid, and we marched over Cithaeron, the ancient mountain that is also our glowering god, and we rallied to the Athenians at Oinoe. We stood beside them against Sparta and Corinth and all the Peloponnesian cities – and we beat them.

Well – Athens beat them. Plataea barely survived, and my older brother, who should have been my father's heir, died there with a Spartiate's spear in his belly.

Four days later, when we fought again – this time against Thebes – I was in the phalanx. Again, we triumphed. And I was a hoplite.

And two days later, when we faced the Euboean, I saw my cousin Simon kill my father, stabbing him in the back under his bright bronze cuirass. When I fell over my father's corpse, I took a mighty blow and when I awoke, I had no memory of Simon's treachery.

When I awoke, of course, I was a slave. Simon had sold me to Phoenician traders, and I went east with a cargo of Greek slaves.

I was a slave for some years – and in truth, it was not a bad life. I went to a fine house, ruled by rich, elegant, excellent people – Hipponax the poet and his wife and two children. Archilogos – the elder boy – was my real master, and yet my friend and ally, and we had many escapades together. And his sister, Briseis ...

Ah, Briseis. Helen, returned to life.

We lived in far-off Ephesus, one of the most beautiful and powerful cities on the Greek world – yet located on the coast of Asia. Greeks have lived there since the Trojan War, and the Temple of Artemis there is one of the wonders of the world. My master went to school each day at the Temple of Artemis, and there the great philosopher, Heraclitus, had his school, and he would shower us with questions every bit as painful as the blows of the old fighter who taught us *pankration* at the gymnasium.

Heraclitus. I have met men – and women – who see him as a charlatan, a dreamer, a mouther of impieties. In fact, he was deeply religious – his family held the hereditary priesthood of Artemis – but he believed that fire was the only true element, and change the only constant. I can witness both.

It was a fine life. I got a rich lord's education for nothing. I learned to drive a chariot, and to ride a horse and to fight and to use my mind like a sword. I loved it all, but best of all ...

Best of all, I loved Briseis.

And while I loved her – and half a dozen other young women – I grew to manhood listening to Greeks and Persians plotting various plots in my master's house, and one night all the plots burst forth into ugly blossoms and bore the fruit of red-handed war, and the Greek cities of Ionia revolted against their Persian overlords.

Now, as tonight's story will be about war with the Persians, let me take a moment to remind you of the roots of the conflict. Because they are ignoble, and the Greeks were no better than the Persians, and perhaps a great deal worse. The Ionians had money, power, and freedom – freedom to worship, freedom to rule themselves – under the Great King, and all it cost them was taxes and the 'slavery' of having to obey the Great King in matters of foreign policy. The 'yoke' of the Persians was light and easy to wear, and no man alive knows that better than me, because I served – as a slave – as a herald between my master and the mighty Artaphernes, the satrap of all Phrygia. I knew him well – I ran his errands, dressed him at times, and one dark night, when my master Hipponax caught the Persian in his wife's bed, I saved his life when my master would have killed him. I saved my master's life as well, holding the corridor against four Persian soldiers of high repute – Aryanam, Pharnakes, Cyrus and Darius. I know their names because they were my friends, in other times.

And you'll hear of them again. Except Pharnakes, who died in the Bosporus, fighting Carians, so long ago that I can't remember his face.

At any rate, after that night of swords and fire and hate, my master went from being a loyal servant of Persia to a hate-filled Greek 'patriot'. And our city – Ephesus – roused itself to war. And amidst it all, my beloved Briseis lost her fiancée Diomedes to rumour and innuendo, and Archilogos and I beat him for his impudence. I had learned to kill, and to use violence to get what I wanted. And as a reward, I got Briseis – or to be more accurate, she had me. My master freed me, not knowing that I had just deflowered his daughter, and I sailed away with Archilogos to avoid the wrath of the suitor's relatives.

We joined the Greek revolt at Lesvos, and there, on the beach, I met Aristides – sometimes called the Just, one of the greatest heroes of Athens, and Miltiades' political foe.

That was the beginning of my true life. My life as a man of war. I won my first games on a beach in Chios and I earned my first suit of armour, and I went to war against the Persians.

But the god of war, Ares, was not so much in charge of my life as Aphrodite, and when we returned to Ephesus to plan the great war, I spent every hour that I could with Briseis, and the result – I think now – was never in doubt. But Heraclitus, the great sage, asked me to swear an oath to all the gods that I would protect Archilogos and his family – and I swore. Like the heroes in the old stories, I never thought about the consequence of swearing such a great oath and sleeping all the while with Briseis.

Ah, Briseis! She taunted me with cowardice when I stayed away from her and devoured me when I visited her, sneaking, night after night, past the slaves into the women's quarters, until in the end – we were caught. Of course we were caught.

And I was thrown from the house and ordered never to return, by the family I'd sworn to protect.

Three days later I was marching up country with Aristides and the Athenians. We burned Sardis, but the Persians caught us in the midst of looting the market, and we lost the fight in the town and then again at the bridge, and the Persians beat us like a drum – but I stood my ground, fight after fight, and my reputation as a spear fighter grew. In a mountain pass, Eualcidas the Euboean and I charged Artaphernes' bodyguard, and lived to tell the tale. Three days later, on the plains north of Ephesus, we tried to face a provincial Persian army with the whole might of the Ionian Revolt, and the Greeks folded and ran rather than face the Persian archery and the outraged

Phrygians. Alone, on the far left, the Athenians and the Euboeans held our ground and stopped the Carians. Our army was destroyed. Eualcidas the hero died there, and I went back to save his corpse, and in the process found that Hipponax, my former master, lay mortally wounded. I gave him the mercy blow, again failing to think of the oath I'd sworn, and my once near-brother Archilogos thought I'd done it from hate, not love, and the Furies gathered round the corpse to punish me for my impiety. And that stood between us and any hope of reconciliation. To Archilogos, I'd raped his sister and killed his father after swearing an oath to the gods to protect them.

From the rout of Ephesus, I escaped with the Athenians, but the curse of my shattered oath lay on me and Poseidon harried our ship, and in every port I killed men who annoyed me until Agios, my Athenian friend, put me ashore on Crete, with the king of Gortyn, Achilles, and his son Neoptolymos, to whom I was war tutor. I tutored him so well that in the next great battle of the Ionian War, Neoptolymos and I were the heroes of the Greek fleet, and we helped my once-friend Archilogos break the Persian centre. It was the first victory for the Greeks, but it was fleeting, and a few days later, I was a pirate on the great sea with my own ship for the first time. Fortune favoured me – perhaps, I think, because I had in part redeemed my oath to the gods by saving Archilogos at the sea battle. And when we weathered the worst storm I had ever seen, Poseidon had gifted me the African-Greek navigator Paramanos and a good crew in a heavy ship. I returned to Lesvos and joined Miltiades – the same who had wooed the Plataeans at the dawn of this tale. And from him, I learned the facts of my father's murder and I determined to go home and avenge him.

I found Briseis had married one of the architects of the Ionian Revolt, and he was eager to kill me – the rumour was that she called my name when he was with her at night. And I determined to kill him.

After two seasons of piracy with Miltiades and further failures of the rebels to resist the Persians, I found him skulking around the edge of a great mêlée in Thrace and I killed him. I presented myself to Briseis to take her as my own – and she spurned me.

That's how it is, sometimes. I went back to Plataea, an empty vessel, and the Furies filled me with revenge. I found Simon and his sons sitting on my farm, Simon married to my mother, planning to marry his youngest son Simonalkes to my sister Penelope.

I'll interrupt my own tale to say that I did not fall on Simon with fire and sword, because four years of living by the spear had taught me that things I had learned as a boy from Calchas and heard again from Heraclitus were coming to seem important and true – that justice was more important than might. I let the law of Plataea have its way. Simon hanged himself from the rafters of my father's workshop, and the Furies left me alone with my mother and my sister.

That would make a fine tale, I think, by itself – but the gods were far from done with Plataea, and by the next spring, there were storm clouds brewing in all directions, all directed to the plain of Marathon.

An Athenian aristocrat died under my *hypaspist*'s sword – Idomeneaus, who comes all too often into these stories, a mad Cretan – he had taken up the priesthood of the old shrine. I went off to see to the crisis, and that road took me over the mountains to Athens, and into the middle of Athenian politics – aye, you'll hear more of that tonight, too. There I fell afoul of the Alcmaeonidae and their scion Cleitus, because it was his brother who had died in our sanctuary and because my cowardly cousin Simon's sons were laying a trap for me. He stole my horse and my slave girl – that's another story. Because of him, I was tried for murder – and Aristides the Just got me off with a trick. But in the process, I committed hubris – the crime of treating a man like a slave – and Aristides ordered me to go to Delos, to the great Temple of Apollo, to be cleansed.

Apollo, that scheming god, never meant me to be cleansed, but instead thrust me back into the service of Miltiades, whose fortunes were at an all-time ebb. With two ships, I re-provisioned Miletus – not once but twice – and made a small fortune on it, and on piracy. I took men's goods, and their women, and I killed for money, took ships, and thought too little of the gods. Apollo had warned me – in his own voice – to learn to use mercy, but I failed more often than I succeeded, and I left a red track behind me across the Ionian Sea. And in time, I was a captain at the greatest sea battle of the Ionian Revolt – at Lade. At Lade, the Great King put together an incredible fleet, of nearly *six hundred* ships, to face the Greeks and their allies with almost three hundred and fifty ships. It sounds one-sided, but we were well trained. We should have been ready. I sailed with the Athenians and the Cretans, and we beat the Phoenicians at one end of the line and emerged from the morning fog expecting the praise of our navarch, the Phocaean Dionysius – alongside Miltiades, the greatest pirate and ship-handler in the Greek world. But when we punched through the Phoenicians, we found that the Samians – our fellow Greeks – had sold out to the Persians. The Great King triumphed, and the Ionian Revolt collapsed. Most of my friends – most of the men of my youth – died at Lade.

It was the darkest day of my life, and it has haunted me ever since.

Briseis married Artaphernes, who had slept with her mother – and became the most powerful woman in Ionia, as she had always planned.

Datis, the architect of the Persian victory, raped and plundered his way across Lesvos and Chios, slaughtering men, taking women for the slave markets, and making true every slander that Greeks had falsely whispered about Persian atrocities.

Miletus, that I had helped to hold, fell. I saved what I could. And went home, with fifty families of Milesians to add to the citizen levy of Plataea. I spent my fortune on them, buying them land and oxen, and then – then I went back to smithing bronze. I gave up the spear.

How the gods must have laughed.

A season later, while my sister went to a finishing school to get her away from my mother's drunkenness, I went back to Athens because my friend Phrynicus, who had stood in the arrow storm at Lade with me, was producing his play, *The Fall of Miletus*. And Miltiades had been arrested for threatening the state – of which, let me say, friends, he was absolutely guilty, because Miltiades would have sold his own mother into slavery to achieve power in Athens.

At any rate, I used money and some of the talents I'd learned as a slave – and a lot of my friends – to see that Phrynicus' play was produced. And incidentally, to win my stolen slave-girl free of her brothel and wreak some revenge on the Alcmaeonidae. In the process, I undermined their power with the demos – the people – and helped the new voice in Athenian politics – Themistocles the Orator. He had little love for me, but he managed to tolerate my success long enough to help me – and Aristides – to undermine the pro-Persian party and liberate Miltiades.

I went home to Plataea feeling that I'd done a lifetime's good service to Athens. My bronze smithing was getting better and better. I spent the winter training the Plataean phalanx in my spare time. War was going to be my hobby, the way some men learn the *diaulos* or the kithara to while away old age. I trained the young men and forged bronze. Life grew sweeter.

And when my sister Penelope – now married to a local Thespian aristocrat – decided that I was going to marry her friend Euphonia, I eventually agreed. I rode to Attica with a hunting party of aristocrats – Boeotian and Athenian – and won my bride in games that would not have disgraced the heroes of the past. And in the spring I wed her, at a wedding that included Themistocles and Aristides and Miltiades – and Harpagos and Agios and Moire and a dozen of my other friends from every class in Athens. I went back over the mountains with my bride, and settled down to make babies.

But the storm clouds on the horizon were coming on a great wind of change. And the first gusts of that wind brought us a raid out of Thebes, paid for by the Alcmaeonidae and led by my cousin Simon's son Simonides. The vain bastard named all his sons after himself – how weak can a man be?

I digress. We caught them – my new Plataean phalanx – and we crushed them. My friend Teucer, the archer, killed Simonides. And because of them, we were all together when the Athenians called for our help, because the Persians, having destroyed Euboea, were marching for Athens.

Well, I won't retell Marathon. Myron, our archon and always my friend, sent us without reservation, and all the Plataeans marched under my command, and we stood by the Athenians on the greatest day Greek men have ever known, and we were heroes. Hah! I'll tell it again if you don't watch yourselves. We defeated Datis and his Persians by the black ships. Agios died there on the stern of a Persian trireme, but we won the day. Here's to his shade. And to all the shades of all the men who died at Lade and Marathon. May they dine with Achilles and Hector and walk forever in the Elysian Fields.

But when I led the victorious Plataeans back across the mountains, it was to find that my beautiful young wife had died in childbirth. The gods stole my wits clean away – I took her body to my house and burned it and all my trappings, and I went south over Cithaeron, intending to destroy myself.

May you never know how black the world can be. Women know that darkness sometimes after the birth of a child, and men after battle. Any peak of spirit has its price, and when a man or woman stands with the gods, however briefly, they pay the price ten times. The exertion of Marathon and the loss of my wife unmanned me. I leapt from a cliff, expecting death on one of the rocks we call Poseidon's Spear.

I fell, and struck not rocks, but water. And when I surfaced, my body fought for life, and I swam until my feet dragged on the beach. Then I swooned, and when I awoke, I was once again a slave. Again, taken by Phoenicians, but this time as an adult. My life was cruel and like to be short, and the irony of the whole thing was that now I soon craved life.

I lived a brutal life under a monster called Dagon, and you've heard plenty of him. But he tried to break me, body and soul, and nigh-on succeeded. In the end, he crucified me on a mast, and left me to die. But Poseidon saved me – washed me over the side with the mast, and let me live. Set me on the deck of a little Sikel trading ship, where I pulled an oar as a near-slave for a few months. And then I was taken again, by the Phoenicians.

The degradations and the humiliations went on, until one day, in a sea-fight, I took a sword and cut my way to freedom. The sword fell at my feet – literally. The gods have a hand in every man's life. Only impious fools believe otherwise.

As a slave, I had developed new friendships, or rather, new alliances, which, when free, ripened into friendship. My new friends were a polyglot rabble – an Etruscan of Roma named Gaius; a couple of Keltoi, Daud and Sittonax; a pair of Africans from south of Libya, Doola and Sekla; a Sikel named Demetrios; and an Illyrian kinglet-turned-slave called Neoptolymos. We swore an oath to Poseidon to take a ship to Alba and buy tin, and we carried out our oath. As I told you last night, we went to Sicily and while my friends became small traders on the coast, I worked as a bronze smith, learning and teaching. I fell in love with Lydia, the bronze smith's daughter, and betrayed her, and for that betrayal – let's call things by their proper names – I lost confidence in myself, and I lost the favour of the gods, and for years I wandered up and down the seas, until at last we redeemed our oaths, went to Alba for the tin, and came back rich men. I did my best to see Lydia well-suited, and I met Pythagoras' daughter and was able to learn something of that great man's mathematics and his philosophy. I met Gelon, the tyrant of Syracusa, and declined to serve him, and sailed away, and there, on a beach near Taranto in the south of Italia, I found my friends Harpagos and Cimon, son of Miltiades, and others of the friends and allies of my youth. I confess, I *had* sent a message, hoping that they would come. We cruised north into the Adriatic, because I had promised Neoptolymos that we'd restore him to his throne, and we did, though we got a little blood on it. And then the Athenians and I parted company from my friends of Sicily days – they went back to Massalia to till their fields, and I left them to go back to being Arimnestos of Plataea. Because Cimon said that the Persians were coming. And whatever my failings as a man – and I had and still have many – I am the gods' own tool in the war of the Greeks against the Persians.

For all that I have always counted many Persians among my friends, and the best of men – the most excellent, the most brave, the most loyal. Persians are a race of truth-telling heroes. But they are not Greeks, and when it came to war . . .

We parted company off Illyria, and coasted the western Peloponnesus. But Poseidon was not yet done with me, and a mighty storm blew up off Africa and it fell on us, scattering our little squadron and sending my ship far, far to the south and west, and when the storm blew itself out, we were a dismasted hulk riding the rollers, and there was another damaged ship under our lee. We could see she was a Carthaginian. We fell on that ship and took it, although in a strange, three-sided fight – the rowers were rising against the deck crew of Persians.

It was Artaphernes' own ship, and he was traveling from Tyre to Carthage to arrange for Carthaginian ships to help the Great King to make war on Athens. And I rescued him – I thought him a corpse.

So did his wife, my Briseis, who threw herself into my arms.

Blood dripped from my sword, and I stood with Helen in my arms on a ship I'd just taken by force of arms, and I thought myself the king of the world.

How the gods must have laughed.

The night before last, I told you of our lowest ebb. Because Artaphernes was not dead, and all that followed came from that fact. He was the Great King's ambassador to the Carthaginians, and our years of guest-friendship – an exchange of lives going back to my youth, if you've been listening – required me to take him and my Persian friends, his bodyguards – and Briseis, my Helen reborn – to Carthage, though my enemy Dagon had sworn to my destruction in his mad way, and though by then Carthage had put quite a price on my head.

Ha. My role in taking part of their tin fleet. I don't regret it – the foundation of all our fortunes, thugater.

At any rate, we ran Artaphernes – badly wounded – into Carthage, and escaped with our lives after a brilliant piece of boat handling and the gods' own luck. Possibly the *Lydia*'s finest hour. And I saw Dagon.

We ran along the coast of Africa and stopped at Sicily, and there I found my old sparring partner and *hoplomachos* Polymarchos. He was training an athlete for the Olympics, and in a moment I made peace with the gods and took Polymarchos and his young man to Olympia, where we – my whole ship's crew – watched the Olympics, spending the profits of our piracy in a fine style, and making a wicked profit off the wine we brought to sell. There, we played a role in bridging the distance between Athens and Sparta, and there I saw the depth of selfish greed that would cause some men – like Adeimantus of Corinth – to betray Greece and work only for his own ends. I hate his memory – I hope he rots in Hades – but he was scarcely alone, and when Queen Gorgo – here's to the splendour of her, mind and body – when Queen Gorgo of Sparta called us 'a conspiracy to save Greece' she was not speaking poetically. Even the Spartans had their factions, and it was at the Olympics that I discovered that Brasidas, my Spartan officer, was some sort of exiled criminal – or just possibly, a man who'd been betrayed by his country, and not the other way around.

With only a little jiggling of the wheel of fate, we made sure Sparta won the chariot race and we left the Olympics richer by some drachmai and wiser by as much as we'd had nights and nights to thrash out plans for the defence of Greece.

So it was all the more daunting when King Leonidas and Queen Gorgo of Sparta asked me to take their ambassadors to the Great King – the king of Persia. That's another complex tale – the old Spartan king had killed the Persian heralds, an act of gross impiety – and Leonidas sought to rid Sparta of that impiety. So he sent two messengers to far-off Persepolis – two hereditary heralds.

And me.

Well, and Aristides the Just of Athens, who was ostracized – exiled – for being too fair, too rigid, too much of a prig . . .

I laugh. He was probably my closest friend – my mentor. A brilliant soldier – and his finest hour will come soon – and a brilliant speaker, a man who was so incorruptible that ordinary men sometimes found him easy to hate. An aristocrat of the kind that makes men like me think there might be something to the notion of birth; a true hero.

We went to the Great King by way of Tarsus, where I was mauled by a lion, and Babylon, where I was mauled by a woman. Of the two, Babylon was vastly to be preferred. In Babylon we found the seed of the revolt that later saved Greece. When we arrived at Persepolis, I knew immediately that our embassy was doomed – the arrogance of the Persians and Medes was boundless, and nothing we could do would placate or even annoy them. I told you last night how the Spartan envoys – and Brasidas, my friend – and I danced in armour for the Immortals, and were mocked.

Our audience with the Great King was more like staged theatre, intended by his cousin Mardonius to humiliate us before the king had us executed.

But luckily, my friend Artaphernes had a long arm, and his own allies. In other places I have discussed him – another great man, another hero, another mentor. The greatest of my foes, and one I never defeated. But in this we were allies – he did not want Mardonius to triumph, nor did he seek to destroy Athens or Sparta. Because of Artaphernes, we had a few friends in Persepolis, and we were rescued from death by the queen mother, who smuggled us out of the city and let us free on the plains – not because she loved Greece, but only because she feared Mardonius and his extreme, militaristic policies.

We ran. But in running, with our Persian escort of Artaphernes' picked men (and my boyhood friend Cyrus!) we left Brasidas to fan the flames of revolt in Babylon, and we slipped home.

In Sardis – after weeks of playing cat and mouse with all the soldiers in Asia – I saw Artaphernes. He was sick, and old, but strong enough to ask me for a last favour – that when I heard he was dead, I should come and take Briseis. Yes – the love of my life was his wife, the queen of Ionia as she had always meant to be. Artaphernes' son, also called Artaphernes, hated her, and hated me.

At any rate, we made it to my ships, and sailed across the wintry sea to Athens. In the spring, the revolt of Babylon saved Greece from invasion, and the leaders of the Greek world gathered at Corinth and bickered. Endlessly. My ships made me rich, or rather, richer, bringing cargoes from Illyria and Aegypt and Colchis and all points in between, and I sailed that summer, going to the Nile Delta and back, and ignoring the cause of Greek independence as much as ever I could.

But in the end, the Persians came. Last night I told you all of the truth – the internal divisions of the Greeks, and their foolish early efforts; the march to the Vale of Tempe and its utter failure; and the eventual arrangement for a small land army to hold the hot springs of Thermopylae while the great allied fleet held Cape Artemisium.

Leonidas, best of the Spartans, held the pass at Thermopylae. And we, as ragtag a fleet as ever put oar to water, held the waters off Artemisium – day after day. Storms pounded the Persians. We pounded the Persians. Once we fought them to a standstill, and on the last day, we beat them.

But at our backs, a traitor led the Medes around the Spartan wall, and King Leonidas died.

The so-called Great King desecrated his body, and took his head. The Great King's soldiers did the same to all three hundred Spartans, and to others besides. Dogs ripped the body of my noble brother-in-law, Antigonus. My sister would weep for his shade, and I would weep too.

No gods laughed. The week after Thermopylae was the worst of the Long War – the worst week many of us had ever known.

For me, it was Lade. Again. The day that haunts me.

And then, last night, I told you of Salamis. Oh, such a day, and such men. But it almost did not happen, and too closely we emulated the divisiveness that led to defeat and treason at Lade. The Corinthians, and many Spartans, too, were more interested in seeing Athens humbled than in defeating the Medes. And after the death of the Spartan king, the lynchpin of the alliance, and his bodyguard of Spartan gentlemen, who were also his partisans in the murky world of Spartan politics – when the Persians were despoiling his body and mutilating his corpse, it was Greece they beheaded. In that hour, even Themistocles despaired, and the voices for dispersing the fleet – the *victorious* fleet – were loud and long.

But luck, and the will of the gods, sent us all to the beaches of Salamis, the isle of Ajax. And there we lay, resting from war, and bickering, for many days.

Not the Plataeans, though. We landed on the Attic shore and marched overland to rescue our goods and our people, because victory at Thermopylae allowed the Persians to overrun Boeotia faster than any of us could have imagined. We cleared Plataea, knowing that Thebes had already betrayed us and joined the Great King, and ran; the phalanx for the isthmus and Corinth, where the league army was forming, and our sailors and marines back over Cithaeron to Attica. But the Saka and the Persians were hot at our heels, and we fought, and Teucer's son died there, here's wine to *his* shade, and we had a long, hard day withdrawing over the passes into Attica, but by nightfall my son Hipponax and my former *pais* Hector laid a fine ambush and we had them.

Indeed, it is part of this story that those two, one the son of my youthful lust and the other the son of a dockside crime lord, became fast friends and great warriors, which was good, as I was thirty-five that summer, and my body had taken enough wounds that almost every morning, something hurt. By the time we went back to our ships, richer by a little loot and a dog, I had been fighting for weeks, and my dreams were dark and my days full of aches and pains too small to make heroic, but those boys shone with youth like Achilles and fought like him, too.

At any rate, we went back to our ships and I went to council after council, listening to Themistocles, the wisest and most annoying of the Greeks as he cajoled, begged, shamed and demanded that the fleet remain intact and face the Persians again to cover the population of Attica, which had been moved to Salamis. Every day and many nights, men talked and talked, and Adeimantus, the Corinthian navarch, demanded that we all run to the isthmus and abandon Attica. I thought he was in the pay of the Medes, but it was difficult to tell, as they sent presents to so many men, and many took them and fought them, too. Like wily Greeks, whose hero is Odysseus.

After days of debate, I took my beautiful *Lydia* to sea to find my friend Cimon, who had tarried to harry the enemy. We needed his voice in the council; he was an Athenian aristocrat, and yet an ally of Themistocles, and he could persuade the Spartans and the Corinthians when Themistocles fell back on insults. I ran east into the sun, hopping from protected beach to islet, all the way around Sounion and up the coast of Attica to Marathon. It was only after several days, hiding on the tiny isle of Megalos, that I spotted his mighty ship-killer *Ajax* on the horizon, fleeing from a crowd of Ionian ships.

That was a great day, for not only did I take a ship of Naxos – or rather, they changed sides – and rescued Cimon's squadron, virtually single-handed, but I saw the brother of my youth, Archilogos, on his command deck, and he waved. That wave meant more to me than victory; it told me that something had changed, and I began to think that perhaps some old wounds might be healed.

We returned to the fleet with our captures, and the winds of politics began to change. Themistocles openly threatened the Corinthians that if they did not support Athens, Athens might just change sides. It was ugly, and all I can say is that men were tired, bone-tired, and fatigue does not make for clear thinking.

And one night, we watched Attica burn, and Athens. Far away, we saw the fires as the Medes stormed the Acropolis and fired the temples. That was the night, by the way, that I understood that my son Hipponax was in love with the daughter of my enemy, Cleitus, the Alcmaeonidae clan leader. And that Hector, virtually my other son, was in love with Iris, a natural daughter of Xanthippus, the Athenian navarch and one of their party leaders. And the priestess of Artemis from Brauron raised her arms so that all Attica lay between them, and cursed the Persians. That was the most powerful curse I ever saw, and the gods listened.

In the end, after another scout of the enemy fleet, we, the professional sailors, were convinced we had the upper hand. But Themistocles' arrogance was greater than his virtue, and for once he spoke badly, and with anger. Eurybiades, tired of the wrangling, made the hard decision, and the Spartan commander of the fleet ordered us to retreat to the isthmus. That should have been the end of everything.

It was that night that many, many plots began to unravel. To this day I do not know the depths of Themistocles' treason, or his brilliance, or both. I suspect both. He proposed that we send his slave to the Great King with a promise of Athenian treachery. I accompanied his slave, and what I heard there led me to believe that Themistocles was capable of actually betraying the league. Perhaps, or perhaps not. Certainly, had Themistocles gathered the Athenian captains and demanded that they change sides like the Samians at Lade, I suspect we'd have gutted him like a fish. He was not 'king' of Athens. At the same time, I discovered that he had, in fact, been negotiating with the Great King for some time.

Bah. There was no knowing the mind of Themistocles. Brasidas the Spartan and I were taken as hostages, and with the help of Ka and his Numidians, we escaped. It sounds bald, put that way. We returned to camp in time to inform Themistocles that the Persians had sailed; tempted by his offer of treason, the Great King had ordered his fleet to attack.

Then, it was too late to run. My friend Aristides returned that night from exile – well, he'd never been far, if you are listening – and he backed Themistocles, and that swayed the league, and every man determined to fight.

And fight we did. Some men say Salamis was larger than Lade and some say smaller. And the truth is, whatever my friend Aeschylus says, that we sank or took fewer than a hundred hulls and lost more than thirty ourselves; we'd done almost as well the third day of fighting at Artemisium.

The difference was that autumn was coming on, and the Persian fleet broke and ran for its beaches, and some say that only his execution of some Phoenicians ended resistance, because the Phoenicians then decided to leave the Great King. Yet I was there, and I think we actually broke their will to fight. I had seen many ship fights since the Long War opened in the east, and ship for ship, we were as good or better. The Phoenicians, the backbone of the Great King's fleet, had lost dozens of ships and more important, dozens of crack crews and expert captains since the war opened. At some point, the Greeks had tipped the balance, and as victory slipped away from the Great King's fleet at Salamis, Poseidon tilted his hand, and gave to us the dominion of the surface of his seas.

We paid a high price. Idomeneaus fell there, in desperate fighting; Leukas the Alban took a terrible wound. Many of my friends fell, and many were wounded. When the Persians overran my ship, I lost comrades in every heartbeat, and Cleitus' daughter, the brilliant dancer and Hipponax's beloved, whom he had smuggled aboard to prove herself – a long story there by itself – fought with a broken oar and then jumped over the side to avoid capture and humiliation.

But we cleared the deck and as our revenge we took the flagship, the hardest, longest ship fight I have ever known, boarding through the rowing frame because she was higher than our ship, and then ...

And then we won. I could scarcely breathe, and Hipponax and Hector, my sons, collapsed, almost unable to stand, but Xanthippus and Cimon held the centre; the Corinthians, late, but better than never – stormed in; and far away to the east, Aristides and Phrynicus and hundreds of hoplites and archers stormed the island in the centre of the strait with the Athenian archer corps – of which you will hear more tonight – and the Persians and the Phoenicians and the Aegyptians and the Carians collapsed. Indeed, only the Ionians, our own Greek cousins, and my friend Archilogos amongst them, fought on, determined to cover their fleet's retreat. But for them, perhaps the Great King's fleet would have been destroyed right there. The wicked irony was that we saw ships that Cimon and I had saved at Lade, covering the retreat of the masters they hated.

Ah well. Their hour was coming.

Regardless, we went to our beaches exhausted but triumphant. There were many small signs of the favour of the gods: Cleitus' daughter had swum the three stades to the beach, alive and unharmed; Leukas had not died of his wounds; I picked up a Persian noble in the water and kept him from drowning, and other small things that made me think that perhaps ...

But despite some celebrations, we readied ourselves the next morning to fight again, as at Artemisium. Why not? I tell you, friends, that as the sun set on our victory, the Great King still had more uninjured ships and crews than we did.

But their spirit was broken. Cimon and I put to sea and scouted their beaches, and they were preparing to run east. They had their masts and sails aboard, and we all knew, then, that we had won.

And in the aftermath of victory, I found that Artaphernes was dying or dead, and his son Artaphernes, who hated me and his father's wife Briseis in equal measure, was racing east to have her killed; while Diomedes, the enemy of my youth, was taking two ships on the same errand.

Well. I was tired, but not so tired that I could not try to rescue the love of my life, and rescue her we did.

And last night, as our evening ended, I told you how the people of Attica were welcomed in Troezen and Hermione and other places on the east coast of the Peloponnesus; how, having rescued Briseis, or helped her rescue herself, I sailed into Hermione to find that my steward, a hero of his own kind, had purchased me a house, and prepared almost everything for my wedding, and that my friends had done the rest. And then, in one ceremony, I wed Briseis, and my son Hipponax wed the daughter of Cleitus, son of Cleisthenes of the Alcmaeonidae; and Hector, son of Anarchos, wed Iris, daughter of Xanthippus, son of Ariphron, whose wife Agariste was cousin to Cleitus and daughter of Hippocrates. I tell you all this genealogy so that you may see that my sons – for so they were both accounted – married Alcmaeonidae whose blood was so blue that it might have been taken for the ocean on a sunny day.

On the night I wed, Athens was an abandoned ruin, Attica had not harvested a crop in a year, and Plataea was a pile of rubble. The Persian army had retreated to winter in Thessaly, because there was not pasturage in Attica for twenty thousand horses. The Persian fleet had scattered, but still outnumbered ours.

At Salamis, we won. But mostly what we won was the right to fight again.

It was the year that Themistocles was elected archon in 'Athens', although in fact the assembly met on a hillside on Salamis. It was the year that Dromeus of Mantinea won the *pankration* at Olympia; the year that the Apiad king of Sparta died fighting Xerxes, and the Hellenes triumphed at Salamis. It was the fifteenth year of the Long War. Men planned, and the Fates spun our yarn, and the scissors were sharp.

It was, although we had no way of knowing, the ultimate year of the war.

Everything was in the balance.

Hermione

Winter, 480–479 BCE

My honeymoon in Hermione was scented in fig and jasmine and mint, wine and wood smoke. It was a wonderful time, with most of my friends around me, and if there were dark days when we remembered all our dead, there were great days when we lay on our couches and drank; when I chased my wife into her bed, or we walked into the agora and played at housekeeping; annoyed my sons and their new wives with our middle-aged advice, and wrangled about politics.

Briseis was a wonderful wife. She made no attempt to overrule my steward, but only co-operated with him. Indeed, she ran my little house with so little effort that she had energy left to join Jocasta in ruling the free Hellenes, or so it was said. Certainly she was not afraid to speak her views to men, or to anyone, and her views were plain: Ionia deserved to be liberated from the yoke of Persia. She and her brother Archilogos were practically the only representatives of Ionia on the mainland of Greece that winter, and they were both brilliant and eloquent. Men listened.

Women looked at her brilliance and her free tongue. Some resented her, but some emulated her, too. It was a winter of women; women's politics, and women's will.

Most of the league of allies was gathered together early that winter in a crescent from Troezen to Corinth, and the leaders of our league went back and forth: Gorgo of Sparta and the old king, Leotychidas, son of Menares of the other line of Spartan kings, the man who had arranged for the deposition of Demaratus, son of Ariston, who saved us at Persepolis and who was friend to my captain of marines and close friend, Brasidas. I know this is all dull, but you need to know your Spartan politics for anything that happened in the 'Year of War' to make sense. Leotychidas was the supporter of Cleomenes, who was the architect of the Spartan strategy of resistance to Persia – and Gorgo's father. Sparta had a war party and a peace party; that is, a party that supported the league and wanted to make every effort to face the Medes, and a party that wanted peace with the Great King. Some of the peace party would accept peace on almost any terms, and others simply wanted to see Athens, viewed in Sparta as an upstart rival, humbled or even destroyed by the Great King.

But I leave the road of my story too easily, and I need to plough a straighter furrow. Here it is, then: by two weeks after my wedding, my honeymoon was still glorious, but the honeymoon of the Free Greeks after the victory of Salamis was coming to an end.

The fight that brought the honeymoon to an end was about rewards and prizes, and thus was typically Greek. In the aftermath of victory, Greeks give prizes to the best and the bravest: to the contingent who were best, and to the man who was most noble. And these prizes are worth as much as, or more than, prizes awarded in the great games. Not that there is money, although sometimes the 'best' fighter in an engagement gets an extra share of the loot, and there was some good loot after Salamis. But it is fame we Greeks crave, and the undying fame of being 'the best' in the fight at Salamis was too much for almost everyone.

I think I'd been married three weeks when the league met in Corinth. I confess I chose not to go. I had a welter of excuses, and the best had to do with the state of my ships, every one of which needed serious repair, new wood, new tar, and a drier hull. And yet to you, my beauties and young bloods, I am not afraid to confess that it was Briseis' laugh and her body and her wit and the shine of her hair on my chest that kept me in kindly Hermione. I had had a surfeit of war and politics, and I didn't need to listen to Adeimantus of Corinth, who, in my opinion, had been paid to betray the Greeks, laud himself as the architect of victory at Salamis.

I stayed home. Aristides went, but left Jocasta. Cimon went, and my former mortal foe Cleitus went, and Xanthippus went, and Myron went for the Plataeans.

I remember the day I heard the news. They'd all been gone a good few days, and Moire and I were in one of our hastily built ship sheds. Outside, the wind howled, and a light snow fell, and it was unseasonably cold, but the whole shed was warm enough that we were stripped to the waist, wearing our *chitoniskoi* like Heracles my ancestor, off one shoulder, because we had a great iron vat of pine pitch heating on coals, and the coals warmed the whole shed, at least by the bow. And while the pitch heated, young Kineas and I, and Hippias son of Draco of Plataea, carpenter and wagon builder, and a pair of Hermionian shipwrights, Dion and Aristion, were scraping away at a new stave for the hull; a course of good Thracian oak near the waterline, a fancy building style that strengthened the hull for just a little weight. But oak is much, much harder to work than spruce or pine, and we were cursing, cutting, fitting, and cutting again. You see, when you fit a new strake into a ship's hull, you can only do so much by measurement. The rest has to be done by feel, and by hand, a wood shaving at a time. It takes hours, but it is better than having a leak.

At any rate, we were finally making good the damage of four great battles and a dozen ship fights. At the other end of the *Lydia*, Giorgos and another party of carpenters, and Sekla and Alexandros, were getting at the patch we'd thrown over the hole we put in her hull one morning at Thermopylae. And bow and stern, yet another work party was carefully replacing the pronounced keel that Vasileos had built in as part of his original design. Every beach landing had marred it, but while it bit the water, less than a hand span of spruce at the bottom of centre strake, it caused our beautiful *Lydia* to track better than other ships and it gave her a touch more bite on the water in a crosswind. Four years of hard use had marred her, but we had no other work, and we knew the fighting was not over.

At any rate, we were working away. There is something very satisfying about the process of repair and maintenance; it is healing, I think, and as the holes in the *Lydia* (and other ships) were closed, and the black pitch was spread to seal the wounds we made in her hull, other things healed. Sittonax, who had taken a bad wound at Salamis and hadn't even risen for my wedding, hobbled down to the ship sheds and was brighter each day. He had taken to sitting with Brasidas, who was himself in a dark place.

That day, the day we heard from Corinth, we finished working for the day and I ordered wine served to all the men working. There were no wages that winter. The Hermionians fed us, and we paid what we could, but there was a commonality to the effort that was itself noble.

At any rate, Brasidas raised a *mastos-cup* and poured a libation. 'To work,' he said. 'I suppose if I am to be a Plataean, I will have to learn to enjoy work.'

Sittonax, who never got his hands dirty, had pitch all over him. He shrugged. 'I'll never understand,' he said in his Gaulish-Greek. 'All you *do* is work.'

I frowned. 'You enjoy war?' I asked Sittonax.

He shrugged – and winced as the pain hit his neck. 'I do, as long as some Mede isn't sawing off my head,' he said.

'And yet, war is full of work, and even now, we prepare this ship for war. War at sea would be wet, I think, without a ship.' I was practising the rhetorical skills that I was not, thanks to the gods, using at Corinth.

'There are slaves,' Sittonax said, and Brasidas nodded.

I thought that Dion, the shipwright, would explode.

But I smiled. 'Do you want to go to war in a ship built by men who hate you?' I asked.

Sittonax raised the cup in salute. 'I take your point,' he said. 'But I'll never learn to love pitch.'

'For me, I love the smell,' I said. 'It makes me think of torches and feast days.' I pulled my chiton up and pulled a warmer wool chiton over the first before picking up my sad old blue cloak. 'I'm for home. Care to join me?' I said to Brasidas.

He nodded. 'I would be delighted,' he said, with more warmth than he usually showed those days. So he and I, Sittonax and Moire walked home, and Sekla joined us.

One of the many delights of Briseis – and my steward – was that I could be endlessly hospitable. Briseis was a noblewoman of Ionia. She craved company, and she wanted to host people every night, as far as our tiny house allowed.

That night, I remember, I arrived to find Jocasta, wife of Aristides, and Agariste, wife of Xanthippus, and Penelope my sister, and her friend Lydia, whose husband had been killed at Salamis, and my daughter Euphonia, all together in my very small '*andron*'. Now the *andron* is supposed to be the 'men's room', at least in cities like Thebes. But in my house it might have been called the 'gynedron' because Briseis kept her loom there, and when we came in out of the snow, there were five of them and their handmaidens all weaving away while discussing the future of Greece, as women do. And as I walked in I heard Agariste say the name 'Themistocles' the way some of us might refer to Hades, and I laughed.

All the work at the loom stopped, and some kisses were exchanged. Eugenios my steward came and took my himation and my two *chitoniskoi* and reclothed me in a brilliant scarlet himation of the softest wool; a wedding present. And he brought warm wool felt shoes for all the men, as the floors were cold. It was a very cold winter, by our standards.

'Can we feed all these people?' I asked him.

He just smiled and bowed his head. 'I'm sure that we can, my lord,' he said. 'I believe we can manage roast lamb, some good barley, fresh bread, two or three wines, raisins and almonds.'

I liked to pretend I had something to do with the direction of my house. 'Perhaps soup?' I asked.

Briseis laughed, and I smelled her jasmine and mint and knew she was close behind me.

'Soup would cause both of our cooks to fall over dead, my dear. I guessed you'd bring five, and Pen hoped you'd bring Brasidas, so we're ready. The ladies will dine upstairs and the gentleman in the tiled room, and then perhaps we'll meet for a cup of wine.'

I turned to gaze with my usual delight on those sparkling eyes, arched brows, and amused lips. In fact, I have never tired of them.

Some things are worth fighting for, waiting for, killing for.

'That all sounds delightfully well planned,' I said. 'Sometimes I think that you should be the one directing the war with the Great King,' I said.

Briseis' eyes sparkled more. 'Had I had the direction of the Ionian Revolt,' she said lightly, 'no Mede would ever have made it to Athens.'

Well. Probably the truth, and her first husband was an utter fool. I killed him, of course, but too late to save the Ionian Revolt.

'What was Agariste saying about Themistocles?' I asked. A thought hit me, hard. '*My sister* hoped that Brasidas would come?' I asked.

Briseis smiled sweetly. 'Your sister admires the Spartan,' she said. 'Her admiration is returned. Given how tenuous is his hold on … happiness, and hers, I think this is best for both, do you not?'

I stood in my own house, slightly shocked.

'And,' Briseis said quietly, 'if for some reason you do *not agree*, perhaps this is not the moment to show it,' she said.

I suspect my mouth moved a little, like a fish out of water. This is what my children tell me I do when I'm confused.

So it was hours before I heard about Themistocles. I lay on a couch with Moire and we talked about ships, and I vaguely remember that we talked about taking a warship and a round ship and trying to run to Aegypt in the spring. We knew that we needed to make war pay. Remember that most of my people had lost virtually everything; that is, the Plataean farmers had their tools and their herds, but the lower class men had virtually nothing, unless they were so provident that they saved silver, and they had families living in the tiny houses and sheds of Hermione and Troezen. I had saved my ships and some of my fortune, but my house was gone, my forge, and a great deal of my wealth.

In fact, ever since the dawn after we heard that Xerxes had fled, men had been taking their families back to Attica. Mardonius, the 'satrap of Europe' who was to have conquered us, kept the best part of the Great King's army, but he had retreated to Thrace and Thessaly for the winter, and as soon as his looters and murderers were out of Attica, people began to return. The poorest, in fact.

But we were Plataeans, and Thebes was a firm ally of the enemy. Our city had been razed – destroyed – and we had no place to go.

Yet.

At any rate, I really only remember this because Brasidas snapped that we sounded like helots. It was among the most ungracious things I'd ever heard him say, and he flushed the moment he said it.

He rose. 'I am no kind of company,' he said. He made for the door, and Sekla blocked the way. The Nubian was smiling, but he was not easily moved.

'You will not make yourself better by leaving,' I said. 'Come, let us join the ladies.'

Brasidas looked crestfallen. 'I spoke foolishly, like a boy,' he said.

I laughed. 'That will teach you,' I said. For indeed, he was a byword for Laconic silence.

I carried a heavy Lesbian amphora up the narrow stairs, and one of the female slaves announced us, and then we went into the women's rooms, which really were our bedroom and dressing room. Hermione was nothing like Plataea, much less Athens; too many people in too little space, with all the press of war behind us. Mores were different. I have heard men say that women learned too many freedoms that winter. All I can say is that some men are the merest fools.

Suffice it to say that we sat on camp stools while the ladies reclined on our two *klinai* and my daughter sat on my lap. She was too big for it and made the stool creak.

And I finally heard the story. Agariste was so well-bred that she pretended to be unable to speak to men without her husband present, until Briseis rolled her eyes and sat up.

'The story is,' she said, 'that the league council voted prizes for the best men and the best contingent at Salamis, like a land battle.'

Most of us raised cups at the mere mention of the name, and Brasidas said, 'Hear, hear', or something like that. I remember I turned my head and looked at him to smile, and saw that he was smiling at Penelope, my sister.

So . . .

I looked back to Briseis.

She smiled and nodded and went on. 'So all the navarchs voted.'

'Except my daddy,' my daughter said in an annoying, slightly cloying little-girl voice. She laughed. 'He's right here.'

'And all of them voted for themselves,' Sekla said. He grinned.

Briseis glared at him. It was a mock glare, and he mock-quailed.

'You are ruining my story,' Briseis said.

'I was trying to be funny!' Sekla said. 'But Greeks . . .'

'Well, that's just what happened,' Briseis said. 'Every navarch voted for his own contingent and himself – the Aeginians, the Athenians, the Spartans, the Corinthians, and so on.'

We all laughed.

Briseis shook her head. 'I'm not done. So, after two ballots, Aristides, who was not commanding any contingent, suggested that they all vote for a first *and second* place. All the navarchs voted for themselves in first place; but all of them voted for Themistocles in second.'

We laughed again.

'But Adeimantus of Corinth threatened to leave the alliance if the men of Athens were awarded the prize. And Themistocles has left the council. He walked off in a rage, and there's a rumour he has gone to Sparta.'

'Sparta?' I said.

Jocasta sat back. 'Well, my husband isn't here, but I think I can speak,' she said. 'Gorgo invited him, and Eurybiades.'

'But . . .' I said.

Briseis nodded. 'But the league council has broken up,' she said. 'In effect, the war party has gone to Sparta to talk, and the peace party had gone home.'

'Peace party?' Moire didn't really follow politics.

I nodded. 'More than half the league either thinks we never should have fought the Persians in the first place, or that, now that we won at Salamis, the whole thing will *sort itself out*.'

Moire nodded. 'I see, the way the lion sorts out the sheep, after he gets inside the sheepfold.'

I raised my cup and drank to him.

'And half of them have been paid good gold for their views,' I said. 'I'm not surprised Adeimantus of Corinth made such an inflammatory speech.'

Briseis nodded to me. 'Regardless, the league council has dispersed.'

So. My honeymoon continued.

But the league's honeymoon was over.

We spent the next month repairing ships. Storm after storm struck us, and one was so bad that we warped all of our round ships into the beach and pulled them well up, two *plethron*, or almost two hundred feet, above the water line. Then it turned out that all three of our little tubs had the worm, and we stripped their bottoms and replanked them. They were too wide for the sheds, and that was cold work, but it made the time fly. Moire and I began to plan our expedition to Aegypt and we began to gather a cargo: simple stuff that would sell quickly, olive oil and wine.

Archilogos joined us for the work, bored and eager for company, and asked to be included for the trip to Aegypt.

'I've been, you know,' he said, with something of his old sparkle. 'And not as a pirate,' he added.

He had a point there.

We were having a difficult time, he and I. We had been best friends; indeed, we had been brothers. But I had been his slave, too. Parse that as you will, it was never a simple relationship, and I killed his father. He blamed me for that for years, although, if you have been listening, you know I only put him out of great, mind-destroying pain. And when his mother died, he blamed me for that, too.

And I was Briseis' lover. My life has taken many turns, and few of them what I expected when I was learning the spear dances from Calchas by the tomb of Leithos. But making love to Briseis in the hours after avenging the family on Diomedes ... I have thought many times of what it must have been like for him, for my friend/master Archilogos, to find me abed with his sister, just a few weeks after discovering that his mother had been unfaithful to his father.

Listen, thugater, and all of you, because these are stormy seas in which to keep my helm. But when you are young, you are full of fire, and yet, I find, curiously prudish. And when you are old, the fires have died down, and you realize that things that seemed worth killing and dying for when you were young are silly, or trite, or the merest custom.

When Briseis and I were discovered, she said things – things about her own possession of her body, and her intentions – that, to be honest, I hated as much as her father hated them. *Men* possess women. A woman's chastity is an expression of a man's power, his honour. Eh?

So must Archilogos have thought, and to have his slave – or his recently freed slave – *possess* his sister was impossible. And to have his sister claim that she possessed herself . . .

In retrospect, thugater, I have come to realize that all my life I preferred women who possessed themselves; in time I hope you come to your own possession. And yet, at the same time, I have some doubts as to the ability of any young boy or girl ever birthed to possess themselves. This is the story of age and youth, I think. The ability to possess yourself – your body and your mind – comes at different ages to different people, but there are few enough at fifteen or sixteen who are anything but a tangle of feelings and appetites.

Of course, I'm so much more mature now.

Hah.

Bah. I am sailing off into the wrong sunset; my lovely daughter is making a motion with her hand to keep the steward from refilling the krater. I had to tell this, to say that Archilogos and I could not simply fall back into being friends. We had to learn everything. It was a little like taking a bad wound, and recovery. Even our footwork had suffered. Everything was troubled, and the simplest conversation could carry an edge.

And all this complexity was made worse by Archilogos' position as a sort of supplicant, an untried deserter. He had been a famous man amongst the Ionians. He had a great reputation with them, and with the Great King and with his officers, even Mardonius. I know what an animal repute is; how it sits on your shoulders, how its weight pushes you this way and that, like a drunkard on a pitching deck in a storm at sea, and robs you of your independence. And he had repudiated his sister and then grudgingly accepted her, and in the end, she had been one of the agents of his change to our side, and now . . .

He was the same man, but he had neither reputation nor honour, and he wasn't sure about anything. I feared for him every day. I feared some foolish hothead would say that Briseis was a whore, a concubine first of the Medes and then of the Greeks; and he'd fight and kill, or die. I feared that some man would question his courage or his patriotism. Or belittle his manhood. He was on edge, and he *looked* for insults, as only a man who fears for his repute does.

Sekla, always careful, always aware of how others felt ... Sekla watched over him the way he looked after Brasidas. I could not. If Archilogos caught me protecting him, he would grow angry, and he would say ...

Things. But thirty-six is better than twenty-six. When he insulted me, I laughed and walked away.

At any rate ...

Work can be like battle, and he and his deck crew were gradually welded into our little fleet as we rebuilt his *Lady Artemis*, where his stern had taken damage in the fighting at Salamis – where he had been on the other side. But his helmsman was a Samian, Cadmos, and he was like Harpagos and Epaphroditos and all the other great islanders I've known: a fine seaman, but also a witty man. Most of his crew were Ephesian and Samian and they discoursed every day on how eager the islands were to throw off the hated Persians and be free.

I'd given my youth fighting in Ionia and I hardened my heart.

'When the time is right,' Archilogos said.

I shook my head. 'When the time is right, the Ionians and Aetolians will have to throw off the yoke themselves,' I said.

Archilogos shook his head, annoyed. 'I don't think it could happen,' he said. 'The tyrants imposed by the Great King are careful men with picked bodyguards of foreigners. I think it would take a league fleet and a league army to bring us to revolt again.' He met my eye. 'I would give *anything* to help effect the freedom of Ionia.'

I was pounding tree nails into pre-bored holes in the hull of the *Lady Artemis*, putting new planks on her. Archilogos was a better aristocrat than I, and tended to watch and 'manage'.

'If the league doesn't meet and plan its strategy,' I said, 'no ship will go east of Aegina. Delos, perhaps.'

Indeed, there was a story making the rounds that a delegation of Ionians had gone to Sparta, and one of the rumours was that an angry Ionian had claimed that the Greeks of Attica and the Peloponnesus couldn't navigate east of Delos.

If anyone had asked me – and outside of my own friends, no one did – I'd have told you that we were in for years of war. Mardonius had the Great King's field army in Thessaly, as I said, and we heard from the winds that the 'Persian' fleet was at Cos. I foresaw years of this: summer campaigns coming at us out of Thessaly and across the fields of Boeotia, and summers of commerce raiding. Moire and I – and Brasidas and even Briseis – were beginning to plan for a future where we had no town of Plataea, and we needed income and supplies.

A nice mixture of trade and piracy.

In fact, I bought one of the Persian captures: a really beautiful light trireme, probably made in one of the Asian Greek cities. We had another month of bad weather, and the hull was sitting on the beach. Aegina bought a dozen captures and Athens kept the rest.

Anyway, the whole winter smells of pine pitch and resin and new-sawn wood, in my memory. And the sea.

Ah, and we drilled. I forgot that, although it played a role in the healing of Archilogos, in as much as he was healed.

We all knew we were in for a fight, and there was very little work except for what I provided in ship repair. We had most of Plataea there, and Myron and Hermogenes decided that we would drill every day and pay the men a wage of one drachma.

I'd like to claim credit for this, but it was Hermogenes' idea. Myron and I and a dozen other 'rich' men – rich by Plataean standards – all put in what funds we could spare. By paying our people, we made them dance and drill, and we kept them together, thinking of themselves as 'Plataeans.'

I had never drilled every day. But Brasidas had, and it delighted him.

'Now we will be excellent,' he said with real enthusiasm. 'We will be ready for the contest.'

So that winter is also tinged with the memory of cold mornings on the beach of Hermione, with a thousand Plataeans, dancing the first *pyrriche* until we were warm, and then dividing into a dozen smaller *taxeis* to learn new dances, practise others that some of us knew, or to learn in new ways.

Of course Polymarchos and some of the other *hoplomachoi* I had met didn't teach with dance. They taught the new way, the way the best *pankration* coaches taught, with postures and drills. Both have their uses. The dance is beautiful, and it also teaches men (and women) to do things *together*, and I also have a feeling, no more, that the dance is easier to learn and somehow works down into the muscles like a good massage. Things I learn in dance are there even in the midst of blood and terror. But on the other hand, in dance, you can never stop and ask questions; and they are very difficult to change, because of customs.

Let me give you an example.

Calchas taught me a great deal about spear fighting, but he believed, at the core, that the stronger – the stronger in *arete*, in excellence – would pound the weaker down; that this was virtually inevitable. He taught me several very strong blows, and by Ares, I have killed many men with his way.

But later, Aristides and Polymarchos taught me that these heavy, committed overhand blows could get me killed, and frankly, I was lucky never to have faced someone who knew how to use them against their enemy. Imagine that you thrust hard into the face of an *aspis*, and your point buries itself in the face of the shield? There it is, held by the soft wood under the face of the *aspis*. Your opponent rolls his shield outwards and your spear is ripped from your hand, or at least taken well off line, and you are open to a variety of killing strokes.

You see?

I have had this happen dozens of times in combat. But no man ever killed me in that brief interval while I tried to remove my spearhead from the face of his shield. Although once I trapped my spear between the thin sheet of bronze facing an opponent's shield and the soft wood underneath, and when I wrenched it free – the head was gone, and I had a stick. This was fighting on Crete. I should have learned then, but I beat the man down with my shaft and killed him with my *saurauter*, the heavy bronze butt spike that makes a fine club.

Aristides fought very differently, and used his spear shaft – even in close fighting – to defend himself, scarcely ever moving his *aspis* at all. This, I later discovered, was how Polymarchos taught. Whereas Calchas taught me to keep my *aspis* moving, to attack with it, to use it to pre-empt an attack.

Which is 'right'?

Well, both work. A dance cannot teach the subtleties of crossing and pressure that would make me decide how to handle an opponent's spear or my own attacks. But individual, patient instruction can.

And then, with dance, I can teach a hundred men the basics of spear fighting in an hour. Or I can use that hour to thoroughly teach two or perhaps three men.

So on the beach, we would divide, and divide again; learn dances, and also go to various men – I was one of them – for some individual instruction in the new way, as I say. Men joked that they were being prepared for the Olympics, especially when Hermione itself produced two Olympic *pankration* teachers and we purchased their services.

We'd been practising for perhaps two weeks, and it was the first day of the feast of the Anthesteria; the way Plataeans celebrate it, we take four days, and all the hard drinking is in the last three, but even after the first day there were some hard heads. Hector was late, and did not take well to the ribbing and the jokes about newly-weds and insatiable young women.

'I didn't know I was training for the Olympics,' he shot at Brasidas.

Brasidas nodded. He went on, putting the men into ranks, discussing something with Hermogenes, and then, when we were all lined up in the cold wind, he jumped on a Gaulish barrel and addressed us. Surprising for a man so often silent, he had an excellent speaking voice, and his voice carried.

'Men of Plataea!' he said. 'Many of you wonder why we work so hard! And train every day!' He smiled, and looked at Hector, who, of course, stared at the ground.

'But there is no greater contest than the one that will face us, this summer or perhaps the next. We will go helmet to helmet with the Medes, and the most excellent will triumph. For the winners, a crown of laurel, and for the losers – shame and death. If we are the losers, we will lose not only our lives, but our freedom, our women and children will be made slaves, our temples will be thrown down, and it will be as if Greece had never been. If we triumph ...' He smiled. 'If we triumph, we will have earned the right to face the Medes again in the next summer, and the next, until we convince them that this beach and our wives and these stony hills are not worth the blood we will make them pay. So I say to you, men of Plataea, that this is the greatest contest that Greeks have ever known, and every one of you should be honoured that you are included. And Hermogenes and Arimnestos and Polymarchos and Triton and all your teachers will show you how to live, and how to win. And where an athlete would pay many gold darics for this training, we pay you to have it. And every day we spend here in training, one of you will learn something that will keep him alive, or enable the phalanx to push a little harder, to fight a little longer, for one man's spear to reap another Mede, and one day at a time we will work for victory. That is why we train.'

He jumped down.

I have a lump in my throat. He *believed*. He loved to train, and a little at a time, he made most of us love it, too.

At any rate, we all cheered for a while, and then we hit each other with sticks.

Three weeks in, Brasidas started us running. Every day. He would put himself at the head of the phalanx, and call out, 'Ready to run?' and we would groan.

Oh, how little we knew of what was to come.

And Polymarchos would stop us, all of us, some days, on some rocky path in the hills above Hermione, and make us lift rocks, or tumble, or fall and rise without our hands, and then we'd run again.

And when we were headed home, and men were flagging, Brasidas would halt us and make us tug at our sweat-stained *chitoniskoi* and even run our fingers through our hair.

'Always finish well,' he'd say. 'Finish as you began. Now sing!'

Archilogos and his crew joined us from the first, and like the work on the ships, it helped bridge all the gaps between us. Many of the hoplite class men of Hermione joined us as well; at first they mocked us, but as time went on, almost two dozen came with us, running on the barren hills.

One day we ran in snow. One day we practised boarding ships, and a dozen of my sailors began practising with slings. Sekla led them, and surprised me by throwing heavy rocks and big clay pots.

'I thought slingers used stones and lead bullets,' I said.

Sekla smiled.

'If you continue spending time with Brasidas, you'll forget how to talk,' he said.

Brasidas smiled at me. He winked at Sekla. 'We like to let you do the talking,' he said. 'You seem to enjoy it.'

Many men laughed. I have no idea why.

The next morning, most of the *Lydia*'s deck crew behaved like small boys with a secret, grinning, hurrying about, laughing too much and looking very serious ...

We all ran, and then we pulled bows for exercise, and Sekla and the crew built a bonfire of driftwood on the beach. It was a cold day.

The slings came out. The newly trained slingers lobbed various things, and then a small boy brought a firepot, the kind you'd use to move fire from one hearth to another.

Sekla put the thing in his sling, whirled it once, and let fly, and the whole firepot flew through the air, struck the bonfire ...

It didn't quite explode. But the results were very satisfactory.

Brasidas raised an eyebrow, and took us for a second run. No one got warm at the fire, and we ran in snow.

That was unpleasant.

At any rate, we repaired our ships, and we trained for war.

It was also after the feast of the Anthesteria, when we were all a little hungover from three days of toasting Dionysus, that Cimon came in with Aristides. They had sailed to Corinth, but they came home on horseback, over the passes of Arcadia from Sparta. They left their ships in sheds to the north. The weather was terrible, and no one could sail, not even daysailing along the coast.

Hermione returned to being the capital of free Attica. That is to say, with Aristides and Cleitus and Xanthippus and Cimon we seemed to have all the powerful men of Athens – except Themistocles, who was lingering in Sparta. Myron had returned, and Hermogenes, two weeks earlier; they'd drilled from the first. Hermogenes, not I, was now the polemarch of Plataea. I hadn't been fired. I'd merely chosen to fight at sea at Salamis.

Aristides and Cimon had stayed for the entire farce of the award of prizes. They were disgusted, but delighted to find the Plataeans drilling for war, and they joined us with a great many of the Athenians around the town, so that by the end of the month of Anthesterion, when Aristides sacrificed for the Diasia for the Athenians and coaxed me to sacrifice for the Plataeans, we had almost three thousand men dancing, drilling, practising, running.

We also began to act as if we were the war council of the league. I think that, in fact, we were, and events bore us out, even though I will confess we were wrong about almost everything we supposed.

We expected their fleet to come at us in the autumn. For myself, I expected the Persians to spend the summer building ships and training, gathering allies, coercing the Aegyptians and the Cilicians to provide more and better ships. So it was my plan to sail to Aegypt as soon as the sun appeared in spring to warm the frozen ground. Brasidas and I thought we'd do what we could to provoke an Aegyptian rebellion. Every one of us who traded knew that the Aegyptians hated the Persians *at least* as much as we hated them. Persia had re-conquered Aegypt just four years before, but we thought – we hoped – that they were still spoiling for a fight.

I thought Aegypt was probably a more fertile ground than Ionia, although I was willing to try there, too.

Oh, it was a matter of weather and sailing. Let me explain. In spring, a good captain who can navigate can take the west winds off Europe and slant down from the Peloponnesus to Crete. These are the winds that allow Crete and Sparta to be so close. And from Crete, as I well knew, it was little matter to take the westerlies across to Cyprus and then down into the mouth of the Nile, which I had done several times, and Moire had done only the year before. A much shorter trip, let me add, from Hermione in the Peloponnesus than from the other side of the Corinthian Gulf, up by Plataea.

But the return voyage is a different proposition. If you wait for early autumn, you can take the easterlies back. That's what some of the huge Athenian grain ships do in these decadent days, but there's another solution, which is to stay in with the coast along Syria and Judea. It can be touchy along the coast of Cilicia, what with pirates and currents, but by coming the long way home, we'd have time to trade and to pick up all the rumours. Perhaps even lay eyes on the Persian fleet – and we'd be coming up on them from the south. The Medes would never expect enemies coming from the south. We'd stop at Chios and perhaps Mytilene, and then pick our way back west to Attica.

Yes, Attica. Already by midwinter solstice, more and more Athenians were preparing to move back into their homes, or rather, to go back and plant and rebuild. Many already had.

We were in Aristides' house one night after the solstice; I lay with my son Hipponax on one couch, and Aristides lay with Cimon on another. Hector was there, and Brasidas, and Amenias of Pellene, who most of us thought deserved the prize for valour at Salamis, and my new brother-in-law Xanthippus, and my former master Archilogos. We made a sacrifice, and indeed, Aristides, who was appalled too often at my lack of aristocratic skills – besides my ability to clear an enemy trireme, that is – was teaching me some of the art of divination by entrails. Fascinating stuff, if a little messy.

As usual, I digress. After we sacrificed in the courtyard, we lay around, drinking too much wine and eating too much *opson* like much younger men. We'd been running all day, and most of them had been debating the move to Attica: its timing, the economic necessity. The people of Hermione were unbelievably generous, but they were going to run out of food, olive oil, and wine. And everything else.

'And half the *thetes* of Attica are still camped on Salamis,' Cimon said. 'They'll be thin as mongrel dogs by spring. We need to feed them.'

'There's grain in the Euxine,' Amenias said.

Archilogos perked up. He was sullen most of the time, but talk of war brought him to life.

'Don't I know it,' Cimon said. 'My pater used to own some of it. How do we get it here?'

'The Persian fleet is at Cos,' I said. 'The Euxine must be feeding them.'

Aristides waved at his steward for more wine.

'So there's a grain fleet,' I said.

'We don't know that,' Cimon said cautiously. 'We don't know if it exists, or when it will sail, or what route it will take.'

'Put a squadron off the mouth of the Dardanelles,' I said. 'You'll have a grain fleet in a few weeks.' I rolled over and did some calculations. 'They must have twenty thousand rowers on Cos. That's almost eight hundred *medimnoi* a day.' Let me remind you that a rich man in Athens had farms that produced two hundred *medimnoi* a year. That's a lot of grain.

'Eight hundred a day?' Archilogos nodded. 'That's about right.'

Of course. He'd been commanding a squadron and attending command councils – on the other side.

'That's more than one grain fleet,' I said. 'That's a grain fleet every month.'

Archilogos sat up on his couch and smacked his right fist into his left palm. 'We can do that,' he said.

Cimon shook his head. 'No. As soon as they know you are there, they'll keep the grain at Byzantium or one of the other towns and send a squadron to clear us away.'

'So it has to be a surprise,' I said.

Aristides nodded. 'The Great King is laying siege to Potidaea,' he said.

Now it was my turn to be cautious. 'All those cities sent earth and water on submission,' I said.

Aristides nodded. 'So they did. And in the autumn, when Artaphernes was retreating with Xerxes, he demanded too much, and Potidaea shut her gates.'

Cimon nodded. 'That's a very strong place,' he said.

I shrugged. 'Never been.'

Amenias laughed. 'Never been?' he asked. 'By Poseidon, Plataean, I didn't think there was anywhere in the great disc of the world you hadn't been. You've been to Hyperborea and not to Potidaea?'

'Where is Themistocles?' I asked.

There was a little silence.

'He's behaving like an arse,' Aristides said, 'in Sparta.'

Well, Aristides was no friend of Themistocles.

But even Cimon, who sometimes voted with the 'wise man of Athens', shook his head. 'The Spartans crowned him in laurels,' he said. 'Some say he is in Gorgo's bed.'

Aristides furrowed his brow. 'None of that in my house, please,' he said.

Amenias nodded. 'Well – I heard it too,' he admitted. 'But I understand him all too well. He should have had the prize at Corinth. And the thanks of every free Hellene. And instead ... we heard a speech from your friend Adeimantus. Now he bathes in the praise of the Spartans. I do not blame him.'

'Except that he is a man of Athens, not Sparta.' Aristides shrugged. 'He is the *archon basileus* for the year. Yet he is not here to lead the council or the fleet.'

Xanthippus nodded. 'Yes. He needs to be here. Perhaps we should praise him more.' He smiled a nasty smile.

'You know he has an escort of Spartiates, like a king?' Aristides said.

'I know that the Spartans don't mind laying it on thick,' I said. When I was there, the year before, they had been in the process of granting full Spartiate status and citizenship to a seer, a man of Elis named Teisemenos, reputed the most wonderful diviner in all Greece. As he had not undergone the *agoge* or warrior training and was a foreigner, it had surprised me that they would 'adopt' him. Plataea gave citizenship readily enough, but the Spartans!

As usual, I have left my course.

'I think ...' my son Hipponax began. Then he flushed and looked around.

Other men smiled. Young men are usually shy at a symposium, and for good reason. But Hipponax was popular, newly married, a very Achilles from Salamis. 'I think that if Themistocles craves praise, he also deserves it.'

There was a little silence, and then Aristides raised the two-handled *kylix* krater. 'Well said, young man,' he said. 'Let us remember Themistocles, the architect of victory.'

And we all drank to him.

'I still think we can take a grain fleet,' Archilogos said.

Cimon fingered his beard, and I had a moment of real fear that he was going to mock Archilogos for saying 'we'.

Or call him a traitor.

Instead, Cimon nodded slowly. 'Potidaea?' he asked.

By the spring feast of Apollo we'd repaired every ship we owned, despite all the exercise and training, and they dried in the sun on the days there was sun, and were pounded with rain and occasional snow on other days. Twice I took teams of oxen over the mountains to Epidauros to fetch more wood. The sanctuary by the sea is very beautiful, even in winter, and more beautiful when almost empty of pilgrims. But no adventure occurred, although once, Polymarchos had me leave a whole load of cut trees up on the hillside, and then he took the whole phalanx up there at a run and made us *carry* the trees down, twenty men to a tree trunk. By Heracles, that was a miserable day, in sleet. And yet we were proud as Ares when we had them stacked by the sheds.

But on my return the third time, chilled to the bone but with enough oak, ash, and pine to repair Cimon's long *Ajax*, I found that Themistocles had been. And gone.

Briseis sat by me and we ate alone. We did, sometimes.

'He said some very provocative things,' she said.

We ate a little, and talked of other things.

'I'm pregnant,' she said fondly. 'My body responds to yours,' she said impishly.

I laughed with joy, thugater.

I laughed, but Themistocles was gone. He had gifts from the Spartans, and they had gone to his head. He had tried to use his powers as *archon basileus* as if he was a tyrant, or the *basileus* himself.

He and Aristides had had a shouting match, which must have been humiliating for poor Aristides, and then he'd gone off to Troezen, and then, we heard, Attica. But that was later.

'A baby,' I probably burbled. Next to my wife's pregnancy, Themistocles seemed like a very small fish. 'What did he say that made Aristides so angry?'

'He said that the Spartans were building a wall on the isthmus, and that they would never fight for Attica, and it was time to consider where all the people of Attica were going to settle.'

Briseis smiled, but I could tell that the words had hurt her. No woman wants to bear a child in a howling wilderness, or in a colony, and the former queen of Ionia had, I think, expected better than to be the wife of a man without land. Although to be fair, she never said so.

'By Heracles my ancestor,' I said. 'Themistocles thinks the Spartans will abandon us?'

'Aristides suggested that this was just one of his schemes – that if we all sailed west to form a colony, Themistocles would be the most powerful man in it.' She shrugged. 'For myself, I did not like what I saw. He was – immoderate.' She spat the word.

This from Briseis, who had made a sort of art of immoderation, once upon a time.

Well, well.

'You don't like him,' I said.

'He puts me in mind of a number of windbags I have known,' Briseis said. 'But if his views on the Spartans are accurate, love, then I am terrified, once for my new people, the Athenians, and another time for my own people in Ionia. Because he said that the Spartans refused to receive the delegation from Ionia, and said that their cities should be disestablished, and all their people moved to the west.'

Our eyes met.

'We'll come through it,' I said. I took her hands.

She leaned her head on my shoulder. 'I never doubted, my husband. Merely ... As always, I wonder why so many men are fools.' She looked at me, unsure of herself for once. 'I want ... Ionia and Aetolia free. Prosperous. As they were when I was a girl.'

Foolishly, I forgot who she was. 'Spare me,' I said, with little feeling.

'Spare you what?' she snapped.

'Spare me a speech about the Ionians,' I said. 'I was there. I fought in every thrice-damned battle. I was there when we sacked Sardis like impious fools, and when we were driven like cowards from the field at Ephesus, and when Miletus fell, and when the Samians betrayed us at Lade. My friends *died*, Briseis. For *nothing*.' I crossed my arms, sad and angry and foolish. 'Ionia can fight for itself.'

She reached for an almond, and it was my fighter's senses that saved me where empathy failed. She reached very slowly, she who was so graceful, and I realized that she was controlling herself very carefully. That she was angry.

'Miltiades and his ilk have used Ionia as a cat's-paw to engage Persia, abused the Ionians' cities, led them to revolt, and now, in our darkest hour, you would abandon us?' she asked. Her voice was quiet and almost sultry.

Youth is a fine thing, but maturity is better, except in the morning when the wind is cold. I actually thought before I answered. 'I do not think that Ionia can be freed from the Persians by force of arms,' I said carefully. 'The league has not even determined an assembly point for the fleet. We don't even know how to defend Greece.'

'Ionia *is* Greece,' Briseis said. 'Sparta and Athens are nests of pirates and mercenaries who live in grass huts, at least when compared to Ephesus and Halicarnassus. Name a philosopher, an artist, a singer, a poet from *Athens*. Much less *Sparta*.'

'Hesiod was a poet, or so I hear,' I said. I was stung by her contempt.

'A conservative old man who knew the seasons and hated women,' Briseis said. 'Perfect. The very epitome of mainland Greece.'

I took her hands again. 'Briseis,' I said.

'Perhaps we should stop having this conversation,' she said carefully. 'I have already spoken intemperately.'

'Briseis,' I said again. I caught her eyes. 'The Ionians fought against us at Salamis. In fact, they fought very well for the Great King. If I were awarding prizes, I'd give the prize for valour in a disaster to them. If only they'd been so good at Lade.'

'Lade,' she spat. 'You say it again and again as if it justifies abandoning the best part of the Greek world.'

'You weren't there. I was. And your *husband* was commanding the siege of Miletus.' I let go of her hands and crossed my arms.

'Are you suggesting that I am responsible?' she asked in an arch tone.

'Yes,' I said. 'I know you. You are far too ... involved to escape responsibility. You are more like Themistocles than I am. You like the game.'

She got up. 'I will not listen to you,' she said.

'If you want Athens and Sparta to help the Ionians, you will need a better argument than that they are nearly barbarians and should save their superiors,' I shouted after her.

Ah, rhetoric. And measure. And good manners ...

It was our first fight.

Gorgo summoned me before the Spartan feast of the Enyalia, where the young men who have passed the *agoge* sacrifice dogs to Ares and join their regiments. and invited Briseis as well.

We went on horseback, although not too fast. Nothing could be worse than blood-mad Spartan adolescents. I was not in a hurry. We had a dozen servants, Eugenios, and I took Giannis and Alexandros and left my sons to their wives and my daughter to her tutors.

Briseis and I were speaking to each other, but only about household issues, and the silence could be quite ... brittle.

South of Epidauros, I thought I'd lance the boil.

'Gorgo will want to discuss the Ionian ambassadors,' I said.

Briseis looked at me. It wasn't a tender glance, but more the look a spear fighter gives a new opponent, or a boxer on the sands of the *palaistra*.

'They should not have been sent to Sparta,' Briseis said. 'I told them to send gifts to Themistocles, and flattery.'

'You told them?' I asked, and things became clear.

She shrugged. 'I advise my brother. Women are not encouraged to meddle directly in politics,' she added, with an utterly false modesty that I loved.

Aha. And aha. 'You are not just expressing an opinion about the liberation of Ionia,' I said. 'You are manipulating—'

'Why is it that women *manipulate* and men *lead*?' she shot back.

Our slaves were getting farther and farther behind, and Alexandros was smiling grimly.

Giannis wasn't smiling. In fact, he looked like a man in almost physical pain.

Many years ago, at sea, I learned a thing – a way of considering a problem. That is to say, in a storm, I learned to remove myself from the crisis and look at the ship as if I was above it; to rotate the ship in my mind's eye, to look for answers. A little headsail? A sea anchor? A couple of oars over the side?

Perhaps I do a poor job of explaining. But I learned to leave the problem and look at it from outside. Later, in dealing with Neoptolymos, when he was first my student, I learned to look at people in much the same way; to get outside my own skin.

Briseis had been the queen of Ionia in everything but name, and she could not, realistically, be expected to become a farm wife in Plataea or a ship-owner's wife in Hermione. Not in a time of crisis. Not when people depended on her.

'The Spartans are not the ones to ask,' I said.

'Who should they have approached?' Briseis said. 'Aristides?'

I pulled at my beard, and thought about what it must be like to be a woman. 'Yes,' I said. 'I think that they should approach Aristides, but your advice was exactly right. First Themistocles, and with gifts and flattery.'

We rode on in silence for a way, looking at the magnificent mountains of Arcadia while I wondered if the locals went to special effort to make the roads bad.

'I would help them,' I said. 'Or rather, I would help you to help them with Themistocles.'

Briseis raised an eyebrow, as if to say *This is a change.*

'Until Mardonius is defeated and the Great King's fleet is dispersed, I doubt that anyone – Athens, Corinth, Aegina – will spare any thought for the Ionians' cities.' I paused, choosing words with more care than ever. 'That is all I meant to say the other night. The rest was . . . wind.'

She smiled. 'Ah, well, I may have used some intemperate phrases in regard to mainland Greece,' she laughed, her laughter ringing off the snow-covered hillsides.

'Are we so barbarous, to you?' I asked.

She raised and lowered both eyebrows, an expression I had always loved. 'Yes,' she said. 'Should I pretend otherwise?'

I smiled ruefully. 'Every woman in Hermione now has earrings like yours,' I admitted. Not just earrings. Briseis, when she dressed as a priestess, looked as if she was from another world. Much of it was in different textiles, better goldwork, but even these things were expressions of the Ionian taste and refinement.

'Husband, you lived in Ephesus,' she said. 'You studied with Heraclitus. Who loved you best, I think, of all his boys. And who was Heraclitus but the living embodiment of the world of Asia and Greece mingled?'

I nodded. 'When I was a boy,' I said, 'I went as a slave to Ephesus, and your father purchased me. I remember that he took me to the Temple of Asclepius, and there I slept on white sheets with a white wool blanket on a bed, and all of it was better than anything I had seen in Plataea.'

She smiled. 'And that was the part of the temple reserved for slaves.'

'I had never seen golden sandals before I went to Ephesus. It was like visiting Olympus.' I shrugged. 'I never wanted to leave.'

Her smile was steady. 'I am a woman of Ionia. You have loved me since you pulled me to the ground in an alley – do not deny it. Ionia is part of me.' She raised a hand, like a man giving a speech in the assembly. 'I call out to the boy who grew to be Achilles – in Ionia. Ionia made you.'

'Ionia also made me a slave,' I said carefully.

'War made you a slave,' she said. 'And then made you free. And then made you a king.'

'I am no king,' I said.

She smiled brilliantly. 'You hold the balance in the league. I see it in the way men speak to you. It is a brilliant kind of power, which you exercise with beautiful restraint. Aristides, Themistocles, Gorgo, Eurybiades, Cimon. Aristocrats and democrats. You hold the balance.' She leaned over. 'All I ask is that you sway the balance in favour of the liberation of Ionia. My brother and I will do the rest.'

'What is "the rest"?' I asked.

'At some point the Ionians will have to rise,' she said.

We rode towards the towns of Sparta, and I was thoughtful.

Euphonia, my first wife, had wanted control of my house and recognition that she was a partner, not a servant.

Briseis wanted Ionia.

But I was not quite a fool, and I realized that what she wanted and what Euphonia wanted were a piece with their aspirations, and that Briseis also wanted to be a partner, not a servant or a bed-warmer. And while I might have been offended, part of me basked in her quite genuine admiration for my role as the balance point in the league. Briseis had always seen me as Achilles, and I was never really fond of Achilles. My hero has always been wily Odysseus.

I looked at her as we rode down over the high pass by Sellasia and smiled. 'Penelope was Helen's relative,' I said.

Briseis laughed aloud. 'So she was, my love.'

I had an audience with the king, Leotychidas. I had expected to meet him with his mess, or a crowd of other Spartiates, as I had the last time. But instead I was ushered into his house and waited on by helots for quite a while, until I began to fret. He had no bronzes, no hangings; the only decoration I found was a small shrine to Aphrodite, with a fine piece of Corinthian tile of the goddess receiving worshippers.

'The king will see you now,' said a helot.

I followed him, noting automatically the bruises he had and his servile reactions. Racial slavery is detestable, no matter how admirable the Spartans might be.

The king was sitting alone in a small, plain room lit by four oil lamps and the winter sun. He looked up.

'Ah,' he said, 'Arimnestos.' He rose and took my hand, as if we were intimates. Since there was no one there to see, I wondered at his lack of reserve, but that's Sparta.

He motioned me to a stool. 'First,' he said, ticking his points off on his fingers, 'I want to thank you for your service with our heralds.' He smiled. 'I'm quite fond of both men,' he said. 'You brought them back alive.'

Well. Who doesn't like praise? Especially from a king of Sparta?

'And may the gods preserve them,' I said.

'At least until the contest,' he said.

I knew what he meant. All the Spartiates used the phrase. *Agon*. The contest. The day when the Spartans and the Persians went man to man and spear to spear. Brasidas had infected the Plataeans with it.

To the Spartans, Thermopylae had settled nothing. In fact, it was a little like the Spartan story of the fight with the Argives. As the Persians had cheated, going through the pass and surrounding the Spartans, the result didn't count. Only a straightforward fight, gentleman to gentleman, would settle the issue.

Salamis didn't count either. Gentlemen do not settle their affairs of honour on ships.

Look, I'm not a Spartan and I never could be. To me, the whole notion is mad, and they are like a nation of drunken revellers. And yet I understand them well enough.

The king leaned back. 'Wine for my guest,' he said. When the helot was gone, he raised an eyebrow.

'Will Mardonius fight?' he asked me, blunt and Laconic.

I probably sputtered. 'How would I know?' I said, or something equally weak.

He looked away in annoyance. 'Of all men, I expected you to know,' he said. 'You know the Persians.'

'The Medes and Persians are as diverse and complex as Greeks,' I said.

The king glanced at me, a glance meant to explain that he was a king of Sparta, over sixty years of age, and he'd had a thought or two in his head.

I flushed.

'Tell me what you think,' he said.

Wine was brought, and the helot moved a side table for me to give me time to think. I had expected Ionia to be the topic.

'I am only guessing,' I said.

'Please,' said the king.

'Then I will say, yes, he will fight. Not only fight, but possibly come back at us.'

The king frowned. 'Come at us?'

'You must believe the same, or you would not be building a wall at the isthmus,' I said.

The king frowned again. 'The wall is merely good sense,' he said. 'Always secure your base.'

I shrugged. 'So you believe that the Persian fleet will stay on their side of the sea.'

He looked at his shuttered window. 'Why will Mardonius fight?' he asked.

'Because he's the satrap of Europe,' I said. 'Because Xerxes says we are all rebels against his authority. Because the way men frame their stories is as important as the story itself. I do not think Mardonius can say, "Alas, Sparta and Athens are too powerful for me, and I'll leave them be."'

'Athens is destroyed,' the king said.

I shook my head.

He raised both eyebrows. 'You think Athens is still a viable state?' he asked.

'Yes,' I said.

He nodded. 'Interesting. Why?'

I shrugged. 'Houses can be rebuilt. The farms are there, the olive trees will still bear, and the vines are hard to kill. The people live. And the fleet is still intact.'

'Ah,' the king said. 'The fleet.'

I waited.

'What if I told you that the Lacedaemonians are in favour of making the fleet the main effort this year?' he asked. 'To pursue the Persian fleet and destroy it?'

I hesitated. It was not what I'd expected, at all. 'Interesting, my lord. I would be interested.'

He smiled very slightly. 'What a very measured response. Almost ... Spartan.'

I twitched an eyebrow. Did Spartans deal better with their wives because neither side made elaborate emotional responses? I wondered this in my newly-wed wisdom.

'I will command the fleet, instead of Eurybiades,' he said.

I didn't understand, but I wasn't going to say so.

Every Spartiate I knew was spoiling for a big phalanx fight with the Persians, as soon as it could be arranged. Yet here was the king of Sparta, suggesting that the war should be won at sea – by attacking the Persian fleet.

'You mean to go after them?' I said.

'If we must,' he said.

There is something that honest men do, when they are lying. It is hard to explain, except that they don't have the experience to 'sell' their lies. The king was hiding something, and I had no idea what it was.

It worried me, though.

But ... 'What of the men of Ionia?' I asked.

The king made a dismissive gesture. 'Oh, they've been and gone,' he said. 'I told them to abandon their cities – we'd find them places to settle in the Peloponnesus, or Illyria.'

Only in that statement did I realize that I was speaking to one of the architects of Spartan hegemony. In a moment I did what I had done with Briseis; I looked at the king of Sparta from every angle, trying to see myself as he would see me. Trying to understand what this conversation was about.

First and foremost, it was about Sparta.

I thought of Themistocles, and the wall at the isthmus.

And I'm proud to say that it did not take me long to see that, if you believed that Athens was 'destroyed,' and you used her fleet to destroy the Persian fleet – before Athens made some other declaration, or took her population to Magna Graecia or some such – you could *secure Sparta's coasts*. At least, if you had a wall on the isthmus, and the Persian fleet was destroyed.

There was no answer to make. He was the king of Sparta, and I was a small-time warlord from Plataea. And I assumed on the spot that Themistocles had seen through his strategy as fast – doubtless faster – than I had.

Unless Themistocles had proposed it. He was a fickle bastard. And Aristides had said how Themistokles wanted the Athenians to move to the west.

Wheels and wheels and wheels.

Greeks.

Briseis and Gorgo.

What more should I say? Both, in very slightly different ways, epitomize everything I think is best in women.

Well, and Jocasta. And a number of other women.

I digress.

They were not as instantly intimate as Jocasta had been with Gorgo, but they could laugh together, and they had many things in common and many differences, too. But it occurred to me that the women who didn't like Briseis were afraid of her; afraid of her foreignness, of her beauty, of her willingness to intrude in the affairs of men, as if her being was a reflection on them. Gorgo was afraid of nothing; so she had nothing to fear from Briseis.

At any rate, I went from the king to Gorgo. Now that she was a widow, she had very little direct power; nothing like what she had enjoyed as the wife of Leonidas. But she was also the daughter of Cleomenes, and had many friends, like Bulis.

I went to her house and found her sitting in her courtyard, surrounded by rose bushes that offered only thorns and no flowers in the dead of winter. There was some sun, and she sat in it with a himation thrown over her, and Briseis sat with her, the two of them sharing a *kline* like symposiasts.

I bowed, and Gorgo smiled. 'Well?' she asked. 'Did he ask you to take the heralds to Mardonius?'

I thought about that. 'No,' I said.

'He will,' Gorgo said. 'Or perhaps he will not.'

'The peace party in Sparta has triumphed?' I asked.

Gorgo raised an eyebrow. 'Better call it the "Sparta First party",' she said. 'They believe they have an iron-clad strategy for saving Sparta, and that it is their duty to follow that strategy. They have all the ephors and many of the Spartiates. Indeed, I understand them all too well.'

'But the rest of Greece ...'

'Is already lost,' Gorgo said. 'That's what they say. Athens is destroyed, a lesson to Sparta. Corinth and Aegina are too weak to stand in the storm. And besides, Aegina and Corinth are both safe as soon as the Persian fleet is destroyed.'

'So, in fact, the preservation of Sparta is at least in part about the destruction of Athens,' I said.

She nodded.

Briseis said, 'And by a twist of irony, my love, the preservation of Attica is now to be tied to the Ionians.' She shrugged, wriggled, and Gorgo looked at her.

Briseis was a patient schoolmistress. 'You must see it,' she said. 'If Ionia revolts, the Great King will have no soldiers to invade Greece. And no fleet.' She looked at Gorgo.

It was cold in the garden. 'I'm not sure I want to go to Mardonius,' I said.

Gorgo sighed. 'You would think we'd lost the naval battle,' she said. 'Not won it. It is as if my husband died *for nothing*. They are going to build their wall and keep the league army inside it, and sweet-talk the Athenians into sending their fleet against the Persians. So that Athens can be discarded later. Or even destroyed. Or even destroyed again.'

I stood and shivered. The garden was cold, and the sky stark, and spring was very far away.

The next morning, as if by chance, I met Pausanias, the new regent, in the agora. He was with his son Plaistoanax, who had just left the *agoge* at the festival, and some other men, and he would have passed me without a glance except that Bulis emerged from their pack and embraced me, and in a minute we were exchanging tall tales – that is, I was talking, and he was smiling. He introduced me to Pausanias.

The regent raised an eyebrow the smallest fraction. 'Gorgo's friend,' he said.

Spartans convey a great deal of information in very few words. He meant to insult me.

I met his eye. 'Yes. Who are you?' I asked with a smile.

He turned on his heel and walked away.

I won. You see, I made him show anger in public, and to a Spartan, anger is weak.

His son stood and glared at me. I laughed. 'See something you like?' I asked, as Bulis' wife had once said to me about ten paces away from that very spot.

I went back to looking at some familiar looking Sicilian pottery. Lacedaemon had once had some of the finest pottery in Greece, but now all she exported was war.

The ephebe – I suppose he wasn't an ephebe any more, but his attempt at a man's beard was silly – at any rate, he stood very close to me, as if the power of his shadow would hurt me. He reminded me of someone. Someone I'd liked, even with his thin beard and his foolish anger.

He followed me to a sword-maker's. Or rather, a sword-seller's – again, all the swords were made on Crete. I looked at a couple; too small for me, although the Spartans like them short. I was looking for something for Brasidas, I suppose. The boy stayed very close.

I kept thinking of witty things to say, and then leaving them unsaid. I didn't need a fight with a boy. You lose such a fight regardless of the actual outcome.

My, how adult of me.

And then Sparthius appeared, gap-toothed and long-limbed, and we had to embrace, and he had always been talkative enough to be a Plataean, and we wandered from stall to stall in the market, and then he turned to the boy and his three friends.

'Hello,' he said.

That was all. All three boys nodded politely and then walked away.

'You know that little sod will be king,' Sparthius said.

'Really?' I asked. Then I shrugged. 'They're all useless at that age. I was. I remember Neoptolymos ...'

War is odd. I lost Neoptolymos at Lade, where all the friends of my youth died. And suddenly I knew that that Spartan boy reminded me of Neoptolymos; and tears came to my eyes. It is difficult to describe how suddenly the hammer can hit you, but for a moment it was as if my friend had *just died*, and the unfairness of his loss, the treason of the Samians ...

Sparthius was not a typical Spartiate. He put his arm around me, in public. And we stood there.

Eventually, it passed.

Lade. It was too much with me. And later that day, I began to think, really think, of how much I blamed ... everyone ... for Lade.

Even Briseis. Or perhaps, especially. By Aphrodite, love is difficult, and I had never looked that one in the eye. I made a halting attempt to talk to Briseis about it that night, and she ... laughed.

'What good would it have done the Ionians to win Lade?' she said.

'Many of my friends would be alive,' I said.

She was quick, my Briseis, and she caught my tone and paused, brushing her hair while a slave held her mirror. 'Ah, love, I'm sorry,' she said. 'I don't always see the rebels as people. But bumbling, inept *idiotes.*'

'And me among them,' I said, trying to keep the tone light.

She shrugged and went back to her hair.

The next day – I don't know, perhaps there were several days, and I've forgotten a few – Gorgo sent for me and told me that Pausanias wanted to meet with me.

'He won't be pleasant,' she said. 'And I'm afraid this means the Sparta First party has triumphed completely.'

'How do you know?' I asked. She was veiled, being a widow with a man. Briseis was not there, so I knew she had something to tell me.

'If they were going to compromise, the king would have sent for you. He's no friend of Athens, but now he's as close to a moderate as there is.' She paused. 'And he thinks very highly of you. Personally, and outside politics.'

Well, she would know. She'd played the game of Spartan politics all her life.

'I will not see my husband having given his life for nothing,' she said. 'These fools think that they can use the Great King to destroy Athens, and they will have back the world of their grandfathers.'

I shrugged and she looked up, and the veil came off her head. 'Oh, sit down, Plataean,' she said in mock annoyance. 'They all say we're lovers anyway.'

'Do they?' I asked.

'Pausanias implied as much in public yesterday, and Bulis checked him,' Gorgo said. 'Pausanias is a good fighter but a very poor politician. For a man of Lacedaemon, he is too transparent. He is easily hurt by the things men say, and he thinks to wound people with his spite.'

'Ah,' I said. 'Very un-Spartan.'

'You should tell him that,' she said, amused. 'On second thoughts, please do not. What I have summoned you to say is, please, please, take no action. Break no noses, exchange no barbed witticisms. I ask you this in the name of all Greece. They want to provoke you. You have a great name in Sparta: friend of my husband, ambassador, soldier.'

'Pirate,' I added.

She smiled. As I have said before, in another woman that smile would have been … an invitation? At least flirtation. With Gorgo, and Briseis, that smile was simply one of the many weapons in a near-infinite arsenal. 'Let's keep that part our secret?' she said. 'He will try to use his thuggish son Plaistoanax to annoy you.'

'My lady, I am immune to the charms of young men,' I said.

She raised both eyebrows. 'How un-Spartan of you,' she said.

But Plaistoanax was not at my meeting. Instead, it was Pausanias, and a dozen or so of his peers. Euryanax was an older Spartiate, tall, well-formed, and a veteran of many fights. Amompharetos was as big as a titan; he stood almost a head taller than me, and had the reputation of being a skilled commander as well as the greatest man-killer of his generation. With him was Poseidonios, another big man, although small by comparison, and among them, beaming with pleasure, was Callicrates, probably the handsomest man in Greece, one of the best fighters I've ever known. We'd been together for days and days during the Salamis campaign, and I knew him well; he was, after Bulis, Sparthius' best friend.

If my reception was supposed to be cold, Callicrates ruined it, striding forwards, taking my hand, and singing my praises to the regent.

Pausanias' face was immobile, and he seemed haughty, but after Callicrates kept up his ebullient flow of praise, Pausanias managed a smile.

'I don't think any of us question his prowess, Callicrates,' Pausanias said.

They all asked me some questions about Salamis; I was bashful, and asked Callicrates to help me with my answers, but despite his bodily beauty, he was not a storyteller, and it was heavy going.

And then, without preamble, Pausanias said, 'So we won't be asking you to take our heralds to Mardonius.'

I'd been prepared, of course. So I bowed, just slightly, imitating

Spartan mores. But I also didn't make any of the snarky comments that I'd considered in advance, like, 'I'm sure I'll find a way to amuse myself this spring,' or something of the kind.

An uncomfortable silence fell. Callicrates looked surprised. 'But the king named him!' he said.

I rather admired Callicrates, but he wasn't the brightest, and he wasn't the man you'd include in a conspiracy. He didn't see the world in terms of plots and shades of grey; he liked me, he liked Pausanias, and that should have been enough.

Pausanias winced.

But he was an honest man. He turned to me. 'It is true; the king named you to escort our heralds to Mardonius. But . . . I have chosen otherwise.'

I nodded. 'I understand,' I said.

We all looked at each other.

I remember once, at a symposium in Piraeus, when one of the men present admitted that he knew his wife was having an affair, and didn't know what to do about it. It wasn't what he said, but the hopeless manner of his saying it, that silenced an entire dinner party, and the party never recovered. And so, here. The silence was thick with accusations and insinuations, but no one spoke.

So when the discomfort was too much for me, I nodded my head again. 'Then I will take my leave, sir,' I said formally. Callicrates embraced me, and even Pausanias took my hand.

We had a long, slow ride back to Hermione. Alexandros had enjoyed Sparta very much, and Giannis less so. Both of them had heard the phrase 'Athens is destroyed' repeated like the deepest wisdom, over and over.

There was snow everywhere, and we took refuge from it in a shallow cave in the hills, scavenging firewood and eating someone's sheep for two days. We were just north of Mantinea.

It was the best part of the trip. By the middle of our second day, Eugenios and Giannis had begun making furniture for our cave.

Briseis joked that we could found a city.

We returned to Hermione to find that the spring was expected, that there were warmer airs, and that most of our friends had returned to the ruins of Athens to begin rebuilding. Cimon had just ridden off north to fetch his ship from the beaches of Corinth, and Aristides was already headed for Attica.

And there was a long letter from Doola and Gaius, brought by none other than Megakles, who brought the first Sicilian cargo of the year in a snug round ship. I read it aloud with Briseis' head pillowed on my stomach while she and I drank wine, and I told her some tales of Alba and tin.

Doola and Gaius had a very successful trading venture going, and, in effect, invited me to join their consortium in another trip to Alba. It made sense, or more sense; Carthage had lost ships at Artemisium and at Salamis, but she had also lost a titanic land battle on Sicily against Gelon. Some men say it was the largest land battle of the age; other men claim it was fought the same day as Leonidas fell, and thus the greatest victory of Greeks over barbarians was fought the same day as the most glorious defeat.

Well, I can count, and I find them to have been fought nineteen days apart, but men like things to have meaning.

Regardless, Gelon's defeat of the Carthaginians had many effects. One was that he knocked Carthage out of the war altogether, or so Doola insisted in his letter.

I lay on my bed, and I didn't really realize that I had stopped reading and was staring into space until Briseis poked me sharply in the ribs.

'I'm sorry, my love,' I said.

'Carthage will leave the war,' Briseis said. 'Or already has.'

'Yes,' I said.

'That means that Tyre and the other Phoenician cities will have to look elsewhere for allies. And will be more cautious.' She spoke carefully, knowing that in three sentences, we would be arguing about Ionia.

But it annoyed me that she didn't think I could see these things for myself. Some days, I thought that Briseis saw me as the merest sword-swinger.

'And they took the heaviest losses at Salamis,' I said. 'And their navarchs must already have known of the losses in Sicily.'

'Of course,' Briseis said, a little too brightly. In other words, she'd already had all these thoughts.

'What if the Great King was left with nothing but the men of Ionia, and the Cilicians and Carians?' I asked.

'Then, instead of having a house, the Great King has nothing but a pile of firewood sitting on dry kindling, and all that needs be applied is flame,' Briseis said.

I laughed. 'I knew you'd say that,' I said.

She put the wine krater carefully on the side table and turned over. 'Really, my husband? You knew I'd use the image of fire and a house?'

'I didn't guess the allegory,' I said. 'Merely the content.'

'And am I wrong?' she asked. Her hand was moving into my armpit. Intending mischief.

'No,' I said. 'No, I think you are right.'

Her hand stopped. 'You do?' she asked.

'Yes,' I said.

Her hand started a very different operation.

'Is this a reward for liberating Ionia?' I said.

'Yes,' Briseis said.

Well, as rewards went, it was a good deal better than a wreath of laurel.

Afterwards, Briseis said, 'You will help me save the Ionians?'

I laughed. 'I think I've already agreed,' I said. 'But Athens and Sparta will take a great deal of convincing.'

Briseis rolled over me. 'You know that in Sparta, people openly claimed you were the queen's lover?'

I wasn't sure what to say. 'I am not,' I said.

She shook her head. 'I know that, silly. I'm saying something else.'

'They're sending an embassy to Mardonius,' I said.

'I know,' she said. 'Gorgo . . . can't believe what is happening.'

She said no more. But I understood her well enough.

It was all about Ionia. And Sparta. And Athens.

A few days later, Archilogos and I took two ships loaded with Athenians and their goods across the gulf to Piraeus. I wanted to test the winds and all the repairs I put into the *Lydia* and her consorts. But I knew that Doola's news needed to be shared, and I wasn't going to peddle it to the king of Sparta. And I wanted to be sure that my Athenian friends knew that the Spartans were sending an embassy to Mardonius.

And didn't want me along.

I will say that, away from the embrace of my beloved, I had a hard time telling myself why I shouldn't take my crews and my people, and perhaps *all* of the Plataeans, and sail for Massalia. Doola had laid it out: that the collapse of Carthaginian sea power changed everything;

that Massalia was now secure, and so was Rome. We could enter the tin trade; with a little luck and ten warships, we could perhaps *dominate* the tin trade.

I didn't need to ask Leukas or Sekla. Near death had not changed Leukas, but he was done with the east and wanted to go home, and Sekla had had enough of war. I read them Doola's letter as we crossed the gulf on a sunny day in Agrionios, which the Athenians call Elaphebolion, the first month that can decently be called spring.

One of those things we talked about was Athenian festivals. We were in exile in Hermione, and we celebrated Athenian festivals, not Plataean ones. It rankled. You might recall that fighting over the Dandala was at the root of our troubles with Thebes. Festivals matter. They make us who we are, whether Boeotian or Spartans or Athenians.

At any rate, winter was not quite a memory, but if we'd been home in Plataea, most of the good farmers would have had their ploughs out in their farmyards, sharpening the blades and checking the harnesses.

Piraeus had not been badly damaged by the Medes; they'd thrown down the two temples, and demolished the small port, but by the time we put our refugees on the beach, most of that had been rebuilt. The old temples were mostly wood, except for the fancy stuff at Delphi and on the Acropolis of Athens.

It was worse up in Athens. I rode up on a donkey and saw whole neighbourhoods around the Acropolis that had been burned down to basement holes, and they had done terrible, blasphemous things to the temples. Indeed, Aristides – whose house was untouched, because the Great King had lived in it – took me up the Acropolis quite deliberately to fan the fires of my anger, and he succeeded. I will not even tell you of the things I saw there, except to say that no man should ever be surprised at the capacity of men to destroy, torture, burn, humiliate.

Mind you, less than a fifth of the city was destroyed. But the temples were hardest hit. Every statue in the Temple of Athena had been thrown down, and desecrated. Horribly. Every building had been burned, and a winter of rain could not wash off the blood and the faeces.

Well, I had been at the sack of Sardis. Horror is not a Persian invention. But before the sack of Athens, I might have been moved to argue that the Persians were better than that.

'In Sparta, they say that Athens has been destroyed,' I said, watching the grim determination with which the Athenians, rich and poor, free and slave, were rebuilding houses.

But not anything on the Acropolis. Not a single collapsed, charred roof beam had been salvaged. Not a burned brick or smashed statue had been moved.

Aristides said nothing.

I watched as a long line of men carried sacks of sand and cut stone; as hundreds of men cleared the hillside around the old Temple of Hephaestus and began building new workshops.

'If I was a Spartan, I might think the same,' Aristides said.

Back at his house, I propounded the news from Doola, and Aristides fingered his beard. 'The rumour you heard – that the Spartans are sending an embassy to Mardonius,' he said. 'Do you think that Sparta would abandon us?'

'Yes,' I said.

Aristides looked out over his courtyard. 'That's what Themistocles says,' he said.

We sat in silence a while.

'You believe this news of Gelon's victory,' he said.

'I do,' I said.

He nodded.

'I think we can win the war in Asia,' I said.

Aristides winced. 'This again? The forward strategy?'

I rocked my hand back and forth. 'Yes and no,' I said. 'Carthage defeated means Phoenicia weakened, and they have borne the heaviest losses in the Great King's war at sea. One great blow in the east ... and perhaps everything unravels. Caria, Ionia, Cappadocia and Cilicia. Perhaps even Aegypt.'

'By Poseidon, Plataean. We sit here in the ruins of my city and you are suggesting the collapse of the Great King's empire.' He shook his head. 'I will settle for keeping the Great King's men out of Attica this spring.'

'We can only do that by forcing him to fight in Asia,' I said.

Aristides shook his head. 'No. There will be a day. A fight. With the Persians. Like Marathon.'

I frowned. 'You would like that to happen, because it would put the hoplites in the front,' I said.

Aristides frowned. He looked at his wine. 'Yes,' he said. 'No more naval fights. No more oarsmen.'

'The king of Sparta intends to lead the fleet this year,' I said.

That rocked Aristides.

'The Spartans desire *the contest* as much as we do!' he said.

I sighed and outlined what I saw as the Spartan strategy. 'The Spartiates may desire a contest,' I said. 'But the state does not have to behave with such ... philosophy.'

Aristides took a few deep breaths. 'I do not believe it,' he said.

'I'll wager Themistocles believes it,' I said.

Aristides' nostrils flared. 'Themistocles,' he said with contempt.

I stayed with Xanthippus and Agariste. Their house had been occupied by no less a person than Mardonius. Some of their belongings had been looted, and a marble shrine had been desecrated, but they had more than most people, even rich aristocrats, and I got space on a floor. I mention this because Agariste opened her house to dozens of men and women, because she had a roof and they did not. Athenians were showing who they really were, that winter.

All the Athenians I knew behaved as if nothing had happened, and yet all of them behaved as if they had a secret – like men cheating on their wives. It's difficult to define, but there was a brittle humour to them, and a sense of injury.

They bought all my Sicilian wine, though.

There were no cargoes in Piraeus, not of any kind, and I rowed west with empty bilges.

The *Lydia* had never been so fast. There were a few things I didn't like, and I wanted a look at that new keel, because she tracked oddly under oars. Odd, and somehow symbolic, that a plank no more than the width of your hand can have so much effect on steering.

Back at Hermione, we rolled her over and sure enough, I'd broken the new keel plank on the gravel beach at Piraeus, and the break had started a leak and probably dragged us off course.

So we replaced the keel plank in oak, a little thicker than before, and tree-nailed to the central rib under the shell of the hull planking, and that made her heavier and stiffer.

Cimon loved the result, and determined to try it immediately on the *Ajax*. 'Beautifully stiff,' he called the *Lydia*.

Megakles wasn't so sure. We both knew how ships flexed, especially in a storm. 'You are trying to make something perfect, better,' he said. He shrugged.

I paid for my cargoes with the money from Megakles' Sicilian wine – in effect, I was borrowing money from him, but he'd decided to join us on the voyage to Aegypt. He was going to take his cargo all the way back to Sicily, or even Massalia.

'Imagine what an ostrich egg would fetch in Gaul!' he said.

Leukas looked pained. I knew he wanted to go home, and I knew that Megakles could get him there.

And I knew I needed him. The really good sailors and helmsmen in the allied fleet were like too little olive oil spread over too much bread, that spring. Sekla and Leukas were all for going to Massalia; both of them had had enough of war, and both had earned the right to leave.

But so many of our best were dead: Paramanos, Harpagos, Idomeneaus; all men who could command a ship, or, in Idomeneaus' case, take one. By himself.

But I wasn't going to beg them to stay. Part of me wanted them to go, to live, to build me a bolt-hole where I could run with Briseis if all went to Hades. Part of me knew we'd be fighting for another fifteen years, and I understood that they'd had enough. By the skin of dreadful Ares, I'm not ashamed to say that I'd had enough. I didn't want to fight again, and sometimes I would sit by the hearth, stare into the embers, and shiver at the black thoughts.

In fact, Briseis' wit and her body kept me sane, some days. And a little wine, too. And my friends.

Bah.

At any rate, Megakles announced that he and his round ship would join us all the way to Aegypt and back, and that put the day of parting off.

Briseis' tummy wasn't even a little round yet. A few farmers had their ploughs out, but no one was ploughing, and the oldest farmer in the village told me that there was one big winter storm left.

Megakles shook his head. 'Nope,' he said. 'Sharp, cold winter – early spring. Or I wouldn't be here.'

We completed our cargoes, put in water and wine and food; we'd use the round ships to allow us to stay at sea. Three triremes, all now rigged as trihemiolas. Three round ships, one quite small and two larger, all round as walnut hulls, all full of cargo and food. We had seven hundred men to feed, give or take. A round ship could just about hold ten days' food for the lot of us, and it wouldn't be pleasant sailing, not that anyone I'd ever heard of had kept the sea for ten days running. At least on purpose.

The league officers were summoned for Corinth.

Briseis was worried that I would lose prestige and command by sailing for Aegypt. I didn't think it likely, but I wrote to Gorgo and to Aristides and to Themistocles, explaining that I was off to earn some money and bring back some information.

Cimon came to see us off, at the very break of day. He gave me an embrace almost as fulsome as that which Briseis had given me in our courtyard, where I had sacrificed a lamb with my new divination skills and learned that, as far as I could tell, we were in for a fair voyage.

'Wish I was coming,' he said. 'Don't take all the prizes.'

I laughed. 'Purely trade,' I said.

'Yes, well, if you trip and fall and happen to board a Phoenician, leave some gold for me,' he said. 'I'll tell Aristides what you are really doing.'

The last sacks of grain were going aboard the *Lydia*, who was warped alongside a temporary pier. It was like a pilgrimage – the first day, you carry too much, but eventually you eat yourself light, eh?

'What am I really doing?' I asked.

'Looking for the grain fleet,' he said.

I laughed. 'I'm taking a cargo to Aegypt,' I said. 'If I do not, I'll be borrowing money to pay my oarsmen.'

Cimon frowned. 'I wish you wouldn't say such things,' he said. 'I may sail for Potidaea after the conference,' he added slyly.

'Ahh,' I said.

I probably rolled my eyes. Aristocrats. Secrets and secrets. Cimon didn't trust someone, probably Archilogos but possibly Themistocles.

And then we were away.

We had the *Amastris*, the former Corinthian, in Moire's capable hands, and the *Lydia* and Archilogos' *Lady Artemis*. Megakles had his round ship *Demeter's Daughter*, and my sons, who needed to learn the difference between skill and command, each had a round ship; Hector took the old but dependable *Leto* and Hipponax the newly rebuilt *Io*. We sailed on a fair wind blowing south and east as if we'd ordered it apurpose, and we sunk the Peloponnesus and then the islands behind us and went right over the rim of the world, to the surprise of almost no one. My oarsmen knew me, and the *Lydia* had a brilliant crew.

The seas were empty.

We ran down the spring zephyrs and raised the northern coast of Crete on the morning of our second day. It wasn't a record-setting run, but it was damned pleasant, and we weren't even tired of salt fish and biscuit when we got into Gortyn's snug little fishing town. We had presents for Hipponax's mother, and for the king of Gortyn himself. I hugged her, and Hipponax prattled about the wedding, and my former lover Gaiana found herself mother-in-law to the bluest blood in Attica.

'Come and live in Hermione,' I said. Her father was aging, and she deserved to be comfortable.

'I hear you wed too, my dear,' she said with a little vitriol. 'Am I to be your aging courtesan, or just ...'

'Gaiana!' I said.

She shook her head. 'No charity, my jolly rover. But I'd like to meet my daughter-in-law, and see the babies. Go and fight your silly war and we'll see you next spring.'

I protested, but not too hard. Gaiana and Briseis under one roof?

At any rate, seven hundred oarsmen drink a lot of wine and they can get in a lot of fights, and I was happy to be away the next morning, in a light rain.

We ran due west for Cyprus. We were calmed a day, and rowed, and then we towed the round ships, a terrible, laborious waste of a day, and we made perhaps a parasang in the whole useless day, but there was no sense in outrunning our food.

But we were not yet ten days at sea when we raised the goddess of love's island, and we ate mutton on the beach there, as I had as a young man, and all the helmsmen felt a deep satisfaction at our navigation. And twelve days out of Troezen, we saw seabirds, and land birds, and on the thirteenth day, we were in brown water and raised the low coast of Aegypt. We hadn't seen a single sail; we'd had the market at Gortyn all to ourselves, and Megakles had joked that if the Persians were so busy making war, men could trade in round ships and leave the warships at home.

But in the mouth of the Nile we found plenty of warships. Most of them were small Aegyptian *lembii*.

I ran in, in the *Lydia*, and met a pilot boat with a deeply officious bureaucrat who was seasick in the Delta. But he made no attempt to see through the fairly transparent fiction that we were Greeks of Magna Graecia, and in no way at war with the Great King, and he marked my lading tablet with his signet seal while he turned a pale green.

I ran back out to sea, where my little squadron was just a nick on the horizon, and led them in, and we made a good show, but there were seventy Aegyptian trieres and as many *lembii* in the Delta, all with yards crossed and stores aboard, and the docks south of Naucratis were packed with marines and oarsmen.

We'd worked this out back at Hermione, and there are no seven hundred oarsmen in the world who can stay silent or keep a secret. So I arranged for them to go ashore in the Greek colony of Naucratis and I paid to have my cargoes brought north from the Aegyptian ports. Archilogos understood all this, and had done it before; suddenly he was indispensable, negotiating with bureaucrats, paying the owners of the small reed Nile boats to move our papyrus and our hides and our ostrich eggs and ivory up to Naucratis.

Aegypt stunned me. I'd been before, in the year we salvaged the Corinthian ship, but I'd scarcely left the Greek shipyards on that trip, and Naucratis could be any town in the Peloponnesus – except for the girls and the incredible bureaucracy and the heat. But in early spring, the wheat was already knee high in the Delta, lush and rich, and the people were totally alien to me, and yet ... another world. I am a head taller than most Aegyptians. They have entirely different gods from Greeks, and yet not as different as the gods of the Syrians. Their peasants are 'free' and yet incredibly poor compared to Greek peasants; the land is so rich that, somehow, it betrays them, and they work very small plots to pay terrible taxes.

They die young. A woman is old at thirty, a man at thirty-five. I met a man who was my own age, thirty-six, and his hair was white, he had a scraggly beard, his chest was almost hollow and he was bent like an old tree in a wind. I met a pretty young matron with a child on her hip, and she told me by signs that she was thirteen. I wanted to imagine I had misunderstood, but Aten, my new servant, of whom more in a moment, told me that thirteen was old enough to be an adult man or woman.

You may recall that I'd had a new *pais* at Salamis. He'd survived the battle, and then run off. Well, he wasn't a slave, and I couldn't keep him. But Eugenios had stayed with Briseis, and Hector was too old and too important to be anyone's servant. So I'd sailed without a boy.

I'd been in Naucratis about an hour when a boy begged alms from me and then asked, in a very good Ionian Greek, if I would like to buy him. I brushed past him without an answer, the way you do with an importunate beggar, but an hour later, when I was watching Archilogos handle half a dozen Nile boatmen, I was handed a cup of very good wine by the same boy.

'I speak Aegyptian and Persian, too,' he said.

He was perhaps ten years old, although Aegyptians are tricky with age and he might have been twelve. He was very small. And brown – brown eyes, brown skin, brown hair, mostly shaved.

'Who owns you?' I asked.

'No one,' he said with a bright smile. 'I own myself. But my mother needs money, and I'm to be sold.'

That didn't sit well with me.

'Free men don't sell themselves,' I said.

He smiled, the way children do when adults say something foolish.

'These men are lying,' the boy said. 'The boatmen. They want more money, so they say that it is early in the year. Your friend doesn't seem to understand that it is not actually early in the year, or perhaps he doesn't understand that they simply want more money.'

I beckoned to Archilogos. 'Tell him,' I said.

The boy repeated his statement, and when Archilogos challenged him sharply, the boy defended himself with real eloquence, explaining the rise and fall of the Nile.

Archilogos still had the man I loved inside him. He rubbed the boy's head. 'So, young pillar of wisdom, tell this unworthy one how he should proceed,' he said in Ionian Greek.

The boy flushed. 'If you are rich, offer them more money. If not rich, let me tell them how they lie.'

'If you tell them they lie, they will not negotiate,' I said. 'If we give them too much money, we will make no profit.'

The boy looked chagrined. 'Ah,' he said.

'But if you were to tell them, as a favour, that we will just leave them be and warp our ships upriver and pick up the ivory ourselves ...' I smiled. 'If you will do that, I will consider loaning your mother money.'

My young scapegrace smiled wickedly. 'You two Greeks keep talking,' he said. 'We'll see how smart a boy of Naucratis can be.'

He went into the taverna.

Archilogos watched him go. 'Where'd you find him?' he asked. 'He reminds me of Kylix.'

'What has happened to Kylix?' I asked. These questions – which both of us asked – could lead to pain, or difficulty, and I no sooner asked than I winced.

He smiled. 'He's a freedman in Ephesus,' he said. 'My sister got him a place in the temple.'

I nodded. 'Good to know someone will survive the war,' I said.

Archilogos laughed. 'That's exactly how I feel,' he said.

There it was, just peeking out – the warmth of friendship.

I could see, over his shoulder, the boy, his head bobbing up and down, amidst the crowd of boatmen.

'Did you ever marry?' I asked.

Archilogos raised an eyebrow. 'Took you long enough to ask,' he said.

'You could just tell me things,' I said.

'When do you have time?' he said pointedly. 'The great lord Arimnestos.'

And there we were again.

'I have time right now,' I said.

He smiled, a little hurt but still, I think, game to try. 'She died. In childbirth.'

'Oh, gods,' I said. 'Avert that misfortune from your sister. My first wife died bearing Euphonia.'

'I know,' he said. 'Briseis tells me all about you. You never ask about me.' He shrugged.'I sound like an arse.'

'No,' I said. I was cursing inside, but the boy was pushing back through all the prostitutes and urchins – Aegypt is a lot rawer than Greece, children – and he passed us without a glance.

A very pretty, very tiny Aegyptian girl wearing only a rope around her waist came and poured wine. Archilogos began to negotiate for her ... favours ... and then turned bright red.

One of the boatmen appeared.

Archilogos was a better actor than I'll ever be. He pretended to be done with the boatmen, and he kept turning to the *porne* and asking her things – indelicate things, ladies – and she was bored, but eager for his custom, so to speak, and she'd make answers ...

No one was laughing but me. The boatman became annoyed. He insisted on something.

'They'll do the whole cargo for our price,' he said with satisfaction. 'This girl thinks we can ... perform ... right here!'

I smiled. 'Different places have different ways,' I said. 'Tell the boatmen that we'll pay a bonus of a silver drachma a man on delivery into our holds, if he's timely and organized.'

'That's adding a ninth to the cost!' Archilogos said.

'Better than having the whole cargo stolen or the fabrics all wet,' I said. 'Never piss off the transport, that's my rule. That girl's about to walk off on you, by the way.' I rose. 'I'm going to go loan some money to a woman. Use our room,' I said generously.

Archilogos laughed. 'I missed you,' he said.

'I missed you too, Archi,' I said.

The boy's mother was ... horrible.

I really know nothing about her, but she was fat, loud, abusive and eager to sell me her son. I'll guess that she'd been a whore, and perhaps I do her a disservice. Or perhaps the life did it to her, and the bearing of a dozen children without fathers. But she was a nasty piece of work, and her love of money gave me a glimmer of how men like Cimon felt about men who spoke openly of earning, by which I mean that her love of the stuff was gross, and I didn't want to talk about money for weeks after.

She did not want a loan. She wanted cash, in silver, paid down. She had a lawyer and a notary to hand, and they had a contract. She'd had a dozen children and she'd sold all but three. She knew the business.

'He'll be happier with you,' she said, and she didn't care one way or another.

It's odd, but much as I detested her – and I promise you, she made me feel like a piece of filth – despite that, her son loved her, and as I came to know him, I detected almost none of the brokenness I associate with bad parents and horrible homes. Perhaps he was just tough. Perhaps in her indifferent way she was attentive. She had paid for him to go to school with priests; she told me that she'd done it to raise his sale value.

Anyway, that's Aten. He cost me about thirty drachmai; cheaper than an Illyrian, and far better trained. He could read Aegyptian and a little Greek; he spoke four languages, and his memory was phenomenal. In fact, his mother bragged that the temples had offered for him but wouldn't meet her price.

Just to make the hot afternoon perfect, she kissed my cheek and whispered that he was a virgin and he'd be a delight in my bed.

Zeus. Perfect.

'Ever been in a fight?' I asked him as we walked out of his mother's tenement.

'Oh, yes,' he said.

'Like it?' I asked.

He shook his head. 'Not really,' he said with brutal honesty. 'I'm small, and bigger boys beat me.'

I nodded. 'Care to learn to fight better?' I asked.

'Oh, yes, master.' He smiled. 'Are we going to Greece? I want to see Olympia.'

'Olympia?' I asked. It turned out that his mother had had a lover who'd been an athlete.

I bought him a dozen linen *chitoniskoi* and another dozen for me, in all the colours of the rainbow. Aegypt is the place for linen, by the gods. I went to the Temple of Zeus and made a sacrifice, and another for the boy.

He shocked me. He raised his arms and called on Zeus-Ammon. He spoke a prayer. Like a priest. The old priest, an aristocrat, naturally, laughed.

'Tell your slave boy I do the prayers,' he said to me, but his comment was not as ill-natured as it sounds.

'Aten, the prayers in a Greek temple are usually said by a priest,' I said.

'Oh,' he said. He was crushed. 'But I am Greek now, am I not?'

We got our cargoes in four days; a long time for me, but a record time for Aegypt. I bought a fair amount of undyed linen, because it was cheap and I had a notion that no one in Attica had done much weaving that year, and I knew damn well that no one had brought in a crop of flax. I had some luxury goods; the bilges of all three triremes carried a whole fortune in glass, beads, bottles, even some cups.

Megakles bought a cargo of high-quality iron that Sekla found up the Delta, beautiful stuff from the south beyond the Red Sea, and we all had a lavish dinner with the Arabian trader who'd brought the cargo up from Eritrea and south. I suppose our original intent was to get information on the Aegyptian fleet, but the dinner was better than that, like the court of Persepolis again. The Arab had almost never sailed in the west, in the Inner Sea, but his tales of the Outer Ocean sounded like myths, except that I could match them with tales of the other Outer Ocean outside the Pillars, and he'd been all the way to India.

Perhaps when my daughter's baby is born, you will all come back to my home and I'll tell you how that story came out: when we sailed to the end of the world. But that night in Naucratis, we listened to a man who'd been to the southern end of the Red Sea, and he shared his knowledge freely; he told us of the overland route from the cataracts on the Nile to the Red Sea, and how hot the Red Sea was in summer, and then described the coast all the way out into the Outer Ocean and down the coast of Africa to what he called the 'Beautiful Island'.

I traded him for the whole route to Alba and the tin. By Poseidon, I didn't think he'd ever go that way, nor did he, but we did allow each other this fame, that among the men at that table, in a dingy taverna in Naucratis, we had sailed ships from Hyperborea to India.

There's more to life than war and spying.

But then, as if for dessert, they also told us in detail about the preparations the satrap of Aegypt was making for war with the Greeks. A hundred triremes, and sixty *lembii*, all to sail in a month.

And in a week in Aegypt I didn't meet a man who was interested in revolt.

We sailed more than we rowed up the coast of Syria, and then, out of nowhere, the weather changed, and we had some very difficult days that turned into a rotten week, and ended with the lot of us in the port of Salamis of Cyprus, although we'd got there by two very different routes: the round ships by sailing across the wind, and the triremes by rowing in some of the highest swells I'd seen in the Inner Sea. In fact, I was surprised and pleased at my own confidence; I didn't have my usual trainers at hand, but the trip to Alba and the years at sea were finally telling. I judged the winds automatically, and kept us afloat and relatively dry, and the rowers only cursed me a hundred or so times.

We had another bad day off the port, making no distance in a heavy wind, and unable to enter the port or beach the long ships.

But Poseidon and Aphrodite were with us, and in the pink light of dawn we got the hulls ashore, the round ships anchored in a protected cove, before the storm hit us again about midday, and it blew for three days, so wild that spume off the wave-tops came into the taverna on the beach.

Megakles shrugged as the sun burst forth on the last day of the storm. It was a red sunset, and betokened the end of the storm.

'Thank the gods we weren't at sea in that,' he said. He looked at me. 'I thought winter was over.'

'A few people are going to be afraid we are dead, if that storm blew through the Peloponnesus,' I said.

Regardless, the road home wasn't a short one. We had to pass through the heart of the Great King's maritime empire. Now that we were off the coast of Syria, the whole enterprise seemed a little foolish – in fact, it seemed insane.

But we made it into the harbour of Rhodos in one dash, to find the place full of ships from the storm, still staying snug except the more daring fishermen. There were a number of warships, and almost no one believed we were Sicilians, but we stayed only long enough to count the warships and refresh our water and biscuits and we were off north.

We spoke to a ship four days out of Miletus, bound for Halicarnassus in our wake; she told us that the Great King's fleet was at Cos and that there was a Phoenician squadron off Samos.

We beached on an islet, ate free mutton that belonged to someone, like the pirates we sometimes were, and contemplated our choices. But in the morning, there was a strong wind blowing off the coast of Asia.

Megakles looked at the sky and tasted the wind with his tongue. 'If I was home, I'd say this was good for two days, or even three.'

I looked at the tiny swallow pennant tacked to my mainmast – my weather gauge.

'If the round ships ran for Delos, you could be home in a few days,' I said. 'Even if the wind changes, as long as you make it into the islands, you are home.'

'And you?' Megakles said.

I shrugged. 'I need to have a look at the Great King's fleet,' I said. 'I always wanted to, and without your slab-sided tubs, we can outrun anything on these waters.'

'You mean to look into Cos?' Archilogos asked me.

Sekla frowned.

So did Leukas.

'Samos, Cos, and Lesvos,' I said. 'And the Dardanelles if I can manage it.'

Sekla rolled his white eyes. 'Damn it,' he said, with real bitterness. 'I thought we were here to make a fortune. And we have the gods' own wind home to Greece.'

I liked to hear him say 'home to Greece'.

'Listen, friends,' I said. 'I am a man of Green Plataea, and a Hellene, and in this hour ...' I looked out to sea. 'In this hour, I'll do what I can.'

Sekla sighed. 'Oh,' he said. 'I want to be done.'

I nodded.

Sekla sighed. 'But I can't be done until my friends are done, too,' he said.

Leukas shook his head. 'By Poseidon, I can,' he said. 'Except that I've been with you mad pirates so long I swear by Greek gods and I dream in Greek and I had a house in Plataea, too. But I want to die in Alba, not here.' He looked at me. 'And I have had dreams of dying here.' He frowned and looked away. 'Bad dreams.'

'Dreams are often worthless,' Sekla said. 'Anyway, it's much nicer here. I was in Alba. It's cold and wet.'

Archilogos laughed. 'This is the great pirate Arimnestos? The Spear of the West? I thought you'd just bark orders and be obeyed.'

It was my turn to sigh. 'I wish,' I said. I looked around my little command. 'Round ships head west, triremes north? Is that decided?'

Archilogos looked under his hand to the north, as if he could see Ephesus. 'You know what I want,' he said.

Sekla nodded to me. 'One more time,' he said.

I was afraid he meant it.

And Hector and Hipponax were the opposite, begging to be allowed to stay, as marines, as oarsmen.

In truth, I wanted to keep them, but I needed those round ships to make it home. And I was secretly pleased to send them out of the line of fire, so to speak, although I was also aware that any Phoenician wolf on the seas could snap them up.

Responsibility is the bane of happiness, in command. The knowledge that two of my best helmsmen – and friends – were only with me out of duty, and personal duty to me, weighed heavily on me. I dreamed of them being killed – drowning in storms, plucked off their rails by sea monsters, killed by enemies – and I knew, awake, that these were not premonitions but my own brain exposing my fears. Or rather, I thought this – I hoped it.

But I worried a great deal.

Despite which, I was determined on taking the great risk: straight along the beaches of Cos, swooping out of the dawn. I knew the waters, and we slipped into a cove on a nearby islet two nights later, with our sails down and our oars rowing soft, and we could see fires on the beaches of Cos. We snapped up a pair of local fishing boats on our way in. We couldn't afford to let them go, despite their protestations of loyalty to the league.

Strategically, by sitting on Cos, the Great King's fleet controlled Ionia, and that's what they were doing. It was obvious to all of us as soon as we were told the location. They were not preparing to attack Greece. They were making sure the Ionian cities didn't revolt. I stood on the beach with Archilogos and Sekla and Brasidas, and we saw the fires twinkling on the beach at Cos, maybe thirty stades away.

'The Persians will gather the whole of Ionia so that the best men can be watched,' Archilogos said. 'The Phoenicians and Aegyptians are camp guards.'

'We'll see in the morning,' I said. 'But let's see if we can singe the Great King's beard. I'd like to burn a few ships, if they are unready. Or take one.'

'Taking one would be ...' Brasidas smiled. 'Worthy.'

'I agree,' I said.

In the first light of dawn, the two fishing boats slipped away, put up their sails, and tacked back and forth until they became the merest nicks on the horizon about the time we launched the warships. Now we were undermanned, with only the top two decks manned, but the strong wind still blew from Asia towards Greece, and my deck crews had our sails laid on the decks, ready to raise them.

We rowed over the mirror-bright water in the pink light of dawn, and I had lots of time to be afraid of everything. Mostly for my friends. I know men who ship with strangers so that they won't have to see their friends die, and I know men who stop learning the names of their mates; indeed, I have done that, but on the other hand, there is no feeling in all the great *aspis* of the world like taking a mighty risk with your friends, daring the Fates and the hand of man in one great throw of the dice.

To the east and south, the fishing boats came in with the headland that marked the end of the great beach and vanished into the shoreline.

Our three warships went for the northern end of the beach. We were running north to south along the coast, and Sekla counted hulls. Most of them were out of the water and upside down, drying in the spring sun and the breeze. A few were upright, and a dozen or so were bows awash, ready to launch.

No one paid us any attention whatsoever for an hour.

In that hour, we ran along twenty stades of beach from north to south, and counted a little over four hundred hulls.

Four hundred ships. And this without the Aegyptians, who were behind us, still in their winter ports.

We stayed a stade or more off the coast, and rowed easy, looking for signs that would identify contingents. Archilogos was far better at this than I, and he would call out when he knew that there was such-and-such, and there so-and-so: most of the tyrants of Ionia; Artemisia of Halicarnassus; and the Red King.

His ship I knew for myself. It was long and red. His contingent was in the middle of the beach, and two of his ships were ready for the sea, with bows in the water.

The sun was well above the horizon. It was the hour in which rich men rise from their beds.

There were men looking at us under their hands; as they were all on the west coast of the island, we had the rising sun behind us.

'Ready?' I called.

Sekla, in the bow, for all his earlier hesitation, was grinning from ear to ear.

Leukas was in the steering oars, and he was more reserved. Rowers were looking at me; my top deck stern oar, who was about a hundred years old and had been with me since the dawn of time, grinned at Leon, a big brute of a man who'd followed me for ever and couldn't be trusted with a stern oar because, despite years as an oarsman, he couldn't keep the time.

''Ere we go again, mate,' Poseidonios said.

Leon grinned, showing the stumps of many teeth. 'Let's fuck 'em, eh?' he said.

Yes, well, Greece wasn't saved by philosophers.

'Hard to starboard,' I said.

We'd practised. We knew what we were about, to the pace; every oarsman knew we'd run in and turn in our own length and then the fun would start.

But the channel current caught us and moved us along the beach, south, faster than I'd expected, so that the Red King's hulls were too far to the north, and we were presented with a row of Cilicians, all beached in the most haphazard manner.

Sekla put up his hand – he was ready.

We were so close to the shore that you could hear men talking, and there was a real danger that the current and the gentle surf would take us in too far. The bottom shelved suddenly and I could see the bottom.

'Ready about ship,' I called.

Sekla began to whirl his sling. There were three of them in the bow.

Now, a sling is a miserable weapon at sea. There are ropes and lines everywhere on a ship, all located in the perfect places to catch on a slinger's weapon. And when you are throwing hot oil, or bitumen, or Poseidon's fear, hot coals, you can *burn your own ship*.

The bow is the only place a man with a sling can use. And then only because the mainmast has no forward stay on the trihemiola, only a back stay.

So there were three of them in the marine box, taking turns.

'Lie on your oars!' I called. We were fifty paces from shore.

'You can't land here!' called an officer in Persian from the sand. 'What contingent are you?'

'Plataea!' called some wag among the oarsmen.

Sekla launched his first pot.

It struck the upturned hull of a Phoenician trireme and burst. Nothing happened, though.

The next throw struck the same hull.

The result was spectacular. With a low *whoosh* like the chuckle of a monster, the whole bow of the beached trireme burst into flame.

Ka and his archers had begun to toss arrows into the chaos. They were taking their time, loosing carefully. They were wagering on shots.

I ran forward, more worried about that small current than about the enemy, and I leaned over the side from just forward of the first bench, watching the bottom.

Sekla was throwing hot oil, and his partners were throwing hot coals.

'About ship!' I called. They'd thrown more than a dozen pots, and there were three ships afire and it was time to go.

North of us, there was quite a commotion, and a great drum was beating, and cymbals.

My crew was magnificent. We turned end-for-end, easy as kiss-my-hand, not so difficult when you have no way on you, and then we were pulling out to sea.

Archilogos followed me. He had no firepots, and he'd contented himself with having his archers shoot at the Phoenicians on the beach.

Moire had stayed off the whole time, watching the beach. He was our security that there wasn't a new squadron coming over the horizon, or coming off the beach where we couldn't see. But he raised a white shield as we turned, to tell me that all was well, and we cleared the shallow water and turned to starboard again to run south, parallel with the coast. On the beach, men were running in every direction. My archers continued to loose at them, causing panic. Columns of smoke rose into the air like a sacrifice to Poseidon.

I wished I had a magic weapon that could reach out a few hundred paces – two stades, say – and set ships afire. The Great King's mighty fleet was as helpless as any newborn babe.

Except that astern of us, the Red King had launched his great red trireme, and there were four more coming off the beach.

He was no slouch.

We continued down the beach at a pace slightly better than a man walking. We were about six stades from the headland that marked the southern end of the main beach, and ...

There was a beautiful black-hulled trireme coming off the beach just off the bow. The rowing was ragged, but they meant business and they came out of the low surf and onto the flat water like champions, already going to cruising speed.

I waved to Nikas, a tall, skinny man of my own age who'd rowed most of his life. My new oar master.

'Cruising speed!' he ordered, and his spear butt began to tap a faster pace.

I only had two banks of oars, and my hold was full of faience and frippery. We did not leap forward, and the long black ship pivoted and seemed to spring.

But it didn't ram us. Instead, its rowers cheered and turned to starboard and they began to pass us, rowing for the headland.

That was Brasidas on the command deck, and Kineas at the helm. They'd landed from the fishing boats with all our marines – many of whom were now rowing – and fifty of our best oarsmen. And under cover of the confusion of our attack, they'd seized the best ship at the southern end of the beach, slaughtered those who resisted, launched and crewed the ship.

She was an oversized trireme, probably Carthaginian in origin, or perhaps Sicilian.

Aboard her, a dozen marines who were not really sailors struggled to raise her boat sail mast. I thought that they were going to lose the thing over the side, they were so inept, and Leukas looked like he was going to weep.

'Mind your helm,' I said.

Indeed, we were coming down on the headland at a great rate, the southern promontory of the island.

Leukas pursed his lips. 'They can't get the sails up,' he said.

I looked over my shoulder, where the Red King and his squadron were coming up on us hand over fist.

In my plan – my beautiful plan – the moment we weathered the point, we'd raise our sails and be gone, as sweet as honey, on that beautiful east wind.

But all of our marines and the cream of my rowers were on board a capture and didn't seem to be able to raise their sails.

And credit where it is due – the Red King got his ships launched like a proper sailor. He knew what he was about, and he and his full crews outnumbered us.

I watched the promontory passing us. Nothing brilliant was coming to me. If I stayed to fight, another three hundred ships would come off those beaches and eat me.

I was not going to abandon Brasidas.

By then, we had a signal book. But I only had a dozen signals – more than anyone else on the seas, but not enough for this situation.

Still . . .

I ran aft and waved at Leukas. 'I'm going to need you and most of the deck crew to go aboard that ship and get the masts up,' I said.

He nodded. 'Right,' he said. And gave me the steering oars. I looked over the stern, cheated the oars a little to put us a little farther south and east before the turn. She answered beautifully. It really was remarkable how much difference a hand-span of keel gave to the *Lydia*.

We rounded the headland still several stades ahead of our pursuers, and another dozen enemies were coming off the beach.

Now, everything in war is in the smallest detail, and that action was no different. Because Brasidas and young Kineas had all our best oarsmen – many of them – and the marines, they were actually rowing *faster* than we. But . . . If we put up our sails, we wouldn't be able to manoeuvre well because, of course, we were in long ships, and they don't turn very well under sail.

Sekla came aft. 'Going to fight?' he asked.

I looked aloft, at the wind pennant, and astern again.

'I intend to put it off as long as I can,' I said. The wind at the southern end of the point caught the bow and I had a tricky minute or two with the steering, and in fact Sekla joined me at the oars.

'Boat sail!' I called. I was about to test the keel's bite, and try to manoeuvre under sail.

Archilogos weathered the point and sheeted home his boat sail and then, in no more than it takes to tell it, his mainsail.

Moire and the *Amastris* rounded the point. He had the same rig I did and all his sails laid to, and the moment he passed the point, his ship seemed to bloom sails, and he turned straight downwind. His archers were already playing long bowls with the archers on the Red King's long ship. But now his archers were shooting into the east wind, and the Red King's archers had the wind behind them, and it was an unequal contest, and men died.

But . . .

But the wind was strong, and all our ships but one had the sails laid to the yards.

The Red King's ships had launched quickly, but I was betting everything that they didn't have a sail aboard any of them, and as Moire pulled away from his opponent, safe behind the strong timbers of the graceful swan's breast of his stern, not a sail appeared aboard the Red King, and when his consorts began to make the turn, they too continued under oars.

One.

Two.

Three.

A long pause, and I began to think of fighting.

Four.

We could take four. The problem was that if any of our ships incurred any damage at all, it was lost, and the crew with it.

But any thoughts of extreme risk dropped away in the next fifty heartbeats, and a dozen more ships rounded the point, tangled, two fell afoul of each other, and I was close enough to hear the whistles and the shrill cries and the anger. But there were ten ships in my wake now, and no matter how badly handled, I couldn't take them all.

Under boat sail alone, we were catching up to Brasidas in the prize. Likewise, Archilogos and Moire were overhauling me because they had their mainsails up, and Archilogos' ship was fast. As fast as the *Lydia*.

I left Sekla in the oars and ran forward, watching Brasidas, praying to Poseidon that his people would get the boat sail mast up.

Instead, with the strong wind astern, they lost it over the bow even as I watched. Instantly the prize fell off; oars tangled and splintered.

'Two points to port,' I called. Leukas was right there. 'Take in the boat sail,' I said.

'Boat sail aye,' he said.

I ran along the catwalk, encouraging the rowers. 'When we go, we're going to have to go fast,' I said. 'Drink some water and be ready.'

Then I ran to the helm. I snapped my fingers at Aten. 'Arm me,' I said.

Of course, he never had. Of course, he was terrified. And of course, I was endlessly patient.

No. I was not.

'Lay us alongside the capture,' I said to Sekla.

Sekla grunted.

Nikas roared at the rowers to get their oars in and *right across*, by which he meant the butt ends tucked under the opposite bench's overhang. So they couldn't move and weren't a danger to anyone.

'Alongside it is,' Sekla said. 'Look at her. She handles beautiful.' He grinned at his own bad Greek. 'With beauty,' he corrected himself, and laughed. 'I'd miss this, if I left,' he said.

We turned to port and then back to starboard, and then the boat sail was down and we were coasting, coasting ...

Astern, the Red King's ships were suddenly coming up very fast, and Archilogos was already ahead of us and Moire was just even, a little inshore.

I grabbed one of the deck crewmen who was not ready to leap aboard the capture. 'Do you know the signals?' I asked him. Molinus, I think he was.

'Leukas'd have me arse if I didn't,' he said.

'Signal *Every ship for itself*,' I said. I had a sudden horror that Moire and Archilogos would turn and fight to cover the *Lydia* and we'd get locked into a ship fight we couldn't win.

'Hang on, sir!' Molinus yelled, even as Sekla began a turn to port that we usually did with oars.

We listed suddenly, and every free man on the deck ran to the high side and threw his weight as far outboard as he could, me included. But the twin steering oars and the keel bit the water and we *turned*.

There was a fair amount of cursing beneath my feet as my oarsmen got some bruises, and some awkward sod had not got his oar under the opposite thwart, with the result that the oar got loose and started breaking bones.

Old Poseidonios rose off his bench, cursing, and dropped into the lower rowing frame to sort things out – with his fists, if all else failed.

I had to trust my people, at this point.

I looked over the stern – over the starboard side, now – and there was the Red King. In fact, he was continuing past me, locked in his duel with Moire. His first consort made the turn to engage us.

We threw two grapnels aboard the prize, and belayed them on our masts, and our way came off on the ropes, slewing the prize around so that she pointed almost due east, but by the time we were lying bow to bow and broadside to broadside, Leukas and twenty of our deck crew were already over the side, on Brasidas' deck and running for the tangle of the boat sail mast.

'Cut the grapnels,' I said. 'Pole her off.'

Molinus was ready with the remaining sailors, and he got us an oar's breadth and Nikas ordered the oars out.

The Red King's consort was a stade away. But he didn't have archers with horn bows who'd shot all winter for sport, and Ka and his lads and their winter recruits began to loft shafts at two stades, in the wind.

The breeze caught the stern, and the port side oars gave their first good pull, and we were around.

Of course, we had no marines, and only two thirds of our oarsmen. And we were rowing into the teeth of most of the Great King's fleet.

By that time, I was making everything up as I went. I'm sparing you the plans I made and discarded every ten beats of my fearful heart, but I made a few, I promise you.

Archilogos took in his boat sail and his mainsail. I knew what that meant. He was coming about.

Damn. It brings tears to my eyes. When men love you enough to die with you.

But I didn't plan to die, and I didn't want help. I planned to run, after I used my superior . . .

The truth was, I was out of superior anything. I'd faced the Red

King's ships a year before, and frankly, his captains were as good as mine. His ships were beautiful, his rowers were expert, and sadly, children, rowing for the freedom of Greece doesn't actually make you any better than rowing for a good wage.

And yet . . .

And yet, we'd beaten them at Artemisium and we'd beaten them at Salamis and we'd beaten them at Chios. I knew how I'd feel if I'd lost three times in a row to another ship, another man. I had an edge, and I had to count on it.

And then there was Tyche. Fortune. Victory's prettier sister.

'Beak to beak,' I said to Sekla.

He grunted the 'Like I needed to be told' grunt.

I ran to Ka, who was coaching two of his escaped Spartan helots – that's a story I've forgotten to tell – anyway, he was helping them be better archers.

'Take all the time,' Ka was saying softly. 'Draw and loose together, my friend. No . . . Too long you held that. Like this.' He rose and loosed, almost, it seemed, without looking, and yet his shaft winged over the waves and went in through the rowing frame. An oar stopped, trailing, and some confusion spread along the oars.

The smaller helot stood and loosed. He was graceful, but his arrow fell paces short of the onrushing enemy ship.

'Better,' Ka said.

'I need you all in the bow,' I said.

Ka nodded, picked up his huge quiver of arrows, and trotted forward, his helots at his heels. There were only three Nubians left, and he'd added five helots over the winter, and no one had told me where the helots had come from.

Nikas took us to ramming speed. It wasn't a very fast ramming speed, as we only had two decks of rowers and there were half a dozen oars not in the water because of our little accident on the turn, but we were moving.

We turned a little to starboard. I realized that I still had only one greave and my helmet was aft at the helm station.

'Aten!' I roared.

The boy was terrified, and of course, screaming at him was not going to help. And there was no time, anyway.

I hate fighting without a helmet. I ran forward, knelt behind the leather screen. Ka and his archers were pouring shafts into the enemy ship. We had eight archers, and by luck or skill, they'd put down all their opponents, so they were uninterrupted as we went bow to bow, our ship slightly out of line. Sekla turned again, very close.

Too close. And the Red King's consort turned too.

We won the turning contest, but nothing about that contact went as anyone had planned. The enemy helmsman had turned *hard* less than a ship's length from the *Lydia* and he'd turned to *port*, looking for a cathead strike or an oar rake. But Sekla's turn, our relatively slow speed, and the pressure of the wind on our bow had turned us to starboard inside his turn to port, and our ram struck their bow almost at the ram. It wasn't much of a strike.

In fact, we probably did no damage at all, and their ship continued on, almost unchecked. All we had done was to strike them on the bow and hasten their turn to port, out to sea. He turned almost end to end as they swept by. Ka and his lads poured arrows into their ship, which was slightly lower. They had their oars in and we had ours in – already coming out when we saw how we were, relative to them.

They threw grapnels, and we cut them.

'Row!' roared Nikas. Old Poseidonios was emerging from the frame, and all the oars were in the water.

The boat sail mast was just coming out of the water behind us, and I could see Leukas, silhouetted against the late morning sky, pointing aloft.

Ka grunted as he loosed, but although we'd taken away a lot of the red ship's speed, she was almost out of effective archery range already.

But the impacts had spun us, and the oarsmen were doing the rest. We were around.

Which was as well, because there were half a dozen enemy ships running for us.

I panted my way aft to Sekla. Aten was crying. He immediately began to try to force my right greave over my shin. I pushed him away and did it myself.

'He's going to ram Brasidas,' Sekla said.

He was, but he had oars trailing in the water, and little trails of blood that were darker than the red paint on the ship's side. Eight archers given unlimited shafts and a full minute in range could do a lot of damage.

Archilogos was all the way around and coming back, his oars beating the water.

Kineas, in his first action, had his wits about him. He had the port side rowers row, and he got the bow of the capture around, into the wind, and facing the rush of his opponent. The bow is the strongest part of a trireme, built to take collisions. Then he got his oars in.

The Red King's consort struck. By then, we were less than ten ship's lengths away and coming on strong, and Archilogos was closing from the other direction, and behind us came so many ships I couldn't stop to count them.

The Red King's consort tried to grapple.

Just north of us, the Red King himself came to the conclusion that he wasn't going to catch Moire, but he could help defeat me, and he began to turn to port.

Brasidas let the grapples come aboard. I'm told he smiled as if he'd won a prize.

After all, he had *all our marines*.

The ram strike did no damage that we could see, the grapples went home, and the Red King's consort boarded the capture.

I turned north, aiming to go bow to bow with the Red King. Showing my side to a dozen enemy ships.

'We need to go up his downwind side,' I said.

Sekla rolled his eyes expressively. He really didn't need me to tell him.

The *Lady Artemis* shot from under the capture's stern as if released from captivity and surprised me. I'd missed her new change of direction; I'd underestimated my childhood friend. He wasn't going to die gloriously by my side. He was trying to give us all a chance.

So now, to a veteran sailor, the game had changed again. Now, any contact between my ship and the Red King's ship that cost him his speed would guarantee that Archilogos and the *Lady Artemis* would strike him, full tilt, a perfect ram, amidships, just a few seconds later, an almost certain one-shot kill.

The Red King turned upwind. He had no other choice, and although he offered me an oar rake, he saved himself from destruction and he bet that I didn't want to tangle with him while a dozen of his friends came to his aid.

I didn't. I didn't even consider it. I was growing up.

'Turn to port,' I said.

Sekla leaned on the oars, and the rowers breathed.

I looked to the south. The rising sun was actually making it harder to see. But I was confident that Brasidas would clear the Red King's consort. I had to hope he wasn't dead or maimed; that he would win; that Leukas would get the boat sail up.

'Signal, *Make Sail* and *East*,' I said.

Molinus cackled. 'Aye,' he said. 'Sails up?' he asked.

'Bide,' I ordered. I got up on the command platform and then climbed the four rungs I'd set into the mainmast, and looked south under my hand.

Leukas was poling off the Red King's consort. And he had the boat sail mast *and* the mainmast up.

'Mainsail, boat sail!' I called, acting as my own sailing master.

The handful of sailors were joined by me, by Aten, and by the nearest oarsmen who knew their business, including old Poseidonios, and we got the boat sail to draw.

Now there were ships turning towards us, and we were moving.

'Mainsail!' I ordered. Again.

Then I almost wept in frustration. Of course Leukas had taken all the best men: the ones who set sails. Molinus and I were virtually the only two men on the deck who knew how to raise the mainsail, and I put old Poseidonios in the steering harness so that Sekla could join us.

We were spread too thin. The whole thing had been a stupid jape. The capture of a single Persian ship was not worth this, and I had endangered all my friends and everyone I loved best for a sort of military prank. And as we raised the mainsail, I could see Brasidas with his own mainsail set and drawing, pulling away to the south and west, and the whole flock of our foes turning to my lovely ship, now the slowest, the last.

Archilogos had sailed away due south. It was another excellent decision; he split the pursuit, and he didn't have to waste speed on a turn, and as the wind filled his big sail, he let the wind push him south and west, almost diagonally, because he had no keel. He made more south than west, and every minute his ship was farther from Brasidas.

Moire was almost hull down to the east.

The only ship that wasn't going to escape was mine.

But we struggled with the flapping linen canvas, and we cursed and we prayed to Poseidon, and it was Sekla who found that two brails had become interlaced so that the sail was more like a chlamys pinned at the neck than a sheet, and then he cut the brails; the thing opened like a seabird spreading her wings, and Molinus got the port side sheeted home just as Ka began to loose arrows again. Because we had a ship closing astern, at almost twice our speed.

But the moment the sail was taut, our speed increased. And remember, our opponents were rowing, and had now been rowing half an hour at outlandish speeds.

Arrows flew.

And then they began to fall away.

It seemed to take hours, as we gained on the three ships closest to us. And arrows began to strike around the helm.

Ka leaned out over the stern, loosed a shaft, and then paused to cut one of the newcomers loose. He examined it.

'Huh,' he said.

Shafts fell like a shower, but all of them fell into the sea astern.

We were away.

Sunset. There were still bare masts astern of us, at the very edge of sight. We were east of Cos in the Ionian, somewhere, and the sun was setting and I didn't have a supply ship or any food.

But we were alive. Alone. But alive.

I joked about throwing Aten over the side as my sacrifice to Poseidon, but the boy so obviously thought I was serious that I had to pat him on the head.

As the sun set in fire to the west, I shook my head.'Archilogos saved us all,' I said.

Sekla smiled. 'Well,' he said, 'that will be good for him.' He glanced at me. 'Now what?'

'Chios,' I said. 'And some food.'

There is no substitute for a good crew that trusts its captain. Sailors talk a good deal about their ships, and ships are lovely things; a good ship is like a gift from the gods. But a good crew is the work of years and Tyche's hand is always on the tiller; it takes luck to build a crew. Two hundred men, unleavened by women. Women are an important source of bonds and loyalty among men, and women, I have noticed, can often say things that men cannot say – things like, 'I notice you are not doing your share of the cooking,' and, 'Have you ever thought that if you did more to impress the oar master, you might be promoted?'

But with no women, you are left to the complexities of men's lives and their aggression and their fear. Battle and storms play their role, bonding man to man as brothers. Good leadership counts for something; but in my view, good leaders are like good parents. Which is to say, a good leader can do a little good but a bad leader can do enormous harm. Look at Dagon.

I mention this to you, my friends, because a good crew got us through the next two days. They were miserable days. We were short of deck crew, missing our whole lower tier of rowers; we had no food and very little water, and the truth was that almost any enemy could have had us. Ka and Ithy and Nemet and their former helots all began to learn the ropes during that cruise, and they were pivotal to the next two days, as we crept from islet to islet in the Ionian with a lookout posted on the mainmast and a general sense that we were a hunted animal. We spent all that time at sea, without sleeping ashore.

No other crew I've ever had would have done it without mutiny, or near enough. I won't say the *Lydia*'s crew did it without a grumble, but we had made a custom of victory and every man knew he'd be paid, and paid well, if we made it.

So we were three days to the southern beaches of Chios, and lack of food and water made every abrasion burn and every injured muscle hurt as if ropes were cutting our flesh from the inside.

We made the squadron rendezvous on the third day, creeping over the sea on a gentle spring breeze, a veritable zephyr, because we didn't have forty men capable of rowing. Listen, friends. I am not going to belabour this; it's dull telling. But three days in a trireme without sleep, food or water is enough to cause murder, mutiny, and desperation. That we made it without those things ...

I was very proud of them.

And when we made Chios, there were no hulls on the beach. I didn't have spirit to spare looking, and we landed. We took sheep, cooked them and ate them, took water from the stream; it was spring, the only time of year when any stream runs clean in Greece.

It took three more days for my oarsmen to rally. Three days wasted, and twice we saw sails on the horizon. On the second day, we had enough rested men to put up a pole-tower on the headland to watch the sea.

And on the third day, Brasidas pulled in, as spent as we had been. But his ship had had two tiers of water amphorae as ballast, and his rowers recovered faster.

He'd seen Moire, hull down on the horizon, a day before, but not

Archilogos and the *Lady Artemis*. And while his oarsmen consumed the pork I'd purchased, the *Amastris* appeared in the distance, identifiable by her dark sail and Corinthian build, and we saved them some scraps, but Moire was a cunning old bird, and he'd landed on the back side of Mystis, a little islet that faces Cos, and fed his oarsmen on the flocks stored there for the Persian fleet. He'd turned his ship into a sort of floating barn, too, penning the animals in his lower oar frames because Brasidas had some of his rowers, too.

But thanks to him, we had hundreds of sheep. We ate like kings, and gave the rest to the shepherds from whom I'd stolen enough to feed my oarsmen. I was out of gold. I had my cargoes, and now I had an extra ship.

Well, Chios is a fine place to take on oarsmen. They're all fisher folk, except the villages that grow the mastic, and the fisher folk take to piracy as well as Thracians take to war.

When I handed over several hundred head of sheep to the herdsmen, their thanks were palpable; they'd expected to be killed, and instead they'd made a small profit, and they gifted us almost forty pounds of white mastic. The stuff is not exactly worth its weight in gold, but it's the best stuff in all the *aspis* of the world for cleaning teeth and freshening breath; ladies like it, and I've even known a few gentlemen; Aristides used it, and so did Perikles.

Briseis doted on it.

Then we moved up the east coast, wary all the way, three ships and all short-handed, until we landed on the same beach where I'd met Harpagos and Agios, and Stephanos and others. And there, we put a couple of planks across two Gaulish barrels, and Brasidas sat under a sail and recruited.

We were honest; we said we were going to fight the Great King. We promised pay at two silver drachmai a day; nothing to an Athenian oarsmen, but a fortune on Chios. A couple of older matrons cursed us for taking their sons, but we picked up two hundred likely lads in two more days.

And of course, someone told the local Persian commander. Chios had been under 'direct rule' for almost fifteen years. There was a garrison in most of the towns. The 'Persians' were mostly Carians and Lydians, but all the officers were Medes. I never thought that they'd be foolish enough to try anything; the people hated them, and whoever the informer was, there were a dozen who kept us informed of the progress the local garrison was making, marching towards us over the mountains.

We had two ships' crews and the makings of the third in our recruits; all of our veteran oarsmen and deck crews had weapons, and most had armour. We had expert archers and we outnumbered the local garrison about eight to one.

One of the local headmen, Aristocles, asked us to let the garrison live. He came to me on the beach as a supplicant, and knelt.

Greeks hate to kneel.

'Great lord,' he began.

'I am no lord,' I said.

He shrugged and stayed on his knees. 'Lord, I am here to beg for the lives of the Persians and Medes who are coming to attack you.'

I waved at Aten for wine. 'Sit,' I said. 'Have some wine.'

I realized that I sounded like Anarchos. I was a crime lord, on a beach. 'Tell me how I can help you?'

'Lord, if your ... men ... massacre the Medes.' He met my eyes. 'The satrap will avenge them. On ... us.'

He had eyes that had seen too much. Well – the Persians had raped Chios. It was horrible. I knew some survivors, and he was clearly one, and he didn't need another generation of people used as his own had been.

On the other hand, I had other concerns. 'Truly?' I asked. 'You know that the Great King's fleet was beaten off Attica last year? I'm not sure the satrap will have time and troops to spare ...'

My village elder drank greedily from his wine cup and then sat back. 'Last autumn, one of the satrap's officers came here,' he said. 'He promised us ... that rebels would be punished. First. Before the Great King took any measures against Sparta. And he reminded us that Athens was destroyed and would never come to our aid again.'

'Athens is being rebuilt,' I said. 'Athens still has a fleet and a phalanx.'

He nodded agreeably. 'Sure,' he said. He didn't believe a word I was saying. 'I will beg if you like.'

I looked away.

'There are several very attractive young maidens in our village,' he went on. 'I could ... send you one. With perhaps a hundred darics.'

'Apollo's bow!' I spat. Now, I never swear by Apollo and it was an odd moment. A disgusting offer.

He was serious.

'You fear the Medes that much?' I asked.

He looked over at the recruiting table. 'Take the young men and teach them to fight,' he said. 'But don't leave us to be killed.'

I summoned Brasidas and Moire.

Moire's eyes darkened with understanding.

Brasidas shrugged. 'He's wrong,' the former Spartan said. 'We can annihilate the garrison and there will be no reprisal. By Ares, with six hundred good men, we could kill every Mede on Chios.'

Well, there was a point.

Moire, who seldom spoke at council, leaned forwards. 'These are our hosts,' he said quietly. 'They have fed us and sent us their young men. Let's get off the beach and sail away. Right now.'

The old man looked deeply grateful.

'That's what you want?' I asked.

'Yes. We will tell them you threatened us and took our young men as slaves. They'll leave us alone.' He nodded. 'There will be no fighting to get their blood up. Most of them are Carian mercenaries. Not bad men.'

Brasidas spat in disgust. 'A fight would blood the new men,' he said.

This was unlike him. 'You need a fight,' I said.

'I need nothing,' he said.

But I understood. Brasidas had been in a dark place since Salamis, and like a drunkard, he thought another dose of the same might cure him. I didn't think so.

'Let the Medes live,' I said. 'Let's go to Lesvos.'

I was embarrassed when the old man threw his arms around my knees like Priam in the *Iliad*.

But we left the beach at afternoon, and fetched Eressos in the sunset.

Well, you all know how I feel about Sappho and her town. We landed behind the great rock, three warships at the end of the day. It was not like my youth. But there was no Mede garrison on Vigla, and while the villagers cowered behind their walls we landed and dragged our ships up the beach.

It's a wonderful beach. Briseis owned farms there, and a house, and I managed to get six hundred men fed and bedded down with nothing but work and persuasion. At Eressos I laid down amphorae of water for several days, traded some of my Aegyptian wares for wine and food, and rowed away on a calm morning, better found in supplies, to train all the new oarsmen. We called our capture the *Eleuthera* or 'Freedom' and manned her from the other ships, so the *Lydia*'s crew was now one third Chian fishermen. But they were on the lower deck, where all they had to do was handle their oars, and they were good seamen, and five days rowing into a gentle headwind trained them to the task wonderfully well. We stopped at Mythymna, and again at Temnos, and then we got two days of beautiful weather and we rowed into the mouth of the Dardanelles.

I was not eager to be caught inside the straits by a Persian squadron. We sprinted from bend to bend, our rowers fighting the heavy spring current running out of the Euxine, and we looked at the ruins of Miltiades' little empire. There weren't even fishing boats. Indeed, it got colder each day, and spring had not really touched the distant hills on the Asian side. We passed Troy on the starboard side and then ran up the Ocean stream for a day, and it was like raiding with Miltiades, except that all the weight was on me.

On our fourth day inside the Dardanelles, we raised Byzantium on the west side. Our sails were down, and we'd stripped away anything that might show on the horizon.

Sekla was at the masthead. He and Ka had the best eyesight, and they took turns. He spotted Byzantium, nestled in among the complex web of peninsulas and channels, and he saw the grain fleet.

We turned away all together, a manoeuvre that I remember being quite creditable, and ran downstream with wind and current behind us, and we made it to Troy in one full day where it had taken us three to run up.

Moire was the best trierarch, and he was never rash. I left him in command, with Brasidas for muscle, and I took the *Lydia*, the fastest ship, and ran for Potidaea. I'm sure I gave Moire a welter of conflicting orders, but I don't remember them, and then I was away.

Ever caught a big fish?

You know the feeling of mixed fear and exhilaration that comes over you when you feel that heavy tug on your line? You could lose it . . . but you have it.

It is one thing to lie on a couch with your friends and propound naval strategy.

It's another thing entirely to find a grain fleet in the Bosporus.

It's a third thing to take it.

*

The Athenians have made a fine thing of Potidaea now, I agree. But back at the climax of the Long War, it was small enough, but virtually impregnable: an island at high water, the very tip of a promontory at other times, and with two glorious beaches to land smooth-hulled ships in all weathers, it was the perfect port for Thrace, at the narrow neck of the long peninsula that reaches far out into the Ionian Sea. I had never been, but I knew where to find it, and we ran there with a fair wind and a following sea. We touched at Samothrace and I made sacrifice to the gods there, and then we made Potidaea in sixteen long, hard hours, although it terrified me to run between the long fingers of the hand of Chalcedon, always watching for a Persian squadron.

We landed under the town after we spoke to the men in a tower off the southern point, and learned that the Persians had launched an attack that afternoon and been beaten off, and that there were three Athenian ships on the other beach.

An hour later, I was sitting with Cimon drinking wine by lamplight while Sekla and Leukas did all the work of landing and drying the *Lydia*.

Potidaea had revolted against the Great King because he'd wrung the town for food and gold as he marched to Greece and then ordered another 'contribution' as Artibazos, son of Pharnakes, escorted the king east again after Salamis.

But I heard all about the siege in snippets, because Cimon had his brother and two more of his captains there, and we were already planning our raid.

It is easy when you are old to see where empires rose and fell; to see little events that were pivotal, and perhaps to add lustre to one's campaigns. I'm sure I do. And I told you several nights ago of the clarity I had in the moment when the Etruscan marine's sword dropped onto the boards under my bare feet when I was a top deck rower on a Carthaginian warship. Sekla likes to say that we won the Battle of Mycale in those moments, because so many of the main players in Greek independence were entangled in the results of that boarding action and that dropped sword.

So. The grain fleet was not the pivotal moment of the war by any means. However, it was a pivotal moment to several small branches of the greater tree, if you like. And from first to last, it was Tyche, and not her elder sister Nike, who reigned supreme. Luck. Luck that we survived stealing a Persian ship at Cos. Luck that no one at Cos thought to warn the Bosporus that there were Athenian ships on the seas. Luck that we found the grain fleet in one go. Luck that Cimon was in Potidaea when he said he would be.

But Tyche, the most fickle goddess, also requires some effort. It was not luck that we'd made a plan, or that Cimon worked his rowers like a mad thing to get them into Potidaea, because the sweet zephyrs that wafted us up the coast of Asia were in his face as he rowed to Potidaea.

It wasn't luck that we'd worked up our crews all winter; that our hulls were dry and newly repaired; that we had good lookouts. All those things allowed us to row with luck, but you cannot force Tyche. You can only make love to her and hope she takes you along for the ride.

We had three or four days of anxious rowing. I cannot even remember how long it was, except that we had no supply ship, because, of course, with the wind against him, Cimon had left his at home, and ours were gone with my sons. Rowing meant we had to stay in with the coast, so we camped the first night in the full and terrifying knowledge that Artibazos and his main army were camped two ridges to the north, out of sight. They were so close that we heard their trumpets in the morning, but by then we had wet our sternposts and we were off and rowing.

We weathered Mount Athos with no room to spare, our only sailing, and then pulled and pulled across the gulf, landing on the beautiful, endless beach above Samothrace. And luck was with us again, because the Great King and his teeming armies had swallowed up all the Thracians, and there were none left to contest our landing or trouble our sentries. We stole their sheep without a qualm, and their goats, and filled our water, and rowed.

Again.

Four days of this.

I rowed every day and my whole body hurt, and Sekla declared me old.

I was too kind to tell him that he had more white in his new beard than any man in the ship.

Ka and his archers continued to make progress as sailors.

We taught them to row, too.

And finally, after what seemed more like four weeks than six days, we raised Troy, saw the ancient hill where Hector died, and landed on a beach that could easily have held a thousand ships. Certainly it still held the *Eleuthera* and the *Amastris*.

'We haven't seen 'em,' Moire said confidently. 'I have a tower out on the headland and two fishing boats up the stream towards the Euxine.'

Tyche. I can't tell you why the grain fleet sat at Byzantium. A pretty girl? A charming boy that the navarch fancied? A great poet, too much wine, a fear of spring winds in the Ionian? I'll guess the latter, but I never knew.

The next day brought us another spring storm, and it blew for two days, but we were snug on the best protected beach for fifty parasangs in any direction, and we ate Asian goats and found them much like Attic goats. Brasidas took some scouts inland one day, and then, when the next day dawned in high winds and heavy seas, Ka stole horses and rode all day, well inland, and returned to tell us there was no army marching to drive us out. The villagers lay quiescent in fear. As long as we were on that beach, almost no one moved, except a few very brave older women who fed their cattle and then, cautiously, approached us to sell us grain.

We swore oaths to them, and they came back with great pithoi of grain on their heads. But they brought no young men or young women; it was clear they viewed themselves as expendable. Troy has seen many bad times.

The third day was the worst, as the wind in the Bosporus was fair for the grain fleet and we were pinned on our beaches, a little too much chop for us to launch. I suppose we'd have tried if the grain fleet had appeared, but it was bitter; we were so close, and we had done so much, and now Poseidon seemed to be offering our enemies a helping hand.

But there was no smoke from the guard tower, no movement on the sea.

I awoke in the middle of the night. Spring was passing; the air was warmer, and I had thrown off the blankets.

Aten, of course, had taken them all. That boy was never warm.

I awoke, unaware why I was awake. I got to my feet and walked, and after a few steps I had it.

The wind had changed. It was warmer, and the wind had changed.

I gave my crews another hour. And then I woke Sekla and Leukas, and we began to prepare to go to sea.

Cimon joined me in the dawn, a wine cup in his hand and we drank, poured libations to Poseidon, and drank more.

We assumed they would be a covering squadron, almost certainly Ionian Greeks. We had six good warships and the Naxian who had changed sides in the autumn for a seventh. We thought we could take any dozen enemy ships.

It was the first morning that Aten armed me competently. He had it all laid out on my spare cloak, and a cup of watered wine, warm, on my camp stool. He closed my breastplate, my thorax, and pulled my chiton up just the way I like it, and he got my shoulder pieces just right, and all the while I chatted to Leukas about marriage and children.

I remember I turned to him at the end. 'Nicely done,' I said, and the boy glowed. 'I feel like a god,' I said.

Aten blushed.

Then I went to find Cimon and his brother Stasigoras, who were standing at a fire with Moire. Moire looked like Memnon from the old *Iliad*: skin dark as ebony, armour as gold as real gold in the red light of dawn.

Miltiades' sons and I had been taking ships in these waters for almost twenty years. We knew each other.

To be honest, we didn't even make a plan. We knew it would all be a matter of wind, current, and position and it couldn't be helped.

We didn't embrace, or say anything dramatic.

Only I remember that the sun was rising, red as blood; something men often say, but it isn't often true. That day, it was; a dark, angry red exactly like blood, and a stiff breeze in our favour. Of course, it might mean that the grain fleet would stay in port, but I had to doubt it. Their sailors were eating more food than my oarsmen, every day.

And I remember that Cimon threw his heavy silver cup far into the sea for Poseidon.

He turned and smiled. 'I wish my father was here,' he said. 'He would have loved this.'

I got a lump in my throat.

Imagine, choking up over that pirate. But by Heracles my ancestor, he was, all in all, the best of the Greeks, and he didn't live to see the final days. But Cimon was right. I wished I might have seen him one more time, standing on the great deck of the mighty *Ajax*, racing in to kill another ship, or ordering us to charge the olive grove at Marathon, while he took the army over the mountains. I remembered then, how he stood and wept that night at the Sanctuary of Heracles, looking at Athens, and said he was with the gods.

'Let's do it for him,' I said.

Cimon laughed, but his eyes were full of tears. 'You say the best things,' he said, and then he ran for his ship, where the stern was already off the beach, and we were away into the red, red dawn, our oars in, our boat sails alone set, moving well for all that over the red seas.

We ran down the Bay of Troy and then we were in the open sea, and the waves were still tall, but no threat to old salts as purely salty as we, and we took down our sails and turned across the wind, drenching our port side rowers in cold water, and rowed into the mouth of the Dardanelles.

If this were Homer, we'd have found the grain fleet there, but they were not, and we crept cautiously up the great Ocean river and, in fact, beached for an early lunch where I had used fishing boats to attack the Persian fleet almost twenty years before. We ate on the black sand, and I poked around and found the blackened timbers, deep in the sand, of a trireme we'd burned on the beach. We made a sacrifice to Poseidon there, and as if in sudden answer, the wind fell and there, just at the edge of vision, was the grain fleet.

There were forty sail. They weren't big ships, but small round ships, and they looked like all the small merchants of the whole of Ionia: ships that would carry two thousand *medimnoi*, and a few big round ships that would carry three times as much.

When we took on the tin fleet it had been different. There, any capture was a fortune.

This was another kind of nut to crack, because we needed it all.

We put to sea. For once, our standing rigging was an encumbrance. There was no wind to speak of, and no way to use our masts or sails on the trihemiolas. The *Eleuthera* and Cimon's ships left their masts on the beach.

Fighting in the Dardanelles is interesting. There's a heavy current in spring, almost ten stades an hour or even more, and the grain fleet was simply floating down in no particular order and all intermixed with their escorts.

But inshore against the banks there is a reverse current. It is only three or four stades an hour at most, but it flows upstream.

I have no idea why. Some jest of Poseidon's, or a casual attempt to help poor traders make a little silver going up to the Euxine.

Regardless, while the grain fleet was hull down on the horizon, my rowers raced us across the flow and we nestled against the far bank like ducklings in a stream fleeing from a predator, a fox or a cat or a snapping turtle, and Cimon, bless him, did the same on his own bank. We crept upstream, touching our oars from time to time.

A ship against the bank of a river is almost invisible. The flash of oars can give you away, or too much movement, or armour.

But we were patient hunters. And they came downstream on the current, blissfully unaware as newborn lambs in spring are of lions in the sheepfold.

About midday, something gave us away. But by then, a third of their ships were past us, and their guard ships, which seemed legion, were all so intermixed that we couldn't count them.

We heard a man call across the water, and another. And oars came out on the nearest warship, a small black-hulled trireme.

Well. My rowers were rested, I had all my marines aboard but Brasidas himself, and Ka was fairly bouncing up and down.

I pointed at the small trireme.

Sekla nodded.

That's all the orders we needed.

We seemed to take a long time to turn and line up with the warship, who was turning towards us across the current, and then, as is always the case in ship fights, time seemed to compact, and everything came faster and faster.

Over the bow I could see other warships turning out of the flotilla, at least a dozen.

They were all coming for me.

Now I probably haven't said this, but the *Lydia* was pretty as a picture, all red and yellow and blue, paint and pine pitch. The spring hadn't stripped her paint, and her colours probably showed a dozen stades over the water.

That morning in the Bosporus, we *saw* the moment at which our adversary realized who he was facing.

We saw because he backed water.

And then sculled, turning end for end as we came on. Backed by a dozen friendly warships, that trireme ran.

Blood on the water for sharks, and the moment a dog turns tail in a fight.

Alexandros called the action down to the oarsmen, and when he said the black ship was running, they growled like mastiffs, and I swear the ship leapt forwards.

Men are at their most dangerous when their enemies flee.

And those first moments divided the sheep from the goats all across the great flow of water. A dozen ships put out their stubby oars and crept away, heading for the mouth of the Dardanelles and the open ocean.

The rest . . .

Ships tried to turn across the current and ran afoul of other ships. Rigging caught other rigging; masts fell, and oars splintered, and men screamed.

I hadn't attacked anyone yet.

Those that ran we had to let go. With only seven warships, and heavily outnumbered, we couldn't afford even a single ship to give chase, and anyway, we hadn't made such a plan. So the dozen round ships that ran all got away, and the inexorable mathematics of the current, the wind, and the oars meant that although we could see them all day, we couldn't catch them an hour after the sun crested the sky.

But by Poseidon . . .

The rest of them wallowed like fools, ran each other aboard, and fell into a great mass, a sort of wooden island, and perhaps they huddled for safety or perhaps they were lubbers because all their best sailors died at Salamis or Artemisium, or perhaps they were fools.

I didn't know all that. I knew that the grain ships were huddling like sheep, but my concern was to defeat the warships, and not tire my oarsmen. When the small trireme ran, we slowed our beat and turned north into the current and rowed, looking for a fight. Moire came up on my starboard and Brasidas on my port side, and we had drilled so much that we could *almost* intermesh our oars. We were virtually oar tip to oar tip creeping up the flow, and enemy began to form against us, but they were scattered across twenty stades of strait.

And they weren't Ionians.

They were Cilicians. Smaller ships, for the most part. Veteran pirates.

Not a patriot among them, and now, faced with us, at odds of six to one in their favour, they were showing no heart for a fight.

They backed water in the current, waiting me out, waiting to see if I was foolish enough to attack at long odds.

Three to fifteen is long odds.

Figured against that, every one of my ships was bigger than their biggest ships, and I was going to have a huge advantage in marines, in quality, in virtually everything.

So after half an hour in which the huddled merchants drifted downstream and we moved with them, in relatively the same positions, with my three ships *just* edging to the middle of the stream and the Cilicians *just* backing away, I looked at Sekla and he shrugged. I caught Leukas' eye and he raised his hand, an Alban sign of favour.

I could see Brasidas. I knew what he wanted, anyway.

I was leaning over the rail of the marine box. I straightened up and waved at Sekla at the helm.

'Let's try them,' I called.

The oarsmen growled.

The oar tempo increased sharply and the rowers, old salts, Poseidonios and Leon and all, and the new Chians, all put their backs in like men with a fortune to gain, which they were.

And the canny Cilician pirates backed water, unwilling to try me. By then, they were in a line stern on to the west bank, with a northern squadron of five ships that were clearly unwilling to come closer, well to the north, and ten ships closer to the grain ships.

Here, I'll lay it out in almonds.

So the Cilicians backed water.

We came on. Fast.

After five minutes my rowers were grunting, and our pace was slacking, but we *were* gaining. It's harder to back water than to row forwards.

Leukas ran forward to me, heedless of any trouble he caused the rowers.

'We're going to wear them out,' he said.

I didn't call him an old woman, and I didn't curse. Nor did I point.

'They can take one more minute,' I said, loudly enough that my voice carried.

It's one thing to be asked to row till your arms fall off and your guts burst, and another to know you have 'one more minute'. The tempo went up; the pace increased, and we gained.

Three against ten, with another five ships to the north, willing to let their mates live or die.

And then, of course, Cimon came. Had you forgotten him?

I hadn't.

He was hidden on the far bank, and when we'd made our first dash for it, he hadn't been ready, and so, once again, Tyche took a hand, and he hadn't exposed himself. And now, for twenty minutes, the Cilicians had backed water *straight towards him*.

I assumed he had to be in the small bay opposite me, since I couldn't see his ships elsewhere.

And there they were. They exploded out of their little bay like wasps out of a hive when a boy strikes it with a stick, bored and foolish, on a hot summer day; and his four ships went to ramming speed in a rattle of orders and the Cilicians were rowing the wrong way, their momentum already committed.

The *Ajax* made the first kill, rolling her opponent over.

All the other ships tried to run.

The Naxian took one, slicing up alongside and all her marines going in one sparkling, bronze-clad wave in the sun, and then Cimon's brother Stasigoras struck, an oar strike into one ship that spun his target around and laid him between two of them, and he boarded both. Cilicians are great fighters, and he chose to fight, oar to oar.

Five of their ships were dead or fighting, and the rest turned to run. But there was no wind, and backing oars is as tiring as rowing fast.

I looked back at Sekla, but he'd already made his choice, and Leukas, no longer the friend of the oarsmen, raised the tempo to ramming speed and the oarsmen responded.

What is fatigue, when the enemy runs?

We had a fortune – fifty fortunes – in Euxine grain, lying to our port side, ours for the taking in a little effort.

I jumped down, armour and all, and trotted along the catwalk until I was a little aft of amidships, where I turned around. From there, most of the top and second deck oarsmen could see and hear me.

'I see fifty talents in silver,' I called. 'In grain alone, and then the value of the ships. I say there will be a fair split of spoils, and I'll skip half my share for you. Now pull!'

Without a doubt, that was my best speech. I especially like the bit about the Freedom of Greece.

Hah.

Our bow spun north, and we went to our best speed in four ship's lengths, and we were like a wolf loose among sheep, and the sheep made bad decisions – they scattered, abandoning the line they had been forming, and two of them went *forwards*, as if they wanted to go beak to beak, and then turned.

Their oars tangled, and Sekla turned us, perhaps a single pace, a flick of the oars, and the grapnels flew. It was too shallow a strike to roll an enemy ship, and I can't remember whether we crushed their oars or not, but Alexandros was by my side, shouting orders, and I realized that for two years I had followed my sons onto decks.

Not that day.

I leapt up on the rail, balanced for a single heartbeat, and leapt.

Our ship was slightly higher than the Cilician, and that saved me. I leapt onto his rowing frame, and got both of my feet down on heavy timbers, but the frame is open and I had too much momentum, and I was going forwards, so I leapt again, my spear already gone. I assume I threw it.

Cilicians are pirates, right enough, and this ship had a free crew, and the moment I went over the top deck oarsmen, they began to stab at me with short swords. One stuck me a blow against my shin, cut my beautiful greaves and left me howling in pain, and I still didn't have my *xiphos* in my hand, and I raised my shield to turn the spear of a man on the central catwalk and kicked the man with the sword. He was below me, and I had hobnails on my Spartan-style sandal, and he screamed.

And I put weight on my wounded leg and pushed, and got *up* onto the platform. Spears were reaching for me, but by then there were ten marines coming over the railing, and heavy black arrows were reaping any enemy marine who showed himself, and I had a few beats of my heart to draw.

Listen, thugater. I had to be first. I wasn't sure of myself any more. Which is to say, I knew who I was and what I was. But I had always been the first on every deck, the first in every fight, and suddenly ...

Well. Age is a killer, just as much as Ares, or more so. And nothing kills you as dead as forcing yourself to do stunts that were foolish when you were eighteen, like leaping from the marine box onto the enemy rowing frame. Alexandros led most of the marines across the ram and onto the enemy stern. Like the practised professional he was. But Siberios had followed me, and he killed a man above me with a magnificent thrust.

Thanks to Siberios and to Ka's arrows I took a breath and my *xiphos* flowed into my hand as I'd practised and I used it across the face of my *aspis* to drive a spearhead away, and then I back cut, but my opponent was canny and turned my blow with his smaller *aspis*. My back felt very naked.

So I turned, cutting at the spear I expected, and I was right, and cleared it, thrust underhand at the now open sailor, probably a deck crewman, who watched his death open-mouthed and fell back into the open rowing frame. I took a blow on my shield, got my weight down to push, took a blow on the horsehair crest of my helmet, and pushed. Then the *xiphos* proved what it was made for, slipping round the rim of the shield, kissing the bronze, as we say when we practise, round and down as our shields locked, and into the top of my adversary's thigh. I felt the soft flesh and thrust into muscle – and his groin – and he fell away and I pushed forwards ...

Siberios was already on the command deck, and he glanced at me ... We tapped shields ...

And we were done. It was a small trireme, and the two of us had tied up all their five marines for a few dozen heartbeats; Alexandros had come aboard unopposed and killed them from behind. He was the only man with blood on him, besides Siberios and me. The enemy trierarch was dead at the helm, and so was the helmsman.

Our ship was close alongside. Sekla threw firepots into the Cilician, and the rowers screamed, but I didn't have the men to hold that ship and the rowers were still fighting. We cut our grapnels and poled off even as most of their rowers scrambled to jump over the side. The heavily pitched ship caught with a roar.

We were away, and I was bleeding onto my own deck. I had to sit while Giannis and Aten got my greave off, and the edges of the cut bronze came out of the wound with a little sucking noise and a spurt of blood and pain.

But they had clean linen, salt water, and honey. I lost blood for a while, and then all the Cilicians were gone. The squadron that hung back to the north turned and ran for Byzantium.

I looked south from the helmsman's bench, and I could see Stasigoras, still between two of them. I pointed, and Sekla spat, and my oarsmen cursed. The battle was done; the grain fleet was ours.

'Come on, then,' I said, or something equally heroic.

The *Lydia* spun with less than her usual alacrity, but then we had the current behind us, and we came down on them like a cavalry charge.

Stasigoras had caught a pair of tigers. His oar rakes had done some damage, but on one ship the rowers had risen off their benches, and so his own ship was swamped, and by the luck of Poseidon, he'd been driven off his own deck and onto the other Cilician's, which had a slave crew and showed no fight at all. And then the Cilician's own rowers had risen. It was a brutal, confused fight, no quarter asked or given, and we landed into the back of it. I remember it because, for the first time in my life, Sekla tried to restrain me, physically, and I shoved him away and went over the ram, the easy way, so to speak, although not so easy when you are armoured and the waves are ready to drink your soul.

But I went up the side, and my leg held me, and the spirit was on me. And then it was a nasty fight, hard to know who was yours and who an enemy; I didn't know the Athenian rowers, and mostly they were naked men, and so were the Cilician rowers.

But I had no trouble picking out their marines, and I went for those. And in truth, the appearance of a dozen fully armoured men in their rear ripped their hearts out of their chests and gave hope and spirit to Stasigoras and his three remaining marines, and it didn't go on long.

Luck, or habit, and I was the one to go for the nearest Cilician's command platform, with Giannis at my shoulder, and in fact he passed me as we went over the top deck benches, a man of bronze, glittering in the sunlight, his red and white and black plume like a banner.

I had seldom seen anything so beautiful in such an ugly fight, and then the two of us were against their navarch and his trierarch in full panoply, and the helmsman and another sailor behind them with long boat spears.

Giannis swept the spears aside with his own, as Brasidas taught, and then went close, as Polymarchos taught, and stabbed over his shield rim, three times, as fast as the strike of a snake, and one of his blows went into the navarch's eye, and when the trierarch attempted to avenge him, I stabbed him through the bones of the wrist, a pretty strike, I must say; leveraged him with the pain and put my bronze-clad knee between his legs and then slammed the pommel of my *xiphos* into his helmet, knocking him unconscious.

The helmsman fell on his knees.

I emptied myself of the daemon of combat with a scream, a long war cry that terrified the helmsman, but it was another of Polymarchos' teachings; that cry can bring you down, expel the daemon. So I did not kill the helpless man, or his mate, and Giannis knelt suddenly in the absence of spirit that can come after a hard fight, however brief.

We had taken them both.

Most of the Cilician's free rowers were run down in the narrow confines and killed, although a few jumped for the side and another dozen cowered at Giannis' feet; once a man takes a prisoner, he's usually safe to take more.

I see I have appalled you, but really, friends, it's not so easy to stop killing as you might think, especially if you've taken a wound, or seen a friend killed. Something slips in your mind, and the daemon runs free, and you are not a man but a raging beast in the grip of Ares, and you kill. Men, women, the unarmed, the aged ...

It takes will, and training, to leash the daemon and stop.

I am proud that Giannis and I stopped. But never imagine it was simple.

At any rate, I looked out over the water, and there was the huddle of grain ships, all way over towards the European side of the channel, and the Cilicians were taken, afire, or turtled.

We had won.

Well, for once, I never doubted it. Things had changed. We, not the Persians, were the Lords of the Sea. Poseidon had turned his back on them.

I thought of Miltiades, then. And how much he would have loved to be there, when the tide turned.

Two of the grain ships sank, and a dozen escaped us.

But one of the ships that did *not* escape us was the heavy merchant *Hermes* of Halicarnassus. And she had her holds full to bursting with bars of silver, uncoined gold, and pearls. She was the pay chest of the Persian fleet, and aboard her were a dozen Persian officials, most of them ethnic Greeks.

That one ship had roughly the value of Greece aboard her, and the documents: tally sticks, musters, and more, the best information we had ever had about the number and contingents of the Great King's army and his fleet.

Just think of it, friends. There were sixty thousand oarsmen on the beach at Cos, give or take a few awkward sods. That was sixty thousand drachmai a day at rock bottom prices. And imagine that there were marines, trierarchs and helmsmen to be paid ... Sixty thousand a day, and this was the pay for a summer of sailing and fighting. Ten talents a day in silver. Twelve hundred talents. Of silver.

Brasidas took her, or rather, went aboard. I remember that he came back aboard the *Lydia*, where I was having my wound dressed. We were trying to get the huddle of grain ships to pole off and form in some sort of order before we lost them in the darkness.

'You need to see this,' he said quietly.

I complained a good deal, which amused him. But he helped me from my ship up the slap-sided round ship, and there, in the hold, I made all the same noises that he claims he made when he saw the stacks of silver bars and the leather bags of gold darics.

I admit I considered not telling Cimon. Because I knew what Miltiades would have done.

He'd have taken the gold and made himself tyrant of Athens, that's what he'd have done.

But Cimon was more of a patriot in many ways than even the great Miltiades, and Cimon had taken his horses and made sacrifice on Poseidon's altars and then gone to fight his ship like a *thetos* instead of standing on his *hippeis* honour.

So an hour later, it was Cimon moaning, as if in pain, or perhaps the throes of sex, in the hold of the *Hermes*. He looked, hefted a sack in his hand, and then turned to me with the happiest smile.

'Now we will win,' he said.

'It's all spoils to our seven ships,' I said. 'We will need to calculate shares.'

Cimon shrugged. 'It is a fortune, and Athens needs a fortune,' he said.

'Athens should go and take one,' I said. 'I'm already out a half share; I promised it to my oarsmen.'

Cimon tugged at his beard and the silver glowed slightly in the dark hold. 'Will you join me in dedicating a share to the Temple of Athena?'

I laugh. I gave up as much hard specie as I've ever had to someone else's goddess. I've never been a follower of Lady Athena; too cold and virginal for me. But it was too much money; a ludicrous sum. No man or woman needs so much money.

We landed on Potidaea's beaches like a great fleet: ten warships and more than thirty round ships. We slipped in at the end of day, and we filled the beaches, and then we had to herd the captured Ionian sailors ashore under the very arrows of their 'allies' the Persians, who had pressed their siege quite close. A storm was brewing off to the south and the sky was crowned in lightning, the very sky-sign of Poseidon himself.

One of the town's captains met me on the beach. I was worried for my ships, and more especially for the *Hermes*, as I was afraid that the Persians would recognize their pay ship and come and take her. After all, their siege lines were perhaps three hundred paces from where we beached our ships.

At any rate, Sekla and I had just warped her right under the town's wall with Leukas and a dozen of our best sailors, and the Potidaean officer came up.

'Navarch, I must protest. You cannot land hundreds of your prisoners into a town on the edge of starvation.' He looked tired, and he put me in mind of the men of Miletus.

I nodded, and beckoned him to follow me, and we went aboard another of the ships we'd moved in under the walls, and I shone a lantern into the hold where the grain lay, its own kind of gold.

'Yours,' I said. 'You can have four. The rest is for Athens.'

'By Artemis!' he swore. 'By all the gods on Samothrace, and all the gods of Olympus!'

He embraced me like a long-lost lover. And called over the side for public slaves and volunteers to unload. Those ships were unloaded in no time, such is the hunger of a starving city, and Cimon and I agreed to give them a fifth ship as well. There were children dying and mothers crying. What can I say? I am very bad at this sort of thing.

We were unloading the last ship when Leukas called my attention to the weather. The tide was running out. Let me add, for those of you who do not keep the sea for your living and pay your due to Poseidon, that tides in our Inner Sea are nothing like the tides out in the great Ocean, but they can run high at certain times of year, and Potidaea is one of those places where they run high.

And low.

The sky was a ruddy orange-black, shot with lightning – more now than when we'd entered the port. Most of our captains, even the ones who were prisoners, were swimming out to their little ships and putting a second and a third anchor stone over the side. A few of the bigger Ionians had the new iron anchors.

'That's going to be a storm and a half,' Leukas said.

I did not need his hard-won fisherman's wisdom for that. The tide was running out so fast that the bay looked like a river, and already there were rocks showing everywhere.

I turned to the mercenary captain, Skyllias. He was a thin, hard looking man with a silver streak in his dark hair and more silver in his beard. He looked Thracian to me, or Getae. But he spoke Greek and wore Greek clothes.

'How far out does the tide flow?' I asked. 'Will my ships be dry?'

'How would I know?' he asked. 'I'm only here to fight. For money.' He shrugged.

Then time seemed to move like molten bronze – slowly and unpredictably. I sent Aten to find me a town elder or a fisherman, and he vanished into the falling darkness, and still the lightning flashed.

By the grace of Poseidon and my ancestor Heracles I still had my people together, most of them on the beach, and we had kept the *Lydia*'s crew and that of Cimon's *Ajax* in the ships with some thought to a Persian attack. I put Sekla in command and told him to get off the beach and find a place to land up the peninsula, in deeper water. He had just his stern touching when we landed in late afternoon, and by the time I ordered him to sea, it took two hundred Potidaeans and another hundred rowers to get her into deep water, with the keel scraping all the way. The *Ajax* was off on her own, from a different spot on the beach, but it still took a few of us to get her off, and when we looked back, darkness was on us, and the Persians were forming in the lightning-shot darkness for an assault.

Of course they were. The bay was now damp sand, and they were no longer confined to a narrow isthmus on which to launch their assault.

I think I was standing with my mouth open when Aten returned with an elderly man in armour. He was Pittakos, like the old tyrant of Mytiline, and he waved at the wet sand.

'It'll be dry as a bone in an hour,' he said bitterly. 'The sea will come back, but not for six hours.'

Well, the *Lydia* and the *Ajax* were away, and with a heroic effort we got the heavy *Amastris* into the retreating water. Moire only had one deck of rowers, but he sculled her around and crept off into the lightning-shot darkness just as the rain began.

And the Persians came at us. There was nothing we could do but leave the remaining ships and run for it, for the town's walls. There was a giant fortune in grain sitting on the sand, with useless anchor ropes stretched to dry anchor stones, and we couldn't do a thing to save them.

Under the town wall, the *Hermes* floated in what was virtually a pool: a little area that the town dredged for deep-draught ships in peacetime.

Artabazos was a thinker; a good tactician and a fine general. He understood the possibilities of the tide immediately. And despite what men now think, he understood how fleeting his chance was. He sent his best men, picked troops, against the open walls of the town, and then he sent a horde of men, with engines for the siege, across the sand towards Pallene and the long peninsula behind the town. There are heights on Pallene, and he intended to take them, install his engines, and pound the town walls from both sides.

If his shock troops didn't just take us.

On the other hand, our little flotilla put a hundred veteran marines in full armour and almost a thousand oarsmen and deck crew into the town.

I've known a lot of fights. I have seen some hard fighting on land and sea; Marathon comes to mind, and the ship I cleared at Lade.

But that night at Potidaea was one of the hardest fights I ever knew. It was the rain, that ruined archery; the darkness, that made every man a potential foe; and the sheer number of Persians. Pittakos said that Artabazos had sixty thousand men. I'm not sure he really did, and I certainly didn't count them, but I know that before the first big raindrops fell, I was on the sea wall, only a few feet high, facing Aegyptian marines with big shields made of hippo hide, as good as hoplites, if lighter armed.

I'd faced them before at Lade. This time, despite missing fingers, a wound in my shin and fatigue, I was higher on a wall and well-rested, and there's something about fighting for a hold full of gold that fills you with spirit.

It's good that I was full of spirit, because it was black as the pits under Tartarus and they had ladders and courage.

In truth, I remember very little. Isn't it an odd thing, that without light, there's nothing on which memory can bite? It was dark and cold and wet, and men kept coming up at me out of the darkness. I could see the reflection of the town's torches on puddles all over what had been the bay; I remember the smell of the torches and the rain.

And it was silent. Or rather, men were quieter than they usually are in war, perhaps because of the darkness.

I had a spear, a good one, with a long, broad blade like a sword, and I stabbed with it, and cut, too, until the haft snapped. Ka stood at my shoulder, shooting into the darkness, and at one point, Aten was under my shield with a torch, and he would throw it down onto the beach and Ka would shoot.

And then the storm hit us. And suddenly it was a different fight, a desperate roar of the storm god's wrath, and the lightning didn't flash, but instead it pulsed like a sacrifice's beating heart, and the light was white and merciless, and you would see a man in one instant and he would be gone in the next, and Ka shot all his arrows and then stood at my shoulder with a long spear. And his helots fought behind us; I had Giannis and Alexandros and Brasidas all around me, and Siberios, the Corinthian who had been with me since what seemed like forever, got his death wound from the Aegyptians. I loved that man; he had been the making of my son Hipponax, and he'd been with me on twenty decks, and he was gone in a lightning-swept instant.

Somewhere else on the wall, the Aegyptians had driven the Greeks back, and they were into the town, dozens of them. They came into our flank, and killed Siberios, but he threw himself, dying, into their spears. A flash of lightning showed them to us, and we turned. Alexandros was like Achilles, and perhaps I was like Hector, and they were not formed close enough for pushing, and we shoved them back off the wall, all our sailors and oarsmen like a phalanx behind us, and I don't even remember the fighting, only the struggle over Siberios' body. I thought he might be alive, but when we'd driven the Aegyptians off the wall, I saw that he had six or seven holes in his breastplate.

It was odd, though, because as the rain fell and fell, it washed him clean. Most men die in blood or ordure, but Siberios fell at the height of a storm. Well, here's to him. He died for the rest of us, fighting like a god. I wouldn't have minded going that way. Too late now.

More wine.

I don't know how long the storm sat over us. Perhaps it was Poseidon, come to see to his town; certainly, after the events of that night, every man and woman in Potidaea hastened to tell me how assiduously they had sacrificed to Poseidon.

But there is no real pause in my memory, and then the Medes hit us. They had spears, and scale armour, and no shields, and they came up the ladders or simply climbed the low wall. Some leapt it. I saw this. And we killed most of their front rank, and then the lightning stopped, and we were alone in the rain-swept dark with a sea of foes.

They grabbed our spears and died. They grabbed our knees to pull us down, they stabbed and hacked, they punched. The Medes ... I hadn't faced them before. I'd like to sing you a tale of my prowess, of every sword cut, but I fought, and I fought, and the rain fell, and I was still fighting. At some point I had slick cobblestones under the iron spikes of my sandals, and at another point we were between buildings, and then, for whatever reason, the enemy broke, and we pushed them back over the sea wall.

That was the fight at Potidaea. I remember seeing Leukas with an axe, clearing the wall, and realizing that I could see him, and that the light was growing stronger; then I saw that Sekla had taken a wound under his arm, and was weak, and Brasidas saved him, going forwards like Ares – a very wet Ares.

But the men we were fighting were no longer Medes, but some other barbarians in skirts and heavy scale armour, their plumes all matted and wet, or perhaps it was their hair; some among them were painted red, or blue, and the rain made the paint run like strange blood in the new light. And they were fighting desperately.

Because the bay behind them was not only full of water, it had whitecaps. The tide had emptied the bay, and the tide had refilled it. And now our foes had their backs to deep water, where they had come up ladders from a damp beach.

My good cloak was a sodden weight around my neck, like a wrestler trying to trip me, and I ripped it off, bending the pin, and threw it at some barbarians and pushed at them. Who knows how many spears I had already used, but now I had my sword, and I got one of their spears in the face of my *aspis*, a terrifying strike that went through the bronze and leather and linen and wood and pinked my arm, but I twisted, as I had more control of the trapped head than my foe, took the slick shaft right out of his hands and cut him down. It's the only kill I remember of the whole night, and then I stood and dripped.

We had cleared the wall. The last painted barbarians leapt into the sea.

And ... sank. Their armour dragged them down.

The last act, if it had been a play by Phrynicus, was retaking the treasure ship, anchored just off to the left. It turned out that the

Persians had used her as a ladder all night, to get over the wall; that's why we kept being attacked from the left. But in daylight, Brasidas and I led the marines in retaking her, and a dozen Aegyptians offered surrender and we accepted.

The Aegyptian officer climbed down off the round ship and onto the sea wall and dropped his sword. And then a strange thing happened.

Ka gave a bellow of rage, stepped forwards, and threw the man into the sea. It was quite a moment. The other Aegyptians froze; the man Ka had thrown sank like a stone. Ka stood above him like a wet, black Poseidon, and bellowed. His rage was clear, but none of us had a clue what he was saying.

Nemet was by me, bouncing up and down on his toes and shouting in some barbarian tongue.

I went and struck Ka. I loved the man, and he'd saved my life all night, but discipline is discipline.

I think I said something well-reasoned like 'What the fuck!'

He slammed me in the head with his fist.

I didn't quite go out, but my knees went and I went down. I heard Brasidas snap orders. He seemed very far away.

And Ithy, usually the flightiest of the archers, came forwards empty-handed and said something. Calmly.

Ka threw his hands up and knelt by me. He began to say things.

I couldn't understand any of them.

It is interesting to get caught up in someone else's story. But sometimes it hurts your head.

As I understood later, that had been the Aegyptian who took Ka's town in the far south, killed his wife or worse, enslaved Ka and his people. A man as bad as Dagon. Ka's mortal foe.

Every man, aye, and every woman, has their own story. Every man is Achilles, and every woman Helen, in some way. I will never know the end of Ka's story; for all I know, he lives still, a great chief among his people. But by Heracles, I know the end of that Aegyptian's story.

Bad luck for him, then. But any Greek could have told him that the Furies never sleep.

Brasidas ordered the rest of our people back from the sea wall, gave his word that the rest of the Aegyptians would be unharmed, and coaxed them ashore. By then the light was strong, and we could see that Poseidon had wrought a terrible miracle in the night. For the engines that Artabazos had ordered dragged across the bay's sandy floor had not made it. One long arm stuck up above the whitecaps, and the beaches as far as the eye could see had a storm wreck of corpses like ugly, fleshy driftwood.

They say Artabazos lost ten thousand men that night. Ten thousand is a number beloved of poets and rhapsodes. I didn't count them, but I know that the poor bloody Potidaeans had to drag all the corpses ashore and burn them, because the stench was so bad it made them ill.

But the storm broke the siege. Artabazos had had enough, and he told Xerxes that the tides showed the will of the gods. Well, that's one explanation. The other was that the winter was over, and Olynthus nearby had fallen to him, giving him a storehouse of grain to feed his troops.

I've also heard that he'd just been informed of the loss of the grain fleet. That'd be deeply ironic, as his soldiers could have had all the grain – and silver – back. Any time. Instead, as the tide rose, the ships floated. Most of the anchors held. Three more ships were lost, smashed on the rocks, their grain lost in the bay. And the barbarians who retook the *Hermes* never went below decks, luckily for us.

But our warships were lost. That is, Sekla saved the *Lydia*; Cimon's helmsman saved the *Ajax*, and Moire got the *Amastris* up the beach miles to the south *just* as the rain surge hit. But the other seven – the Naxian, our new captures, and two of Cimon's ships – were all trapped on the beach, overrun by the Persians who fired them, and then the hand of Poseidon came in with the rain and swept over their burned timbers. We didn't salvage a thing.

The gods give with one hand and take away with the other. We were five days, or more, in Potidaea, because we had to shift grain and crews – remember, we'd lost ships, but scarcely a man – and help to clean up. Artabazos marched – or squelched – away on the second day, while we were still getting new masts into the *Lydia*, who'd been dismasted by the storm.

Well, there's many ways that the gods mock men, and this was not the least, that spring: that we sailed for Piraeus from Potidaea with thirty grain ships, the *Hermes* crammed to the gunwales with silver, and only three warships to defend them.

On a more positive note, we let all the Ionians go, expect that almost half of them changed sides and took service with us. The rest set off, a sodden and dejected lot, to join Artabazos. And to tell him of the loss of all the gold and silver, no doubt. We re-crewed all those little ships with our fighting crews, and we had the best disciplined merchant fleet ever seen on the Inner Sea for ten fine days. We had food and wine, and it should have been a fine time, except that Cimon and I spent it all in a cloud of fear, watching the horizon for imagined squadrons of Carthaginian and Phoenician warships come to retake the *Hermes*.

But we raised Salamis in late afternoon, on the last day of the month. And we landed at Phaleron, on the same beaches where the Great King's fleet had lain the night before the battle.

And then Cimon and I walked up to Athens like any other sailors. There were no horses to be had, and it's about ten stades, all uphill, and we mocked each other for our weakness, and we panted, two sailors unused to land.

I remember our last fear. There were no Greek ships at Phaleron or on the beaches opposite at Salamis, and we wondered where, on all the great bowl of the sea, the Greek fleet might be. The spring was rolling on, and summer was at hand, and the fleet should have been together; and it occurred to us that we'd been away almost seventy days, and that anything might have happened, including the extinction of the alliance.

But Athens was full of men and women carrying things. Indeed, we two, with staffs, walking, were virtually the only two people in the whole of Athens not working. Here, men salvaged a roof beam; there, four women were carefully taking tiles off a collapsed roof and stacking the unbroken ones; there, two women baked bread in an oven untouched by conquest; a dozen sweating men, naked, worked to haul the fallen pillar of some past victory from across the road so that loads of timber from the countryside could pass.

Aristides was leading the work gang, and he was stripped as naked as any other man. And not a dozen paces away, Themistocles directed another group salvaging a house that had not been badly damaged.

Aristides was too busy to take any notice of me until I tapped him on the shoulder.

He saw me, saw Cimon, and gave us one of his rare and precious broad grins.

'Aren't you a sight for sore eyes?' he said, or something equally banal.

Cimon made a sign. I didn't know it then, not yet being an initiate of the mysteries, although of course, now I know. He gave the 'crisis' sign.

Aristides called out to Phrynicus. The playwright was pulling in a rope harness, like an ox, with Aeschylus. He dropped his rope, came, and took command.

Aristides picked up his chlamys and threw it over his shoulder as if he'd been eighteen, and stepped into the road with us.

'We have taken the grain fleet,' Cimon said. 'It's on the beach at Phaleron.'

'Now, Athena be praised,' Aristides said piously.

'We also got all the silver for the Persian fleet,' I added.

He stared as if Apollo, clothed in glory, had just appeared before him.

'Somewhere between sixty and ninety talents of silver,' I said.

Aristides, the Just Man, the very exemplar of aristocratic good behaviour, threw his arms around us both, and burst into tears.

Sometimes after the sublime, one is reduced to the most extremely normal. In my case, I hadn't lost a ship, although I now had some time to spare worrying about Archilogos, last seen sailing south and west from our little disaster off Cos. When we took the Persian treasure ship, we had no idea how bad things were in Attica, or indeed, throughout the league. In fact, I'd have said ... Well, you've heard my views. I thought we were in for a long war, but fairly secure for all that.

But it was a hard spring, and harder because Attica was one of the granaries of Greece and Boeotia another. Thebes sold her grain north, to the Great King and Mardonius in Thessaly. No one had farmed Attica in a year. And there was no food forthcoming from the Peloponnesus.

There were all sorts of ugly rumours in Athens about the Spartans sending a delegation to Mardonius.

At any rate, our grain probably saved the *thetes* and the slaves from starvation. And the silver ... gave Athens an insurance policy.

That was all for another day; indeed, there was a rumour that Mardonius was sending the king of the Macedonians as an ambassador to Athens to negotiate with them.

That was all very well, but I still had two ships with their holds full of fripperies from Aegypt: glass, some of it smashed to pieces in various hard landings, storms, and ramming attempts, but a good amount in perfect condition. Four hundred Athenian hoplites took charge of the *Hermes* and it occurred to me that neither Themistocles nor Aristides could be trusted when it came to money, and that my oarsmen needed to eat. I had no word of my sons or Megakles, either. Or Archilogos.

Just when your head is in the clouds and you think all day about concepts like freedom and dignity ...

No one on the beach at Phaleron was buying, nor in the busier port of Piraeus, either. They wanted grain, and timber for building. No one wanted perfumes, linen, or glass.

So I took my ships back to sea and across the bay to the beaches of the Peloponnesus, all the way to the south coast, where helot slaves of Spartan masters bought my wares as if there was no war, and coloured linen was their sole delight. Several Elisian merchants made up a consortium and bought all my perfumes.

And then, at last, I could turn for home to Hermione. We landed on the beach at midday, and Briseis came down to meet me, clad in a marvellous wool that shimmered in the sun. She was just starting to have a belly, and her skin was lush and her lips warm on mine, her tongue the very taste of victory in my mouth, and we came perilously close to making love in the ship sheds. But Plataeans came running down to see their men, and we paid them their wages, but none of their prize money, on the beach, and Briseis sat by me as I paid my way through almost four hundred men. And Megakles was there; Hipponax with his bride, who was also nicely rounded and still had the arms of a boxer; and Hector with his bride, who was far more pregnant, somehow, and yet had the square shoulders and upright carriage of all the Brauron girls. Briseis admired them; said Sappho would have loved the Brauron priestesses; admitted it was a wonderful institution without a rival in Ionia – rare praise for her.

I had a small ivory Aphrodite for her that I'd found in Naucratis, and she immediately liked Aten, complimenting him on this and that and sending him on small errands so that she could reward him.

I remember leaning over as I paid the last man – Brasidas, who was not too proud to take his gold darics. Listen, we were all deeply honourable men and committed to the fortunes of Athens and of Greece, but some mysterious hand – which I'm going to wager had belonged to Leukas, who was a very practical fellow – some mysterious hand, as I say, had moved quite a few of the bags of Persian gold onto our *Lydia*. And, in fact, the rest of the bags of gold had vanished into the *Ajax*; apparently Cimon had no more confidence in politicians than I had myself.

At any rate, I remember leaning over and whispering to Briseis that she was a pirate queen at last, and she laughed her marvellous laugh and weighed a leather bag in her hand.

And this is out of order, but Megakles had made a ferocious profit by selling most of his goods to Sicilians.

I was just considering whether it was time to count it all and share it when Briseis' hand ran up the inside of my thigh.

'I have waited quite a long time for you, husband,' she said in a low voice. 'Perhaps you could take me home ... before you come back to all this ...'

And on the walk to our little house, Briseis leaned over to Aten.

'When we walk into the house,' she said, 'do not allow anyone to follow us. Do you understand? Then run and buy yourself a sweet. And don't come back for an hour or so, yes?'

Aten laughed. 'A sweet, mistress? That's enough for—'

Briseis smiled at him until he was quiet.

We came to our little house, climbed the steps, and Briseis paused on the threshold.

'Men talk and talk about sex,' she commented to the air. 'And then they sail away ...'

Well, I can be blind, and deaf. But ...

Some things are worth waiting for.

We didn't make it out of the entry hall, which was so small that ...

Never mind. It was glorious.

An hour later, we were on our bed, and she lay as she liked to lie, with her head on my chest.

'You brought me mastic!' she said. Her delight was obvious. An ivory Aphrodite was the sort of thing any rich husband might pick up; remembering how much she valued her mastic was the real gift. I know. I have been around.

Four months pregnant, she was radiant. I ...

Never mind. Really, I'll only embarrass you. Except that just as new intimacies were being discovered, she raised her head.

Where's my brother?' she asked.

I always see Briseis through the eyes of love and lust, attraction, beauty. It is very difficult for me to separate her, in my mind, from her body and her use of her body, which had always been one of the strongest bonds between us. Even as I mention her – and you blush, daughter of my heart, because I speak so of your mother – I see her before my eye, not as a matron of forty or even of fifty; not as your mother, who sat in a chair at meals, and glared at me – even now, years after her death, I know that were she alive for all this praise, she would glare.

No, I see her in the eye of my mind at seventeen, or twenty, or thirty-five; naked, and proud of herself, or fully clothed in all the magnificence that her taste and her riches and her wardrobe could provide, shoulders straight, neck firm, head high, eyes never downcast except when she willed it. My appreciation of her was always physical; I do not blush to say it.

So when we were wed, I confess that I expected to become bored of her; carnality, in my experience, passes, and I had assumed that years of denial had kept my passion hot. Is that too cynical for you, my young friends? Well then, rest assured that as you age, you find other reasons to love your partner than hips and legs and breasts and lush lips. Then there are children, property, the management of property, and education. Many, many things bind you; look at Jocasta and Aristides.

Well, that didn't happen. So much for cynicism. My body's attitude to hers never altered. I was never bored.

This is all too much, I can tell. But there's a reason to this aside, which is that in that winter, at the very climax of the war, I was learning more and more, with a new burst of maturity, to look at those people around me and try and see them as themselves, or, just as difficult, to try and see them through the eyes of others. Aten, for example; I found him a near-perfect servant, but Brasidas, who I loved, detested him for his apparent effeminacy, and the more I looked at Aten through Brasidas' eyes, the more I worked to bring Aten to a more Greek notion of manliness, because Brasidas' contempt was, I noticed, shared by other men. At the same time, with a little help from Briseis, I tried to bring my Plataean friends to understand that there were many ways to be a 'man', and that Aten was not a catamite.

But perhaps the greatest work was to see Briseis through other people's eyes; men and women. I noticed, for example, that Sekla and Brasidas adored her, while Myron, for example, seemed to squirm in her presence.

When she was nothing but my 'spear-won' Ionian wife, Xanthippus and Agariste seemed well-disposed towards her, but as Briseis befriended Jocasta and became popular, especially with younger aristocratic wives, Agariste distanced herself and then ... I began to hear things said.

Dion the shipwright obviously feared and disliked her. And he adored me, and needed my custom.

Sittonax would sit by her for an evening, talking of nothing. But Sittonax was a man who preferred women's company to men's, something I have seen often among the Galles. And of course, this would be accounted effeminacy and even a close kin to cowardice, among Greeks, except that Sittonax had killed enough men to crew his own trireme in Hades, so no one said a thing. And, come to think of it, Idomeneaus openly kept a boy as a lover and had once gone into battle wearing eye makeup, and no one ever accused him of effeminacy more than once.

Heh.

And Styges, who had been his catamite and loved him well, was now a deadly man and a hero of Salamis, and was looking to wed. I have left him out of this story so far, because he went over the mountains to Olympia for the winter to accomplish an oath he'd sworn to Idomeneaus, and he returned only in late spring, and I found him when I returned from the markets of the Peloponnesus, working bronze in the ship sheds with Tiraeus, repairing panoply and cooking pots. It was small work, but prices in Hermione were climbing by the day.

I'm making heavier weather of this than usual. Suffice it to say that I was interested in why some men loved Briseis and some hated her, and to say that to have Agariste – whom I respected, and who was the mother, by proxy, of Hector's wife – as an enemy was not a comfortable thing. I wanted to understand, and understanding drew me to observe.

So the next two incidents came in a timely way, as if sent by the gods. Styges complained of the prices, in front of sixty men who owed their wages to me, and all the work stopped in the shed, and a great many men looked at me. I shan't make too much of it; Styges was not out of line, and it passed, but I had registered his comment. I stopped Myron and Hermogenes in the agora and we had an impromptu discussion.

'Most of the Athenians have returned to Attica,' Myron said thoughtfully.

I looked at him. 'Do you think we could return to Plataea?' I asked.

Myron shook his head. 'No,' he said. 'But I think we have earned the right to some deserted village in Attica, if only for the duration of the war.'

Hermogenes nodded. 'We won't be a polis in another year,' he said. 'We'll all be bondsmen. Or your oarsmen, Arimnestos.' He shrugged, and held up a hand. 'I mean no offence. But we are ... not bondsmen. We're Boeotians.'

I was tempted to muster up anger; but in fact, I understood the deeper truth of his assertion. In another year, we would start to lose the very things that made us Plataean. And the costs were outrageous. It wasn't really the 'fault' of the Hermionians. They had fed all of us through the winter. Stocks were low.

I went home with Myron, very thoughtful, discussing when, if ever, the league would meet. The agora was full of rumours that the Spartans were sending a embassy to Mardonius, too. The pretext was that they had received a prophecy from Delphi and they were sending an embassy to ask Mardonius for restitution for the death of Leonidas.

Perhaps. But everything was brittle, that spring. Truth and trust were as rare as grain. And I hadn't brought any of the grain we'd taken back to Hermione. Men looked at me a certain way. If Thebes had 'Medized' then I was held, I suppose, to have 'Atticized' and helped the Athenians when I should better have been helping my fellow Plataeans.

On the other hand, friends, it is also vital for a leader to remember that people like to complain, and that you do not always have to worry about everything they say. And, in fact, Myron was dismissive of the tone about the grain. He understood as well as I that it was all about Athens; that if Athens fell, we were defeated, and if Athens stood, sooner or later Plataea would be free.

But it was that same day, as I came, very thoughtful, from the agora, that I found Briseis weaving, with Sittonax reclining on a *kline*, and young Perikles seated watching her with every sign of appreciation while his particular friend Anaxagoras, an Ionian, read a scroll aloud; something by Heraclitus, no less.

Perikles leapt to his feet as I entered and plucked up a herald's staff. His whole lineage were hereditary heralds.

Myron looked stunned.

Perikles struck an orator's pose.

'Jocasta, high priestess of Athena, summons Briseis, priestess of Aphrodite, to the Festival of Athena in Athens,' he said pompously. Then, almost as an aside, 'Foreign priestesses are sometimes allowed to come in the parade, and it is considered a great honour, most years.'

Just for a moment, I thought Briseis might mention that you could still smell the smoke of the sack of Athens, or perhaps I thought that she'd remind the big-eared young herald that Athens was a collection of pig sties at the base of a steep hill compared to Ephesus.

But she smiled brilliantly. 'Of course, you had to wait until my husband was present,' she said. Her comment had a wry edge, as if to mock the notion.

Perikles shrugged. 'I suspect that Aristides and Themistocles both want him to come, and this was the agreed on formula,' he said.

'Meaning that you do not need me at all?' Briseis shot back.

Perikles saw the gulf yawning at his feet and hurried to back away. '*Despoina*, I assure you that the high priestess of Athena requests you with all honour, and it is for this and this alone that I was sent,' he said in his herald voice.

Briseis gave a very slight sniff; her nostrils flared. Sittonax grinned. Anaxagoras gave a condescending smile; he was Ionian, and he would have been Briseis' ally in any argument about the barbarity of mainland Greeks. Myron frowned.

Now, I have noticed over the years that some men resent it when any man is chastened by any woman, and I was sorry to see that Myron was one of them, but there it was.

Briseis was not done. 'Perhaps,' she said calmly, 'I shall come to Athens for the festival, and my husband will stay here, looking after his ships and preparing for the league meeting.'

Perikles grew pale.

She loved doing this to people. I had grown up with it, and in fact, I think she learned it from her father and from Heraclitus. He did the same, forcing boys to declare themselves.

Myron glared at me. I smiled. It's really good to be a hero. You do not always have to answer; not to your wife, not to your officers, and certainly not to the archon.

'The High Priestess . . .' Perikles began. The boy was quick-witted, but she had him, and his mouth opened and closed twice, a little too much like a big fish dragged on dry land.

'Wine, Aten,' I said imperiously. Then I sat by Anaxagoras.

'Perikles, put down the staff and speak to us like an Athenian. Briseis is correct; I have a great deal to do here. I am, in fact, waiting for the league to meet. So is Myron, here. And, if I may be frank, I was *just in Athens*.' I waved Myron to the other *kline*.

I noted that he actually made a little circle around my wife, as if to give her space.

Perikles placed his staff carefully against an oil lamp rack and seemed to relax.

But it was Anaxagoras who spoke. 'The Lacedaemonians have sent an embassy to Mardonius,' he said.

Myron nodded. So did Briseis.

'We know,' I said.

Perikles was looking out at our fig tree, as if he was pretending not to be there.

Suddenly, with my new-found powers of observation, I saw that Anaxagoras was communicating directly to Briseis.

In the wheels within wheels of our lives, I was being forced to see that there were no longer two sides in Greek politics. We had all been used to Sparta and Athens.

Now we had Ionians. Through Briseis and through Anaxagoras and a dozen others like them, they were almost sitting at the table.

'We think the Spartans are offering to allow Athens to be destroyed,' he said. 'Again.'

I probably raised an eyebrow. 'So?' I asked.

Perikles spoke up. 'You have seen the Acropolis,' he said. 'But most of the best houses are intact, and we've rebuilt most of the town on the lower slopes. Piraeus and Phaleron are virtually intact. And Sounion.'

I looked back and forth between them. 'What are you saying?' I asked.

Perikles looked away.

'Aristides and Themistocles are gathering their allies,' Anaxagoras said. 'Among whom they may now count a few Ionian cities. Men speak of you as the saviour of Potidaea, Arimnestos. Delos is now free. Naxos too.'

Briseis seemed to stand taller.

I realized that I had a hard, angry look on my face and I wiped it away and replaced it with a calm face.

Myron looked at me. 'Athens cannot fight alone,' he said. 'Even with a ragtag of Ionians behind her.'

I decided that this was not the moment for straight talk. I had a few thoughts in my head, and just then, my *andron* was not the place to share them.

I looked at Briseis. Her lips were parted. She was on the point of speech. And she had held her tongue. Our eyes met.

It might have been a brilliant moment to have a public disagreement on the fate of Ionia. Instead, she laid her bone shuttle carefully on the stool by her feet and took a prepared needle from Aspasia, her handmaiden, and began to put in tiny stitches of embroidery.

From the depths of her concentration, she said, 'Of course, Perikles, it will be up to Arimnestos whether we go.' She said it so easily that no one would ever have guessed that it cost her anything.

'Briseis and I will discuss it,' I said. As she had been gracious, I was determined to meet her; a public admission that I consulted my wife on political matters . . .

Myron rose to his feet. 'I am not invited, I see,' he spat. He looked at me. He, too, was ready to say unspeakable things.

'Not my fault,' I said quietly. 'Come anyway. It's a war, Myron, not a popularity contest.'

Briseis smiled at Myron. 'They only invite me to cover it, Archon,' she said. 'They do not want the Spartans to know. Please do not be offended.'

Maybe because he disliked her, her shot went home. Myron was not a bad man; not really a windbag, either. He deflated.

'Just come,' I said.

Perikles was still looking out of the window.

Anaxagoras, bless him, spoke up. 'Of course the archon should go. Perikles feels he cannot say these things, but I can. This is the true meeting of the league, sirs. And Xanthippus plans to have the fleet gather at Aegina.'

'Will the priestesses of Aegina be at the festival of Athena?' Briseis asked.

Perikles smiled. 'Of course!' he said. 'And for the first time that anyone can remember.' Anaxagoras gave a wry smile.

Myron softened. Then he looked at me. 'Aegina and Athens make common cause?' he asked.

'The skies may fall,' I agreed.

A week later; the third week of Theiluthios, not quite Hekatombaion in Attica, just shy of summer, and even amidst the ruins, they were preparing for the Panathenaea, the greatest festival of Athens. All the jasmine was in flower; the hillsides were still green and not yet brown. The sun was warm, and Attica was beautiful, despite the scorch marks. We stayed with Aristides, and I got a taste of what those great Athenian houses were for, as we had my train, including Briseis and Euphonia, Eugenios the steward, and Aten and Aphasia, as well as Hipponax and Heliodora and two of their slaves. As I watched them together, I had time to think that it had been Hector that Heliodora had first looked at – that nothing was ever simple, between people, or nations.

At any rate, we filled Jocasta's house, and she was gracious, efficient, hospitable, and delightful. And I sat and held her wool as I always did – in a Greek house, it's virtually the only way that a married man and a married woman can share any intimacy of conversation.

And Briseis laughed, more ill at ease than I'd ever seen her. 'He never holds my wool,' she said.

Jocasta laughed. 'I imagine he has other ways of talking to you,' she said. She went back to wool winding.

Briseis gave me an odd look. 'Here I hold myself the very avatar of Aphrodite,' she said to Jocasta, only half in humour. 'And I find that I'm married to a man who can flirt with the queen of Sparta and the greatest lady in Athens.'

Jocasta gave her the kind of arch look that my mater did so well.

'Really, Briseis,' she said. 'I do not flirt. And I cannot imagine Gorgo does either.' She gave an aristocratic sniff.

I had never seen Briseis actually lose an exchange. She looked ... chastened. I didn't think it was possible. But in my new-found skills of observation, I saw that she really admired Jocasta, and took her words as a criticism.

Women's lives are as complicated as men's. No great surprise there.

It was our third or fourth day in the wreckage of Athens. The assembly was meeting on the Pnyx, the natural amphitheatre on the next hill from the Acropolis. As it is natural, improved only by some stone carving around the bema and a little reinforcement at the back, it was beyond Mardonius to destroy it. Which, as Aristides had just said that morning, in a brilliant and very un-aristocratic speech, said a good deal about the roots of democracy.

I was watching Briseis attempt to befriend Jocasta while at the same time trying to understand her. They'd spent the winter together, two housewives in a small town. But now that we were in Athens, Briseis was confronting the true power of the Athenians, and Jocasta's power.

Nothing is simple.

Jocasta was older than Briseis, older than Gorgo, her children grown, her husband at the pinnacle of power. And something about her life of discipline had prepared her for this moment; when all Athens was in ashes, she was as calm and capable as when the Acropolis gleamed with paint and marble and gold. I think Jocasta might have been a harridan in some situations; and perhaps, in others, Briseis would have been a virago. Or perhaps men simply distrust power in women.

But that spring, as the flowers bloomed, women had a great deal to say, and men listened. It is one thing when you plan the conquest of someone else's home. But when you plan the last ditch defence of your own home ...

Your wife may have things to contribute.

The fourth day we were there, at my urging – and remember, Hipponax and I were both Athenian citizens, and so was Myron – the Plataeans were given four small towns in the deme of Acherdus, near enough to Eleusis to live until the Great King was defeated and Plataea restored. It was hard by territory claimed by Megara and, of course, there was policy in settling us there; we could defend it. But let me say that the Megarans were nothing but hospitable to us; I still own a house there; so do most of us. It was very generous of Athens, and yet it was also excellent policy.

With a scroll from Myron, Hipponax departed that very afternoon on the *Lydia* across the gulf. With public grain and land to farm, the Plataeans would be better off in every way working to build something in Attica than lingering as refugees at Hermione and Troezen. And Acherdus was near enough to the coast that I could beach ships there. With half a dozen round ships and four warships, we had the ability to move the Plataeans very quickly.

But on our fifth day in Athens, the king of Macedon came.

Macedon is a curious place. In an odd way, I'd just been there; some people account Potidaea as part of Macedon. But the Macedonians had been subordinate to the Great King for two generations; Alexander gave earth and water as tokens of submission as soon as he was asked, and he led cavalry against us in each campaign.

Yet, at the same time, he was accounted Greek by most of us; he spoke Greek, and he drank wine like a gentleman and dressed like a civilized man. And the Macedonians were not like the Thebans; no one blamed them for backing the Medes, because they really had no choice. They were hemmed in by Getae and other Thracians, and Mardonius swept right over them in the year that Tisicrates of Croton won the *stadion* at the Olympics.

The king of Macedon looked like a very rich Athenian cavalry officer and not like a Medizing tyrant. He wore a little more gold than Aristides would have, and his horses were magnificent. He also spoke like a teacher or a sophist; too eager, I think, to show his Greek education, he sounded more aristocratic than Cleitus, my new brother-in-law.

I saw him enter the city, because Aristides took me and Hipponax on horseback to join the escort. Hipponax was so bad on horseback that he made me look good, and I wished for Hector, but we had two days of riding to practise, and we weren't an embarrassment by the time the king of Macedon and two hundred of his *hippeis* rode down the pass. We met them out by Marathon and escorted the king across Attica.

I could see that he was very interested in the rebuilding. He was very cautious, too; dignified, even.

He stayed with Xanthippus and Agariste, and we all had dinner together on couches, and he spoke nothing but platitudes. But I remember that he took a long draught of the wine, and looked up sharply.

'But surely this is Sicilian?' he asked.

Aristides smiled. 'Why, yes, it is.'

'You have had ... ships? From Sicily?' he asked, and there, I thought I knew him. He wasn't as cocksure as he seemed. *Xerxes and Mardonius fear we will make common cause with Gelon of Sicily.*

'Several,' I said. 'Gelon of Sicily is my guest-friend.' Bragging, if you like. But fairly true.

He looked at me. 'I don't think I know you, sir,' he said. But by Zeus, I had his full attention.

Aristides was by me on the *kline* and he motioned with his arm. 'Arimnestos the Plataean,' he said.

Alexander nodded. 'Ahh,' he said. 'The noted mercenary.'

Somehow, in that one phrase, he made me sound very low.

But Aristides' hand closed on my left wrist like a vice. Politician that he was, he was a fine fighter and a very fit man, and his clear *no* was sufficient for me. Especially with all my new-found maturity.

I made myself laugh. 'If I'm a mercenary,' I said, 'I suppose I fight for the Great King.'

Heads turned.

The king of Macedon frowned. 'I don't think I understand,' he said.

'Well, it's generally the Great King's ships, or those of his allies, that pay me,' I said. 'I understand that Greek is a difficult language, my lord. The word you wanted was "pirate".'

My implication that his Greek was poor stung him. 'I know the difference between a pirate and a mercenary,' he spat.

Cimon laughed. 'Apparently not!' he said, and all the Athenians laughed.

Even Cleitus.

Alexander flushed.

I just looked at him. I was pretty sure I could put him down. He was alone amidst Athenians and Plataeans, and none of us saw any reason to make him comfortable. He was, in every way, the enemy.

And later that evening, when Jocasta and Agariste and Briseis wanted to see, we took our wives to meet him, and he tried very hard to look down the front of Briseis' lovely Ionian chiton. Now, I have known many men to ogle her breasts, and every other part of her, but never one so obtuse about it.

No, I didn't like him.

Regardless, the next day we all met on the Pnyx. It was not a full meeting of the assembly; it was merely the greater boule or council of five hundred; mostly aristocrats, but not all. And there were a handful of women present: Jocasta, as the High Priestess of Athena, and Briseis, because it was hard to stop her, and two or three more with their attendants. And it was that morning that Myron and I were 'elected' to the Athenian boule by a sort of back-arsed rule; it was wartime, and we were held to represent our four villages in the deme.

Well, they weren't my rules, so I didn't care much.

And that same morning, a dozen Lacedaemonians arrived. Their coming was a surprise, and we understood that they were already at Eleusis, unannounced, and that my father-in-law was escorting them. Cimon and I took a dozen men and borrowed horses and rode out to meet them. One of them was Bulis, who slapped my back. But the rest of them were men of the other party, men I didn't know well. One was the regent's son, Plaistoanax, of the Agiad house; the annoying boy from the agora in Sparta. Men said he was one of the leaders of the faction that wanted Athens destroyed, which made him an odd choice as an ambassador. I pretended that I'd never met him directly, and Bulis introduced me, and the Spartans were all invited to attend the conference with the king of Macedon.

'He's on his best behaviour,' Bulis muttered. 'Sparthius is back there with the baggage.'

From this rather long speech I gathered that the Sparta First party was still in the ascendant, but that they had limitations, because Bulis and Sparthius were virtually the leaders of the party of Leonidas; the last two of his *hippeis*. They'd missed the disaster at the Gates because they'd been with the fleet; they were with the fleet because they were also close to Eurybiades and because their time with me made them 'sailors' by Spartan standards. I remind you of all this to show that it is not just women's relationships that are complicated.

So I rode back along the column, saluted Sparthius, and was back on the Pnyx by the time the sun was high, with a dozen dusty Spartiates. I was covered in early summer dust myself, and Briseis wrinkled her nose and I knew I'd just ruined a fine chiton that she'd woven. But she snapped her fingers and Aten appeared with water, a sponge, and a himation; in moments I was fit to appear in an assembly, and Aristides gave me a friendly nod.

'That woman is good for you,' he said. 'A year ago you'd have tried to appear in your riding clothes.'

'You sent me to fetch the Spartans!' I said.

'I sent Cimon and he's already changed,' Aristides said. He bowed his head to the Spartans as they assembled, and a dozen helot slaves gratefully took pitchers of water and began to clean their masters.

There had been hours of routine business to transact that morning, like my appointment to the boule, and Myron's, and a hundred other matters. But when the Spartans were ready, and not before, the king of Macedon was summoned.

The Pnyx is always loud; the rock walls reflect sound. And Alexander was clearly annoyed; he had expected a small audience, and I could tell that he wasn't best pleased by crowds or by democracy, even what passed for democracy in Athens.

I was close by him when he turned to Themistocles. 'I think it might be best if I represented Mardonius just to you; or perhaps you and Aristides. What do all these people have to do with this?'

Themistocles raised an eyebrow. 'Everything, my dear Alexander.'

Alexander just sighed, like a farmer with a long field to plough and not much daylight.'Let's get on with it, then,' he said. He walked to the steps of the bema and mounted to the speaker's place, and most of the crowd fell silent.

I say *most*, because there's never been a speech given on Pnyx to total silence. No, I lie; when Miltiades made the final speech for war in the Marathon year, I don't remember anyone speaking. But otherwise, there's a constant undercurrent of business deals and carping comments and satire and backbiting. Greeks. Especially Athenians. They love to talk.

But poor Alexander made two false starts. It's difficult to speak from the bema, and harder when the walls echo so well because it's relatively empty. He started in a booming voice and frightened himself and he trailed off.

'This, Athenians, is what Mardonius says to you ...' he began, and stopped.

Two men towards the back were debating the ownership of a load of roof tiles – a precious commodity at the time.

Briseis laughed, and her woman's laugh floated over the crowd. Men turned their heads. There weren't usually women in the Pnyx.

'Ahem,' Alexander began again. 'Men of Athens ...'

People laughed. It was just poor timing – Briseis' laugh, and his phrase 'Men of Athens.'

He grew a little red in the face, and said, very loud and too fast:

'This, Athenians, is what Mardonius says to you – there is a message come to me from the Great King, Xerxes, saying, "I forgive the Athenians all the offences which they have committed against me; and now, Mardonius, I bid you do this – Give them back their territory and let them choose more for themselves besides, wherever they will, and dwell under their own laws. Rebuild all their temples which I burned, if they will make a pact with me."

'This is the message, and I must obey it (says Mardonius), unless you take it upon yourselves to hinder me. This, too, I say to you: Why are you so insane as to wage war against the king? You cannot overcome him, nor can you resist him forever. As for the multitude of Xerxes' army, what it did, you have seen, and you have heard of the power that I now have with me. Even if you overcome and conquer us (whereof, if you be in your right minds, you can have no hope), yet there will come another host many times as great as this. Be not then minded to match yourselves against the king, and thereby lose your land and always be yourselves in jeopardy, but make peace. This you can most honourably do since the king is that way inclined. Keep your freedom, and agree to be our brothers in arms in all faith and honesty.'This, Athenians, is the message which Mardonius charges me to give you. For my own part I will say nothing of the goodwill that I have towards you, for it would not be the first that you have learned of that. But I entreat you to follow Mardonius' counsel. Well I see that you will not have power to wage war against Xerxes forever. If I saw such power in you, I would never have come to you with such language as this, for the king's might is greater than human, and his arm is long. If, therefore, you will not straight away agree with them, when the conditions which they offer you are so great, I fear what may befall you. For of all the allies you dwell most in the very path of the war, and you alone will never escape destruction, your country being marked out for a battlefield. No, rather follow his counsel, for it is not to be lightly regarded by you who are the only men in Hellas whose offences the Great King is ready to forgive, and whose friend he would be.'

So when Alexander had made an end of speaking, the envoys from Sparta came forwards. They were as agitated as Spartan gentlemen were allowed to be; Plaistoanax, their leader, might have been said to be shaking. He, however, did not speak. The speaker was one of Cleombrotus' cousins, a man I had met in Sparta, Euryanax. He was not shaking, but grave, dignified, and measured.

He said, 'We on our part have been sent by the Lacedaemonians to entreat you to do nothing harmful to Hellas, and to accept no offer from the barbarian. That would be unjust and dishonourable for any Greek, but for you most of all, on many counts; it was you who stirred up this war, by no desire of ours, and your territory was first the stake of that battle in which all Hellas is now engaged. Apart from that, it is unbearable that not all this alone, but slavery too, should be brought upon the Greeks by you Athenians, who have always been known as givers of freedom to many. Nevertheless, we grieve with you in your afflictions, seeing that you have lost two harvests and your substance has been for a long time wasted.

'In requital for this the Lacedaemonians and their allies declare that they will nourish your women and all of your household members who are unserviceable for war, so long as this war will last. Let not Alexander the Macedonian win you with his smooth-tongued praise of Mardonius' counsel. It is his business to follow that counsel, for as he is a tyrant so must he be the tyrant's fellow-worker; it is not your business, if you are men rightly minded, for you know that in foreigners there is no faith nor truth.'

These are the words of the Spartans. They had an odd, arrogant ring to them, especially spoken in the windswept Pnyx to five hundred men who had, every single one of them, fought at Salamis.

Aristides and Themistocles exchanged a look, and Themistocles, as the archon, announced that the people of Athens would answer first to Alexander and Mardonius, and that Aristides would deliver the oration. This is it, as best I remember it.

He mounted the bema carefully, with dignity, and he looked at us for a while. He was almost accorded silence. Then he turned to Alexander, and his voice was perfectly controlled, and it cut like a whip.

'Do you think us fools?' he asked. 'We know of ourselves that the power of the Mede is many times greater than ours. There is no need to taunt us with that. Nevertheless, in our zeal for freedom we will defend ourselves to the best of our ability. But as regards agreements with the barbarian, do not attempt to persuade us to enter into them, nor will we consent. Now carry this answer back to Mardonius from the Athenians, that *as long as the sun holds the course by which he now goes, we will make no agreement with Xerxes*. We will fight against him without ceasing, trusting in the aid of the gods and the heroes whom he has disregarded and burned their houses and their adornments. Come no more to Athenians with such a plea, nor under the semblance of rendering us a service, counsel us to act wickedly. For we do not want those who are our friends and protectors to suffer any harm at Athenian hands.'

And Aristides came down off the bema to massive applause from every man and woman present, including the Spartans.

Such was the answer of the Athenians to Mardonius, but now Themistocles mounted the steps.

He addressed the Spartan envoys and said, 'It was most human that the Lacedaemonians should fear our making an agreement with the barbarian. We think that it is an ignoble thing to be afraid, especially since we know the Athenian temper to be such that there is nowhere on earth such store of gold or such territory of surpassing fairness and excellence that the gift of it should win us to take the Persian part and enslave Hellas. For there are many great reasons why we should not do this, even if we so desired: first and foremost, the burning and destruction of the adornments and temples of our gods, whom we are constrained to avenge to the utmost rather than make pacts with the perpetrator of these things; and next, the kinship of all Greeks in blood and speech, and the shrines of gods and the sacrifices that we have in common, and the likeness of our way of life, to all of which it would not befit the Athenians to be false. Know this now, if you knew it not before, that as long as one Athenian is left alive we will make no agreement with Xerxes. Nevertheless, we thank you for your forethought concerning us, in that you have so provided for our wasted state that you offer to nourish our households.

'For your part, you have given us full measure of kindness, yet for ourselves, we will make shift to endure as best we may, and not be burdensome to you. But now, seeing that this is so, send your army with all speed, for as we guess, the barbarian will be upon us and invade our country in no long time as soon as the message comes to him that we will do nothing that he requires of us; therefore, before he comes into Attica, now is the time for us to march first into Boeotia. For if you allow Mardonius again to penetrate Attica – and be warned, men of Lacedaemon, that we hold you and our allies responsible – then we will think again on our own actions.'

When Themistocles was done speaking, it was obvious that he had mortified both embassies. Alexander had rolled his eyes like an angry horse through Aristides' speech to the Spartans, and he asked to speak again, and was denied.

I was standing quite close to him, and he turned to me as if we'd always been friends.

'Are they mad?' he exclaimed. 'Do they know the Great King's power?'

'As to that,' Cimon said, 'I fear you may find it less than you imagine this summer.'

'Less than I imagine?' Alexander exploded. 'By Zeus, you Athenians are puffed up like adders at your little victory last autumn. In a month, Mardonius will be here. Again. There is nothing you can do to stop him. Even now, Thebes advocates the total destruction of Athens and all Attica – every tree cut, every field salted. How will your ever-vaunted fleet stop Mardonius and the Great King's army?'

Sparthius had detached himself from the Spartan embassy, and he walked over to where I was. For all I know, he was looking to have a cup of wine when the windbags, as he called them, were done.

But he stopped, two paces from the king of Macedon.

'We will stop Mardonius,' Sparthius hissed between his missing teeth. 'Tell your master that he cheated at the pass of Thermopylae and denied us the contest he seemed to promise. Tell him that every Spartiate dreams of the day when he has an Immortal on the end of his spear.'

Alexander of Macedon drew himself up and looked down his long nose at the Spartiate. 'I have no "master",' he said. 'And I think you will find that your ephors have other views.'

'Really?' Cimon said. 'Enlighten us.'

Alexander froze, a man who had said utterly the wrong thing.

'Yes,' Aristides said. He had come to perform the rituals to close the oule. 'Yes, my lord. Tell us, and the *Spartan embassy*, of the alliance you have with the Spartan ephors.'

Now silence fell over the whole of the Pnyx, and it was eerie. For the whole of the conference, there had been hammers and saws all over the slopes of the Acropolis, but now there was nothing but a single, long cry: a seabird.

Sparthius laughed, and his laughter was more dangerous than all the glares of all the kings of Macedon ever born. 'Don't count on some whispered promise from old men,' he said. 'We lost our king. We will avenge him in blood.'

Cimon smiled grimly.

Aristides nodded.

Themistocles took a deep breath.

The Spartan embassy knew something had happened, and they could, no doubt, see Sparthius and his deep red cloak. But now Bulis came towards us, and then Plaistoanax and his handlers.

The king of Macedon was trying to walk away, and the crowd was stopping him.

And Sparthius was as angry as I have ever seen him. He turned on the regent's son.

'This,' he spat, and the 's' was a long sibilant, 'this is the result of all the dirty politics. That this creature can stand in public and say that we will *not fight*. They killed my king, and this ... ' Sparthius stepped forwards until he was very close to Plaistoanax. 'Swear to me that there is no alliance with Mardonius, or by all the gods, I will become an Athenian this day.'

Four hundred and ninety-nine Athenians craned their heads to see the Spartans fighting among themselves.

I was watching Alexander. And thinking, *You just revealed our worst fear was true.*

He was writhing, his face moving. His fury was part and parcel with his fear, I think.

Themistocles' eyes met mine over Alexander's head. He didn't look triumphant, although all winter it had been his voice that had warned us that the Spartans were selling Athens to the Great King.

Perhaps none of it mattered to what happened later. Often in the affairs of men and gods, talk is cheap, and men talk, make deals they never intend and betray themselves later; men make promises they do not mean; men swear they love women when in fact they do not, and perhaps the ephors never intended any support to Mardonius.

Or perhaps they did.

But if they did, they chose their tools unwisely, because Pausanias' son was brave as a lion, for all his pimples. He was young, the fire was high in him, and he looked at Sparthius, a famous man, a fighter, and he shook his head sharply.

'I swear to you, Sparthius. We will fight to the last drop of our blood for the league. And if Athens stands with us, we stand with Athens,' he said. He glanced around, and if he was dissimulating, I didn't see a sign.

So. Perhaps it didn't matter.

Or perhaps right there, under the altar of Hermes, everything changed. I will never know.

'I swear,' the boy said. He raised his hand. 'By Hermes, and by Zeus, the god of kings, and by my forefathers back to Heracles, I swear that my spear will be next to yours, Sparthius, when the day comes, and the contest.'

'Son of a bitch,' Themistocles said quietly. 'I don't believe it.'

But Bulis was smiling. It was a calm smile.

I suddenly had a vision, almost like a priest, of Gorgo: Gorgo, sitting in her cold garden, dressed as a widow. Gorgo was sitting with Bulis. And she said, *They are sending Pausanias' hot-headed son? Fools. When the Macedonian has spoken, Bulis, you or Sparthius provoke him. Get it in the open. And then . . . Then we'll see what Plaistoanax does.*

Perhaps it was not like that. I will never know. But Bulis looked awfully smug, for a man of Lacedaemon.

And that night, when we were all gathered, Aristides took me by the hand and led me to where the king of Macedon stood with his captains.

'Come, my lord. I wish to show you something. You may return to Mardonius and tell him what you have seen.' Aristides walked with the king. And Themistocles was there, and Cimon, and Xanthippus – it was his house. And Sparthius.

We walked out of the courtyard, and around the back of the house by torchlight. There was an outhouse, and Alexander joked that he knew the way. No one laughed. We walked up a small hill, where Xanthippus had his outbuildings.

'Ordinarily, what we are about to show you would be in the treasury of the Temple of Athena Parthenos,' Aristides said. 'But of course, that was looted, destroyed, and defamed. You know what they did on the altars of Athena, O king of Macedon? They raped a man and killed him. And left his body to rot. Yes? You understand, king of Macedon?'

We were standing by a small shed, by torchlight. I think that the king of Macedon was afraid for his life.

'You know what your Great King did to the king of Sparta?' Sparthius asked. 'He took the body and defiled it, cut off the head, and spread the entrails on the ground.' He smiled. 'You think we will make peace because some old men see an opportunity for power?'

'If you kill me—' Alexander said.

'Kill you?' Themistocles asked. 'Don't be a fool. We want you to take our message back to Mardonius.'

I knew that he had stage managed all this. I knew his hand; I knew his plotting. He was playing all the sides, but ultimately, he was the *archon basileus* of Athens, and he was Athenian.

They opened the shed. There were steps going down into darkness.

'Why must I go down?' Alexander asked.

'Because your duty to your master compels you,' Themistocles said.

We walked down the steps. Only five of us fitted – it was a cold cellar, or some kind of storage shed. Actually, I've been back since, and it was an old house, carved into the living rock of the hill, from the time of the Trojan War, and it was dark and sinister by torchlight.

I confess I was sure we were going to kill the king of Macedon.

Instead, at the base of the stairs, there was a door. Themistocles grasped the handle. And threw it open.

Inside was all the treasure that we'd taken in the Dardanelles. Fifty talents of silver, and gold and pearls.

'Alexander,' Themistocles said softly. 'This is the pay chest of the

Great King, king over kings. It is all the treasure he had to pay his fleet off Cos. But our fleet has already struck. Ask Mardonius how he plans to pay his men. And ask him, too, how the Great King's fleet will co-operate with him, when they are too afraid to cross the sea? When the rowers are not paid, and the Phoenicians have other cares? Ask Mardonius why Athens should care? If the worst comes, we can sail away, and *still be rich*.'

He turned to Sparthius. 'We do not need Lacedaemon's largesse because we have our own funds, and the Great King has *most kindly* provided us with grain.' He nodded. 'But we will be best pleased to see the hoplites of the league march over the isthmus. Soon. Because the king of Macedon is a harbinger, and Mardonius means us ill.'

Alexander shook his head again. 'Even now, you could be the Great King's favourite ally.'

And Aristides said, 'Never.'

That week, Themistocles set the fleet rendezvous for Piraeus, and then, after consultation with his Aeginian allies, moved it to Aegina. We were all painfully aware that Mardonius was already marching, and that the league's phalanx was two weeks away. Or more.

In fact, I've made all this sound mature and measured. And in a way it was. The Athenians had dignity, amidst their ruins and their new construction. But at the same time, we knew that the Athenians couldn't hold Mardonius alone, and we knew that it would take the Spartan embassy a week to get home, and another week to even get the league's troops to move.

And there was immense pressure on Themistocles, too. He was the *archon basileus*, and he was an arrogant sod. He'd promised everyone that he'd keep Mardonius out of Attica so that they could rebuild. And now it looked as if Mardonius might return with fire and sword.

On the other hand, no one – and I mean *no one* – in Attica suggested any form of rapprochement or collaboration.

So the next two weeks passed in a flurry of concerns. The Plataeans landed on the beaches of Eleusis and formed a long train walking inland to settle in their villages. It was too late for a spring planting, but possible to get a barley crop in late autumn, with luck, and as fast as we allocated plots, men were ploughing. And women, too, because of course, the hoplite class went to Corinth, not Eleusis. The league army was forming at Corinth, or so we heard. Hermogenes sent me word by his oldest son, Bion, that the only Spartans at Corinth were building the wall, and that Adeimantus said openly that no man of Corinth would fight for an inch of Attica.

The problem was that the army was forming, but it was not marching. We heard that Cleombrotus was to command, and he was clearly in no hurry. And messengers told us that no Spartiates or even Peloponnesian allies were at Corinth. That is, there were seven thousand helots under Spartan officers building their precious wall.

Friends of the league in Thessaly sent word that Mardonius was marching.

We all knew how fast he could move. This time, the Athenians were far better prepared. The cavalry of Athens, which was reckoned excellent by Greek standards, rode as far abroad as the plains of Boeotia, and my son Hipponax rode with them on horses provided by Cleitus – there's some irony there. Shipping was concentrated on the beaches of Eleusis and Piraeus far more efficiently than the last time. I saw some familiar looking round ships in the Bay of Salamis and wondered if I was ever going to see a copper from my greatest heist.

Myron led the Plataeans in their temporary villages. As it was clear that Mardonius was coming, no one tried to build anything more than the hastiest of shelters, but it was agreed to plant barley, as we didn't expect the Persians to stay long. As they would have the league army coming up on their flank, we assumed they'd either never make it into Attica or they'd be ejected before they could do much damage.

Well, most of my oarsmen were Plataeans, and we didn't have to be at the isthmus. So we hauled ploughs. It would make a good comedy for a bacchanal; half a thousand oarsmen and sailors trying to help farm wives with ploughing while their husbands were playing soldiers. They were the worst farmers ever, and I suspect they'd have liked to play husband in more ways, but we kept them on a short leash and provided free wine in a tent camp. The ground got ploughed, and the barley got planted.

It filled the time. I mean it. I never stopped moving, and it was as if I lost two weeks of my life. Briseis stayed with Jocasta, a perfectly rational choice, if one I didn't especially like. Aten went back and forth between us with little presents – I sent her a pressed flower, she sent me an amphora of good wine.

Thirteen days. I only ploughed, myself, twice; Draco's granddaughter mocked Leukas and said that if I'd stop being a pirate she'd have me as a farmhand any day, because I was one of the few there who *actually* knew how to farm. My sister Penelope complimented me on my ploughing and then told me to get my sailors penned up before all the maids were pregnant.

When the farm work was done, I drilled them with Brasidas. I had thought he might go to the isthmus for the league army, but he shook his head and looked, not at me, but off towards the mountains. It was odd, but from one place in our four villages, we could make out the back of Cithaeron. We had women there who had never expected to leave Plataea in all their lives, and here they were, six hundred stades from the rubble of their homes, ploughing foreign ground with strangers, and laughing about it. At any rate, that one hill, where we could see Cithaeron, became a sort of shrine for Plataeans. First there were flowers, and then someone sacrificed a rabbit, and ten days in, Myron and I got some locals to move an old stone. It might have been an altar of the old people, before the Trojan War; it was a big piece of stone, but we had borrowed Athenian oxen and some things are more important than war or work. Then most of my sailors spent an afternoon picking rocks out of our new fields and moving them to the new sanctuary, and we built a low wall, and there was the first Sanctuary of Cithaeron ever built in Attica, and perhaps the last.

Anyway, Brasidas had taken to swearing on it, perhaps because he wanted us to know he was Plataean, and when he turned his head, it was in the direction of Cithaeron. 'I couldn't stand on the isthmus and watch Sparta betray Greece,' he said.

I think my eyes almost fell out of my head, so fast did my head snap around. 'You think that Sparta will not march?' I asked.

He pursed his lips. 'I think that I would prefer to belong to a polis where no one has to ask.'

So. We worked. We drilled. We were fit, and tired all the time. And then, at the very brink of the month of Hekatombaion, messengers came with the order to evacuate.

We were all veterans by that time, men and women together. Donkeys were loaded; no one had brought much. Myron gathered all the non-fighters, we formed two columns, and the sailors, armed, became the rearguard, because the Oinoe road ran through our two central villages and for all we knew, the Persians would come across the pass that day.

Instead, Cleitus, once my enemy, cantered up with my son and fifty more rich boys on good horses, all leading second and third animals. They had the corpse of an Athenian over one horse and several men were wounded.

'Your son rides like a sack of flour,' Cleitus said, dismounting. 'But he fights like Achilles reborn.'

He looked at my phalanx of sailors, formed beside the road. 'A pleasure to see, but there's no need. There's a handful of Saka over by Plataea, but their main force is camped at Thebes tonight. They'll march for us tomorrow.'

We fed him. 'You had a fight?' I asked.

Hipponax shrugged. 'We were down by Thespiae, and the fucking Thebans attacked us.'

Cleitus raised an eyebrow.

Hipponax took a breath. 'The Theban cavalry attacked us.'

I was impressed – with Cleitus.

My son proceeded to tell the story of a mixed cavalry and infantry skirmish. He never mentioned himself, and he certainly praised Cleitus.

Well, well.

I tried not to be jealous as he lauded Cleitus as a military commander.

When he went to get more soup, Cleitus smiled grimly. 'My son-in-law validated his marriage in a single afternoon,' he said. 'He saved my life in the fighting. I was down, and he stood there – in a cavalry fight – and killed Thebans.' He shrugged. 'Makes paying the dowry seem worthwhile.'

Cleitus and I had a hard time loving each other. But his Laconic praise was genuine, and I grinned. 'He's a good spearman,' I said. 'Sometimes a pain in the arse.'

Cleitus looked at me as if he feared a joke. 'Must run in the family,' he said.

I admit I laughed.

The next day we were aboard our ships. We rowed two hundred women and donkeys across to Salamis, and it was as if we'd come home. The same beaches, and in our case, the same fire pits, as the women of Plataea moved into the camp that my squadron had had. There were no Brauron girls on the next headland; Brauron was in ruins, and the priestesses had not even attempted to gather the girls that year. But Lady Thiale, the high priestess, was on the beach, and she met Briseis and Euphonia the day we landed, and so, by the time I had my people sorted, Euphonia was bouncing up and down and asking if she could, please, go with Thiale.

In fact, Thiale had asked a number of her older girls to help with dances; not just for the daughters of aristocrats, but for all the Athenian girls of every class who were on Salamis. Like Briseis and Jocasta, Thiale was determined that women would contribute.

Morale was low. It is fashionable now to pretend that we all kept a stiff upper lip and went back to Salamis in lockstep, knowing that victory was at hand, but that's a crock of horse piss, and the truth was that as the boats landed people at Salamis, more than a few Athenians thought that they would never go back to Attica.

Women like Thiale worked miracles. Dancing was for everyone, but exacting dancing like that taught at Brauron was for the elite. Yet ... Cleisthenes in his political reforms had told the hoplite class that they were as elite as any, and Thiale seemed determined to make that as true for daughters as for sons. So Heliodora, nicely rounded in her fourth month of pregnancy, and a dozen other newly married 'old girls' joined my daughter and a number of other 'bears' in teaching the dances to groups that could, at times, fill the beach.

I offer this to say – life went on. Athens never surrendered, although the temptation must have been there, because the night after we fell back to Salamis – again – we could see the fires. The Persians were burning the repairs that these people had just made. Another summer of work – gone.

Briseis was very impressed with Thiale, and did all she could to help. As I have said, it was the summer of women; Jocasta was everywhere, and Briseis, and you'd have thought that women had always played a major role in the politics of the city.

It was that week that Themistocles fell from power. He fell as soon as we saw fire in Attica. It was, perhaps, unfair, but democracy, for all that I support it, can be deeply unfair. Themistocles had promised the people of Athens that he would keep Mardonius in Thessaly, and he'd failed, or rather, his Spartan allies failed him. The unfair part is that I, who didn't really like or trust him, knew that in this case he'd done all that could be done, and that the Spartans were deeply divided and indecisive at the best of times, and worse now.

Regardless, the assembly met on Salamis and stripped Themistocles of his rank as *archon basileus*. He stunned me by accepting this demotion with good grace. In fact, he turned to me and shrugged.

'I failed them,' he said. 'I deserve it.'

'Is this Themistocles talking?' I asked.

Aristides shook his head. 'Arimnestos,' he said, 'we are enemies in politics, but in this, I understand him perfectly. He won the battle here, and the league spurned him, and he was angry. But he lost Attica to the Medes; even if it is not his fault, he bears the responsibility. Yes?'

Themistocles nodded. 'I wanted to command the fleet,' he said. 'The Spartans would give me an escort like a king, but they wouldn't give me command. I knew then that something was rotten.'

That afternoon, with the smoke of Attica in our nostrils, we voted for Xanthippus to be *archon basileus* for the balance of the term. After consultation, it was decided that he would go to the fleet with Themistocles as his 'advisor', and Aristides would take the phalanx over to the mainland when the league army came.

I was in every council, that summer. As a member of the boule, however tertiary, I had almost unlimited political rights, and I used them. But it also carried responsibility, and the boule chose me as the go-between for fleet and army.

It wasn't a role I fancied. I rather hoped to be given a squadron in the fleet. But I owned my own ships and I had friends in every camp, and Aristides himself wanted me to be the messenger. The summer before, the linkage between the army and the fleet had been essential. We had every reason to expect it would be the same.

So when Mardonius marched his army into Athens proper for the second time, I was just launching the *Lydia* off the beaches of Salamis. It was an odd morning, and the gods were close. Time seemed to have no meaning. Girls were dancing on the next beach; the smoke rose from our cooking fires to mix in the high air with the burning farms of Attica, and it was as if the Battle of Salamis had never happened, as if Thiale had never cursed the Persians, and as if our long ships had never defeated theirs in the deep bay. I kissed Briseis.

She laughed into my mouth in her accustomed way and scandalized her friends in her accustomed way. 'The Ionian ambassadors are with the league fleet,' she said.

I wondered how long she had known that.

'Help them,' she said.

I kissed her again.

We had beaten the Medes at sea, and I had married Briseis. I banished all the dark thoughts and Moire and I went to sea.

Plataea

Summer, 479 BCE

The league fleet lay at Aegina, short only of those contingents that came from the Peloponnesus. Corinth had provided sixty ships the year before, or near enough, and the rest of Peloponnesus perhaps thirty.

That summer, Aegina hosted us on her marvellous beaches, and we had more than a hundred ships of Athens, all better crewed than the year before; Aegina had almost sixty herself, and little Hermione sent three, apparently because no one had told her council that the Peloponnesus was going to be slow. I had four ships of my own there, and my new ship, the one I'd purchased, was crewed with Hermionian marines and Sekla had her. We called her the *Nike*. Now, there were perhaps fifty ships in the fleet called *Nike* that summer, because Greeks can be deeply unoriginal. So ours was 'Plataean *Nike*', and there was not, I regret to say, a single Plataean aboard except Sekla.

At any rate, we had the *Black Raven*, the *Amastris*, the *Lydia* and the *Nike*. The rest of what had been 'my' ships were crewed by Athenians. The Plataeans were off to dry land, to fight as their forefathers fought.

The *Black Raven* and the *Amastris* were both heavy ships, fit for the middle of a line in a pitched battle. Sekla's lithe *Nike*, on the other hand, was fast – as fast as the *Lydia* – although lacking the upper deck and standing masts, or perhaps because of that. At any rate, it's not ships but crews, and Sekla had good oarsmen and good sailors, and so the two of us became the messenger ships.

But I had a fifth ship in 'my' squadron, because we landed at Aegina to find Archilogos and the *Lady Artemis* well up on the beach.

Archi met me at the edge of the water and we talked at each other at a stade to the heartbeat, so to speak.

'I thought you were done for, there,' he said.

'I think you saved us all,' I said. 'That was as pretty a piece of ship handling as I've ever seen.'

There were other men around – Xanthippus, for example – and I told them all of the fight off Cos, and how, at odds of ten to three, Archi had turned his ship and attacked, disrupting the enemy attempt to envelop us and saving the lot of us.

Archilogos bathed in my words.

And Xanthippus turned to him, as if he hadn't seen him all winter in Hermione, and invited him to the trierarchs' conference. Who doesn't love praise?

But Archi needed it. He needed to have his reputation back.

He had also brought half a dozen Ionian envoys: men from Lesvos and Chios and Samos and Rhodos. They begged to be heard.

I listened to them speak in detail, and I confess that all I heard was hot air – the same sort of piss-poor planning and empty promises of the Ionian War. They swore that all Ionia would rise; that they could destroy the Great King's fleet once and for all.

And perhaps worse, I could see that Archilogos didn't believe them any more than I did. He had spent the spring sailing across the Ionian, criss-crossing it, looking for support, and not a single ship had joined him. Just ambassadors.

That evening, we learned that Mardonius had sent an embassy to the Athenians on Salamis. We were told that Aristides had ordered the assembly to meet to hear the ambassador's words in public.

It was Alexander of Macedon all over again; or at least, the offers were the same. The ambassador this time was Mourychides, who came from this very town on the Hellespont. That's another story. He made his offer: peace, if Athens would make peace, or war, and the utter destruction of Attica.

One member of the boule raised his voice and proposed that Athens accept the offer.

I never met him. I'm sorry for what happened. But the assembly turned on him, and ripped him to pieces. I gather that every man in the assembly was covered in his blood, and it happened before the very eyes of Mardonius' ambassador.

And the women of Athens – even Jocasta – went to his house, and killed his wife, his sister, and their children.

That was the summer of the climax.

That, not Salamis, was the razor's edge.

Athens held the line. Athens refused earth and water. Athens tolerated no dissent on this one issue – that there would be no peace with the Great King.

The barbarians burned everything they owned, and they did not flinch.

When we heard, perhaps ten hours later, men wept openly, and some poured ashes on their heads. Xanthippus groaned aloud. Not because a man had been publicly executed without a trial, or innocent women and children torn limb from limb. We wept because Athens was doomed.

Because weeks had passed.

Because the Spartans had betrayed us.

The Ionians begged and begged me for an audience with Xanthippus.

'This is not the day,' I said.

Archi said the same. And in that terrible hour, we were reconciled. Archilogos knew what we were suffering.

The leader, if they had a leader, spat at me, 'I am a powerful man. I do not need to be kept from the archon of Athens like a beggar.'

And Archilogos stepped between us, because I might have done something violent.

'Herodotos!' he said. 'These men have lost their cities, while you still enjoy yours. These men have been fighting for *years*. *This is not the time!*'

Even the Aeginians, who, all things said, had more reason to hate Athens than any other city in Greece, expressed sorrow. And the navarch of Aegina, who had more than done his part at Salamis, said, 'Who has time to hate Athens? There are so many Persians to hate first.'

It became a byword, that summer.

The next morning, the council of the fleet, supported by the Assembly of Athens, voted to send a ship to the army on the isthmus, and a delegation to Sparta directly, bypassing the so-called 'Council of the League' which was led by – you guessed it – Adeimantus.

I was present when Xanthippus charged the delegates – of whom I was not only the transport but a member – to tell the ephors of Sparta that no prevarication would be accepted.

Xanthippus was sometimes shallow and petty. But that summer, as Athens burned – again – he looked at the six of us.

'Aristides, Themistocles and I are in agreement,' he said. 'And I have told the Aeginians. If the Spartans will not march, we will take our people and go to Magna Graecia. We will never *help* the Great King destroy the Peloponnesus.' He nodded. 'But we will not lift a finger to stop them.'

'Zeus sator!' cried Cleitus, who was also one of the delegates. 'I could almost help the Great King land on the coasts of Sparta.'

And I said, 'I could almost agree, but what of Troezen and Hermione? They welcomed us.'

Cleitus nodded. 'You speak well, Plataean. Very well. Let us go and "reason" with the men of Sparta. But I, for one, will never forget.'

And Xanthippus' son Perikles nodded agreement. 'Never,' he said.

We were almost a week into the port of Sparta; what should have been a short trip was ruined by two small storms and a day of full calm. The delegates debated what to tell the Spartans, as the loss of a week was a great deal. Xanthippus had told the Spartans they had two weeks to send their army, or Athens would quit the league. One of those weeks was already gone.

Cleitus was the head of our delegation. I found it difficult to listen to him; sometimes, difficult to be close to him. And yet, I kept agreeing with him. He insisted that all of the delegates bring their panoply, as if going to war, and he said we were going to go before the ephors dressed for war. I thought his point was valid. And I still couldn't stand him.

We arrived in Sparta to find them celebrating the Hyakinthia; that's one of their finest festivals, or so I understand. Lots of dancing, anyway; Euphonia would have enjoyed it. I gather it's all about the beauty of Helen, and despite that, being Spartans, they have some of the dancing done by young boys.

I say no more.

But the ephors refused to meet us for two days, on the grounds that they had religious obligations. Cimon was for leaving, on the spot. Cleitus said we had to have expected this.

For once, I was against Cimon and with Cleitus. I took Cimon aside. 'This is for everything,' I said. 'Only the result matters. Not our feelings, not our vanity.'

Cleitus nodded to me. 'I worry when we agree,' he said.

We voted, and we chose to stay.

On the third day, the ephors met with us. We were all in armour, and we made quite a show. And the ephors did not like our armour.

They talked among themselves, with their whispering voices like the dead animated by the wine of Odysseus at the mouth of the underworld. Finally one of them rose.

Cleitus was invited to speak. He strode forwards.

'I will not practise rhetoric,' he said. 'When Mardonius sent us the king of Macedon, you sent an embassy to beg us to stand firm for Greece. Your ambassador swore an oath to come to our aid.'

He looked them over. The old men sat very still, very dignified in their red, red robes.

'We know of no such oath,' said the oldest ephor.

The others nodded.

And all of the delegates thought the same dark thought.

'Ah,' said Cleitus. 'Very well, then. Now . . .' He paused. 'All Attica is destroyed, and Mardonius camps in the rubble of Athens. And still your army does nothing.'

I'll give them this – none of the bastards smiled. They did not give away by the twitch of a fingernail that they had played any role in the destruction of Athens. Nor had they.

They simply let it happen.

Cleitus raised his voice. 'The assembly has once again met and voted. This time they voted with stones and blood, men of Sparta. No Athenian will give earth and water to the Great King.'

Not a twitch from the ephors.

'We will never surrender, nor will we join in alliance with the man who defiled our temples,' Cleitus said. 'However . . .'

He said he would not employ the tools of rhetoric, but he couldn't help himself. In that moment, I rather admired him, despite the little matter of my mother that lay between us.

The ephors sat up. They were like dogs at a feeding.

'If Athens has not heard from you in ten days,' Cleitus said, 'We will take our ships and our people and sail away.' He looked at them. 'We have the treasure and the fleet. We will leave.'

The eldest of the ephors rose. 'What of the oaths you have sworn to send your fleet against the Great King this summer?' he asked.

Cleitus paused. Later, he told me that rage rose in him, and choked him, that they dared.

I rose to my feet and stood by him, although he was, in many ways, one of the men I hated most in the world.

'We know of no such oath,' I said.

Every head turned. Every one of those ancient bastards turned and looked at me.

But Cleitus nodded curtly. 'Exactly,' he said softly. And Cimon came and stood with us, and he *laughed*.

The ephors looked at each other.

'We will need to discuss this,' their elder said.

'You have ten days,' Cleitus said.

'No one tells Sparta of an ultimatum,' he said.

Cleitus shrugged, as if tired. Perhaps he was. 'I make no ultimatum,' he said. 'If Xanthippus has not heard from us in ten days, the fleet will sail for Italy.'

There followed five days of the most intense politics I have ever known, and every day I wished for Briseis. Not because she could work miracles, but because I took actions of my own, and I needed an ally; someone with whom to discuss all the things I was trying to do. I would have settled for Brasidas or Sekla or Leukas or Styges. I had none of them. I had Cleitus, who I didn't like, and Cimon, who was very withdrawn.

The Athenians were utterly demoralized. We'd stood up to the ephors, but we were treated like lepers, and it was fairly obvious that the ephors intended to let the days run out and take no action. To this day I do not know if this was from policy, or outraged vanity.

But I did what I could, on my own, because none of the Athenians had friends in Sparta. Cleitus had had a friend, but he had died at Thermopylae, and Aristides had friends, too, but he was not with us.

So I did what I could.

First I met with Bulis and Sparthius.

'I would weep,' Sparthius said. 'I really should. That little shit swore an oath on his ancestors, and now he's using the ephors as an excuse to break it.'

Bulis shook his head. 'He's not happy, though,' Bulis said. 'In fact, he's angry at his father and the whole faction. He wants to fight.'

I looked at the two. We were at Bulis' house, sitting under an awning at twilight. It was a sharp contrast to Attica. There was still a festival happening, and gaily dressed men passed us, waving. Bulis' very attractive wife passed through in a superb himation. She waved.

'Save the world, will you?' she said to me. 'If the ephors wreck this, he claims he's moving to Persia.' She kissed me on the cheek. 'I don't want to move to Persia.'

She went out to the festival.

I leaned forwards. 'Is there any way to work around the ephors? Surely most of the Spartiates want to fight.'

Sparthius shrugged. 'Now we see the limits of our form of government,' he said. 'Without Leonidas to lead the Spartiates, they will simply obey.'

'No one will obey Gorgo?' I asked.

Both men shook their heads.

'By Athena, gentlemen, we must do better than this.' A thought struck me. 'Surely there are other members of the Peloponnesian League – the allies of Sparta – who will see sense. They can't want the Persian fleet on their shores. Hermione. Troezen. Elis.'

Sparthius looked at me with his eyes far away. 'It is a point,' he admitted.

'Megara?' I asked.

'No,' Bulis said. 'The Megarans do as they are told.'

'I know someone who might be with us,' Sparthius said. 'Tegea.'

A day later, a party of Tegeans rode in over the passes, with some other men from the league and many of their wives – that is, the Peloponnesian League, not the League of Corinth. They didn't come for us; they'd been invited to attend the festival, as Briseis and I had been invited to attend the Panathenaea that had never happened.

I dragged Cleitus, who was in a black mood, to meet the Peloponnesians, and they were appalled – literally – to hear what was proposed. We had to explain it six times. And even then, I do not think their leader, Chileos, would have budged. He was a product of the Peloponnesus; he couldn't see past his Lacedaemonian propaganda, even with Bulis and Sparthius arguing with us.

But then Gorgo played her hand.

She invited all the Tegean women to her house.

I wasn't there.

But the next day, Chileos sent me a note. It said, 'Let me see what I can do.'

That was day nine. It was a long, long day. A beautiful day in the magnificent Vale of Sparta. I borrowed a horse from Bulis and rode – for pleasure. I agree, it was out of character. Or perhaps all the riding I had done with the embassy to the Great King had had an effect. But I rode up the vale to Mystras and then across the valley, stopping to have a cup of water at the springs. In the distance I saw a dust cloud. Even during the festival, the Spartans practised and drilled.

Mid afternoon, I was riding easily over the fields north of the city, and I saw a rider, and I knew her immediately – it had to be Gorgo. She was fully clothed in a cloak and a big petasus-hat, but she rode like a centaur.

I crossed a few fields, with helots cursing me, and met her by a low stone wall.

She waved.

I rode up until my horse was nose to tail with hers.

'My slaves said you were riding,' she said. 'I doubted them.'

'Well you might,' I agreed. 'Although,' I said, amused despite the end of my world and the Furies gathered around me, 'this horse is the best I can remember riding.'

She turned her mount. 'I wanted to find you and say that I have done everything I could.'

I grinned. 'I knew you would,' I said.

That's when she told me about the Tegeans and their wives.

I nodded. I told you it was the summer of women.

We rode along a path at the edge of the stream bed – dry in summer, of course.

We rode to a small shrine, which proved to be a sanctuary of Heracles.

'Really, I just wanted to pretend for a few more hours that the world was sane,' she said.

I laughed, and thought of Heraclitus, and of Briseis. 'I am happy that you, the queen of Sparta, see me as a representative of sanity,' I said. 'Many might not.'

She smiled. 'I like your wife,' she said.

'As do I,' I said.

I made a small sacrifice at the shrine, and we rode back to the city, or the towns or whatever the Spartans want to call them. It was the last day of the festival.

'I'm in disguise,' Gorgo said.

Only in Sparta could a queen go riding with a man not her husband, in broad daylight, during a major festival, and no one say a word. Spartan women have rights that Ionian women would only dream of.

I left her at the edge of the agora, on her horse. She was looking over the crowds, and she tossed the big hat back over her shoulder like an Athenian boy, and her horse gave a little curvet, and she turned the beast to control him, and then glanced back over her shoulder at me, and gave me a smile.

'I'm off to sacrifice to Tyche,' she called.

I never saw her again. Well, once, but that's another story.

I rode back to Bulis' house to return the horse. His wife smiled and said Bulis was out, which, in retrospect, was true, and wonderfully Laconic. I went back to our borrowed house, had dinner with Cimon, and slept well.

The next morning Cleitus led us to the ephors, and we presented ourselves. They didn't make us wait a moment. We were ushered directly in.

All of them were there, in their red himations. It was difficult to believe that these had once been hale men, warriors.

Cleitus walked briskly forwards. He was like a soldier on parade, or perhaps like a boy, a brave boy, going to his punishment in school.

'What is your answer?' he asked.

'Answer?' asked an ephor in his old man's voice. 'What answer?' he asked.

'Will your army march?' Cleitus shot, like a spear thrust.

The ephors looked at each other, and I waited, as if for a blow.

'Our army marched yesterday,' the ephor said. 'The whole army of Sparta, with seven helots to every Spartiate, and the men of the Peloponnesian League are marching.' The old man looked positively evil. 'Didn't your friend Queen Gorgo tell you as much?'

Well. We were stunned. And for the most part, delighted. But Cimon didn't believe them, and I confess I was suspicious. Cleitus thought we were tomfools and said as much.

'They're Spartans!' he said. 'They wouldn't tell a blatant lie.'

I was going to remonstrate, but then I had a better idea. 'I have my panoply,' I said. 'And they are on their way to the isthmus. Tell Sekla to meet me at Corinth.'

'What are you going to do?' Cimon asked.

'I'm going to go and impose on some Spartan mess group,' I said. 'If they turn around and come back, or linger at the wall, I'll be right there.'

Cimon laughed. 'Better you than me. I'm for the fleet.'

The other delegates shuffled their feet.

Cleitus met my eye. 'Good,' he said, 'I agree. I'll send your ship to Corinth after she runs us home.'

And it was done.

I went back to Bulis' house and borrowed the riding horse I'd borrowed the day before, packed my armour in wicker baskets on a donkey, and bought a small horse for Aten. It took little enough time, and then I was off on the road to Tegea. It was as if I was riding home to Hermione, for a while; we passed Sellasia, and Megara, and came to Tegea just a day after the Spartans left.

The Lacedaemonians are very efficient, at least by Greek standards. When they intend to march, with all their allies, they send messengers ahead by horseback, with an appointed day for the allied *taxeis* to muster, and then the Spartans march, and all the allies are met on the road, so that the league army gathers strength like an avalanche on a hillside, and so that no ally marches without the direct order of the Spartan commander. The Tegeans, well warned in advance, even while we Athenians had no idea what was happening, had turned out, almost three thousand hoplites, and were waiting, all formed, when the Spartiates and helots and *perioikoi*, the 'second class' Spartan hoplites, came marching up the road.

We missed this by half a day. Aten and I stayed a comfortable night in the house of Chileos, who had already marched with the phalanx. The next morning we rode out at dawn, and by afternoon we came up with the rearguard, which was, of course, all Spartan.

I dismounted, gave my horse to Aten, and walked or jogged up the column until I found Bulis.

'May I travel with your mess to the isthmus?' I asked.

He grinned. 'You always make trouble,' he said.

I shrugged. 'I mean no trouble,' I said.

He looked over the column, which kept moving. Men waved at me, or greeted me.

'You are a foreigner, and you want to march with us.'

'The Tegeans are foreigners,' I said.

'Allies,' he said.

I sighed. 'Couldn't you have mentioned to us that you were marching?' I asked.

He frowned. 'No one told you?' he asked.

'Not even your helots,' I said.

He smiled. He was pleased, the bastard.

He sent me up the column to Pausanias with a helot as a guide, and we found the regent and his peers walking like any other Spartan near the head of the column.

'Plataean,' he said, when he took notice of me.

'I would like to walk with you to Corinth,' I said.

He looked at me for a moment and nodded. 'Fine,' he said.

That was all. But it told me everything. It told me that the Sparta First party had been forced to act, and having been forced, they were, in fact, acting.

I have left a great deal out of my account, I find: how Cleombrotus died, while in command of the Spartans at the isthmus, and the confusion that his death must have caused; two deaths in the royal families in a single year. Cleombrotus was Pausanias' father. I know that Cimon, who loved the Spartans, said to me later that had he known that Cleombrotus was dead, he would have been less aggressive in his dealings with the Spartans.

I will close this part of my tale by saying that what I saw, and still see, was a struggle not between Athens and Sparta, or Sparta and Persia, but between the kings and the ephors for power, not unlike the endless struggle to be first among equals in Athens. I have heard smug philosophers declaim that this vicious infighting is what makes Greeks such great men; perhaps, but if those pompous windbags knew how close we all came to utter disaster in the winter of the last year of the war, they would not prate so.

It may seem odd to you, but that was one of the happiest weeks of that year. For all I pretend to hate them, the Spartans were good company, if you ignore the helots and the oppression. The Spartiates are all gentlemen, whatever their failings; they train in a hard school, and they are very well-behaved. It is rare to meet a man who is sullen or wicked; the *agoge* deals with all that, and probably files off all the burrs. I won't say that I came to love them; they can be intensely impractical, and just when you warm to them and their slow, careful humour, one of them will suddenly hand his spear to a helot and say 'polish this' without so much as a 'please'.

The first night on the march, I had just eaten my second or third meal, with a Spartan mess group: black broth and black bread, all delicious after a day's march but food barely fit for farm slaves. We had a fine fire burning away, and we were in hills in the north of the Peloponnesus, headed for the isthmus. The night was still an hour or more away, the fire was very pleasant, and I took out my sewing kit and set about fixing the liner in my best helmet.

There are various forms of liners. My favourite, and the form used by Anaxagoras, is a plaited straw cap inside a leather cover. In most helmets, the leather cover will stay inside the bowl of the helmet, held by nothing but friction. But for some reason, it kept slipping.

Now, with most armies, this wouldn't have mattered. Most hoplites have their equipment carried by slaves, and they only arm when they are in the face of the enemy, so to speak. But the Athenians and the Spartans – and the Plataeans – tend to march in their armour. It prevents difficult surprises, and saves time, and slaves. So I was marching in my good bronze thorax, and wearing my arm guard and my greaves, with my helmet tilted back on my head. I was as heavily armoured as the most heavily armoured Spartiates; a few wore thigh guards, but hardly any and they were mostly older men, and many of the younger men had less armour than I. Among the *perioikoi*, the allies and second-class men, there were leather corselets and some quilted linen, but among the Spartiates, nothing but bronze.

So I sat with my back against a comfortable rock, playing with my liner until I found why it kept coming out. The straw was new; it would be weeks, even wearing it every day, before I'd need to change it.

So I began to fiddle with the liner to find an attachment point against the bronze. There aren't many holes in a helmet; on purpose, of course. But there are two where the crest attaches, and I found a way to sew the top of the liner through the crest holes.

I was about halfway through this finicky operation when I looked up, because everyone had fallen silent.

'Can I help you, gentlemen?' I asked.

Bulis looked away in obvious embarrassment.

Diokles, one of the men of the mess, laughed. 'I have a greave that annoys me,' he said. 'Can you fix it?'

The others laughed.

They were mocking me.

Well, in truth, they were *trying* to mock me. Nothing more comic to a Spartiate than mere *tekne*.

'Probably,' I said, with what I hoped was a Laconic air.

They all looked uncertain, except Sparthius, who slapped his thigh. 'Well, send a helot for your greave. He will fix it, Diokles. He's quite a good bronze smith.'

They all looked startled, as if Sparthius had said something *dirty*.

Bulis winced. 'I told you,' he said. I had no idea to whom he directed this comment.

But Diokles sent his helot for his greaves. They came back, and he came and sat by me.

I didn't really need him to put them on. His whole right instep was bloody.

I rubbed my thumb on the instep, and glanced up at the helot. He was missing most of his teeth, and had an impenetrable expression of stupidity that experience with slaves taught me was feigned.

I sent Aten for my little leather bag of tools. I take them everywhere. I couldn't forge hot metal with them, but they are very handy: a small pair of metal grips, made of steel and not iron; several files; a bottle of pumice and a bottle of oil; some linen tow. Nothing fancy.

The edge of the man's instep was sharp. I held it up in the firelight, and I could see file marks.

Someone had filed the edge of the greave where it lay against his skin until it was sharp.

It was the matter of a few moments to round and smooth it.

Then I had him pop the greave on his shin. Greaves really do pop on, if you don't know; you hold them open with your arms and pull them over your shins, and they return to shape if the metal was properly hardened and close on the shin, supported by the shape of your calf muscles. Bad greaves hang on your instep and your ankle bones, and they hurt, as I have had cause to mention a number of times.

This greave was too open; it had been made well, but perhaps overused.

Or someone had simply bent it too far open.

I said a prayer to Hephaestus and ran my thumbs over the metal. Then I bent the greave closed, not open, and forced the inner edges past each other, as far as I could.

I held it there a little while, and then looked at it. My sunlight was fading quickly.

'Put it on,' I said.

He did, without any comment. He nodded at me.

Then he turned and began to speak to another man.

His intention was clear, so I didn't trouble to tell him that his helot had clearly altered his greave to hurt him.

Very dangerous, annoying your slaves. Especially when you march to war.

Sparthius came over and sat by me. After a while, when I was done with my helmet and put all my things away, he handed me his own *mastos* full of wine.

'You have to do this, I think,' he said.

I sipped wine. 'Do what?' I asked.

'Play the Boeotian bumpkin for the Spartiates,' Sparthius said. 'Every man here knows who you are. A priest of Hephaestus at Olympia; Ambassador of the League to the Great King; a Killer of Men. What are they to think, when you repair their bronze?'

I probably raised an eyebrow. 'Perhaps they think I'm a man of many skills?' I asked.

Sparthius took his wine cup back and looked over at Diokles. 'Perhaps they think you are mocking them,' he said. 'We are very proud. Perhaps you could ... not make so much of yourself?'

I was set to splutter that I was not making anything of myself; that I had fixed a man's greave and got no praise for it. But Sparthius saw deeply; I had indeed looked for an excuse to remind them that I worked bronze. I had known what I was doing, fixing my helmet at their fire.

'In the *agoge*,' he said, 'we learn to be *alike*. We learn to live and work and fight and hunt and dance – together. All together. And we come to resemble each other. We do not strive to be ... different.'

'Perhaps I should go,' I said.

'Perhaps you should just be a trifle more polite,' Sparthius said.

You see? I did. I still had a great deal of maturity left to learn.

We entered Corinth by one gate and left by another, and fifteen stades later we came to the wall. The helots were putting the finishing touches on it; it had crenellations, and was a magnificent construction: almost nine stades of wall across the isthmus. Another three thousand helots joined us there, and another five hundred Spartiates and some more *perioikoi*. The Corinthians fell in there. But there were no Plataeans there, and we halted at the wall for less than an hour as canteens were filled.

Pausanias summoned his commanders, and he summoned me by name.

The commander of the Corinthians – Adeimantus, no less – and the commander of the Tegeans, and I were the only officers not in the red cloaks of Sparta. Pausanias may not have been my favourite

Spartiate but he was an excellent, efficient commander, as I'd discovered in six days of marching. He got straight to business.

'Mardonius is in Attica, and he has been informed of our army's march by traitors from Argos,' he said. 'He is marching towards us. Tonight his army will camp at Eleusis. Tomorrow he will be at Megara. The Megarans have begged us to stop him.' He looked around. 'I need a thousand men to run to Megara,' he said. 'The Plataeans have already marched.'

'Alone?' I asked.

Pausanias nodded. 'I'm told there are Athenian cavalrymen with them,' he said. 'The Corinthians declined to march.'

He looked straight at Adeimantus of Corinth when he said that, with such obvious contempt that, had it been directed at me, I might have died of humiliation on the spot.

Adeimantus shrugged. 'The phalanx of Corinth would not desert its post at mere rumour,' he said.

Pausanias didn't even rise to the justification. 'A thousand picked men who run can be there when the sun rises,' he said. 'A thousand picked men to stiffen the Plataeans. Arimnestos, I mean no dishonour.'

'None taken,' I said. 'But I will run.'

He nodded as if he had assumed as much. This is the trouble with being a hero. No one says, 'By Ares, Arimnestos! An old man like you thinks he can run to Megara?' No. They just assume you can do it.

'But I should start now, so that the Spartiates don't pass me by too much,' I said.

The giant, Amompharetos, laughed. 'You're a strange one, foreigner. But funny.'

Pausanias frowned. 'No, all will start together,' he said, as if, being a foreigner, I would have no idea whatsoever of discipline.

But then I saw the merits of the Spartan system. Euryanax, the same man who had spoken for the Spartans at Athens, stepped forwards. 'I will lead the picked men to Megara,' he said.

'Go,' said Pausanias.

I don't think a quarter of an hour passed before we were running. I stripped my greaves and gave them to Aten, who also had my *aspis*. Nor did we run as if we were running the *hoplitodromos*. Instead, we ran at a good jog that ate the stades and the parasangs, and we had about a hundred stades to go.

An athlete or a message runner can run a hundred stades in four or five hours. But men carrying armour, even men in high training, run more slowly. And even young Spartiates have to rest.

The messengers set off first, two on horseback, two running. They were gone out of sight before we even set out. And Euryanax was an excellent soldier, as are most Spartans; he took measures to ensure that our food and some helots would catch us up, and started a column of helots on the road.

In my mess group, every man volunteered. I have heard since that every Spartiate volunteered, and all the Tegeans. And I have to say that I liked what I saw of the Tegeans. They were, in effect, the Plataeans of the Lacedaemonian League. They lived close to Sparta, and they were a little less extreme, but good, reliable men. Farmers.

Euryanax didn't select individual men, but mess groups. It was fast, and easy. He did tell off several hundred of the youngest, because they had some special organization within the *taxeis* that I assume was like our *epilektoi*. But he chose our mess group, and suddenly everyone was smiling at me.

Sparthius was old enough to be carefully stretching while his helot packed him a food bag. But he grinned at me. 'We all know we've been selected because we're with you,' he said.

I was rueful. 'I'm going to die,' I said. 'I'm a poor runner.'

He shrugged. 'What can any of us do, but our very best?' he said.

And then we were off.

The Spartans ran in a loose formation, but for the most part, they let the young men take the lead, and then the older mess groups followed. Men carried their weapons, and most kept a helot to carry their *aspis* – sorry, but it is no pleasure to run with an *aspis*.

Aten vanished in the first ten stades, and when I looked back, I saw one of Bulis' helots carrying my *aspis*. I slowed and let the man catch me up, and thanked him.

His expression didn't change. But in a low voice, he said, 'The foreign boy cannot run.'

Well, the foreign hoplite wasn't so great at running, either.

Ah, you ask why I didn't just ride my horse.

Spend a week with Spartans and ask that. I just couldn't face admitting myself so weak. I admit it.

So I put my head down, and ran.

On the one hand, I was not the slowest. Spartans are professional warriors. Many of them have taken wounds, like mine: wounds to the legs and shins and thighs. Euryanax was one of them; he was not fast.

On the other hand, they were in far, far better physical shape than any other Greek hoplites I know of, even my precious Plataeans, and most of them simply ran off and left me, Sparthius and Bulis included. By the time we were on the coast road and into Megaran territory, I couldn't even see most of the Spartiates. The sun was going down, and the whole thing seemed ridiculous, and more ridiculous if Persian cavalry snapped up the lot of us. Against that, the coast road is as narrow as the pass of Thermopylae, and there's not an ambush site for parasangs – steep cliffs, a narrow road, and no room to manoeuvre. It wasn't insane.

By the thirtieth stade, Euryanax and I were running together, and we were not even pretending. We were keeping each other at it, the way much younger men do. I know now that he has a bad wound in his left foot; in fact, he has only three quarters of his foot. But he never complained. He just ran. Or rather, hobbled very quickly.

Well, I was not much better. The old wound hurt, but a spring of fighting from ships had not prepared me for this kind of physical exertion. I was not weak, exactly, but I was not strong. I blessed Brasidas, though; we *had* run all winter, and without that, I would have been humiliated.

We ran. With us were most of the helots with the *aspides*. Ponder that if you will – they were slaves, they had the shields, and they ran as fast as we. In fact, my guess – helots don't talk, at least to free men – was that they knew they were safe from punishment if they were with the commander.

Evening came on. It was past midsummer, and the sun was slow to leave us, and fatigue is no friend to courage, so that, as we ran into twilight, I had plenty of time to imagine my little Plataean phalanx dead or captured, the Medes riding everywhere, the town of Megara fallen.

We ran.

As the road climbs onto the ridge over the sea, roughly halfway between Corinth and Megara, there was a stream under the road. I slowed when I smelled the water, and with one glance at my companion established that we both wanted water, having drained our pottery canteens.

The cessation of running was better than sex or food or fine wine. But I was as quick as I could be – I clambered down and filled my canteen, and then his. Above me, I heard the Spartiate order the helots behind us to rest and drink.

I came back up and gave him his canteen. I emptied mine, he emptied his, and I filled them again.

Darkness was less than an hour away.

I got back on the road through the crowd of helots. My legs were already starting to stiffen. I thought we were about two thirds of the way to Megara. I knew I could do it. In fact, I knew I could walk the last thirty stades in a couple of hours and still sleep.

A helot handed me a sausage skin. It was filled with a mixture of honey and sesame and meat – the oddest taste, but delicious. I ate it. Then I ate another.

I know this is dull, but I want you to understand what it is like to run a hundred stades.

I did some exercises from the Plataean *pyrriche* and ate another sausage casing of the honey-stuff, and then I put my canteen over my shoulder. In some odd way, a miracle had happened. I felt wonderful. A god had entered my body.

Euryanax clearly felt the same way. He smiled. We had yet to exchange a sentence, nor did we then. He pulled his canteen strap over his breastplate.

And we started forwards into the last of the twilight.

An hour later, we began to catch younger men walking. They were not defeated, and when we caught up to them, they started running again. And twice we walked, ourselves. And all the men gathered with us walked, too.

Darkness fell, but we could see the lights of Megara twinkling on the plain, and we laughed. Men began to sing.

By Apollo, singing is the most wonderful thing.

They sang a hymn to Athena, those Spartans, and then a piece by Tyrtaios, and then songs I didn't know; they settled into singing all the songs of the Hyakinthia that had just ended in Sparta. I sang the ones I knew and ran on, and the stades flowed away, and I was with the gods, floating along, aware that my legs were not entirely my allies but unwilling to stop.

About an hour after darkness we came to outposts: a pair of Athenian cavalrymen. A stade later I found my son Hipponax. He talked, and I breathed. The Spartans had a camp, if a field with rocks in it can be called a camp, but there were Persian cavalrymen abroad in the darkness and it was vital to stay in order.

Euryanax nodded to me. 'Fetch me the Plataean commander,' he said, as if I had not just run for seven hours.

I sent Hipponax, on horseback. I admit it. Sometimes you can work smarter instead of harder, and I swore to myself on the spot that I would never, ever, seek to prove myself to other men again.

Hermogenes appeared in a quarter of an hour. The Plataeans were five stades away, and that was just too damned far for my legs, and I lay down between Sparthius and Diokles, stretched my legs as long and hard as I dared, and went to sleep.

When I awoke, my *aspis* and helmet and greaves were at my head, and they had been polished.

Diokles' helot gave me the slightest nod.

I smiled, and then the pain in my legs hit me.

Let me just say, because Spartans are not immortals, that every man present groaned. There was no Laconic silence that morning. We sat and rubbed oil into each other's legs, spat, cursed, and complained. I complained a lot more, I admit it.

The sun wasn't up yet. We had more honey-sesame sausage. Most of us drank a lot of water and pissed it away, and then helots came around with wine.

Neat.

I'd never fought alongside the Spartans before. And it was a great honour – Diokles asked aloud if anyone could remember a foreigner serving in the ranks.

And it turned out that several men could, and there was far more conversation than I'd ever heard – because matters of culture and tradition are one of the few topics that make Spartans garrulous. A dozen gentlemen-rankers had to tell stories about foreigners they'd known.

And then we were forming up. Bulis put me in the second rank. He told me later that he thought perhaps I would be better in front, but that he felt I was too aggressive to be there. Bulis was a good judge of character.

The sun was rising over Attica, and the Spartans formed a shallow, four-deep line and advanced. We had hundreds of armed helots on our flanks, and we moved over the big ridge by Megara, staying, on purpose, in the difficult ground. Near the top we linked up with the Plataeans, who took the left. Farther along the ridge were parties of Athenian *hippeis*.

I considered, again, running off to join the Plataeans, but by then

I'd been assigned a place, and I chose not to, although the tug was strong.

We came over the top of the ridge, and there was Attica. And as far as the eye could see, there was smoke. This time, the Persian burning and looting was utterly unrestrained, and they found lots to burn – all the reconstruction, and more besides. Their first assault had confined itself mostly to temples and areas of wealth. The second time, they let their various barbarians off the leash everywhere.

Down to our right, hovering off the beaches, were sixty warships – all Athenian. All packed to the gunwales with marines, or Athenian hoplites.

And all along the road in front of us, at the base of the ridges that rose to the left off towards Cithaeron, were the Persians. But you must not think we were looking at an organized army, although no doubt, off to the east, towards Eleusis, there were the Immortals and the Noble Cavalry, marching somewhere together. But facing us was a cloud of barbarians, knots of men, foraging, looting, and burning the easternmost fields of the Megaran state.

For once, my officers had made their plans without me. Hermogenes and Xanthippus and Cimon and Euryanax had agreed on a plan, and I'd been asleep.

We went down the ridge, and into them.

Let's make this simple.

They ran.

By the time the sun was high in the sky, we were dealing with knots of cavalry who tried to hang on our flanks and shoot arrows, but by then we were in western Attica, with rich, walled farms, wood from lots of standing trees, and fields, and the worst cavalry country imaginable. The helots were excellent at this game, and so were the youngest, nimblest Spartans; the Plataean skirmishers were valuable, and the Athenian *hippeis* knew the country. Twice they flushed enemy cavalry from ambushes and into our loose formations where we slaughtered them, outnumbering them dozens to one.

But mostly, they ran. And mostly, it was all I could do to keep up.

Somewhere off in the mid-morning haze, Mardonius discovered, I assume with shock, that there was a Free Greek force operating on the flank of his army. Now, he had a hundred thousand men or more, perhaps; we were perhaps three thousand on land, and sixty ships. But remember that Mardonius had no fleet, so anything at sea was irresistible; that he was far, far from his source of supply; and that he had no idea how many of us there were. Cyrus, my friend, told me long after that traitors from Argos informed them that the Spartans were coming, and magnified their numbers; and of course, we had a whole Spartan *taxeis* that morning.

So often, war hinges on these moments. With good information, even in the dense farmland of western Attica, Mardonius' crack cavalry could have turned on us, swept away our flanks, isolated us from the Athenian ships, and inflicted a sharp defeat on us.

I think it would have ended the war.

The loss of a thousand Spartans and allies? And all the Plataeans?

Cyrus told me that it was the Thebans who settled the issue with Mardonius, begging him to ride back over the passes to Boeotia, where his army could be supplied. And telling him that he didn't dare face the army of the league in the broken country, where his cavalry would be of no use, and that they needed to fight in Boeotia, where the cavalry could ride as they would.

Or perhaps it was the gods, finally taking a hand because Greece had had enough.

It was almost noon, and I'd just wetted my spear for the first time that day, coming up a low, cone-shaped hill. We were in a wide open order, moving in difficult terrain, which the Spartans practise. We were tired; running all day in armour takes a great deal out of you. Especially when you have run a hundred stades the day before.

And suddenly the hillside was alive with Thracians. They were big men, covered in tattoos, fast on their feet, and armed with javelins and swords. And yet, at the crest of that breast-shaped hill, they were as surprised as we to find an enemy. Later wisdom said they were Mardonius' first counter-attack, to try and stabilize the collapse of his wide-flung net of foragers and arsonists.

Bulis went down in the first rush, knocked flat by a Thracian's shield bash, and we were closing – the Spartans came together like a flock of birds rising from the ground, and I stepped over Bulis and very carefully killed my Thracian. I say carefully, because I was tired, my legs were like lead, and I didn't need a long fight. I caught his wicker shield with the edge of my *aspis* and put my spear in his throat-bole, the best, simplest attack.

There was pressure against my back and I went forwards, and forwards again, but the Thracians were already running.

We halted. None of us wanted to try running down fresh Thracians. We had men wounded, too, and we'd lost our helots. We halted, dressed our ranks, and Bulis stood up and pushed forwards, uninjured. Jokes were made, backs were slapped, and Euryanax roared for silence.

Ahead of us, down at the base of the hill to the east, Mardonius was forming his army.

And by Zeus, his army was huge. It took our breath away. There were about a thousand Peloponnesians.

There were about a hundred thousand barbarians.

But as we stood on our little hilltop, Cimon appeared out of the brushy ground to the south with most of the Athenian *hippeis*, almost six hundred men. Horsemen raise a lot of dust.

And by the gods, as if they'd been summoned, the Plataeans and some Tegeans and some Megarans – almost another two thousand men, well formed because they were on the more open ground – came up on our left, on the next two hills in the gentle ridge that ran north–south.

It was noon on the nineteenth day of Hekatombaion. Our red cloaks flashed in the sun, the light sparkled on our bronze and that of the Athenians, and Greek formations kept coming up out of the low ground along the ridge, driving Mardonius' skirmishers before them. We could see his whole army, and they were myriads. He could see almost nothing of our army because of the terrain. All day, we had killed perhaps two hundred barbarians, but we'd driven his people like hunters drive prey, and in that hour, when first Greeks and barbarians confronted each other on land for the possession of Greece, it was the barbarians who flinched.

Mardonius thought he had the whole army of the league across his flank, and he turned and ran for the passes to Boeotia.

And in six hours, the league was reborn. There is no euphoria like that of victory.

We couldn't pursue. First of all, it is foolish to pursue an army of a hundred thousand men with five thousand. It's like chasing a fleeing lion by yourself.

But Euryanax showed his wiles. Before our muscles froze up entirely, he withdrew, a file at a time, down the back of the range of rounded hills that faced the plain. We marched away, and the *hippeis* of the Athenians galloped along our front, raising a remarkable dust cloud.

When it settled, we were six stades back, on the next rib of hills, with our flanks secure in the foothills and olive groves of Megara.

And the Persians didn't follow us. To this day, I'm not sure they understood that we were gone. But Euryanax shifted the stakes. While we stood on the ridge, we were offering battle, and had nowhere to run if the Persians decided to try us. But after we moved – we still threatened Mardonius' line of march, but he couldn't see us, couldn't count us, and if he came at us, the odds were excellent we could slip away into every narrowing terrain; the coastal plain narrows against the heights and the coast.

There was considerable muttering from the Spartiates. I was feeling snappish with pain and fatigue and post-battle darkness, and I turned on Diokles.

'You want to fight them at odds of twenty to one? For me, it would be sufficient to see them beaten, or merely leaving Greece.' I nodded at Euryanax. 'He cares for his soldiers the way a good herdsman watches over his flocks.'

'I wouldn't know,' Diokles said. 'I've stolen some sheep, but herding them is for slaves.'

'Hmm,' I said. So many opportunities to be angry. 'How many Spartiates of fighting age are there, Diokles?'

He looked at me. 'Who knows? Perhaps five thousand.'

I nodded. 'If Euryanax engages and his whole force is destroyed – do you think your helots might revolt?'

A change passed over his face, like a cloud over ground that had been in bright sunlight.

'What a terrible way to think!' he said.

I shook my head and said no more.

As Mardonius began to move away to the north across our front, there were more voices raised to suggest that we should pursue. But the Spartans had been the core of our force, and they – we – were very tired. Further, the real push for Mardonius to retreat was the combination of the Spartans and Plataeans and Athenians to his front, and the Athenian fleet hovering off the coast – brought, may I add, by Sekla, who ran from Corinth to Aegina in record time to bring Xanthippus in mid-morning. The distances are not long, but the timing was remarkable. You cannot plan for things like that; the gods appoint them, or they do not; but you can help the process with good people and good leadership, and to me, Sekla deserved the laurel for the dustless victory at Megara.

But in mid-afternoon, the Athenian phalanx began to land under Aristides, carried across from Salamis by Xanthippus. There was no opposition, and we could hear them cheering.

I'd like to tell you that I walked down to the beach to meet Aristides, but in fact, I lay under the shade of my *aspis*, almost paralyzed with muscle ache and fatigue, with the added benefit of knowing that it would all be worse the next day.

In late afternoon the main body of Peloponnesians came up behind us, and we shifted ground to the right, backed out of the battle line, and marched, file by file, into our original places in the Peloponnesian phalanx as it formed. It was, to me, a stunning piece of manoeuvre, as it offered several opportunities for total chaos, and yet, it was quite orderly. It wasn't as orderly as, say, the way well-trained oarsmen board a trireme; but it worked, and what I noted especially was that Euryanax and Pausanias had paced off the frontage of the whole phalanx with great accuracy and so all of their manoeuvres worked as neatly as when a bronze smith measures the sheet and cuts it before he makes the breastplate.

Just at the edge of darkness, we all moved forwards to our original position, about six stades. By then, we were an army, but there was widespread complaining; many Spartans decried all the shifting back and forth, and the Tegeans complained that they ought to hold the left of the line, and everyone complained that the Athenians were on the right of the line, the place of honour. Of course, the whiners didn't seem to understand that the Athenians were *landing from ships* and were, thus, on the right; nor how silly it would have been to make them march all the way to the left end of our line.

And, in fact, the Plataeans were on the left of the army, with the Peloponnesians just to their right. As we crested our last ridge, we could still see the dust of Mardonius' rearguard, headed up the passes to Cithaeron and Plataea, and I could see from the edge of the plain all the way to where the last sun sparkled on the Athenians' steel spear points and bronze helmets.

And suddenly, we were a mighty army. There were almost twenty thousand Peloponnesians, Spartans and all, with more on the way; there were almost ten thousand Athenian hoplites, all that could be spared and still man the fleet. Corinth was there; even Aegina landed a contingent; there were Plataeans and Megarans and other small *taxeis*, all coming up from the isthmus, even Arcadians and Aetolians. All in all, we might have had fifty thousand hoplites and another ten thousand little men, *psiloi* and suchlike, and the Athenian archer corps, almost five hundred lower class men equipped as Scythians. The Athenians also had a corps of horse archers, but as many of them were themselves Saka or the sons of Saka warriors, they were kept on Salamis as police lest they be tempted to betrayal.

The Athenian *hippeis* were the only cavalry, and my son had already told me that their servants carried *aspides*, infantry shields, because they expected to dismount when the fight came. Five hundred Athenian gentlemen were not going to tangle with Mardonius and his fifteen thousand expert cavalry, no matter how brave and aristocratic.

Whatever our shortage in horsemen, though, we were a magnificent sight, and as the Spartans were closing up and reordering their ranks, I asked permission to depart. Several men slapped my back or shook my hand, and then Aten, who looked far more tired than he should have, carried my *aspis* and I trudged out of the Lacedaemonian phalanx, down into a shallow gully, and somehow forced my thighs to get me up the next hill.

And there were the Plataeans. There was Hermogenes, and there, Hippias, son of Draco, and Empedocles, grandson of the Epictetus of my boyhood, and there was Myron, Tiraeus, Styges, and a hundred other men I knew.

'We thought you'd run off and fallen in love with a boy,' Hilarion said. He was almost an old man, now, and his sense of humour hadn't changed. 'Become a Spartiate. Married Aten, here.'

Men laughed, because the boy-love of the Lacedaemonians was proverbial in Boeotia, whereas in Sparta, it was the boy-love of Thebes that was proverbial – and indeed, I suspect every town accuses the next of some wickedness or other.

At any rate, there was more back-slapping, and more embraces. Night was falling, and many Plataean hoplites didn't have slaves, but instead, a younger son, or a young brother, and the work was done well and quickly, and frankly, I did nothing.

But just as a cup of chicken soup was touching my lips, Aten hurried out of the darkness and told me that my presence was required by 'the commanders'.

I drank the rest of my chicken soup, and thus missed the first half hour of the interminable command meeting, the first of many, many days of them.

When I hobbled down the slope, I found Aristides and Pausanias with Euryanax, Hermogenes, Chileos of Tegea, and a dozen other polemarchs and *strategoi*. The Athenians had done a clever thing, and only sent Aristides. So Aristides didn't have ten quarrelling *strategoi* at his heels, just his secretary, Apollion, and a slave to carry his stool. Adeimantus was there, and a dozen other Peloponnesian officers, and they provided plenty of bickering. Indeed, I think there is something peculiar to the genius of the Greek nation that we enjoy arguing about nothing while the barn burns or the barbarian invades.

They were just re-fighting the order of march, with Chileos insisting that the Tegeans had the right to be on the left, and Aristides was mostly not listening. He was talking to Euryanax, and Pausanias was trying to follow both conversations at once. It was full dark, and hard to see.

I sent Aten for Eugenios. I knew he was in camp; he was the perfect steward, and I expected that I'd return to find a tent and more chicken soup and anything else I wanted, too.

I stood, anonymous, for as long as it took several Peloponnesians to revisit various ways they'd been wronged in the day's march.

Pausanias asked where I was. Euryanax said that perhaps I'd had to run, and several men laughed.

'Takes one to know one,' I said.

Euryanax laughed. 'That's a fair cut,' he answered. 'Here he is.'

Aristides peered at me in the gloom. 'The league appointed you to maintain links between the fleet and army,' he said. 'I need you to know what is going on.'

Well, being patronized by Aristides is part of being his friend. I ate a snappy reply.

'I'm here,' I said.

Then, at a nod from Pausanias, Euryanax gave a good little speech, and told everyone how well the army had behaved that day, and how important it was that Mardonius had retreated. There was a healthy dose of propaganda to it, but there was truth in it as well.

When he was done, Pausanias stood forth. 'I propose to pursue at first light,' he said. 'I want to press straight down the road to Thebes and either force Mardonius to fight or cut him off from his grain supply.'

Well, no one could be heard to directly oppose the Spartan. He ordered the Plataeans and the Spartan *epilektoi* to lead the pursuit; the Spartans would have all their helot *psiloi*, and the Plataeans, of course, would be on home ground.

I was by Aristides. 'So … we attack?' I asked.

Aristides may have nodded in the darkness, but I saw nothing.

A little later, Eugenios came, and at my orders, started a large fire among the rocks, and served out wine. Only the gods know where he found that wine, but the 'officers' shifted ground until they were gathered around the fire. With warm firelight on their faces and wine cups passing around, the atmosphere improved.

Having explained his very simple plan, Pausanias allowed some discussion, which was, as far as I could tell, mostly shirkers like Adeimantus trying to find reasons not to pursue the Medes or prosecute the war at all. Pausanias allowed each speaker to say his piece, and Adeimantus tailed off into a long ramble; other men began to talk over him.

One of them was Aristides, who took the time to explain to me how much it meant for the Spartans to have come.

'Xanthippus and Themistocles are saved, politically,' Aristides said with a smile. 'As soon as we saw the red cloaks, everything changed. There were bonfires last night on Salamis, in celebration.' He leaned closer. 'You did a brilliant job,' he said.

I smiled. 'Most of the credit goes to your wife's devoted admirer, Queen Gorgo,' I said. 'And the Tegeans. You owe them.'

Aristides nodded. 'There aren't enough of them to be on the left of the line, however noble they may be,' he said. 'But I'll remember what you said.'

'And the fleet?' I asked.

'Waits only news that the army is together and marching to launch east, against the Persian fleet,' Aristides said.

'You want me to go?' I asked.

'Your *Lydia* is waiting on the beach. I will see to it that there are horses here for you.' He put a hand on my shoulder. 'You wanted a command?'

I shrugged. 'Here we are at the climax,' I said. 'And I am a hoplite and a herald.'

Aristides stared at the fire for a moment. 'There aren't many men as widely known. Or trusted.'

I probably sighed. I wanted to seize the command of the Plataeans from Hermogenes. I knew I could, and in fact, looking at the man by the fire, I knew he'd be relieved. He felt like an impostor.

Hermogenes hadn't been a polemarch long enough to know that

everyone is an impostor. All that imperturbable mask of command – all acting.

'You want me to leave tonight?' I asked.

Aristides said nothing, and I knew he did. I groaned. I remember that much. I groaned from sheer weakness.

I think Eugenios groaned too.

But my son appeared out of the dark, took me by the hand, literally, and hobbled with me to a small paddock of thorn trees, and we rode off into the darkness. I had the good sense to leave my *aspis* with Eugenios. The rest I wore, because I could borrow an *aspis* but I couldn't borrow a thorax that fitted perfectly, or a helmet I fancied.

Then we rode to the beach, where I walked aboard the *Lydia*. In the darkness, Sekla got her off the beach, and I fell asleep on the aft benches. When the sun rose, we were off Aegina, and I drank a cup of neat wine and swam to try and loosen my stiff joints. The pain in my hips and thighs was less than I had feared. I blessed Brasidas in person, and told him the whole tale, and Sekla, and Leukas, and then I went ashore and repeated it for the king of Sparta and Xanthippus and Themistocles.

Ah, yes, the king. He was the technical commander of the fleet, although he brought only thirty ships, and everyone knew that if Xanthippus and Themistocles left and took with them the Athenian ships, there was no fleet. In fact, the fleet was much smaller than the year before: a hundred and nine Athenian ships, almost sixty Aeginian ships, thirty from the Peloponnesus and a dozen other ships, mostly defectors from the Ionians. The smaller states couldn't man ships and send a phalanx too; look at Plataea. Well, except that we did, in a way. Me.

Archilogos and I had several hours to talk while the league commanders discussed their strategy. Archilogos had already argued for an aggressive strategy against the Phoenicians and Cilicians, to allow more Ionians to defect, and he talked about his weeks of sailing independently, and how he'd tried to raise Ionia, or at least plant seeds of doubt.

'I'm going back,' he said. 'Themistocles wants me to try Lesvos and Samos again. I'll land. I have money for bribes,' he said in a whisper.

'Zeus, take care of yourself!' I said. 'If you are captured ...'

He was concealing something from me – his eyes were evasive. 'I will, brother,' he said. I loved it when he called me brother, and we embraced, and any suspicions I had were dispelled.

Leotychidas of Sparta summoned me. He was the fleet commander; he was also king of Sparta, and an old ally of Athens in many ways. He hadn't left Sparta until the army marched, because he knew as well as Gorgo how close we were to fracturing, but as soon as he knew that the red cloaks were in the vales of Megara, he and his ships landed at Aegina. He covered a grin when he saw me, and I greeted him in the name of Pausanias.

'You'd think we could have found some Spartan messengers,' he said wryly.

Themistocles nodded. 'And then no one would trust you,' he said. And I realized that he was right, as was too often the case; a Plataean go-between guaranteed that there was no conspiracy to wreck Athens; at least, not while I was paying attention.

I then gave the officers of the fleet a full report on the last three days on land. Xanthippus had landed marines on his own, without orders, and then moved the Athenian phalanx to the mainland under Aristides' orders, but the king of Sparta approved.

Compared to the army, there was very little discussion in the fleet. Of course, Adeimantus wasn't with the fleet, either. And something profound had changed after Salamis. The Athenians and Aeginians, ancient enemies, were solid; they were aware that they would stand or fall together, and that meant that three quarters of the fleet was united. They even practised fleet manoeuvres together.

There was another aspect, too. It was *not* like the year before. Artemisium and Salamis gave us a tradition of victory; Archilogos and a dozen other Ionian trierarchs told us that the Ionians were begging for liberation.

In the army, there was considerable hesitation about meeting the barbarians head to head. The Spartan rank and file wanted 'the contest' more than a night with Aphrodite; the Corinthians and the Arcadians were not so sanguine.

But in the fleet, the oarsmen talked only of getting to grips with the enemy, and finishing the war. In fact, there was some very real class pride among the oarsmen – 'little men' of 'no worth' who knew that in their strong hands and backs lay the freedom of Greece. Not a trierarch stood on his command deck but he knew that he'd won against this enemy three times.

And, because I'm a braggart, I'll add that our little raid in the early spring had a certain effect in reinforcing all this. I may have exaggerated the relative helplessness of the enemy fleet at Cos; perhaps I was bombastic. And gave the impression that the enemy was supine. But let us view this realistically, from the comfort of our couches, and with a good cup of wine passing from *kline* to *kline*. Taking Potidaea had been of the very first importance to the Persian high command; they had committed almost forty thousand men to the siege.

But they didn't send a fleet. And when it became clear that the Greeks would supply the city by sea ...

The Persians abandoned the siege. To me, and to the other old pirates like Cimon, that meant that they were afraid of us.

And by Poseidon, my friends, we meant to give them every reason, that summer. On his couch in Sparta, making policy, Leotychidas might countenance the degradation of Athens. But once he was at the helm of a fleet, with the Persians before him, the king of Sparta wanted nothing more than to get to grips and finish his enemies – to win the greatest victory in the history of men.

By the gods, my heart was with them. That fleet all but had its laurels granted. They were veterans; they had survived the dark days, and now, they knew each other. The chaff was gone. Only the sailors remained, and they were determined to make something. Among the Athenians, there was open talk of dismembering the Persian empire; of a rescue of the Ionian cities. And the Spartans writhed.

I wanted nothing better than to sail with them; I had one of the finest ships, although Athens and Aegina also had some superb vessels. But I was again disappointed when the king of Sparta laid out his plan of campaign. He was intending to go to Delos, gather any defectors from the Ionians, train his oarsmen for two weeks, and then go for the jugular: a straight attack on the enemy fleet base at Cos.

It was everything I wanted in a plan. It was *the* forward plan that Cimon and I had advocated for four years. It would avenge Lade and end the war. And almost certainly free Ionia.

It was everything I desired, and everything Briseis desired, and in fact, in the execution of it, I could see the hands of Jocasta, Briseis, and Gorgo.

But I was not to go.

I was ordered back to the army, so that they would be informed of the timing and purpose of the fleet.

Cimon was riding with the *hippeis* and I was going to march with the Plataeans, while younger trierarchs fought the battle of which we had dreamed.

I considered an explosion of rage.

Perhaps it was my best hour, as a man. There was the freedom of Ionia and the revenge of Lade, and I did my duty as assigned, for no better reason than that, in the last summer of the Long War, a lot of men as good as I were doing their duty. I was offended that they didn't want me with them; I felt as if all my work and fighting at Artemisium and Salamis was forgotten. I am petty enough to know when other men are petty; I knew my brother-in-law Xanthippus resented my reputation.

But . . .

I also knew that if either the army or fleet lost, we were finished; that for all the fleet's euphoria and confidence, it only took one misstep to wreck the league and end it all.

So I swallowed my pride and rage. I walked down to the beach and ordered my ship to sea in a strong voice, and Sekla put a hand on my back, and suddenly tears filled my eyes, and I felt like an arse.

Brasidas walked aft. 'Well?' he asked.

I shrugged. 'We go to the army,' I said.

He made an odd face, the edges of his lips downturned, as if in a frown, but his eyes light, as if smiling. 'The army?' he repeated. 'Excellent.'

I probably raised my eyebrows, or cursed, or both.

'I trained the Plataeans,' he said simply. 'I want to be with them.'

He made me ashamed of myself.

We rowed into the wind all evening and landed at Piraeus before the sun set. Once again, the people of Attica were reoccupying the smoking ruins of their city and their countryside.

They gave me a great deal to think about. In Piraeus there was a statue of Poseidon; the Persians had thrown it down, and the head was broken off. As my ship landed, a sweating crew of older men, too old for hoplite service, was raising the statue. They got it erect before we were alongside the stone piers, and some of my deck crew cheered, but that was nothing to when a young boy shimmied up a ladder against the nearby wall and placed the head. My crew cheered, and so did every sailor in the port.

Ships were landing grain, and livestock, and people.

It was odd, but it made my throat swell and my eyes water. They assumed we would beat the Medes. They were not afraid to rebuild.

Again.

All into the long evening, as we rode our horses west and north to my father-in-law's house – pardon me, friends, that's my first wife Euphonia's father – all evening, we watched men working, throwing up sheds, creating hasty enclosures for sheep and goats. And in another way, I saw something of the futility of Ares. Two things that the Persians hadn't spent time to do – they had not girdled and killed the olive trees, and they had not thrown down the endless stone walls that enclosed the best pastureland. Of course they hadn't! Either job would have taken an army of myriads many weeks to accomplish over all of Attica. But failure to do these things robbed their victory of meaning. They destroyed luxuries like temples, but the trees remained.

There were only slaves in the house. His wife Niobe was long dead, and he himself, despite his age, was riding with the *hippeis* or fighting with the hoplites. But his slaves all knew me, and even as they were clearing the central rafters, which had crashed into the house when the roof burned, they were polite enough to serve me soup – far better than anything I'd eaten with the Spartans – and give us a bed.

I'm not telling this well. We had four horses, so I had Brasidas and Leukas and Aten. Sekla and I debated marching the whole crew, oarsmen and all, over the mountain. We knew the way; we'd fought along that road before, together. And my one crew, suitably armed, would put another two hundred men in the phalanx.

Against that, Sekla and I knew I might be sent back immediately. And I hoped – really, I think, all of us hoped – that we would be sent to the fleet in time for the battle. For as much as the Spartans desired a great land battle to settle it all, where all the nice gentlemen could fight together and leave their social inferiors to the dirty work, I wanted a naval fight that would finish the Persians as a sea power forever. The way I saw it – and still see it – beating Mardonius would only allow the Great King to come at us again, and again, until either all that was left of our culture was the ability to make war, or until we failed and lost our freedom.

But if we crushed his fleet and took the sea, why, he'd never be able to come back; or if he did, it would be at such a remote time that my grandchildren – your children, thugater – would never have to worry.

But remember, my dear. Remember that Leotychidas and Aristides and Pausanias all agreed on one thing: that the great battle needed to be fought by hoplites. Because if the oarsmen freed Greece – goodness, what would we be then? And yet, for all that I'm a little tyrant now, I'd have been happy to try a state like that. A state where even oarsmen had the vote.

I'm leaving the furrow again, am I not?

Very well. We rose the next morning, and every part of me ached, and my missing fingers plagued me with ghosts of pain, and my thighs burned from riding. Aging is not a pretty process, and every morning I seemed older.

I've never been good at getting older.

And as we rode over Cithaeron's shoulder, there were a lot of ghosts. It's funny, because not all the ghosts were of the dead. Here is where I heard that Empedocles was a prisoner; here, I made love to the lame girl who was, in some way, sent by the god Apollo; back there is where my father stood against the Spartans; and just there is where my brother died. This pass, from end to end, was redolent with memory, and at one point, looking at the foliage, I realized I was looking at the very trail from which I had left the pass to fling myself into the distant sea, and I wondered that I didn't see the fleeing shadow of myself, running from Euphonia's death.

We came to the very top of the pass: the place where convoys turn their wagons so that they can brake their way down the far side; the place where men hurry to pass the slowest animals, the overladen donkeys, the lame horse. Here is where we found the boy's corpse. Here is where I met Tiraeus.

From the top of the pass, there is a little used path running west on the knife-edge of the ridge. It runs, after some turnings, to the very top of Cithaeron, amidst the clouds.

I had a sudden feeling, as you do when Zeus throws his mighty bolts to earth, or when Poseidon earth shaker rattles the dishes. My hair did not quite stand on end, but I understood.

I turned to Brasidas and Leukas. 'I'm sorry,' I said. 'But I am going to ride this excellent horse up there, to the peak.'

Brasidas said nothing.

Leukas frowned. 'Why?' he asked.

'That's where my family's altars are,' I said. 'I go to sacrifice.'

Brasidas nodded. 'Good,' he said.

Leukas sighed. I suspect he'd had a simple life as a fisherman, although I'd never really asked him a thing about it. I thought, right there, at the top of the pass, that I was an arse for never asking.

'Leukas?' I asked.

'Boss?' he answered in his Alban-Greek.

'What was your life like before you joined us?' I asked.

We rode along the high trail. It was many years since I'd been this way. Usually, I walked, ran, or rode to the top of Cithaeron from the beehive tomb, the Tomb of the Hero. This was another way, and in many ways harder.

We rode along, moving with our animals, watching the ground fall away. It was a beautiful afternoon. I wondered if he'd decided not to speak.

'Well, I'd been taken as a slave, you know,' he said.

I nodded.

'Sometimes I wonder what would have happened to me if you hadn't come,' Leukas said. 'And then, sometimes I wonder what would have happened if I'd taken a little silver like Daud and stayed in Alba or Galle.' He shrugged. 'Before they took me, I was a fisherman. Not a bad life.' He smiled. 'But I think that now ... it would bore me to death. You've ruined me, boss. I want good wine, and a pretty girl, and I doubt that I would be able to take the shit my local chief dribbles on all his "people". I dream of going back, and then I think ... ' The Alban laughed. 'I think I'm ruined for being someone's peasant fisherman. I think I'd make trouble, and some of the gentry would have to kill me.'

Brasidas listened as if the Alban was from another world. 'Perhaps you could go back and kill the gentry, and become the chief,' Brasidas said.

'Poseidon's spear. What for?' Leukas asked. 'I don't want to lord it over people I grew up with. Fuck that.'

'You could change the form of government,' Brasidas said, as if this was a reasonable thing to assert.

Leukas nodded. 'Why?' he asked.

Brasidas sighed. 'So that you could have justice.'

Leukas shook his head. 'If we beat the Medes,' he said, 'I'm going to offer marriage to ... a person.' He paused, and actually flushed. 'And if she'll have me ... Well, I aim to own a ship. I think I have what it takes. I can run to Aegypt and back, twice a year.' He looked at Brasidas. 'That's plenty of justice for me. I don't need to kill anyone at home. Aphrodite's tits. Who cares?'

Brasidas caught my eye when I turned to look at Leukas. 'Is this game for everyone?' he asked. 'May I play too?'

'You'd have to talk,' I said. 'Out loud.'

He didn't even smile. 'Before I joined you, I was a mercenary for Syracusa. I faced the Carthaginians several times, and I felt that I had given distinguished service, and yet, on every occasion, when praise was handed out, other men seized it and kept it. So I had none. I dreamed of returning to Laconia. And of course, when I did, I found that it was no longer my home, and I could never go back.'

Leukas laughed. 'See? I don't have to go home to know that.'

Brasidas looked at the Alban for a long time, perhaps two hundred heartbeats, as our horses picked their way up the second great ridge, and we entered the trees on the main slope.

'I think perhaps you have told me something important, Leukas,' Brasidas said. 'I still want to go home to Sparta, kill some people, and make right a wrong that happened.'

I thought I was about to find out what it was that held him apart; what it was that Bulis and Sparthius misliked. It was a mystery, and I wanted it revealed.

'What's that?' I asked.

Brasidas shook his head; one firm shake.

'No matter,' he said. 'What Leukas says is the important thing. The wife; the life. Sons and daughters. Good conversation with men who are my peers and friends. Killing an enemy? Not worth it. Righting a wrong?' He looked off towards the Peloponnesus. This high up, you could at least imagine you could see Sparta. 'Soon, all the men who know the dirty secret I know will be dead.' He shrugged. 'And frankly, it is far too late to ever right the wrong that was done.' We rode on. 'And now, I cannot help but admire Gorgo, who I should view with contempt.'

Perhaps we talked all the way up the slope, although that's not how I remember it. And I remember the moment at which we all had to dismount. There had been a storm – or a sign of the wrath of the old god of the summit. The oak trees were shattered like straws thrown into the wind by a farmer sorting grain from chaff on his threshing floor; they lay all a-tangle.

'Cithaeron,' I said aloud. The trail vanished into the blown-down tree trunks. It had happened at least a year earlier.

Leukas swore in his own tongue. 'We can't get through that,' he said.

I looked at the blow-downs for a while, and walked back and forth. 'We can get through,' I said. 'It's only two stades to the summit.'

The barrier made me all the more sure that I needed to make my sacrifices. I had a new bride, and I had not sacrificed. I had acquired a son and perhaps two more beyond that, my boys by Briseis. If that wasn't just her tale. I am an old storyteller myself; I have been known to make an unpalatable truth more palatable.

At any rate, I picked my way among the fallen trees, and at one point the three of us had to move a tree, and at another point I cursed and wished for an axe, but in two hours we made it two stades.

And there was the family altar, on the last of the slope, just beneath the summit.

The altar isn't much, if I have not described it before: a stone, formed, I think, by the gods or by the forces of nature, but on one side a raven has been cut into the living rock, for the Corvaxae. And the name of Heracles is written there in the old Boeotian script, and there's a natural hollow in the rock, long ago stained iron-brown from the blood of sacrifices. And a little distance away, just up slope and under an enormous oak, was the ash pile from the burning of the sacrifices. It is nothing like the mound at Delos or Olympia, but it's high enough.

I used to stand as a young man, fresh from a run with Calchas, staring at the ash pile, and thinking of what it meant that my ancestors had killed so many animals. And not just animals; as a boy I found a human femur there, and wondered.

At any rate, the storm, or the wrath of the god, had broken a branch from the great oak, and dropped it on the altar. But, as I have said before, it is amazing what three or four healthy men can accomplish, and in very little time we'd moved the branch and broken it up for firewood, and cleared the altar and the area around it. Only the one tree grew this close to the summit, and the rest of the ground was clear.

But the storm had cleared the summit to the north, knocking down almost every tree on the ground below the summit down towards Plataea. It was eerie. I felt naked on the summit, looking off north over the Dance Floor of Ares to the distant city of Thebes and the mountains beyond. It was like being a god; I thought of Miltiades the night after Marathon, when we stood in the high place above the Sanctuary of Heracles.

And old Cithaeron sent me a deer, a young buck of two or three winters. That animal all but walked onto my spear; it was not even hunting. I took him as a sign from the immortal gods, and I carried the buck up the mountain from the edge of the blow-downs where I killed him and gutted him. Leukas had snared a rabbit, a fine young animal in the peak of health. Another sign.

I made a bundle of his hide and all the fat and some of the bones on the ancient altar, and I sang the old Plataean prayers, some of which are dark and some of which are beautiful, and Brasidas, who was quick at songs and poetry, began to join in. And the old paean to Olympian Zeus, the really old one, was so fine a song that Leukas caught on, and Aten, and we sang it three or four times as darkness fell around us.

And then, using my *kopis* as a small axe, I cut the firewood fine and started a hot fire, and then I made my offering to Cithaeron and to Zeus, and as the smoke from the burning fat rose – most pleasing, I'm told, to the gods – I sang the Plataean hymn to Cithaeron by myself while Aten, more prosaically, cooked the best cuts of venison for our dinner.

Leukas and Brasidas gathered brush, and we used our spears to make a little shelter, more a symbol than anything that would stand heavy rain or high wind. We were at the very climax of summer, and there was little danger of rain.

I noted all this, and yet I sang on, completing the full ritual, not as Aristides had taught me, though I added many of his aristocratic flourishes, and not as my father taught me, although I stayed to the family order of service, but as Calchas had taught me; the priest of Leithus and an old Boeotian aristocrat, steeped in our people's arcane and sometimes bloody past. And I poured wine to his shade and said his name aloud, and so pregnant was that night with power that I thought he was there with me as I made the last burning and opened the throat of the rabbit. And as the red blood ran over the stone, I offered wine again, to my father and all the Corvaxae who had prayed here and were now ash: my mother and my first wife; my uncle Simon; my father's father Simonides, and his father Heraclides and his father Kineas, back and back as far as I knew, and their wives and all our mothers, as is the way of the Corvaxae.

I forgot no name.

To the birth of Heracles.

And to them I added new names: Briseis, daughter of Hipponax, and Hector, son of Anarchos but nonetheless my son, and Hipponax, my son by Gaiana; and both my sons by Briseis; and Penelope's son

Andronicus by Andronicus of Thespiae, who died at Thermopylae with the king of Sparta.

And then, without intending it, I began to say other names. Paramenos was the first, and Harpagos, and Agios, and then they rolled out of me like a river released from its banks, a spring flood of names; all the men I'd led to death. I could not stop from weeping. I wept, and my tears fell on my fire, and the voice of the paean was strong behind me, and that was Brasidas. As I remember it, the night was full of voices, strong voices of men and women who had died early and lived hard.

And then I knew what I was praying for, and it was not my sons or the Corvaxae.

I was praying for Greece.

I raised my arms like the old figures, and I faced each of the four quarters, and I asked the gods to save Greece. And a Spartan, an Alban and an Aegyptian boy raised their voices with me, and all the dead that swirled around Cithaeron's height added their shrill shades to the hymn.

And then I threw the corpse of the rabbit on the fire and bowed my head.

And when I lowered my arms, and raised my head, I was standing facing the north, looking out over the plains of Boeotia.

Darkness had fallen.

And there were fires.

As long as I live, I will probably never see a sight like it, and often I have wondered whether this vision was a gift of the gods. Because I could make out the Vale of the Asopus. I could not see Green Plataea herself, hidden at the base of the great mountain, but I could see the line of the Asopus river, and her little tributaries that water the plain of Boeotia. And I could see fires.

A myriad of fires.

I could see the Persian camp, across the Asopus on the road to Thebes. And I could see the Greek camp, also sparkling with fires. Both hosts were great. The combination was incredible, as if all humanity, from Aethiopia to India, had come to the rolling hills of Green Plataea. The campfires were uncountable, denser than stars in the sky, and extended beyond my sight to the north.

Brasidas came and stood by me.

We stood there for some time. There was nothing to be said, so we said nothing, but looked at the Greek camp and the Persian camp, their relative positions, and their extent. The Persians were on the road to Thebes, and their fires covered the plain. The Greek camp was almost beneath us, in and among the complex of ridges where the Athens road over the pass debouched into the plains at Erythrae.

Aten called from the campfire, and said that the dinner was ready.

And that broke the spell, and we chuckled.

Or perhaps it did not, because when we had eaten – feasted, really – and poured more libations, we gathered our cloaks against the omnipresent wind, and shared the canteen of fine wine that Aten, who was really a fine boy, had brought all the way to the peak. We passed the clay canteen as if it was the finest gold *kalyx*. And although we were all pious men, we mocked Leukas when he inadvertently spilled too much wine on the ground.

After a while, the tension was too much for badinage, and we fell silent. The rituals had tired me. I stared into the fire. I felt ... clean.

'All those names,' Leukas said. 'Men you killed?'

Brasidas gave him a hard look.

Leukas shrugged. 'I knew Paramanos,' he said. 'I knew some of those names.'

Brasidas gave a grunt that was meant, I think, to stifle conversation; perhaps to protect me from having to answer.

It is odd when two friends each seek to help you in diametrically opposed ways. Brasidas thought that I needed silence, and Leukas thought I needed talk, which typifies them, I think.

'Men I led to death,' I said. 'My friends, who fell.'

Leukas gave a wry smile. 'Damn. Well, it's a magnificent place, boss. If I eat a spear, you'll say my name to the gods up here? I fancy that. I fancy even the gods in Alba might hear you.'

I nodded. 'I will, too,' I said.

'I think about it a lot,' he admitted. 'Since the belly wound at Salamis. I think about dying and death, and how, when I'm gone, it's over. Never used to talk about this shit, neither.'

Brasidas grunted again, but this time in amusement, I think. Spartans are not just warriors; they are aristocrats, and they are trained to philosophy and they think, too. Some of them. Brasidas, certainly.

I took a long pull from the canteen. Count it in Cithaeron's minor miracles, but the canteen didn't seem to empty that night, under the stars, with the Persian host laid out at our feet.

I lay back on one elbow. 'Brasidas,' I said.

He looked at me and reached for the canteen.

'I think you should let go of whatever it is,' I said. 'I can guess —'

'Do not, please,' he said.

'Very well. But … You know of my story of my return from the Ionian war?' I looked at him, because by that age, I could not always remember what story I had told over and over, or altered … I do alter them sometimes.

You must know that by now.

Leukas made the head nod that meant he'd heard the story too often.

But Brasidas shook his head.

I pointed down the mountain. 'I came back from slavery and war to find that my cousin had seized my farm, married my mother, and taken everything that was mine. My uncle had murdered my father and sold me into slavery.'

You all know the story. I'm sure I told Brasidas at greater length. After all, it is a great story.

I met his eyes by firelight. 'And then I went to the assembly of Plataea with my friends and demanded that he be tried for murder and cowardice,' I said. I reached to Aten for the canteen. 'Because Heraclitus taught me that I had to subordinate my will to the gods and to other men to be able to live as a man, and not a predator. That's not exactly what he said, but that's what I took from it. And I think that this injustice … It has stolen from you the belief in the laws of Sparta – in the kings – that should run in your blood.'

He nodded, no more.

I handed him the canteen. 'I will try and be Heraclitus for you. Sometimes a man betrays his city. Perhaps he opens a gate to the enemy, or he takes a bribe to have poor work done, or he refuses to pay his share for a trireme.' I looked around. 'But sometimes I think a city betrays a man. There is no revenge for this. Would it be fitting for you to bring Sparta down? Would any woman with a babe on her breast thank you for your justice?' I shrugged. 'All you can do is go. Can you imagine a vengeance that would hurt those who actually betrayed you?'

'Most of them are dead,' Brasidas said. He looked into the fire, and then at me, and then at Leukas.

'You are no more a bag of bones and blood, or a thoughtless thug, than I am,' I said. 'Revenge is for weak men with no lives. Help me beat the Persians. And then live.'

He looked at me. 'Revenge is for weak men? What philosopher said that?'

I nodded. 'Me,' I said. 'Years ago, I realized that when I was living a good life in my own house, farming, working every day, making love to a woman I loved – all of that fell away. It was of no value. There is no one to impress; what does my wife care if I sheath my sword in some man who once insulted me? Do my farm slaves care? My children? They care that I am fair and firm; that I not squander money or drink myself into a debauch; that I do my work well, raise my children to be excellent, treat my wife with respect. Only on the deck of a pirate ship do I need to fight and kill constantly to show other men how worthy I am to lead them. Then I must worry constantly about the whispers, about younger men who come to take my place; or I must kill to justify the killing I have already done.'

Aten coughed. Leukas nodded.

Brasidas looked at Leukas. 'It sounds like wisdom,' he said, 'but I notice you've had that canteen a long time, brother.'

Leukas smiled and handed it over the now smaller fire.

Brasidas took it and poured a libation. 'To Ares, to whom I swore an oath.' He looked at us. 'If we defeat the Medes, I will hold myself released from that oath. And I will ask Penelope, widow of Antigonus who fell with Leonidas, to marry me. And I will learn to farm.' He shrugged.

I wanted to embrace him, but there was something very close to the edge in him. So I just smiled, and took the canteen.

In the morning, we picked our way through the blow-downs for several hours, and then I, who had grown to manhood on these slopes, lost my way on the north face where I'd killed fifty deer, and we wandered back and forth until at last I found trails, although perhaps not the trails that I knew. We'd come too far west, onto ground that in fact I'd probably seldom seen, and we walked back east, leading our horses, and found trails I knew well a little after noon. Because of this error, we didn't come down to the tomb, as I intended, but came to the edge of the plain much farther west, almost over by Thespiae.

All I can say is that it's a big mountain, and I'd been away.

We could smell smoke all day, and towards evening we came down the mountain past the older Sanctuary of Demeter, from my grandmother's time, and ran into our first Greek patrol. They were

Spartan helots, a dozen of them with a *perioikoi* officer, sweeping along the edge of the old cart track from Thespiae in the afternoon light.

The officer knew me, although I didn't know him.

'You need to be very careful, sir,' he said. 'There are Persian and Mede cavalry everywhere but right in our camp, and they strike without warning. It's usually safe in the woods, but we lost a convoy coming from Attica this morning. I was sent to look for another road over Cithaeron.'

'Did anyone ask a Plataean?' I asked.

He shrugged. 'You'd have to ask my *taxiarchos*, or even Pausanias,' he said. 'I'm doing the job I was set.'

I pointed to the tomb, just visible to the east among the trees. 'There is a web of trails on the slope behind the tomb,' I said. 'A man who knows the ground could bring a whole mule train over Cithaeron without going to the roads. And this here is a cart track that runs east to the main pass to Oinoe.' I shrugged. 'The Athenians call it the Three Oaks, because in my father's time the main trail split up there and came down three ways. They are still there if you look for them.'

Cassandros, as he was named, nodded. 'I'll go over the shoulder of the mountain, because I was ordered to,' he said. 'But you could do me a service and tell Pausanias just what you told me.' He smiled ruefully. 'I guess someone should have asked a Plataean, at that.'

We rode on, taking more care. We rode past the place where we – that is, I – screwed up the ambush of the Saka; where Teucer's son died. And then down into the first little valley, across the stream and there was Plataea. We were coming at her from the west. I stopped. There ...

I mean, once, there had been a city there.

You know, I'd watched Attica burn. Twice. I had watched Thiale, priestess of Artemis, curse the Medes with her arms raised in supplication to the gods, and all the fires of Attica between her hands, and I thought that I felt for the Athenians. I thought that I understood.

But I didn't understand until I stood at the base of Cithaeron, where a man gets his first view of Plataea, and there was ...

A pile of rubble. A little smoke.

Some of it was still smouldering.

The walls were knocked flat, and turned to rubble, and every house demolished. Myron's house, and the house in which I had welcomed the queen of Sparta. Every house. My forge, and the iron worker's across the street, and my little row of dwellings where Styges and Tiraeus shared, and every other dwelling, high or low, free or slave.

Rubble.

In fact, what made it so unbelievable is that at a distance, it was as if Plataea had never been.

In a moment, all my fine pronouncements about revenge were swept away. I wanted to kill them all; to kill them barbarically.

And yet, the very worst of it may be that in fact, no aliens did this. Not the Persians, not the Medes, not the Aethiopians or the Indians or the Aegyptian marines or the Cilicians or the Immortals.

No. The fucking Thebans destroyed my city. It is less than fifty stades from Thebes to Plataea. They look like me, they pray like me, they drink the same wine. Many of them wear things my father made, or I made, or Tiraeus made in our shop.

All through my youth, every time a man said 'Thebes' aloud, every grown man would spit.

I looked at the smoking rubble of my youth, and I hated.

An hour later, after passing the ruins of our Temple of Hera, thrown down by the Thebans – Zeus, what kind of people are they, to destroy the temples of their own gods? And, I admit it, after kneeling by the desecrated altar and praying to Hera and my mother, who was a priestess and to whom I never prayed, for revenge, for the goddess's hand on the scales – I stood at the little cliff where our acropolis used to stand, with the towers added by Myron when I was young. All gone. But still the very best view of the Vale of the Asopus.

The fields of Boeotia are the very best ground for war in all the world. That is why men call them 'the Dance Floor of Ares' – because armies come to Boeotia to dance. And, if you look south and a little west from Plataea, you see the Boeotia most men imagine – flat as the floor of a temple, a patchwork of grains: barley, wheat, millet, hay for animals, in four or more colours of gold and brown and green. To me, it is one of the most beautiful sights in all the world.

But turn slightly to the east, and the view changes. The ridge, which reaches forwards from the base of Cithaeron, ends with the acropolis of Plataea above the plain, but to the east is another ridge, and it is like a reaching hand; instead of ending in a single rise like Plataea, the ridge to the east ends in five smaller ridges that spread like fingers. Every one of them is low enough to climb in a matter of moments, but every one of them is high enough to hide men and animals, and the top of the ridge has several small sanctuaries and their attendant groves of old forest; in my youth we called it Sanctuary Ridge. There is the old Sanctuary of Hera, where my mother loved to go alone; there is the Sanctuary of Heracles, where I used to pray when I lacked time to climb Cithaeron. But beyond to the east, I could see nothing, and indeed, I knew that the countryside rolled in folds with relatively steep little ridges running almost parallel all the way east to Hysiae and Erythrae and the Greek camp.

And in front of all this rough ground lies Asopus Ridge, which reaches from the east at almost a right angle to the ridges of Plataea and Sanctuary Ridge. This *is* as odd as it sounds. In most of the world, we do not have two ridges or three that run at different angles and yet have such steep sides. But Asopus Ridge was somehow formed by the Asopus; it lies between the mountain and the river, and hides the river from Plataea.

So, despite the acropolis of Plataea being the highest point for dozens of stades in all directions, I could see nothing of the ground to my east and south; I couldn't even see the Greek camp just a dozen stades away at Erythrae, and I could not see the Persian camp at all, even though it was really less than ten stades away, on the main road to Thebes. I could see a smudge of smoke to mark the enemy camp; and I'd seen all the fires the night before. But the camp itself was hidden. Even from the height of Asopus Ridge, which was, I promise you, none too high, it was very difficult to see into the ground behind the answering ridge on the far side of the Asopus, and the Asopus herself is more of a sluggish ditch in midsummer than any kind of a torrent.

'I wonder what Pausanias is playing at?' I asked.

No one else spoke, and our horses' tails swatted futilely at flies. I shook my head and saw a cat, dead, in the ruins of my town. The cat had been killed by a knife or sword.

What kind of man kills *an enemy cat*?

Thebans.

Also from the acropolis, we saw the spurts of dust that marked enemy patrols. There were dozens; it was as if Boeotia had an infestation of worms or ants that threw up dust. They were everywhere.

I dismounted, and so did my friends, and we stood on the abandoned acropolis and watched the Vale of the Asopus for as long as it takes a man to prepare and eat a small meal. I mention that because we ate the rest of the garlic sausage in our packs, drank water, and picked bits of sausage out of our teeth.

We picked out two parties close to us: a small party working around the town to the west, in the direction of Corinth, and a larger party, perhaps fifty horses or so, that was in the dead ground between Sanctuary Ridge and Plataea – by the way, for those of you new to war, dead ground is ground into which you cannot see because of intervening terrain. See?

We elected to work our way off to the left, even though that took us away from the Greek camp, to pick our way past the smaller party and then gallop across the open ground to the east. This had many points to recommend it, but the most important was that I could ride past our farm; I knew the ground by heart.

We moved on foot; past the Temple of Hera and across the little valley, and then up the hill where our farm was. From the gate at the base of the hill, I could see the Saka cavalry down by Epictetus' farm. They were halted, looking at something. Men had arrows on their bows.

Suddenly we were playing cat and mouse for our lives. It was like a sea fight; it started very slowly, and suddenly everything sped up. Were they looking for us?

We came to our hilltop.

The farm was gone. My tower – gone. The Thebans and their rotten allies had burned my shop years before, but Simonides and Achilles and Ajax, all my cousins, rebuilt the place and did a pretty fair job.

All their work was gone, now.

I thought of Achilles, who, if he was alive, must be with the phalanx, near enough to know exactly what had been done to ten years of his work. Hard work.

Some bright sprig of a Theban had crucified a lamb. We must have left one behind, or Simonalkes had, when we took the flocks to Corinth.

Poor little thing. It was mostly rotted. All this destruction was old, probably almost a year, right after the Persians overran Boeotia.

Stupid *fucking* Thebans.

I admit it. I find it difficult to hate the Persians. And very easy to hate the men of Thebes.

At any rate, we moved carefully through the ash and dust of the farmyard, and slipped up the hill into the olive grove and the vineyard.

Which was untouched. Destroying vines takes effort.

Stupid fucking *lazy* Thebans.

Well, it wasn't mine any more, but it made me smile to see the vines and trees. They needed work – massive work. No farm likes to be abandoned for a year.

No matter. Either we'd win, and then do the work, or we wouldn't win, and some other men would have to trim the olives and cut back the vines.

From the vineyard, I watched the Saka. I'd faced them before, and they were canny, dangerous fighters. So we stood in the vineyard, cloaks around our horses' heads, and waited them out, and they puttered around for an hour and rode away north, towards the Asopus, because while they suspected someone was there, they couldn't take the risk of being ambushed so far from their camp.

War. The very best of games.

I gave them a finger of sunlight after they seemed gone, and then we slipped north after them, and made our way through the old wood lot and then down into the plain where we were vulnerable, but the sun was slanting down, and although I'm no great horseman, I had spent a season with Cyrus, riding through the high country above Sardis in the year I took the Spartans to Persepolis, and I knew a lot more about hiding from horsemen than I had as a youth. I used the hills as a backdrop, moved too slowly to raise dust, and we made decent time along the reaching fingers of Sanctuary Ridge.

We could smell the Greek fires cooking mutton when we tripped over an ambush, just south of Hysiae where I had planted my Milesian colonists many years before. I knew the ground; these were farms of men I knew and liked, and above me, in the complex tangle of ridges that rose into the pass, were their wood lots and their vineyards.

Like most fights you survive, it was a cluster of errors from the moment we started. The enemy cavalrymen – not, thank the gods, Saka, but Thessalians – were facing the wrong way. They'd put themselves too deep in the brush at the base of Erythrae Ridge, hoping to pounce on foragers coming out of the Greek camp at its lowest quarter.

Really they needed to go to Cyrus' school, because they hadn't left a trooper to watch their backs and they hadn't left themselves a clear means of escape if their ambush went bad. There were a dozen of them.

There were four of us, and one of us was a boy who didn't like to fight.

But the moment I saw the dark petasus in the brush to my left, I knew I had to attack. It's a hunch, a guess, an instinct. The patch of ground in which they hid was too small for a big troop; the man in the petasus was clearly not a Saka or a Persian, so there would be no bows.

Nor did I actually think these things.

I saw the hat, heard a horse snuffle, felt my horse respond, and I had a javelin in my hand. I looked at Brasidas and he nodded; Leukas cursed. Leukas is an expert, deadly man. He simply does not like to fight. This is very intelligent of him.

I like to fight.

I gave a long screech, a war whoop like those the Thracians use. And there was the nearest Thessalian, much closer than I had imagined, his back to me, his horse's head turning, his long dusty cloak making him almost invisible.

My javelin went through his cloak – and his kidneys, too.

All his mates began to react, and Brasidas cut into the brush from a slightly different direction, confusing them and killing another with an overhand thrust of his javelin.

I had to leave my *lonche* in my first victim, and my *kopis* under my arm was short and not very useful for a cavalry fight. But another man, trying to escape Brasidas, crashed into my horse, side to side, and I locked my right arm around his throat and tore him from his beast while my left stripped his long sword from under his arm. The strap on the scabbard snapped as he fell to the ground, and I drew the weapon, a long, light *kopis*, and threw the scabbard on his cooling corpse.

Leukas, with stunning practicality, had seized the horses of the three men who had dismounted. One of them was captured. He had dismounted to defecate.

Grin all you like. Nasty way to die. But we took him, and another man that Brasidas ran down, and the rest fled.

Here's the thing about little war, friends. In that thick brush, we might have been the whole Athenian *hippeis*. Since they hadn't left a man to watch, there was no way whatsoever for them to know what hit them.

I'd run, too. But if you wait to get a headcount, you're dead.

At any rate, we took our captured horses and prisoners and rode directly up to the Greek camp. Almost immediately a dozen Spartan helots emerged from the cover of some rocks; they'd been close enough to touch the whole time. They had no officer, and for a moment I feared they were deserters until the gap-toothed lout who led them gave me a lopsided grin.

'Was gonna take 'em all,' he said. 'When they turned for their camp.' He shrugged.

'Or die trying,' I said.

'Yep,' he said.

We went back to camp with the helots as our safe conduct, and before the sun set another finger, I was sitting with Hermogenes and Empedocles and Simon and a dozen other Plataeans.

My Thessalian prisoners sat on their haunches and looked terrified. They had every reason. Mardonius had decided that we were all rebels against the Great King and was killing any Greek taken in arms, even slaves caught transporting food from Attica and the Peloponnesus.

I let them stew. Besides, they raised my status immediately. No one else had taken an enemy prisoner in two days.

I drank watered wine and handed the canteen to Brasidas. 'I've only been gone five days,' I said. 'What's happened?'

Hermogenes looked grey with fatigue, and most of the Plataeans looked no better. 'I think . . .' Hermogenes looked around. He wanted support.

No one helped him.

Bad sign.

'I think that perhaps Lord Pausanias has bitten off more than we can chew,' he said.

An hour later I stood before the Spartan commander and his staff officers. Many things had changed: I'd brought prisoners; the war was on.

I was greeted with every courtesy, led to the mess fire, and handed a cup of truly execrable broth.

Pausanias was locked in some sort of argument with his military seer, Teisemenos, one of the few foreigners ever offered full Spartiate status, as I think I've mentioned. So instead, Euryanax, his cousin, sat with me. Bulis waved; Sparthius came and lay full length by me, as a show of social support if nothing else.

'How is the fleet?' Euryanax asked.

I bowed formally. 'My lord, the king of Sparta, Leotychidas, and Xanthippus of Athens, in full agreement, sailed the day before yesterday for Delos. There they intend to rally any Ionians who change sides. And attack.'

Pausanias turned his head slightly.

Euryanax tugged at his beard. If I have not mentioned it, the Spartan officer had the finest, blackest beard in the whole army, and the longest, most perfectly groomed hair. In a woman, this might have denoted vanity. Indeed, I sometimes wondered about Euryanax. And yet, he was an excellent officer, and what did I care if he spent too much time grooming his hair?

Spartans. Not like Boeotians.

At any rate, he tugged at his beard. And shook his head. 'The king has gone over to the attack?' he asked, as if incredulous.

'Yes,' I said.

He looked at me, long, and hard. He did not say *You wouldn't lie to me* But that's what I read in his looks.

'So,' he said. 'Now the wrestlers clinch.'

And at that, Teisemenos came and was introduced. He was probably the single most famous seer in Greece. He'd almost won the Olympics as an athlete; he was strong, handsome, well-built and well-spoken. But his gift of divinity shone in his eyes, and you had to wonder why he'd even tried for the Olympics when it was so obvious that he was god-touched.

He looked at me and smiled. It was a broad, friendly smile, not the usual response of a man you've just met.

'Beautiful sacrifice,' he said. 'Cithaeron heard you. Every bird in the heavens heard you.' He held out his hand.

I won't bore you with tales of his divinations or his prophecies. Listen, of course he might have heard that I'd made sacrifice on Cithaeron. An observant man might have seen my fire the night before; Leukas might have mentioned something to a slave who told another slave. I'd been in camp an hour.

Believe as you will. I only had to look in his eyes.

'I want to attack,' Pausanias said.

'The first army to cross the Asopus will lose,' Teisemenos said. 'I have told you this for three days.'

Pausanias looked at me. 'Plataean,' he said. 'Welcome to the army. How goes it with the fleet?'

'They sailed east with high hearts, unified in purpose, determined to conquer,' I said.

'Lucky them,' Euryanax said. 'The men of Lacedaemon and the

men of Athens are the only hoplites in this army. Adeimantus does all he can to divide every council. We have no cavalry and in a few days we will have no water. Mardonius is killing us by ten thousand cuts, one cut at a time. I want to get to grips with him before a contingent marches away. Or, by the gods, goes over to the Medes.'

Well. I'd been at Lade.

I knew my Greeks.

'It is not my place to command the army,' I said. 'But I have known hoplites to fear being shown up by oarsmen ere this.'

Pausanias smiled grimly. 'You sound like Aristides,' he said. 'And you are right. But those who can be shamed need no shame to stand their ground.'

I nodded. 'I can vouch for the enemy cavalry all around you,' I said. 'The valley is full of their men.'

He shook his head.

'I thought you were marching on Thebes?' I asked.

Euryanax laughed. 'Mardonius is no tyro,' he said. 'He retreated until he had secured his flanks and his supply, and not a stade further. He halted on the other side of the Asopus, astride the Theban road. Yesterday the Theban phalanx came up, adding another fifteen thousand hoplites to his numbers. Enough hoplites to face all the Spartans or all the Athenians.'

The seer spoke again. 'All the signs are clear. Offer battle on this side of the Asopus. Offer it until he accepts.'

Pausanias frowned. 'So … it's not the attack I am to avoid, but merely crossing the Asopus? I can offer battle on Asopus Ridge?'

'And move to better water,' Euryanax put in.

I said nothing, because really, I was just a messenger.

Pausanias looked at the seer and twisted his mouth, not a facial tic you usually found in the men of Lacedaemon; too unhandsome. From which I gathered that the stress was getting even to a Spartan commander.

'Very well,' he said. 'Summon the military council. And let's have these prisoners of yours.'

He nodded at me, as if we were old friends.

I was going to salute, the Spartan way, and then I realized I'd seem like an arse, pretending to be a Spartan. So I bowed slightly, and left him with my prisoners.

*

I found my tent, my excellent Persian linen tent, assembled, erected, and full of Plataeans I knew. My steward, who was now a free man and a hoplite, was unapologetic. Tents were few and far between in the Plataean phalanx. Eugenios gave me a cup of excellent wine and Aten laid out my bedroll and saw to the horses, and I was home.

I was deeply angry. Seeing your home destroyed is horrible; it's like a beating or a rape, a violation. It unmakes some part of you, and I was shaken, and my spirits were low, and my little victory over the Thessalians wasn't enough to light the fires in me. I sat and drank, and my friends, the friends of my boyhood, walked wide around me.

I've said this before, but I had left little Plataea and done too much to be one of them. Hippias, son of Draco, could make jibes; Empedocles, son of Epictetus, could slap my back; his brothers could smile, or hand me wine; but I was not one of them. It hurt, and hurt especially that night.

Brasidas came and sat by me, and Leukas.

'Right now,' I said, 'What I want is revenge.' I tried to sound self-mocking, and instead it came out as the grimmest threat.

Brasidas nodded.

'Perhaps the man at the bottom of the mountain is not the same as the man at the top?' he asked.

I managed a smile. 'That was worthy of Heraclitus,' I said. 'At least in part because I'm not even sure what you mean.'

Leukas laughed.

Eugenios reappeared with two wax tablets and half a dozen scrolls. The scrolls were all straightforward: documents on two slaves I'd manumitted. Don't think me some sort of good master; I merely sold them to themselves when they earned out. I'd always done it with slave oarsmen.

A bill from Syracusa. I had to laugh aloud, because it was like a note from a past life. The Pythagoreans believe in such things, you know – that you may live many times in different bodies, sometimes a man, sometimes a woman; a priest, an aristocrat, a peasant, a slave. Not my idea of religion, but every man must have his own.

I leave the dance as usual. It was a bill for so many amphorae of wine, contracted by Doola and countersigned by me in a dockside taverna, and it seemed as if it was a message from another world, and again, my eyes filled with tears, thinking of Doola and Vasilios and Megakles. I had good friends out in the west.

I handed it to Leukas, and he guffawed.

And then I jumped to my feet. I'd opened the wax tablets: beautiful tablets, in a fine hard wood with Aphrodite worked very prettily on the covers.

Inside was a note from Briseis.

When you read this, I will be on my way to Lesvos with Archilogos.

Our child is safe, and so am I. I love you.

This must be done. Am I to sit home and spin, while you liberate Greece?

I stood there for a moment, staring at the wax by firelight.

And then I began to breathe.

'Bad news?' Brasidas asked.

I looked at that tablet for a long time.

Am I to sit home and spin, while you liberate Greece?

If I had wanted a different wife, I might have had one. I thought of Gorgo, of Jocasta.

Of Briseis.

'In an odd way,' I said, 'It makes me happy. Terrified, but happy. My wife has gone to Ionia to help raise the Greeks against Xerxes.'

'I honour her,' Brasidas said. He lifted the wine cup – my wine cup. 'To Briseis.'

We all drank. Hermogenes had just come up. We embraced.

'I want you to be polemarch now,' he said.

I shrugged. 'The assembly chose you,' I said.

He sat heavily on a camp stool. My camp stool. It was odd, and a little comical; I had all this equipage because I was rich and made war for a living, and all the Plataeans could benefit from that.

'Pausanias means to offer battle tomorrow,' Hermogenes said. 'Ares' dick, brother. I was your *hypaspist* once upon a time. I feel like a fake.'

'You are a fake,' I said, dripping a libation to Ares and his dick. 'So am I, and so is Leukas here. Brasidas may be the real thing ...'

Brasidas smiled quietly.

'Or he may be a fake like me. Hermogenes, no one is a born leader. Look calm, don't show anyone your sweat stains, give orders in a clear voice, look pleased all the time. See?' I drank off the cup. 'Easy.'

Aten appeared, filled the cup, and handed it to Hermogenes.

'Pausanias hinted that you should have been at the council,' Hermogenes said. 'Myron hinted that I should just send you.'

I frowned. 'What does Pausanias plan?' I asked.

'We're going to march out of here in three columns: Athenians on the left, with us and the Megarans. Corinthians in the centre, with a lot of the Peloponnesian allies. Spartans on the right, with the Tegeans. There was a long argument—'

'About the Tegeans?' I laughed. 'Again?'

'And all the Spartans shouted for the Athenians to hold the left. Aristides tried to make the Tegeans feel better, but they're pretty hot.'

I shook my head.

'And the men of Hermione were annoyed. They asked to stand with us in the battle line. Pausanias dismissed their request. They have almost three thousand hoplites, and more than half are men who trained with us last winter.'

I got to my feet. 'That I can fix. Are they in the centre with the Corinthians?'

'Yes,' Hermogenes said.

I nodded. 'I'll be back. Eugenios, keep my cloak warm.'

Myron, by now one of the oldest men to march with the phalanx, waved. 'Mist tomorrow,' he said in his low voice.

Hermogenes followed me into the darkness. 'Will the Medes fight?' he asked. 'Will it be tomorrow?'

I was still angry with the world. And with Briseis, for making me be afraid for her. I could hear the whole argument we would never have. I knew it was silly. I knew that she was merely imposing on me the same fear I imposed on her. I knew, in fact, that she could, alone or with her brother, affect the fate of Greece.

I also knew that Lydia was full of men who would rape, kill, enslave or humiliate her merely to make friends with Xerxes and his officers.

I didn't have time to dwell on any of it. 'Do I look like a seer?' I snapped.

Hermogenes put a hand on my arm. It was warm, like the man. Hermogenes was afraid of many things, and failure not the least of them. But he wasn't afraid of me, or my anger, and that steadied me. 'We have some weak fools in this army,' he said softly. 'I worry even about getting all these men formed. How deep shall I form the Plataeans? We have a little shy of a thousand men.'

The Long War. When we'd mustered to face Sparta, all those years ago at Oinoe, we'd had at least fifteen hundred in our *taxeis*. At Marathon, even more, and we'd made up our losses in freed slaves. I'd brought us good men from the fall of Miletus, and a lot of my former oarsmen and marines.

And now, facing the day, and the battle, we only had a thousand hoplites. We'd been in every fight since the Vale of Tempe. We'd lost men to sickness, hunger, drowning, the enemy, and frankly, there were men sitting on Salamis or back at Hermione because 'service in the phalanx' had never been intended to be every year, all summer long, for years and years, and men were losing their will to fight. On the other hand, it was the best armoured, best trained phalanx we'd ever had. We'd seen more combat than any town our size. We had men who'd faced the Medes at Marathon. And again at Artemisium, and a few at Salamis, too. We had picked up the Thespian survivors; a few hundred had surrendered after the Spartan king died, been stripped of their arms, and escaped.

'Eight deep,' I said. 'With half file leaders ready to close front so we can stop cavalry and widen frontage.'

He grunted in the darkness. 'Good. That's what I thought.'

I walked over to the men of Hermione, found their *taxiarchos*, Diodoros, and chatted with him while his *pais* served us wine. I didn't know him; he hadn't trained with us, but many of his friends had, and he shrugged.

'Troianus says that he learned more from your teachers than he knew there was to learn,' he said. 'So why not be with your Plataeans?'

So the two of us walked through the firelit, smoke filled darkness to the Lacedaemonian camp. They had sentries, but so did the Athenians and the Plataeans; they had well-organized mess groups.

They were having an ugly argument, at least, the Spartiates.

Standing listening to another family argue is never good policy. And Pausanias looked none too happy with the debate, so I walked over, more boldly perhaps than I felt, and stood by him, and he turned to me.

'Plataean?' he asked.

'I came to beg a boon about the formation of the phalanx,' I said.

Pausanias walked out of the firelight with a good grace. He left Euryanax and the giant, Amompharetos, bellowing at each other.

So much for Laconian virtue.

'How can I help you?' he asked.

'I wonder if the men of Hermione could stand by the men of Plataea,' I asked.

'I have already said no,' Pausanias said.

I nodded. I was trying to be gracious. 'I thought only to explain why.'

There was a pause, and I had the sense that Pausanias had had an entire day of this: request after request, demand on demand, favour on favour.

'Speak,' he said.

'All of Plataea wintered in Hermione,' I said. 'We trained all winter together.'

He gave me a hard smile. 'How many times?' he said. 'Four? Five?'

'Every day for seventy days,' I said.

We stood in silence. 'That is how Spartans train,' he said.

Without pausing to contemplate, I said, 'We learned from a Spartan. Brasidas.'

There was a long silence. 'That name is not a gateway to my good graces,' he said. 'Nor is he a Spartan, but a foreigner, by his own decision.'

I'm glad it was dark. Because I rolled my eyes and made a face.

'Pausanias,' I said, 'We are on the razor's edge, and none of that matters. Dead Spartan kings mean no more than ancient Argive history. Today you yourself told the Tegeans that you preferred to have the Athenians hold the left. Whatever stands between you and Brasidas—'

'You are dismissed,' he snapped. 'Plataean, I have no idea why you feel you can address the regent of Sparta as an equal, but we are not equals.'

He turned and walked back to his fire.

I took a couple of deep breaths.

'What an arsehole,' said Diodoros. 'So in the morning, we'll just cross the ground between us and form on you. Fuck him.'

Sometimes, I can forget what Greeks are like.

'That would leave a four hundred file gap in the centre of the line, would it not?' I asked.

Diodoros grunted.

I put a hand on his shoulder and walked him back to his fires. Military camps are very pleasant, at times; it is not for nothing that men remember them fondly. In the absence of death, there's much less work than at home, on a farm. Men lie around fires and drink. There's no one to tell them what chores need to be done.

The night before a battle, there's an edge to all of it. It is hard to explain unless you have been there, but the game, and the price of the game, make the wine all the sweeter. I suppose there are some poor bastards so scared they can't sleep. Or drink.

It's after a battle that it's grim.

But before? The worst danger is staying up too late and not getting enough sleep, or fighting with a hangover.

Anyway, we walked across the camp, and it took a long time. I was in an army full of men I knew. We went from fire to fire, and I probably drank too much, and I talked, and men talked to me.

Hermogenes was right. We had some awkward sods, and some whole contingents who were brittle, or worse, openly mutinous. Pausanias wasn't a fool, but no one in Greece really had the experience to handle an army of this size.

Most of the men from smaller towns had never seen anything like this. They'd never even been in a proper phalanx. They didn't really know how to form the *synaspis*, a manoeuvre already fifty years old in Sparta and Athens, where your half file leaders lead their half file forwards to double the density of the front ranks.

I see a lot of blank looks.

Here we go with almonds, then.

Pais, get me some without honey.

Perfect. See here.

Sixty-four men. The best armoured men, the steadiest, the veterans, are in the front rank and the second rank. Some *taxiarchoi* put their youngest, hottest blood in the front rank.

Myself, I was one of those young, hot men, and I say it is a miracle I lived to make old bones. I want older men, who will take few chances, standing in the front. Old men in good armour who can endure the press, the stink, the death, and the weight of fear, and stand their ground.

Bah.

At any rate, the second rank is as important as the first, and they need good armour too.

After the second rank, you have to be awfully unlucky to eat a spear.

See? A nice square, eight men by eight men.

Now, each man stands with the width of his *aspis* between him and the next file. This is the 'normal' order, the old order. When you form, the *strategos* or the *taxiarchos* bellows for you to open your shield – that's the order – and you extend your left arm until the rim of your *aspis* bumps the next man's right shoulder. See?

In some circumstances, we can push our *hypaspistai* into those spaces, or archers – that's how they did it in my grandfather's day.

And I've done it myself, in the cavalry fight before Marathon.

But some time in the last five or six Olympiads, someone – the Spartans say it was Arcadians – began to do something different. They appointed half file leaders. These are well-armoured, brave men, but they are put in the fifth rank of eight. So now you have to have two front ranks of good men, and then a fifth rank of good men. Because on a given command, the fifth rank push forwards, with the sixth, seventh, and eighth. Like this.

Do I have to move all the almonds?

Now our little phalanx is only four deep, but sixteen wide. But packed very densely, so that a man can only stand sideways to his opponents. And so there is no gap for a horse to penetrate, and all the shields overlap. Those overlapped shields will stop the best arrow driven by the greatest, strongest Persian noble archer.

Of course, you can do this twelve deep, in sixes, or sixteen deep, in eights. The point is that wherever you want, having moved fairly easily in a loose formation that allows men with spears and shields to climb stone walls or go around an olive tree – important matters when your battle line is twenty stades long, I promise you – wherever you are, you can halt, and make your loose formation into a dense wall of men tipped in iron, armoured in bronze, impenetrable to arrows.

After that, you do not move too fast, but you can do some basic manoeuvring.

My father taught all this to the Plataeans, but Brasidas brought us even more flexibility: ways of filing off to the right and left so that we could go through a gate or past dense woods, and reform rapidly; a hundred little manoeuvres that allow a phalanx to move as if they were Thracian peltasts and then halt and, in the snap of your fingers, become a wall of killers.

Pay attention to this. The fours and eights and sixteens may seem confusing, but I promise you that they were life and death for us.

Where was I?

Ah, yes. The smaller cities.

They hadn't a clue. I won't name names – these things are still sensitive – but there was a city with armoured aristocrats, no demos, and only about three hundred total hoplites, and they were a mob, with no drill and no desire to drill. They'd fill up the rear ranks with freed slaves and poorer men with no armour, sometimes without even an *aspis*.

And that nasty fight I'd overheard in the Lacedaemonian camp was brought on because some of the *perioikoi* were not much better. And Euryanax wanted to force them to drill, and other voices said to send them home because they were an embarrassment. And these were the second class men of Sparta.

In other words, although we had a huge number of hoplites – probably the largest hoplite army every assembled – many of them were actually worse than useless, because they would insist on being in the front rank and then they would fold. Or that's how many of us saw it.

It was ... the fleet before Lade. And Artemisium.

You might say, this is the bad side of being Greek.

Anyway, we walked around the camp, and I got an understanding of why Hermogenes – and Pausanias – were so on edge.

By the way, I was very proud of myself that night. I was as mad as a stallion at Briseis. The more I thought of her sailing away with her brother, the angrier I became; that kind of sick, weak anger that makes you ashamed of yourself later.

And Pausanias offered me the perfect vent for my annoyance. He was an arse, and I walked away. One of the things you learn, when you make war for a long time, is how fragile an army is. Once, I almost killed Cleitus because I hated him more than I hated the Medes.

I was foolish to be angry at Briseis, and I knew it, in my head, and I would have been a fool to have a spat with my commander on the eve of the greatest contest. So I walked away, and I didn't even carp to Hermogenes.

Fine, roll your eyes, my daughter. Briseis once told me that men's anger was all drama, and women, who were not allowed to show their feelings so openly, were much better at managing people. She had a point, although at the time I told her to go and lead a phalanx.

Eventually we made it back to our side of camp, and there was Aristides. He was silent, while around him were the men I'd been with the last ten years, on and off: Cimon and Cleitus, Phrynicus, Aeschylus, Aristides' nephew Aristides the Younger, whom I disliked, and young Perikles, who, like many ephebi, was being put in the phalanx.

Think of it. They had one hundred and twenty ships in the water, each with twenty marines and a hundred and eighty oarsmen, all citizens. And then they had ten thousand men in their phalanx. They had more citizens in the field than any other state; really, more than four times as many as the next state. Because their democracy gave them a reserve of manpower unmatched in the world.

At any rate, I went to Aristides and we embraced, and wine was put in my hand. I was almost unable to walk, but he poured a libation to Heracles, and what could I do but answer in kind and drink, and then I told him, with a boyish pride, of my sacrifices on Cithaeron, because I always wanted to impress Aristides.

They already knew all my news: that the army would march down to the edge of the plain and form and offer battle.

There wasn't really much to say, if you were Aristides. Our whole civilization was going to ride on one throw of the dice, and he, as much as Pausanias, was one of the commanders. He was almost silent after his libation.

We looked out over the plain. There wasn't much to be seen; Asopus Ridge blocked our ability to see into their camp, and there was only a dull glow.

Maybe we talked. I only remember standing with him, looking out at the night.

Then he turned to me. 'I have a letter for Jocasta,' he said. 'Will you carry it? If I fall . . .'

Let me add that Aristides was the Athenian polemarch. And that meant he would stand, alone, on the right front of the great phalanx.

They all die, Athenian polemarchs. Well, not always, but damned often. It's part of their way; that the man who first voted for war should run the greatest risk.

I took his little parchment scroll. Then I sat in his tent and wrote my own, and it was odd. I wrote to Briseis as if she was there; I apologized for my anger when she could never have seen it, and I wished her every fortune with the rising of Ionia. And I told her to name you for my mater, if you were to prove a girl. Which I note you did. Or my father, if you proved a boy.

And then I went and lay down in my tent. I listened to other men snore for a long time, and then a hand was shaking me awake, and for a while, it was Idomeneaus, and we were about to fight Marathon.

I missed him, because he could kill *anything*.

But the hand belonged to Brasidas. And by him was Gelon, who I had freed on the morning of Marathon.

'Pausanias is asking for you,' Gelon said.

I hadn't seen Gelon the day before, and we embraced and then, naked but for a chlamys, as if I was some cheese-eating ephebe, I ran across the camp to the Spartans.

Euryanax was there, and Pausanias was with his seer.

'We want to try something different,' Euryanax said.

It was still dark, and I was cold, despite the time of year, and I could feel the moisture in the air. And the tension, which was so great that it was as if heavy ropes were stretched across the sky, vibrating. Even the Spartans were tense. Afraid? Only an idiot is not afraid before combat. No matter how good you are, a child with a pea can take you down. Bad luck, an error, a burst armour strap ...

Anyway, everyone was too loud, too aggressive, too much on edge.

Cimon appeared out of the darkness, with a handsome young man in superb armour with him. I didn't know him, although, as it proved, I knew his father Lacon. His name was Olympiodorus, and he led their *Ippobatoi*, their chariot-warriors. Now, Athens hadn't used a military chariot in hundreds of years, but they still had the games, and the fittest, best young men were the chariot-riders.

He was brash, but he had the mark of Ares on him. I knew him immediately.

He was me.

Athens breeds some. Look at Cimon, or Miltiades.

Anyway, young Olympiodorus stood there while Cimon buried me in praise.

Euryanax laughed. 'Stop! A man as great as that has no need to fight again. He'll walk off and leave us.'

He looked at Pausanias, but the Spartan regent wasn't looking at us.

Euryanax winced. 'So, our notion is that at each end of the line, we build a small local reserve, in case the cavalry gets around our flanks,' he said. 'We've already chosen our reserve: picked men from several contingents, mostly Tegeans and Spartiates.' He looked at me. 'The regent wants you to command the reserve at your end of the line. Three hundred men.'

'The Athenian *epobitai*?' I asked.

'And the Thespian survivors,' Euryanax said. 'We know them. Fine men, eager for revenge. And we know you, Arimnestos. Almost like one of our own officers. And you have a certain man with you who we also know.'

'Brasidas,' I said.

Cimon gave a sigh, as if I was trying his patience, and Euryanax looked at the sky for a moment. It was lightening.

'Good, I accept,' I said.

'Take your ground between the Plataeans and the Megarans, but a spear cast back,' Euryanax said.

Then, I gave the Spartan salute.

I can be a difficult man, I agree.

I turned to Olympiodorus. 'Can you obey my orders?' I asked.

He looked surprised. 'Yes,' he said.

'Are all your lads young?' I asked.

'Yes, sir,' he said.

We started back for the other end of camp.

'We intend to keep our archers in reserve as well,' Cimon said.

I had forgotten that Athens even *had* archers. But they had more than four hundred citizen archers.

Of course, the Medes had sixty *thousand* archers, so no one was going to send the poor Athenians to stand in the battle line. But I remembered how well they had served at Marathon, and as soon as Styges and Aten had me armed, I jogged up the hill to where the Athenians were having their own command conference, hooking Hermogenes by the arm and dragging him.

'We're not Plataeans,' I said. 'We're basically Athenians. Don't be proud.'

'Have you ever known me to be proud?' Hermogenes asked.

I grinned into the darkness, but he could see me. We got to the Athenians' command fire about the same time as Cimon and Aristides, both fully armed except for their helmets.

Aristides looked like a god. He was tall, and the annoying dignity that he wore every day, that made men call him a prig, a prude, a martinet, was like a cloak of authority that morning.

He nodded to me. 'I understand you are taking all of my best young men?' he said.

I bowed my head. 'If you approve,' I said.

'Keep them safe if you can,' he said.

Then he laid billets of wood on the ground. Later I heard he'd cut them himself. There was the Athenians' phalanx, ten thousand strong; he was forming twelve deep and eight hundred men across the front, a frontage of almost four stades. Then the phalanx of the Megarans, eight deep, four hundred men across, a frontage of two stades. Then the Aeginians, eight deep, one hundred wide, half a stade. Then the Plataeans, eight deep, a frontage of two hundred men with the addition of some Athenians and some Thespians. It's worth saying that nowhere else on the battlefield were there contingents that integrated as well as the Plataeans and the Athenians. But if you look at the pieces of wood, and add in the archers waiting at the back left corner of the Athenian Phalanx and the *Epibotai* – my small *taxeis* of selected men, at the back of the center behind the Megarans – we had the Athenian phalanx on the left, and the 'Athenian Allies' (which is, I confess it, a funny thing to call the Aeginians, but true nonetheless) on their right, in two almost equal blocks, allowing Aristides some flexibility of maneuver.

'Who links up with the centre?' I asked, when he was done laying it out. 'And who, exactly, is at the left of their centre?'

Aristides looked grim. 'I don't know, and neither does Adeimantus. Or he's not telling.'

There was muttering.

Aristides looked around. 'I've already made my sacrifices,' he said. 'They were very good. Remember that the enemy is not perfect; that where we are divided by city and deme, they are divided by nation and language. Stand your ground, look to the right and left, remain aware at all times of how to get back to this ground, and look for my signals and my messengers. If anyone has slaves they do not need, please send them to me as runners.'

He then outlined the plan, as best we understood it: for the Greek army to move forwards out of the ridges in front of Erythrae and offer battle. We were going to move down three not-quite parallel valleys. I knew them all well, and right or wrong, I liked Pausanias' vision that he could fan us out from our camp and then form the line swiftly, with the spacings already set – and with a simple route to the rear if we had a disaster. He left a strong force in camp, as well, mostly Peloponnesians, and many of the smallest, worst contingents.

Just as the eastern horizon began to turn pink out over Tenagra, we marched. I was in my armour, and it was magnificently polished, and I had my helmet on the back of my head as I stood, leaning on my spear, looking at the fine young men and the older Thespians I had been given. The Thespians were men who had surrendered and had all their equipment taken, and now they were a patchwork of old helmets and mismatched armour, and here and there was an old Boeotian shield, because every spare *aspis* had been pressed into service. But they had done this before, and the young Athenians had not. A few of the Athenians had fought at Salamis, and the rest had no actual experience at all.

I chatted to them all. Some of the Thespians knew me, and two – precious to me – had served under Antigonus with the Plataeans at Marathon. I made them officers, and I had Brasidas and Styges, and I'd borrowed Achilles from the Plataean phalanx. The world had come a long way for me to *want* one of my cousins at my back.

I also had young Perikles. Of course he was in the *epibotai*. They were all rich kids. And he was already an officer, a file leader.

So after I'd walked around and talked and let myself be seen, calm and cheerful, I called my officers together.

I'd forgotten how much I loved it.

My officers.

No ships, no oarsmen.

Just the spears and the men who used them.

'I expect that we will need to be able to march by files and form like a thunderbolt,' I said. 'Everyone know how to march off by files?'

Perikles raised his hand, and some others looked blank.

Aristides appeared, with Aten. I knew he must be in a hurry; he had roughly a hundred times my level of concern.

'Brasidas,' I said. 'Practise filing until it's our turn to march off.'

He nodded.

I jogged to Aristides. It was just light enough to see his face.

'If the Corinthians fail to appear,' he said, 'or if they are badly formed, I need to know that you will go directly to the Plataeans, and seal our flank on that side. Or find the Corinthians and plug the gap.'

I nodded. 'I'll start at that end of our line, shall I?' I asked.

'You'd make me happier,' he said.

I saluted him.

'I can't see you as a Spartan,' he said.

We were the last to march off the ground, and, in fact, because the other contingents were filing down the tracks, I waited extra time, while Brasidas ordered them to advance by files from the right, halt, and form; files from the centre, halt and form ...

Goodness, this too?

So if the polemarch stands on the right end of the line, and the whole phalanx is in files of eight men – right?

He orders the files to follow him. He walks off in any direction, and the first, rightmost file follows him, and then the next, and then the next, and then the next, until the whole phalanx is one man wide and thousands long in a file.

When he orders them to form, the second file leader runs to the front, and links his shield to that of the man on his right – the leader of the first file. All seven of his men race up and join him.

The third file's leader races up and locks his shield to the second file's leader …

Right. Easy. Most phalanxes can execute this.

Harder from the left end of the line. Then the leftmost file leader leads off, and all the files follow him. The result is the same. Except that when you halt, now everyone forms from the left to the right.

Hardest of all, marching off from the centre of the phalanx. Then the file leaders really have to watch; they must *alternate* right, left, right, left in full files. This is hard in practice and horrifying in fog or dust or bad light. It is a risk, even with trained men.

But by Ares, it doubles the speed at which you reform. Because your centre file halts and the files come up *on both sides*. It's also much better if you don't know how much space you have between that vineyard and that olive grove.

Men pretend infantry combat is simple, but that's because they've never tried to form a phalanx. The phalanx is a superb tool, once it is formed.

But there are many, many things that can wreck it while it is still just a vulnerable mass of marching men.

We set off in *double files from the centre*. This was a Spartan manoeuvre, and one that took practise, but Brasidas and Styges stood and pushed men into the correct positions as they marched, and a *taxeis* of three hundred is very small. And I formed only six deep.

Then I cut across the camp. I didn't follow the Athenians.

Instead, when we were in the Corinthian part of the camp, I got to see that the Corinthian phalanx wasn't even formed, although it was getting there. I had several friends among the Corinthians, and I waved at my guest-friend Lykon, son of Antinor, and his friend Philip, a Macedonian serving with us; both of them were once my wedding guests.

There were all the men of Hermione, formed twelve deep and looking formidable. They were ready to go, bristling with impatience in the dawn light. I waved.

Men in the front rank shouted.

Then I turned down the valley that the Corinthians were supposed to use to deploy.

Adeimantus was not yet in his armour, and he shouted at me.

I turned to Brasidas, who had Sitalkes the marine at his shoulder – a long story, and not for here. And Sittonax, too.

'Go!' I said.

Brasidas called in lungs of brass, 'Follow me!' and turned down the Corinthians' deployment trail, and began to *run*.

I walked to where Adeimantus stood yelling at me. He had a dozen *taxiarchoi* around him.

I stopped within range of his spittle. By luck, I caught him between breaths.

'The Athenians are already on the ground,' I said. 'If you come up to find my corpse, know that I died because you were late.'

Then I turned and ran after my men.

The sun was finally over the rim of the world when we emerged from our valley. We were late; the mist had burned off.

And I was about to fight for my life in the fields of my youth. It's odd, but war was, by and large, something I always thought to do somewhere else. But here we were, camped around the town of Erythrae, where I liked to buy wine in better days. Of course, the Thebans had burned it. And the other end of our camp – the Plataean and Athenian camp – was at Hysiae, another little town that had been made bigger and richer by refugees from Miletus. Also destroyed, and I confess that the roof beams made good firewood and we were happy to repurpose their outhouses.

War generates a great deal of shit.

We moved at a run, because Brasidas was like that, and we were running along the 'broken ground' at the top of the first ridge to the east, while the other contingents were down in the valleys. I could see everything.

I was immediately concerned by how easily we skimmed along the ridge tops. I knew the ground; it looks broken because it's worthless for cultivation, but it's no more difficult than the lower ground. Sure, there are tracks along the little streams . . .

Right, let me describe this again.

Put your left hand on the table palm down and spread your fingers wide.

The table is how flat Boeotia is.

Behind your hand is Cithaeron, rising away to great heights. The terrain is terrible for cavalry, and difficult even for men.

Our camp was under your thumb.

Plataea is just to the left of your little finger. Your fingers are the little ridges coming off Cithaeron; your little finger is Sanctuary Ridge.

Now lay your right arm on the table so that your elbow is a palm's width from your left hand. Rest it comfortably, with your right hand flat, palm down and fingers together, in a line out from your left hand. See that? Your arm is Cithaeron's lower slope, and your right hand is Asopus Ridge, out by the river. If you imagine the Asopus flowing sluggishly to the outside of your right arm and hand, you've got the whole picture.

We were marching out of our camp down the little valleys, moving to spread our line and get onto the good ground at the base of the ridges, where we could deploy, and still cover our flanks from the cavalry. Aristides guessed that the whole army of the league had a frontage of about four thousand hoplites, drawn up eight deep.

I need to remind you that no one in Greece had ever done this before. Everything pinned on one roll of the dice; no idea what we were doing. The Persians fought battles on this scale.

We were too poor.

And yet, as the sun burned in the east, as I trotted along, dead last in a long double file of fit young men in armour, my heart rose enough to make it burst from my chest and fly to the sun. As far as I could see, east and west, were men in bronze, moving steadily forwards. I could see four columns from my vantage. They weren't well matched; the Spartans had marched early and the head of their files, also doubled, had already halted well to my right and their files were forming, so that the whole Spartan and *perioikoi* phalanx looked like a river flowing into a delta, a river of red cloaks and bright armour, and the delta was where the files were thickening out and forming their line. Beyond them I could see the ruins of the Temple of Eleusian Demeter that had been built in my grandfather's time, up on the next ridge, which was higher and full of thorns and old trees. Pausanias reckoned no cavalry would come over that ridge. I misliked that it towered over the Lacedaemonian position.

At my feet, the Corinthians were last in the race, but what made this worse was a set of accidents of ground that had, now that I saw them, probably escaped Pausanias and Aristides. The Spartans had the shortest distance to travel to form a line, and the Athenians had the easiest ground to cover, which meant that the late start of the Corinthians was about to be compounded by the worst trail and a long journey. Their phalanx had almost five stades to go, and they were coming in single file.

I couldn't see the Athenian phalanx, but I could see the Megarans splitting off and beginning to form in the new light. Again, by an accident of ground, they were at the very end of a spur; the ground behind them was too rocky for them to form, so they went out ahead of what would, eventually, be the line. Hermogenes couldn't see them; I could see the double file of the Plataeans climbing the ridge behind the Megarans, walking to the right. The Plataeans were the rightmost *taxeis* in Aristides' line; a signal honour.

And then I saw the first horsemen.

It was as if a school of tuna suddenly struck at baitfish on a calm summer day. One moment, there was the Greek army, virtually alone on the high plateau south of the Asopus, and the next moment, the horsemen crested Asopus Ridge, thousands upon thousands of them, and they halted on the ridgeline across the valley.

I made myself breathe. I had stopped, and my young men ran on, oblivious to the enemy.

I stood and watched for as long as it took me to snatch a dozen breaths, and watched as the Persian cavalry commander, somewhere over there, took in what he was seeing, made his decision, and came on again in a rising column of dust, perhaps fifteen stades away. As far as I could see, there was only cavalry, in a wide, thick column, perhaps two hundred horsemen across and many, many horsemen deep. I knew where they were and why, because behind them, on the other side of Asopus Ridge, lay the ford in the Asopus, wide enough for two hundred horsemen, and where Teucer killed my cousin Simon with an arrow in the fight at the ford where we crushed his mercenaries.

There were an incredible number of horsemen, and more off to the west, spurts of dust and no more, riding over the ridges, and again, far to the east, over by Plataea, more dust.

So – they had scouted us in the darkness, knew we were moving, and came to try us. Or, the gods had decreed it be a day of battle. Later, Cyrus, my friend, a Persian officer, told me that he didn't know; he was ordered to form his troop in total darkness, but then there followed a terrible long wait, and he heard Artaphernes the

Younger blame the Medes for forming slowly. Who knows what men thought to do? In a battle as great as this, the gods arrange the outcomes.

But I will add that, if this is true, then the Medes' slow cavalry saved Greece.

As the head of the great Persian cavalry column crested distant Asopus Ridge, the Spartans were mostly formed and the Athenians were forming quickly. The Plataeans were still crossing the scrub, and the Corinthians were not yet even on the field.

And the Megarans were mostly formed, but far out on the plain, almost alone.

The Persian cavalry commander was Masistius, with whom I had swaggered swords the year before. I'd met him twice. I won't pretend I knew him that early in the morning, twelve stades away, but he was a brilliant cavalry leader and he didn't hesitate. He went for the Megarans the way a lion goes for a single gazelle, separate from its herd.

I saw all this in ten shallow breaths. I also saw the Plataeans, and the Athenian archers farther back, and ... And the five stade gap in our line.

I can only add that, brilliant and decisive as Masistius was, I can only guess that he was as anxious to come to grips with the Greeks, to kill us, and prove himself, as the Spartans were. Had he sent that column into the *empty* ground to the right of the Megarans, he could have entered into our lines, and caught our worst contingents strung over five stades of smooth ground in single file.

But the folds of the earth didn't make this obvious, and so instead he went for the Megarans. To kill some Greeks.

The dice were rolling.

I ran after my lads, still thinking at a furious rate. Three hundred men can change everything, or nothing. Even formed very tight, we'd have open flanks and be easy meat for cavalry on the plains. Formed very shallow, perhaps two deep ... We'd only die.

I turned to Aten. 'Run to the Athenian archers. Right there. See them?'

'Aye, lord.'

'Run all the way. Fetch them to me. We will be right here, at the mouth of this valley.' I waved. 'Go!'

Bless the boy, he ran. He stripped off his chlamys – a little brown boy, naked – and ran for the Athenian archers five stades away. He was Aegyptian, and a slave. And all Greece was on his shoulders.

And he *flew*.

I was thirty-six years old, with bad wounds in my legs, and I flew too. I ran to catch Brasidas, running over broken ground. No point in shouting. No one in a helmet can hear anything.

I ran. One rock under my sandals might have brought me down. Or just age, or fatigue.

And bless him, Brasidas must have had an extra sense, or some goddess at his shoulder told him to turn and look. But when I was halfway up the column, my lungs ready to burst, I saw his great horsehair plume move, and in moments the running column stopped, and men bent double to breathe, and I was passing them, still running, because every beat of my heart mattered.

Brasidas waited. He looked – saw the Persian cavalry, saw the Megarans.

I could read it all in his body language.

I came up with him.

'Right there!' I roared. 'Form at the olive tree!'

There, at the base of the little valley where, in the fullness of time, the Corinthian phalanx might debouch onto the Asopus plateau, there was an olive tree, alone, and to my right was a small stand of trees, and to the right a ditch, widened and deepened by Plataean farmers, a small stream bed that might hold my left flank for a few moments. We were three hundred paces behind the Megarans. Too damned far to help them, but close enough to be caught in any disaster.

But I wasn't going to lose the damned battle in the first minutes because I didn't try.

'Athenian archers,' I sputtered between heaving breaths.

'You should run more,' Brasidas said.

We were formed at the base of the little ridge before the first Persian squadrons came in sight. I stayed high on the ridge long enough to see Aten's little body merge with the Athenians' archers. I realized that I should have told him to run on, after the archers, so that Aristides knew what I knew.

Battle is merely a contest of mistakes. The army that makes fewest carries the day.

And then it all began to roll along, faster and faster. I could see the

Persians as they came up onto the plateau from the valley this side of Asopus Ridge. They were not as well ordered; young men want to be first to kill a foe, whether they be Persian or Greek or Aegyptian, or probably Aethiopian. The column itself was thickening as the contingents went faster and spread out.

Perhaps Masistius lost control of them. Perhaps he had no plan; perhaps he intended to end the war in one charge.

I followed the last Thespian into line: the sixth man in the rightmost file, a file led by Brasidas with Sitalkes behind him. I got to my place and stood alone, with no file behind me, the rightmost man in a line fifty men long. At the other end of that rank, Olympiodorus waved at me.

And then pulled his helmet down.

I pulled down my hinged cheek pieces.

Put my *aspis* on my shoulder.

Three hundred paces away, the front squadron, the Persian nobles, made the earth shake. They had not slackened reins. They rode straight as arrows for the front of the Megaran phalanx. Behind them, the rest of the great column slowed.

By Ares and my ancestor Heracles, I knew those Persians. I knew what fine soldiers they were, and we were about to face them man to man.

Off to my left, the first Athenian archers were racing along the ridge top, may Athena bless every one of them.

And Hermogenes was forming his phalanx next to mine, on the far side of my little ditch. The speed of the Plataean arrival and formation surprised me, and if a desperate man can be delighted, then I was delighted.

Damn, the Plataeans were good.

They ran *straight to their places*.

They formed like iron filings drawn to a magnet.

Phalanx warfare is ponderous. It involves careful planning, and a long, heavy fight; endurance, patience.

I hoped these young men and Thespian survivors trusted me.

I hoped that the Persians didn't charge me while I was moving.

I ran from my place to the centre of my little phalanx. The man in the centre of fifty files had a red-painted helmet. Brasidas' idea.

'Files! From the centre! Follow me!' I roared. I didn't wait to see if they did it right. The dice were rolling, and the Plataeans were now in place to do what I had been willing to risk my three hundred on;

further, they could now cover my approach to the Megarans.

I ran behind the Plataean phalanx and men waved, or called out, and at the back left corner I slapped a dozen shields as I passed, and men called my name, and there were cheers.

Now I was running *towards* the Athenian archers. As soon as I turned the 'corner' of the back of the Plataean phalanx, I ran at an angle to my front, watching the Megarans.

The Persians charged home.

There was a dust cloud, an agony of sound: horses' neighs, screams, men shouting, the sound of metal on metal and on wood and on flesh; the cacophony of Ares.

And then the Persians burst out of the cloud. Some were laughing, and some were not; many had thrown their spears and one daring young man turned in his saddle like a Saka and shot back over the rump of his horse with a bow, and then they were clear of the dust cloud, thousands of them, and the Megarans were still there.

I tore my eyes away. And turned. 'Form your front!' I screamed at my little phalanx.

We were twenty paces in front of the Plataeans, well to their left, almost directly behind the Megarans. The rocky end of the ridge rose just to my left, and I could all but reach out and touch the stones.

'Hold here,' I called to Brasidas, and raced off.

I've looked at that little ridge a hundred times since. It always makes me tired just to look at it. It's only three times the height of a man, and I went up it, over rocks, in a bronze thorax.

The gods helped me, perhaps.

An elderly Athenian in Saka costume with a wispy grey beard hauled me over the lip of the last rock and laughed.

'Like old times,' he said with a broad grin. I didn't recognize him at all, but I grinned back at him like a madman.

'You in charge here?' I asked.

He looked around, more like the shop steward in a well-run iron foundry than like a soldier.

'I guess I am at that,' he said.

'I need fifty of your best,' I panted. 'I'll put them behind our shields. The rest of you work to the end of this ridge and stay in the rocks and drop arrows into the horses.'

'I love it when you armour boys need us,' he said. He thumped me in the back, and I saw a lot of very proud Athenian men; not rich enough to be hoplites, but *there*. When it mattered.

I thought of the day before Marathon.

He began to call out names, and younger, mostly smaller men, came to me. I could wait; I told him so, turned my back, and fairly jumped down the little cliff, and my thick felt socks and well-spiked sandals saved me, allowing me to get down the rocks alive and very, very quickly, and the Athenian archers leapt down behind me.

Brasidas already had them formed, and more than that, he'd already ordered the front rank to take one step forwards. With a little prodding, the Athenian archers ran down the rank between our first and second ranks and fell in, each behind a hoplite.

And Leukas stepped up behind me. 'You look lonely here, boss,' he said.

In front of me, the Medes emerged from the storm of Ares. The Megarans were invisible now, and the dust rose as high as the top of the ridge or higher, and it was so thick that in the haze, all you could see was a dull flash of bronze, or hear the scream of a man losing his soul through his mouth.

My front rank was shuffling. It was not that they were cowards.

It was that no one had ever faced that much cavalry. And it sounded like a slaughter.

I was afraid. Afraid of death, afraid of defeat, afraid for Greece.

And then I was back in the moment. Pretty sure the Megarans were holding, because *otherwise the Persians would be charging me.*

Pretty sure ...

The dice were rolling, bouncing, in the hands of some playful god.

I'm not much for battlefield speeches, but I had got better at them. And my boys were rattled; I was rattled myself. Plus, soldiers hate anything new, and the archers weren't ours, and as a body we hadn't been together for more than two hours, and now I needed them to be a regiment of Achilles and his Myrmidons. With archers.

I trotted out to the front. To my left, I could see a man without an *aspis*, but in good panoply, running towards me. I noticed, too, that when the cavalry struck the Megarans, they didn't really close; they sort of collapsed against the Megaran shield wall, and mushroomed out of the sides, and then the squadron broke up and retreated, opening away from the Megarans to the flanks and then reforming way back north on the plain. I took that in, in a glance. It was a mechanism, and suddenly I understood it.

I got to the centre front and opened my cheek plates and took off my helmet. I didn't hurry.

Everything matters.

Look calm.

Use humour.

'Everyone warmed up?' I called.

People laughed.

I turned and pointed my spear at the Saka, just preparing to charge. 'We're going at them,' I said. 'We'll tuck in to the Megarans' right flank like a calf taking milk and let our archers pick a few off. If they leave any alive, maybe we'll charge. If we charge, **no one goes more than thirty paces!**' I bellowed the last in my 'storm-at-sea' full-throated voice, and men flinched.

I thought I had them in the right place.

'This is for everything,' I said suddenly. 'Do your duty, don't flinch, and I'll bring you all home.'

I was lying, of course.

They roared.

Their roar was itself a weapon, because two hundred paces away, the Persians, busy reforming – and reforming cavalry is no picnic, because horses are so stupid they make ephebi look brilliant – anyway, the Persians looked at us.

I turned to run back to my place and suddenly I knew where I'd met the Athenian master-archer. I felt like a fool or an old man. He'd saved my life at Marathon. His name was Leonestes of Piraeus.

I saw that as a good omen, and the man certainly knew his work. Arrows were already arcing out over the Megarans from the rocks at the very point of the ridge.

The armoured man ran up. 'We're desperate!' he said. 'Hard pressed!'

'We're coming!' I shouted. 'Look at the archers,' I said, and pulled my helmet down.

Irony is a marvellous thing, the tool of the gods. The Persians were the greatest archers in the world.

Hah.

The Athenian archers were shooting into the dust at first, and I have no idea what effect they had. I was running forwards.

My little phalanx buckled and flowed, the front waving like a loose string.

And the Persians were looking over their shoulders at us. We were coming up on their flank, and we were nicely tucked up against the edge of the bad ground. This is the advantage of small numbers.

Three thousand men cannot hide in some rocks, but three hundred men can, and we kept that bad ground close.

We were only two hundred paces from the Megarans when we started. We crossed the ground at a jog, and that's not a lot of time for a cavalry commander to make a whole nest of complicated decisions and change directions.

Someone did, though. A Mede officer, anxious to make a name, or perhaps bright enough to read ahead, came out of the column to the east – a long curtain of dust that ran off towards the Asopus river. He had about a hundred horsemen with him, although they looked and sounded like thousands.

I kept us going long enough to be sure they were coming for us.

'Halt!' I called. I ran to the front, held my spear parallel to the ground and, with a lot of coaching from Brasidas and Olympiodorus, we wheeled through perhaps an eighth of a circle, so that our front faced the oncoming Medes.

Maybe fifty beats of my heart. And my heart was beating very fast.

I led them through the wheel with my back to the horses, and the earth moved.

But my young men were too callow to know how dangerous it all was. More veteran hoplites might have felt differently. Those young men assumed I knew what I was doing.

The archers all nocked an arrow.

'Half files, front!' I roared.

The half file leaders didn't have archers behind them, and the archers needed a little room to shoot.

Too bad. My feel for it, and I had very little experience by which to judge, was that the six deep, slightly open formation might be penetrated.

Closed up, we were only three deep, but there was a wall of shields.

Our incremental wheel had aligned us perfectly.

The Medes were about thirty paces away when the archers loosed. Most of them were kneeling *under* our shields. We'd never practised this. At least one bow smacked heavily against an *aspis* and the arrow fell to the ground in front of us.

At least one bow broke.

But for that, two horses went down, right in front of their charge, and the storm of shafts – fifty shafts seems like very few, until you see them open the front of an unshielded cavalry charge.

The falling horses were like rocks in a torrent, channelling the charge and creating chaos. Other horsemen fell over the falling horses. Men began to rein in, to slow, and immediately their whole charge gelled and slowed as if they were all driven by one will. One rider, brilliant in gold, came on almost alone, and he had a fine riding whip in one hand and a long javelin in his other. He came for me.

Of course he did. I was alone at the end of my little *taxeis*.

He intended to ride around my unshielded side. Too late, he saw the rocks, and swerved, and made a superb throw as he turned his horse.

I knocked his javelin out of the air with my spear.

And he was gone into the dust. If the Medes had all come on like him, we might have been threatened.

Instead, as they clumped up in front, the better archers loosed a second volley, and they emptied a great many horses – say, ten. It looked like a hundred, but there were only thirty arrows in the air.

Ten men wounded out of a hundred is a great many.

And of course, they'd already reined in. A few bolder souls threw their javelins, but they'd all charged the Megarans at least once, and many men were out of spears.

I bent down, eyes on the enemy, and fetched the Mede's javelin. It was beautiful; gold and silver work, well-balanced.

I reversed my fighting spear and stuck it point down in the sandy soil, but the Medes broke. Their morale was fine; they were professionals, and we hadn't broken, and they were shocked that we had archers. They just rode away.

But we whooped.

I did too, I admit it. And I began to remember what little I knew about fighting cavalry. I'd faced Lydian cavalry once or twice in Asia. And Gauls.

So . . .

It was coming back to me.

'Sidestep!' I commanded. We were only a few dozen paces from the Megarans. 'Come on! Don't get fancy!' I called.

It was slovenly and sloppy and it worked fine. We sort of wormed our way to our shield side until there was very little gap between us and the Megarans, and they cheered. By this time they had endured half a dozen charges and they had twenty or thirty men down. That may not sound like a great many, but remember, those would be their best, front rank fighters, and the enemy had squadron after squadron charging in succession, throwing their javelins and looking for an opening.

I've said it before: a man can only be brave for so long. Charge after charge of cavalry. Men dying every time.

It's like something Pythagoras could have made an equation to work.

As we came up, the Indians charged. They were handsome men, dark brown, unarmoured, on beautiful horses, and they threw javelins from very close, in very good order, at a trot. They probably killed more Megarans in their careful attack than all the Persians and Medes had in their galloping charges.

But they had no armour for man or horse, and they didn't come at our front, and we overlapped them. Most of the Athenians shot eight shafts; at least one lad loosed ten. We flayed them, and it happened so fast that, as they tried to 'mushroom' to the sides to reform, their order collapsed. We'd hit a lot of horses. And some officers, I'll guess.

I glanced at Brasidas. Olympiodorus was too far away, right next to the Megarans.

'Charge,' I said in a normal voice, and Brasidas' helmeted chin went up and down decisively.

'Ready to charge!' I called.

There was an Indian about a horse length away from me, trying to figure out what had gone wrong with his beautiful regiment, and trying to get back in his place in the ranks. A good soldier.

Most of the archers just dropped to the ground. A few were pushed.

'*Charge!*' I roared.

We slammed into their chaos. We weren't that many and they were not beaten.

They should have run. Horsemen lose every advantage when they are caught at a stand. There weren't enough of them. There were six spear points for every horse, six weapons facing every rider. And they were imagining themselves safe – they were trying to rally back and reform for another movement. Infantry, after all, doesn't charge cavalry.

The good soldier opposite me died in the first moments, and dozens of his brothers went down fighting. They had no armour and some had no sidearms after they expended their javelins, and to compound their disaster, they were brave.

When they broke, they broke from actual collapse, and they

couldn't control the direction of their flight. They broke into the face of the cavalry column, trapped by us and the Megarans, and they went right into the face of the newly reformed Persians under Masistius.

That was all lost in dust. I went forwards, killed a couple of men who weren't defending themselves, and was so unthreatened that I went the last few paces counting aloud to thirty.

'Halt!' I trumpeted. That was it for my throat.

I looked for Brasidas. The dust was so thick I couldn't see a spear's length.

But other voices took up my shout, *halt, halt, halt!*

Rally! In your places!

So many voices. They were young, and Athenian or Thesbian, and they were full of vinegar, and I loved them.

I heard Brasidas and ran to him, and somewhere I realized that I had left my fighting spear stuck in the ground and I only had a pretty javelin, but that mistake stood me in good stead, and I ran all the way back to the spear. So I knew exactly where I wanted my people, and I got Brasidas to shout for them, and they came in and formed. It wasn't pretty, and there was no 'drill' to it, but we'd only gone thirty paces, and the cavalry column was in total chaos.

But even as we formed, the Megarans were leaving. They'd stood their ground, and they assumed we were there to replace them. They didn't run, either; they marched off by files, carrying their dead. Their polemarch went by me and he saluted with his spear.

I admit it: what I said aloud was, *Well, fuck me.*

Most of my people heard me. Which was a mistake, because I was not calm, or humorous. I was scared and angry.

It was all luck and chaos. The Indians broke into the cavalry column and Masistius took time to sort it out. If that hadn't happened, we'd all have died right there. We didn't have the men to cover the ground.

On the other hand . . .

On the other hand, we should never have been there in the first place, right? I mean, the Megarans were way out on the plain, far from the Plataeans and the Athenians.

We could just retreat.

'We could just retreat,' I said to Brasidas. I pointed at the Plataeans.

'Not until the Megarans are clear,' Brasidas said with a gesture. 'And . . .'

I followed his Laconic gesture.

The Corinthians were *still* not in place. This is the effect of time in combat. I felt as if hours had passed; in fact, perhaps a quarter of an hour. The Corinthian file leader was not yet on his ground. It would be *half an hour* before the allied army had a centre.

'Fuck,' I said again. No other word does justice to the moment when you realize that you and your friends have to die to save everyone else. It's fantastic in an epic, but it's just not that good in the dust and blood.

'Archers!' I called. Brasidas ran down the ranks, and so did Olympiodorus; in our charge, our archers had been stepped on and they were surly, and felt forgotten.

'How many shafts?' I asked.

Most of them had eight, some six, some ten.

I ran back, looked both ways, and saw the Athenian phalanx. It was enormous, and it was edging towards me.

'Back,' I called, and Brasidas got it. We were much smaller than the Megarans, and we fitted in less ground. Closer to the low cliffs of the ridge.

'Front rank, pick up a javelin!' called Brasidas. 'Or a rock.'

Good idea. I was standing there with a javelin in my hand and I hadn't thought of it.

We backed into the edge of the bad ground and formed as close as we could. We had time; men drank water, fiddled with their helmets, ate half a sausage. One bold soul pissed into the rocks.

And then we heard the trumpets, and we knew our time had come.

'Steady!' I called. So did Brasidas, and Olympiodorus. They were young. They all started calling 'steady' as if they were officers.

Fine with me.

The Persians were in their third charge. Their horses were tired. They hadn't had any water. I know these things from Cyrus. So they came at a trot, in good order, and they emerged from their own dust cloud to find that, instead of a wall of Megaran hoplites, they were facing a relative handful of us.

They slowed.

Right, of course they slowed. They had to assume that the rest of the phalanx was broken; they didn't want to charge the steady survivors. Cavalry are apex predators. They attack the weakest, not the strongest. That's how they win battles.

Masistius was looking for the broken Megaran phalanx.

But there's not much time to make decisions on horseback. And we'd retreated back to the edge of the rocks, which meant that we were much farther under the umbrella of all the Athenians on the bluff above us. And Masistius didn't really know any of that. It's possible he never even noticed the Athenian archers.

He decided to finish us, and he ordered the cavalry column behind him to come forwards.

Ares, I didn't know any of that. I only know that the Persians slowed long enough to give us time to get our order close, and for the archers to get a second shaft out and point first in the ground, and then they came on.

Masistius had a white horse, and he wore a great deal of gold. He led from in front, and he was armoured under his magnificent robe of white and purple silk. I knew him now; he was forty paces away, urging his horse to a great effort.

Our archers loosed.

I'd say twenty arrows hit his horse. I saw it; this isn't hearsay. That horse looked like a hedgehog when it raises its bristles.

But it had a great heart, and it came on two, perhaps three more strides, dead, and still running.

Our archers killed that horse, but the Athenians in the rocks *flayed* the Persian nobles, knocking down perhaps one in three of the men in front, and instead of a volley, it was a continuous rain of single shafts, aimed by men who were facing no threat at all.

The Persian charge faltered.

Masistius' horse fell, and he went sprawling, twenty paces in front of our line. There were a dozen Persians close with him; the rest were already hanging back, because they knew when a charge hadn't worked, and their horses were done.

It is all in those moments.

'Charge,' I croaked.

It wasn't my best decision. I forgot – that I didn't have the *Lydia*'s marines, or the Plataeans at Marathon. I had three hundred men who didn't know each other, and fifty archers in our ranks who couldn't fight hand to hand.

But Masistius was *right there* and leaders matter.

Masistius died in the first seconds, stabbed by a dozen men. Olympiodorus swears he killed him; he was there, but I suspect it was Brasidas whose spear point went in and out of the great Persian's eye after his scale shirt turned a dozen thrusts.

It doesn't matter.

We killed him. We killed the dozen men around him, his standard went down, his trumpeter died, and not a one of his bodyguard ran. They died with him, swamped by three hundred hoplites while our fifty archers looked for somewhere to hide.

Almost immediately, the next squadron, the Medes, charged us. They could see nothing in the dust but bronze. Who knows what they thought? But the Persians hadn't ridden clear yet, and no one knew that Masistius was down, and now there was no one to tell them what to do.

And my young men bunched up in a huddle to finish the Persian general's bodyguard and the Medes rode right in among us, and then men fell like rain on a spring day.

I was shouting for them to form, to form, and Brasidas, and Perikles, and Olympiodorus, and even Sittonax in his Gaulish-Greek and Leukas in his Alban-Greek, but we were too late and our men too ill-trained for the finesse that charge would have required.

And then it was just fighting.

I can remember the moment at which I went from officer to fighter. The dust over the column changed, and as in a nightmare, the dust formed into men on horses. Thank Ares and Athena, they had only their swords and *akinakes*; their spears and javelins were gone, and their horses were tired. And they seemed uncertain, probably as deceived by the absence of the Megaran phalanx as Masistius. But we had no order; there were more gaps than *aspides* in our shield wall, and one man, in gold and white, the man who'd tried to take me with a spear cast, came out of the dust wall, saw my crest, and came for me. It was very personal. He knew that I was the officer; he knew that he was a hero.

Simple.

He urged his tired horse to a gallop and the horse responded, because he *was* a hero and he had a superb horse, and he leaned forwards, face locked in a smile. He had a long, light *kopis* in his hand, and not a short *akinakes* like many of the other Medes, and when his horse was five paces away I threw his spear back at him. At his horse, really.

It was a good cast, and the horse shied, took the spear above its right front leg, and went down, and my adversary was off before the horse was flat. He lost his turban, but not his sword, and I went after him, but he got his feet under him and cut at me. His blow went two fingers deep into the oak rim of my *aspis*, and he ripped his weapon clear before my short *xiphos* could get at his fingers.

I was aware of another opponent and I had to turn a spear on my *aspis*, so someone still had a spear; a horse crashed into me out of the dust and I was down.

I knew that white robe was still there, so I rolled over my *aspis* as Polymarchos had taught me, and never was that more vital. I stumbled, getting to my feet, but I was up. I still had my weapon, and there he was, following me, agile, sure he had me, and he thrust, a long, flowing thrust, a sure sign of a trained man.

I knew Persian swordsmanship. I had faced it all my life, and I'd trained with Cyrus. I cut into his thrust, again going for his fingers with my lighter blade, and he recoiled, his rush spoiled.

I was alone in the dust at that point. A horse emerged from what my brain screamed was the wrong direction, behind me, where my archers should have been. He had no spear, or the story would have ended there, and I slashed his leg to the bone with my sword and he screamed, his horse reared, and white robe came *under the horse* and only my *aspis* saved me.

And then all the years of training flooded into me, and without any conscious thought I went forwards into his cut, *aspis* angled, reaching, punching, and my sword low and hidden from him, and he began to back away. I had a shield and he didn't; in a fight like that, once the first moments are over, it's terrible not to have a shield. His smile was gone; he was looking for help.

But there were more horses, more men, and they were pressing in, and I had to back away, keeping the swords off my helmet with my own sword. I took several blows, too, but my heavy horsehair crest held them. See the notch here, in the bronze of my crest box? That was a Mede, and how frustrated he must have been.

And then it was a crush of horses, and I had no idea where white robe was, and I went under some Mede's horse's belly and plunged my sword into the poor thing, and its guts all but fell on me as I slipped past, and the mare screamed and died.

I must have gone the wrong way in the dust, because now I was surrounded; there were only Medes, and white robe was nowhere to be seen. I slammed my *aspis* rim into a booted leg and the man grunted, cut at me and missed, and I threw him from the horse's back with my sword arm, and he cut at me from the ground and then we were both on the ground, and I rolled to get the *aspis* off my arm, wrenched my shoulder, tried to grab for him with a three-fingered left hand and missed my grab, and he tried to draw his *akinakes* and it wasn't there, and I killed him.

Something hit me in the back. Because, in that moment, I wasn't fighting, I felt it, and I rolled, and I couldn't even see the horse above me. My helmet was twisted on my head.

Then Sittonax appeared out of the dust and cut with his long sword and I wanted to cry, I was so happy to see him. It was like coming home, like my wife's embrace ... I got to my feet, crouched, found my *aspis* – aeons were passing and no one was killing me.

I got my helmet off. And dropped it. Something was bent, and *there* was my *aspis*, and there were hoof beats in the dust, and Sittonax was at my shoulder and he turned me. We went forwards, or back, into the brutal fight around the body of Masistius.

Until that moment I hadn't even known. But the Medes knew by then that their lord was down, and they fought for his corpse like Trojans fighting to retrieve Sarpedon's corpse, and there were dozens of mounted men in the press, and we were to their right, and a little behind the closest press, an ugly surprise to the Medes on the fringe of the mêlée. And now, without a helmet, I fought better; I wasn't taken by surprise, and I had my wits about me, and my people were in great danger, and I started to kill.

And here's a thing. From the moment the man in the white robe came out of the dust, until Sittonax appeared over me whirling that long sword, I can remember the course of the action. It was personal.

After that, I remember only the methodical assault the two of us made on the Medes; mostly we slashed horses who threw their riders.

We killed. I baffled sword cuts with my *aspis* or my sword, and always I attacked their horses.

And then something happened, and suddenly we were neck deep in Medes, Persians, and Saka. The word had spread. And the force of the press had pushed me back, and back again, towards the corpse, and there, of course, was Brasidas. My clearest memory of that whole day is Brasidas standing astride the corpse, his spear broken, killing men with his *saurauter* used as a deadly mace, his *aspis* out, held high as if he was teaching ephebi to use a shield. Even as I watched, he smashed a horseman to the ground, and lost the *saurauter*; he punched with his shield at another horseman, and in the same tempo reached across his body and drew his *xiphos*, and his cut rose from the scabbard into the base of the Persian's chin.

If blood and war can be beautiful, then Brasidas was Aphrodite.

But his look when I tucked in by him was just what I imagine mine had been when Sittonax appeared. And in the next few beats of my heart, Sitalkes appeared at my shoulder, Perikles closed up at Brasidas' other side, and a dozen Thespians came together as if summoned by some arcane trickery, with Leukas at their head.

And we fought.

Brasidas says they came in waves, and I remember no waves, but continuous action, but there must have been a pause, because suddenly I had my heavy spear in my hand, brought to me by an Athenian boy who seemed to me absurdly young and handsome.

We began to back the corpse away, and then they were all over us: a maelstrom of Persians, Saka, Indians and Bactrians and Medes, and many of them dismounted in the dust and then it was very, very personal. I have, to be honest, never seen anything quite like it; they were like raging beasts, their humiliation at losing their general pushing them to acts of madness, and they climbed the dead horses in front of us and men leapt onto us as if they were acrobats. A Bactrian bore me to the ground with my sword in his guts, his cardamom breath still spewing hate at me, and rage, while his mate tried to kill me with a spear held two-handed and Perikles smashed in his face with his shield rim.

Then Brasidas was gone, and I was over the corpse. A Mede and a Persian had the feet, and they were dragging it away, a tragic thing of gold and gore, and those magnificent Tyrian robes that made the corpse so easy to spot in the dust. Leukas had the head and was pulling against them.

I put one down with a flicked spear thrust, overhand, and there were men to replace him, and I was damned if I was going to lose the corpse. I went forwards instead of back, got my left foot on the corpse's chest, and my spear thrust and thrust until I threw it, overhand, into their masses, and I pushed them off the corpse with my *aspis* and raked their unarmoured legs with the metal studs on my sandals and I had a sword, someone else's sword, and Brasidas was back. Sitakles took a turn clearing the corpse, and there were cheers – Greek cheers. I saw Perikles' crest flash by, and then there were, of all people, Styges, and Hermogenes, and a great crowd of red-cloaked Plataeans, spears up, pushing the Medes off the corpse. I didn't see it, but ten paces to my left, the whole Athenian phalanx gave a scream – I heard their *eleu, elue, eleu* coming out of the dust, and then the enemy was gone like a gust of wind on a summer evening. Gone, and the dust cloud, rising to the immortal gods, hid their retreat.

I fell to one knee. I was by the dead man's left side; he was face down, and he looked surprisingly good for a piece of meat that a thousand men had fought over for far too long.

The dust began to settle. The Greeks were cheering. There was Brasidas, already down, sitting on his *aspis*. He was exhausted; there was no bravado, no pretence of Lacedaemonian elegance. He'd given it his all, and his face was grey under his tan, his helmet on the ground, and his braids full of dust.

Sittonax still had his sword, and it was bent. He was trying to straighten it, and the blade snapped, and he cursed in Gaulish, and then threw the thing in the direction of the enemy, sat like a dropped sack of sand, and burst into tears.

Perikles was on his knees.

Sitalkes was right by me, puking on the ground.

Leukas was hugging his knees.

And Olympiodorus was staring at a stone. He was sitting on another, and an archer was wrapping his leg. Something had crushed in his greave; blood everywhere.

More dust settled. Men said things. It was as if I was deaf.

I'd lost a lot of boys. They lay in little heaps, sometimes atop each other, sometimes ...

Fuck this.

I killed them. I killed them when I ordered them to charge. I've been comforted for the last twenty years, as Aristides and Pausanias and Brasidas insist my action was right.

What is worth the death of a hundred young men?

I lost a hundred men. In one action. For a corpse.

Wine.

I probably wept. Or perhaps I did not. I have little memory beyond Brasidas, on his shield.

And then Hermogenes came back from chasing the Medes, and the backslapping began. In some ways, it was as hard as the fight. I was exhausted, not a word I use lightly, and the dead boys in their shiny armour were right there, and I really wanted to be dead myself.

I tried to swallow it.

You know, I've relived it a hundred times. Sometimes I have a regiment of my best men, led by Brasidas and Idomeneaus, with all the brilliant hoplites I've known and led, and we take the corpse and not one of us dies. And sometimes I don't give the order to charge, and Masistius is plucked up by his bodyguard and rides away; and sometimes I die. And sometimes I get to see all the dead boys.

They were too young, too ill-trained. Fit, athletic, and unprepared for the feast of blood to which I took them.

Ah, well. I have a lot of blood on my hands, thugater, and I never really promised that the story would be happy. But next to the dying boy I sent into the dark, all those years ago after Sardis, the windrows of dead Athenians haunt me. Sometimes in the dark, they come together, and I am lying by an Athenian boy in the dark, and he thinks I am his mother or his father while I put him down.

Briseis knows.

The rage of Ares, my friends. Bah. It should be the blackness of Ares, the sorrow of Ares, the emptiness of Ares.

The rest of the army was never engaged. The Lacedaemonians saw no action at their end of the line, and saw only the dust cloud. The Corinthians still like to brag that they won the 'battle'. What they mean is that they were an hour late to their positions, and as they began to form, Hermogenes, that best of *strategoi*, correctly gauged that he could go forwards, because the centre was finally safe. And Aristides was coming; I knew that. He extended the left files of his phalanx until he was only four deep, to hold the ground, and sent his right files into the edge of the mêlée for the corpse, a very subtle manoeuvre worthy of the Spartans.

And Hermogenes has told me a dozen times that we only faced the cavalry alone for about ten minutes, and perhaps less. By Athena, by Apollo, by Heracles my ancestor, those may have been the longest ten minutes of fighting I've ever known. It was chaos; it was bitter.

We killed a lot of cavalrymen, though. Especially at the end, when they grew desperate, and hundreds of them dismounted to take the corpse, and Aristides and Hermogenes caught them. Almost four hundred died then, and another two hundred before, so that there were, in fact, heaps of enemy dead, as poets all too often brag.

I 'came to' from the battle darkness, or the post-battle darkness, to find that Aten was getting my thorax off so that Aeschylus could look at my back. He and Phrynicus were front rank men, in the right files – Marathon men. Imagine: when they went into the Persian cavalry, there were the two greatest voices of Greece, side by side.

Well, to be fair, Simonides was there, too, with the men of Hermione, of all places. Not my story.

Plataea was so big that there were too many stories for me to tell.

They got at my wound, anyway, and it was nothing more than a spreading bruise. And there was wine, and water, and I drank greedily.

Phrynicus was looking at the corpses. He looked at me, drank some wine, and looked again.

'Like Lade,' he said.

'We didn't lose!' I said.

Phrynicus shrugged. 'I was unconscious before we lost,' he said. 'I just remember the blood, and the dead.'

My Thespians had held together longer and better than the Athenians and had lost fewer than thirty men, and they were stripping the enemy dead with a will, nor did any man say them nay. They deserved a reward; they had survived humiliation, capture, and escape, and that day was their revenge. There were men among them I knew – distant neighbours, but friends of my sister Penelope's – and Troilus put his hand on my shoulder, a man my age and one of the 'gentry' of little Thespiae, and frowned.

'Good,' he said. Nothing more than that.

I think he meant that we did well. Or that we fought well. Maybe that he'd just regained his pride. Maybe that he was alive, and that was good.

Maybe all those things.

And the worst of it was the praise. Even the Athenian survivors praised me. It was ... grim. It was not my finest hour, and I do not remember it with pleasure, and right or wrong, no man should have to make such a choice.

Enough breast beating. It was war, and men died. I pour this to their shades, and I beg their forgiveness, but their bodies were the coin I had to spend for the freedom of Greece, and I gave them with both hands to the god of the dead, and the Medes were beaten.

Parse it as you will, the Medes were beaten. We had the corpse of their great cavalry commander, and Aristides had it cleaned and embalmed – we were not barbarians, to mistreat a corpse – and then he put it in a cart and paraded it in front of the army. We offered battle again, on the high plateau between Hysiae and Plataea, and on the second day, not a single foreigner showed his face.

Cyrus told me later that Mardonius could not believe that Masistius had been lost; that Artaphernes the Younger made up elaborate tales to justify the commander's loss; that most of the Persian cavalry cut their hair in mourning, and the manes of their horses. Morale in the enemy army plummeted.

And the next day, our army held a council. I was there, and I contributed nothing. Pausanias said he wanted to move the army forwards to the island. The island is the high ground of Asopus Ridge; we call it 'the island' because it has water on three of four sides: the Asopus in front, facing the enemy; the stream of the Spring of Apotripi on our left; and the Spring of Demeter on our right. All three had water in them.

And Pausanias praised us. Most of all he praised the Megarans, who had lost more than a hundred men facing six charges from the enemy cavalry. And he praised the Athenians; Olympiodorus, and the Aeginians. His eye lit on me, and he mentioned that there had been Thespians, too.

It was at that meeting that I realized that Pausanias was jealous of me.

That had a bitter taste, and I wanted to tell him that he was welcome to all the 'glory'. And petty or not, the fact remained that I had led the men who saved the day, and my name was not mentioned.

Euryanax told me later that Pausanias was under terrible pressure from the senior Spartiates because they had not been engaged; because we mongrel Plataeans and Thespians and some Athenian boys had driven off the very cream of the enemy army hand to hand, as most of the Spartiates dreamed.

In fact, that night I had a crowd of admiring Spartiates at my fire: Diokles, of all people, and handsome Callicrates. They were ranting (for Spartans) about how they'd missed their moment. Apparently they imagined that the Persians would simply withdraw, having lost one of their heroes. When I told Bulis that Brasidas had killed Masistius, he went and embraced the former Spartan. And Sparthius told me that Pausanias was petty and had allowed himself to be annoyed by my reputation.

My reputation!

And yet, Pausanias was no tent-sulker, no petty tyrant, and if he chose to dislike me, he was doing as well as anyone could have to direct the army. The council approved his notion of moving forwards to Asopus Ridge.

We moved in darkness on the army's fifth day in Boeotia. The sun was still hours away, and this time Pausanias came in person to the Athenians, and then to the Corinthians, to move their columns forwards. And that morning, as the sun rose, the Athenian phalanx crested Asopus Ridge to stand in full view of the enemy, and the Corinthians came up beside them, and then, majestically, slowly, with their ranks neatly formed and their red cloaks on their shoulders, the men of Lacedaemon came and deployed as if celebrating a feast in Sparta.

We stood in full view of the enemy for an hour. And then Pausanias, by arrangement, had us retire from the crest; he merely had us move back a hundred paces. His intention, as he made clear, was simple deception; he didn't want Mardonius to be able to see us, count our numbers, or identify our contingents.

Behind us, another army of slaves and servants brought up our supplies and built us a camp.

I think I need to say something about armies and camping in Greece.

The Persians have tents. Their camps look like sprawling cities, with wedges and pyramids of white like orderly mushrooms across the fields of Boeotia, or Aegypt, or Syria or wherever the Great King's armies march.

Greeks don't use tents, for the most part. Greeks treat war as a temporary phenomenon; we expect to march out and get it over with. Or perhaps those Greeks who make war professionally prefer to do so from ships, so that, like sea turtles, we carry our camps with us.

Regardless, most hoplite class men march for war with a leather or cloth shoulder bag full of garlic sausage, onions (they keep, even if they smell) and hard cheese. He has a cloak over his shoulder and his slave carries a spare. He has a spear; maybe two spears.

He doesn't carry a tent. Nor does his *skeurophoros*.

Here's another thing worth noting: you, my young guests, live here in the Bosporus, with four seasons and a nasty bite in winter and rain all the time. But in Boeotia and Attica and most of the Peloponnesus, there's rain only in winter, and farmers feel blessed if they get a good rain in late spring to moisten the seed. By the fighting period at midsummer, after the feasts, you can sleep on the ground without a cloak nine nights out of ten. The only risk to your health is the rocks. So many hoplites or their slaves carry a sort of quilted mattress; other men make piles of grass or branches of trees, but again, you can walk a long way in Greece in midsummer and find neither soft grass nor springy branches. But there's always a fine supply of rock.

So the Greek 'camp' was mostly cooking fires. There were tents: I had one; Aristides had one; Pausanias had one, and so did Adeimantus. Perhaps we had thirty tents. For sixty thousand men, free and slave.

I mention all this so you'll understand how quickly we could shift our camp. By the time we'd offered battle and moved back to the safe side of Asopus Ridge, the fires were lit, and a supply train was just winding down from the main pass by Erythrae.

I was bored, and my spirits were low. I spent too much time thinking of the young men who were dead, and as anger builds anger, I also spent too much time thinking of Briseis, and her apparent desertion. All sorts of wild fantasies entered my head, and I allowed myself to dwell on them.

The supply train coming down the switchbacks from Attica gave me something to watch. There were about five hundred donkeys and mules in that train. One day's grain for the whole army, or a little less.

We needed grain every day.

I looked at them coming down, and noticed that in advancing, we were now eight or ten stades from the base of the pass, and we'd also come a little west, over towards Plataea. A very secure position.

Maybe too secure. We were on a fine high ridge, protected in front and flanks.

And since we had no cavalry, we couldn't cover Erythrae or the opening of the pass behind us.

I chewed on my beard awhile. Brasidas was drilling the survivors of our 'selected men', to whom had been added seventy volunteers from Hermione, and a dozen Ionians, all men who had deserted from the Great King's army or fleet, and all fairly dour. I should have been with them, but I was stewing.

But the supply train worried me. It's one thing to know ground, and another thing to see how an army fits it. We fitted Asopus Ridge like a good pair of greaves. We had a frontage of about four thousand hoplites, as I've said before; something like four thousand paces. That fitted neatly into Asopus Ridge and left us a small *taxeis* to act as a reserve or to watch the flanks in case some daring Mede thought to ride around us.

We fitted, but we were somehow farther from Erythrae than I had anticipated. And instead of confronting the Persians on the road to Thebes, as I had imagined, we were sitting on the very end of the high ground that rolled north from Cithaeron, and the Boeotian plain seemed to mock us with its vastness. Listen, when two Greek poleis fight, they send heralds and agree to a battleground.

No, it's not stupid. It's quick and easy. Saves time, and sweat and stupid marching.

I began to worry that Pausanias was depending too much on Mardonius committing to battle like a Greek.

The donkeys continued to crawl down the switchbacks, and continued to make me think. Every donkey load came from the Peloponnesus. Remember, no harvest had come in Attica for a year; in some parts, two years.

The supplies came from Corinth, which was lukewarm for the war at best, and past Argos, which was Sparta's ancient enemy and had declared for the Great King.

Suddenly I felt cold.

That night we ate well, as a great flock of sheep had been driven over the mountains and was feeding us excellent mutton. I wondered who was paying. And we drank wine I'd brought and ate good bread.

The next day was the seventh that the army had spent in Boeotia, and we were sitting on Asopus Ridge. Pausanias began to sacrifice. He had the seer, Teisemenos, with him, and the seer sacrificed his way through a small flock. Aristides was there, and I decided to join them without invitation.

Teisemenos was one of the best seers I ever saw at work. He was thorough, and quick, and he explained everything as he went, so that attending one of his divinations was like a lesson in divination, and even in the history of divination.

'This is a fine specimen. It is essential, for this sort of thing, that the animal be spotless, in the very peak of health – look at that liver. And look at the blood. Beautiful. Already I feel the confidence that the god wants me to feel. See the flow of the blood, see the jewel-like nature? It does not tell us a thing – except that in its beauty we have a foretaste of the truth we will learn. And let me say, gentlemen, that the blood is running in a single stream. We have not yet opened the main cavity, and already we see that the god respects the subject of our question – the river.'

He flicked his knife expertly down the centre of the chest cavity, flayed back the skin with elegant strokes, and then peeled the skin back himself to spill the intestines. I have seen men use slaves for the messy bits, but not Teisemenos.

'Kidneys perfect in shape. Liver unspotted; no disease. Look at the shape of that; see the lobe? And look at the strands of fat, exactly the shape of Asopus Ridge. See? Everyone look.' He stepped back, his bloody hands still holding the flaps of skin. 'I never accept just one sign from an animal; it wastes the life and the god's effort. So let us look at the contents of the intestines.'

He did this with three kids, all a few months old. His prognostication: 'We should not cross the Asopus by any means.' He looked around, his voice as commanding as if he, not Pausanias, was the general. 'If Mardonius attacks us here, we will be victorious. If we leave this ground to attack, we will be defeated.'

Scoff all you like. I was tempted myself. When you have an army of heavy infantry at the top of a high ridge with the front and flanks covered by ditches and water, you may confidently assert that the army should stay where it is; I would myself, and I don't need to get blood under my nails to make such an assertion.

But the thing is, I saw the lobe on the liver, and the river of blood shaped exactly like the Asopus.

'Will the god tell Mardonius to attack?' I asked.

Teisemenos frowned. 'What an impious idea!' he said. 'Gods don't lie.'

I was tempted to quote Hesiod or Homer. It seemed to me that the gods told lies all the time: Zeus lied to Hera about his infidelity; Ares lied to Hephaestus; Hermes lied to everyone.

Pausanias grinned at me. It was the first thaw in our relationship, I think. 'I'm fine with the god telling Mardonius a few lies,' he said.

Teisemenos spread his hands. 'Mardonius will be destroyed by his own hubris. The god needs no falsity; the man holds his doom within like seeds in an apple.'

I didn't stagger, but *that* was prophecy. Pausanias blinked.

I think Aristides wiped his hand over his brow.

It is sometimes terrifying to meet the *other* and sometimes, it's just a matter of military strategy.

*

That evening I felt better. My taste for war returned, and I knew that we needed to take some action. So I split our *taxeis* into two wings and we went to the ends of the army, carrying only javelins, and slipped across the Asopus while the slaves got water. I was very conscious that the plains on the other side would be full of cavalry, but you don't win by leaving your opponent's outposts undisturbed.

We went up the ridge on the far side, about a thousand paces apart: no armour, no *aspides*, moving fast, like raiders. Brasidas, leading the other column, surprised an outpost and killed or captured a dozen men. My end of the ridge was meant to be occupied; we found a brush screen and an observation point, and on the down slope we found horses, which we took. For some reason, a dozen Paeonian cavalrymen abandoned their horses and their post. Again, I'm sure there's a story there, and I have no idea what it is.

We slipped down the other slope, and every one of us was staggered by the sheer size and opulence of the camp that met our eyes. It was ditched and fortified. Perikles, who was with me, had set himself to count fires. His Ionian friend Anaximandros trotted along, head up like a good hunting dog, counting aloud.

Olympiodorus was the 'leader' of our column. I let him give the orders while I made up scenarios of disaster and solutions as we moved – where to run, where to make a stand. Like most young men, Olympiodorus wanted a fight.

I didn't want a fight. I wanted to know what the hell Mardonius was doing.

Sittonax, without permission, took a horse, mounted, and rode off.

Full dark was falling, and the moon was not light enough for action, and I waved my blue cloak as the withdrawal signal. Brasidas saw it, and we were away, slipping down the ridge again. The ridge had many contours; we vanished into the gullies.

It was sheer luck – good luck, the very favour of the gods – that Mardonius had sent archers to harass our slaves at the river. We saw the arrows and heard the screams in the last light, and our panicked slaves, across the river, broke and ran for the safety of their masters.

I was the first in the long file of half-armed hoplites, and I was three quarters of the way down the ridge on the Persian side of the Asopus, about two hundred paces behind the archers. I could hear them shout, and hear the sound of triumph and the chatter as the archers shouted to each other, taking shots at the fleeing slaves.

'Form your front,' I said quietly.

It's something that I have noticed, that men can be a herd. As the men at the back saw the men at the front forming their line, they simply followed along, almost becoming automata. They didn't need orders. My orders probably only carried to the first ten men, but in fifty heartbeats we were forming.

'Ready to run,' I said. 'Run them down. Rally on my horn call. Pass it down.' I had a hunting horn on my hip, a present from my former father-in-law, a pretty thing dyed red and green.

Still the archers were unaware. It seems impossible, but it is like walking up behind a friend in a foreign town; he doesn't expect you, so why should he look for you?

Those moments are agony, though, when you are in command. Victory is right there, but disaster may be behind those rocks. Is there a covering party? A sentry? If they see us, will they risk some arrows? Most of my people were unarmoured, and had no shields. I hate those moments, and yet I love them. Alive. Never more alive than in the moment before the charge. Everything is so clear, and all the crap falls away, and there you are.

I took a deep breath. I remember thinking that somehow I had landed in a campaign where running was an important military skill, and I was not a great runner.

'Charge,' I snapped. I didn't shout. I knew that as soon as I was off, they'd follow, and they did.

We probably crossed a hundred paces of ground before the archers, focused on their massacre of slaves, noticed us. A few arrows flew, but most went over. Unarmoured, running men are very fast.

And we flowed over the ground like hungry wolves.

I was slow. Men passed me, and more men, and I was practically last.

That suited me. I could watch. I watched the rocks, but they concealed no covering party. I watched the hill behind me, and there, suddenly, was cavalry.

I slowed, watching the cavalry in the dusk. They saw us; they were trying to decide who we were.

The archers were dying. I didn't need to turn my head to know that very few of them were going to escape. Brasidas was yelling for prisoners.

The cavalrymen started down the ridge. There were at least two hundred of them, and they looked to be Persians or Medes.

I ran into the back of a massacre and ran through to the edge of the river. Then I stopped, tried to wind my horn and failed, making a noise like a cow making love. I had to stand in the middle of a battle and slow my breathing. I almost gave up, but I mastered my breathing, and blew.

Heads turned. As luck would have it, most of the killing was done.

I blew again, a long note.

'Cavalry!' I shouted. 'Get over the river!'

I couldn't see Brasidas, as he was five hundred paces distant, but he heard my horn, and his whole wing went over the upper ford, where we'd once fought Simon, and then he turned and ran to us along the 'Greek' bank of the Asopus, safe from the cavalry.

Since Brasidas was safe, my *taxeis* needed no second urging, and we splashed through the ford ourselves.

The cavalry rode down the ridge and the darkness deepened; the shadows had almost become night, and it was too dark for archery. We got across the ford and began to form with the right wing, but the cavalry had already decided that they didn't like the odds; they were drawing rein and slowing. They were Persians, and a few loosed arrows, but, thanks to Apollo, we took no hits. It was full dark, and we were not backlit – a very difficult target across the water.

But now I had a new worry: that they'd charge us when we tried to withdraw. Cavalry is fast; I could still lose a lot of men. This is where war requires constant care. No, forget that – everything in war requires constant care. It is like smithing, or farming; you can't take your eyes off the work.

So, as we were already formed, I had our *taxeis* withdraw by the wings. First one, and then the other, one moving while the other stood. It wasn't fast, but after five or six repetitions, all the file leaders got the manoeuvre, and as soon as they saw the other wing halt, they'd turn and filed off down the interval, so that we moved almost like inchworms: move, halt, move, halt.

Of course, the Persians stayed on their side of the Asopus. But it was a good little manoeuvre, in the face of cavalry, and by the time we made it to the top of Asopus Ridge, we were intimate with it.

That was the evening of the seventh day. The prisoners we took told Pausanias that Mardonius had spent the day making sacrifices to both Greek and Asian gods.

*

The eighth day dawned with an alarm. The Persian horse was crossing at both fords; we had *psiloi* – little men – on the crest of the ridge, watching. So we leapt to arms. My selected men were fast; they were, in fact, becoming the elite body they were supposed to be. We were the first to reach the crest, and what we saw worried me deeply.

Mardonius had split his cavalry into three big blocks. One crossed at the upper ford and went east, not south; they weren't attacking us. They were going around us.

The second crossed at the lower ford and rode west. Towards Plataea.

Only the third, all Saka, crossed and came up the ridge.

Asopus Ridge is only a ridge because Boeotia is so very flat. Itself, it's as tall as six men and the slope is gradual. It's not bad for a horseman; annoying, with scrub and some rocks, but not even steep enough to break a charge or wreck a cavalry formation.

And the Saka didn't care anyway. They were superb horsemen, and they came on like a flooding tide racing over sand. They didn't have formations. They merely rode.

The Saka are the eastern Scythians, from the steppes far north of the Euxine. They ride from birth, and shoot bows better and heavier than Persian bows.

My *taxeis* numbered almost four hundred that morning. We now had some newcomers: twenty men of Elis, too late to be placed in the Peloponnesian phalanx, and some more Plataeans sent by Hermogenes, including my cousin Achilles. Best of all, Sekla sent all the marines from the *Lydia*, so we had Antimenides, son of Alcaeus, and Polymarchos the fight-trainer, and Alexandros, and Ka and his helot archers. Men were saying that there had never been anything like our *taxeis*: men from all over Greece, serving together. I laughed with my dour Ionians, because we'd all been mercenaries and we knew that Greek mercenaries always got along just fine with each other, when they were in Asia.

It was getting along in Greece that made trouble.

At any rate, the Athenians' phalanx was forming and so were the Megarans, now recovered from their first fight, and the Plataeans were coming up the ridge *in order* because Hermogenes was taking no chances. I smiled fondly. He was a very good polemarch, cautious and clever. Perhaps better than I was. I liked that he ordered his phalanx at the base of the ridge, just in case the enemy cavalry came at him. He treated war the way he treated craft. He was going to keep his men alive.

The Saka tried us anyway. One moment, they were a hundred paces away, and the next, they were right in front of us, at a gallop, shooting down into our ranks. I'd already closed up to the *synaspis* or closest order, and still men died; Perikles was suddenly in the front rank, and Sitalkes took an arrow in the leg and was out for the rest of the campaign. I wasn't looking, but the way he tells it, a woman on horseback came right down the line of shields and leaned over her horse's neck and shot down into his leg.

The moment he fell, two young men tried to put their horses into the gap he made falling, but we were at the closest order; the shields overlapped, and Alexandros stabbed one of the horses in the chest with his spear. The line sealed itself and the Saka rode away like a frightened flock of starlings. Ka robbed two Saka of their lives and dropped another as they turned away, all from inside my shield.

The helots got another pair. All told, we put down six of theirs, and captured one, and they killed or wounded four of ours. It seems nothing, except that those seconds of fear wear you down; they hurt us.

They didn't come back, though, and I suspect that they didn't like Ka and his friends, because for the rest of the day, they rode up and down the line. They killed a dozen Corinthians, a pair of men of Hermione, and almost twenty men of Lepreos, way off on the right. The men of Lepreos were unlucky, and some poor bastard flinched, or lost his head, got shot, and in a flash the Saka were into their formation, killing. They had a small *taxeis* and they were formed only a few men deep, and they were wrecked, and broke. The Tegeans had to charge and restore the line.

It was a long, hot day; we didn't have enough water, and all the stupid men without canteens were parched.

See, you just pass that off. Spend a day in the Greek sun without water while Asians on horseback try to kill you. It is miserable. It saps your will.

I sent a file at a time all day for water and just to 'do something'. The file would trot to the rear, drop their *aspides*, and move back down the ridge to camp, and then go to one of the streams for water. We only had fifty files. Sometimes I sent two at a time.

I got a sunburn.

It was wonderful having my marines back; I had someone to talk to all day, without pretending to be the great man or the distant commander. I turned them into the right file of the *taxeis*, so that I had both companionship and security in combat, and when my sons turned up at midday with Sittonax, I made them my own file.

Sittonax, a better scout than any of us, had taken his stolen horse and ridden all the way around the Persian camp, riding away from any patrol that chased him. He had measured the size of the camp and said he thought they had eighty thousand men or a little more, without slaves and women.

My sons had come all the way from Corinth, where Megakles had finally landed, weeks late.

Since we had all day to stand in the sun, and we had ten archers, we also spent the day practising various places for the archers: out front, in the ranks, behind, under shields. It passed the time. Once, when the Saka made a run at the left end of the centre, where the men of a dozen small cities stood, all too proud to form a single phalanx, we turned and trotted out of the line, leaving Hermogenes to cover the gap, and ran two hundred paces to the left and set up on the fly, with the archers standing quite boldly out front to shoot into the flank of the Saka.

But the Saka have been making war for a long time, too. Before the tenth or twelfth arrow was off our bows, the whole herd of Saka were riding out of range. No fools they.

Here's the thing. There were only about three thousand Saka at any time on that ridge. They rode up, shot their arrows, and rode back to camp for a fresh horse and more arrows. There were thirty thousand of us, or more, and we couldn't do a thing to hurt them, except that the Athenians had a corps of archers, and I had eight and the old-fashioned Plataeans had a couple of dozen; the Arcadians and the Aetolians also had some archers. As the day wore on, we sent messages back to camp and got any of the *psiloi* who had slings or bows to join us, and they made quite a difference, because even a few missiles coming back changed the game for the Saka, but all in all, they hurt us and tired us, and we barely scratched them.

It was a long day.

We returned to camp to find dinner cooked, at least for my lot; we ate bean soup, ate bread, and collapsed to sleep. My sunburn annoyed me.

*

The ninth day dawned, and a lot of the fears I had for my army came home to roost.

The first fear, the one I always had, was internal division. A day of getting shot up by the Saka, almost without reply, was enough to hurt morale and start the tongues wagging. I could have predicted it.

The second was that amateurs always want to get war over with, but professionals are patient. Sadly, we were the amateurs, and the Persians and Medes were the professionals. Mardonius was happy to take all summer. On the eighth day, the Saka lost perhaps fifty, and the Greeks, as a whole, about the same. But we stood in our armour all day, and fear causes fatigue. And meanwhile, his cavalry columns roved the countryside to our flanks.

We were in a virtually impregnable position. Mardonius was not going to favour us with a frontal attack.

Instead, he was going to annoy us. And make us do something stupid.

And while we had no water and stood in the sun, his massive corps of infantry sat in the shade and played dice.

His food was coming from Thebes, just forty stades away.

Ours was coming over the mountains from Corinth.

On the other hand, in a grander sense, we were winning as long as we didn't lose. Every day brought us a thousand more hoplites. They were pouring in now, all the small cities were coming, even Aetolians and a few Illyrians. Every city in the Peloponnesus was there, with more men filling the ranks every day; there were even a few men from the east, from Thessaly, Phocaea, and Potidaea. By the time the sun rose on the ninth day, we had a frontage of more like six thousand than four thousand. Asopus Ridge was growing cramped.

And most of the amateurs wanted to attack.

Pausanias held more sacrifices, with the same results. And on the ninth day, the Saka were back, with Bactrians. The Bactrians had a go at the Athenians' phalanx and got shot up badly by the Athenian archers. They chose to break past us, and Ka and his lads emptied more saddles. This raised our morale.

We were no longer in the main line; by then we were in reserve, watching the 'joint' where the Corinthian and Peloponnesian centre met the 'Athenian' left, although that was not what you called it when the Aeginians were listening. We were bored and hot.

Perikles popped up beside me like a toy, Anaxagoras at his heels.

'Why don't we go and loot the bodies?' he said, like the god from the machine in a fancy tragedy.

It was a very popular idea, and I sent all the fastest men to do it while the rest of us covered them. It was no big deal, but it annoyed the surviving Bactrians into coming closer, so that Ka dropped another.

This is hardly pivotal stuff. The war didn't change.

My point is that war can be like this, too. On and on. Little stuff, raids on water, skirmishing. For months. And Greeks are not good at sustained effort.

Regardless, Perikles and his party got a dozen shirts of excellent scale armour off the dead Bactrians, and before the day was much older, ten lucky Thespians had slightly soiled scale shirts. So I guess something did change for them. And it passed the time.

And of course, Brasidas never let up. The enemy was in sight, and we were practising withdrawing the Spartan way, or advancing by files from the centre and reforming, or facing to the right and left, which is, I promise you, no fun with a three foot *aspis* and a nine foot spear. Nor were we the only contingent practising; there were even men running up and down the line.

But some time in the afternoon, disaster struck. The daily grain convoy was coming over the pass from Attica, and the Medes struck out of the brush, a thousand horse against slaves and servants and hoplites walking unarmoured by the donkeys. The Medes butchered the lot and spoiled the grain. They killed five hundred citizen hoplites and another thousand slaves and servants.

And later in the afternoon, there were Saka patrols at every watering area, and we lost more slaves and some hoplites just filling their canteens. Suddenly the Spring of Gargaphia, behind the Corinthians, was the only 'safe' water.

So before dusk, with Aristides' permission, I took my *taxeis* and all the Athenian archers under Leonestes and cleared the bank of the Oinoe. I doubt we killed ten Saka, but we drove them off, and then all the servants could fill canteens.

But there was no grain. And many long faces. We'd lost five hundred citizen hoplites in a matter of moments. It was like being robbed; it made men feel helpless, and helpless men make bad decisions.

And Adeimantus demanded a meeting of the army council.

*

Once again, darkness was falling by the time the army retreated off the ridge. It had been a hard day for the centre, and they'd lost men; our flank was completely safe after the Bactrians learned their lesson; we had the archers, and the enemy didn't want to take the losses to face them.

When we met, Adeimantus spoke first. 'My men are taking all the casualties,' he spat.'Those were Corinthians dying up in the pass, and Corinthians dying to the Saka bows, and Corinthians' slaves butchered at the riverside. I demand that we leave this foolish position. Let us go back to the isthmus, where we have a wall and supplies.'

'Maybe they'd have taken fewer losses if they'd marched on time,' Euryanax said. He wasn't as patient with Adeimantus as Eurybiades had been.

Adeimantus flushed. 'We have a huge army,' he said. 'And we're standing here doing nothing.'

Aristides shook his head. 'We are not doing nothing,' he said. 'We are winning by not losing.'

'Bullshit,' Adeimantus said. He was so angry he was stripped of rhetoric. 'Bullshit. We're standing around dying while the Medes laugh.'

Aristides shook his head. 'Not true. Your men are taking the most casualties because you are amateurs at this, but in time—'

'What?' shrieked Adeimantus. 'You blame brave patriots who died? You say that they are not victims, but that they are responsible for their own deaths?'

Aristides shrugged. 'Yes,' he said. 'If they knew how to make war, they would be alive.'

Pausanias stepped in before there was violence. 'Adeimantus, you must have noticed that neither the Athenians nor the Spartans have taken casualties from the barbarians. They have archers, and experience of dealing with horsemen, or good discipline and better tactics.'

Adeimantus spat. 'Then let them take our ground tomorrow. I say it is because we are on the shallowest part of the hill. Let the brave Plataeans come and take some losses, or the Spartans.'

'Spartans have died,' Pausanias said, dangerously.

Aristides nodded at me. 'We will switch ends of the line,' he said. 'Do it before first light. Imagine the shock of the Saka when they encounter our archers on the right, instead of the left.'

It was agreed, after some more argument. It was clear that the

Tegeans, who had no love for Athenians, disliked the Athenians moving to the right of the line, and thought it was a slur on the whole Peloponnesian League. I think, for Pausanias, it was the compromise that allowed him to hold his ridge another day. Pausanias was convinced – he told me this himself – that if we stood there long enough, hubris would drive Mardonius to attack.

I hoped he was right.

In the darkness we rose, unfed, and marched two thousand paces to occupy the ground of the Tegeans while the Athenians, proud as peacocks, took the ground of the Spartans. The Spartans took our ground, and the Corinthians moved along; the Athenians and their allies had a frontage of about two thousand men, by then, formed eight deep. The Spartans and their *perioikoi*, and the Tegeans, only had a frontage of about fifteen hundred. That nudged the Corinthians off the flat ground and seemed to make them happy.

The Saka came before the sun went high, and they went straight for the position held by the Corinthians.

On the tenth day, that was held by the Plataeans, and they had fifty archers, and in less time than it takes a man to make a case in the law courts, the Saka had ridden off for richer pickings. They roamed off to the right until they'd taken fair losses, and then, with a trumpet call, the whole Athenian end of the line drove forwards and the Saka ran all the way across the Asopus.

It felt like a victory, but of course, it was an insult to the Corinthians. And, of course, the Plataeans didn't lose a man, and neither did the Athenians.

Men shouted for Aristides to lead us across the Asopus, and we saw messengers fly to the rear from the Saka, demanding support, I'll guess.

Instead, we retired back to our starting line, tired but cheered by our little victory. And as soon as we retired, the Saka came back. They ignored us and rode for the other end of the line, where their arrows began to flay the archerless centre. Again. A few dozen Saka went through a gap in the line, rode through our camp killing servants and slaves, and rode away across the Oinoe. And in late afternoon, despite Pausanias' precautions, we lost part of another supply column to the Bactrians.

Victory can be sudden, but defeat is often incremental. As we slipped back to our 'camp' that evening, there was, again, no grain waiting for us, and there were enemy archers on every water source. My men were tired, and the Athenian archers were already running short of shafts, but we swept both streams and made sure that the slaves could get water, but the catastrophe was settling on us. There was almost no food in camp. There wasn't enough water, and tired, hot men with sunburns are touchy and difficult; no water and fear makes it much worse.

We were dying the death of a thousand cuts.

That evening, we heard that Mardonius had sent a herald to the Spartans, a Theban, to insult Pausanias and accuse him of cowardice. And before night fell a messenger came and ordered us to reverse ends of the line again, as we had in the morning, and so once again, listless and without enough food or water, we rose too early and marched back to our original positions.

I asked Aristides to remount the Athenian *hippeis* and flood the ground to our left with *psiloi*, little men with slings and bows. There, in the rough ground that Plataeans never farmed, they could ambush horsemen and we could gain a little breathing space.

It was full morning, and the sun was high. I had food: garlic sausage I carried myself. I was eating one and Aristides was eating a large piece of dried beef, and we were both looking west towards Plataea. My sunburn was so bad by then that my beautiful helmet was hanging from Aten's shoulders, and I was wearing a large red petasus. My face was almost as red as the hat, and Aristides was no better, and neither were most of the men who stood or sat all day in the brilliant sun, helmets tilted back on their heads, watching the Persians from across the river.

There seemed to be a million of them. They moved in mobs; aside from the guard regiments on the right, the rest of them seemed to wander where they would, in clumps, which was perhaps how we looked six stades away, too. But there was all their infantry, which we hadn't seen yet.

I pointed to the west, where there were horsemen all along the Plataean plain. 'Give me the *psiloi* and the *hippeis* and I'll drive them off the hills,' I said.

Aristides looked at it for a long time. 'This is not how men make war,' he said bitterly. 'This is foolishness. Mardonius will not try for us because our position is impregnable. As is his – we cannot attack. Just as the omens say. We should be in a place where we can come to grips and reach an end.'

I shook my head. 'We are at grips,' I said. 'Mardonius has found a way of bringing us to our end.'

'This? These raids by barbarian auxiliaries?' Aristides actually spat in disgust. 'You want me to send the very flower of Athenian youth, our richest men, to clear some broken ground of these . . . these Saka?'

I shrugged. 'Yes. Or perhaps it is time for Athens to have some cavalry who are not so politically important. Zeus, Aristides, if the Persians cut us off from food another day, the Corinthians will begin to slip away. At least the Corinthians. We need to occupy the ground between the army and the passes. Or choose a pass and cover it.'

I'll remind you that there were three passes over Cithaeron: one comes down at Erythrae and is the best; one comes down behind Hysiae and is the worst; and one, seldom used because of its length, comes in above Plataea. I had a notion that if we could control the ground around the Hero's tomb, where Idomeneaus had been priest, and Calchas, that we'd have access to food and reinforcements.

Aristides tugged at his beard. 'No,' he said finally. 'I cannot risk the whole cavalry class under a Plataean. It is a political problem, my friend. There is no Athenian who understands what needs to be done in that difficult ground; it would take a social miracle to make the little people co-operate with the aristocrats, and none of them would take your orders.'

'Cleitus,' I said.

Aristides looked at me. 'Yes, he might do it.'

'Send him in command. I'll back him,' I said.

Aristides smiled. 'Sometimes, we Greeks are great men. So you and Cleitus have actually buried your swords? You please me. But Cleitus is not Hipparchos, and . . .'

I grunted. Please don't imagine, friends, from my frequent criticisms of the Spartans, that I thought more highly of the Athenians. Politics ruled them; it was a miracle they had an army in the field at all.

So we took no action. We sat in the sun; priests made sacrifices from our dwindling supply of live animals, and Mardonius' cavalry crossed the Asopus for the third day in a row and attacked. That attacks were desultory; the Saka were used up. We were not the only ones suffering, and I suspected that the enemy had arrow supply problems. If you are a barbarian horse archer, how many quivers of arrows do you bring on campaign? Two? Three? And these men had been away from home for more than a year.

But as the sun began to slant down, the enemy struck. There were shouts behind us, and the Medes, a thousand strong, burst into the rear of our camp and began slaughtering our servants.

I didn't wait for orders. I sounded my horn and my *taxeis* turned and filed off, and we began to trot towards the camp.

We were two thirds of the way down the back of Asopus Ridge when the Persian cavalry went for the spring at Gargaphia. The attack on the camp had been a distraction; I should have known, because Mardonius had a pattern of using Persians for anything that mattered, a pattern that showed that his army had problems too.

I was already way down the southern slope of the ridge, and I could plainly see the Persian cavalry killing water carriers and slaves around the spring. But the worst of it was that even as I watched, they dismounted and began to foul the water; they had bags of excrement and dead, rotted animals which they threw in, polluting the stream and the spring.

I had four hundred hoplites and they had twice my numbers and more in cavalry, but loss of that spring might doom my army. I had to try, and Brasidas thought the same, as did the whole right file of marines. I sent Aten running for the Athenian archer corps and Leonestes, and we wheeled to the right at a trot and I sent my half files forwards and then spread out the order. That was to move faster; it was also because, fearsome as the Persians were, I'd had days of fighting cavalry and I was no longer as impressed as I had been.

Then we all trotted forwards.

The Persians stopped fouling the stream and took us seriously, and before I'd spread my files, they were all mounted. Many of them had bows, and arrows began to drop at us, but most of them simply formed two big squadrons.

We were uphill of them on a big slope with clumps of brush and rocks. It was not ideal cavalry country.

'When I sound the horn, close on the centre, rear rank turn and face the rear,' I said. One of the many things we'd practised over the last four days.

Four and fifty hundred men, only three deep, at half file intervals, take up a great deal of space: almost as much as the whole front of the Athenians' phalanx, for example. And by jogging at them, we deprived them of time to make careful plans; to envelop our flanks, for example. The Persian officer had about fifty heartbeats to do something, and then my spear was going to be in his throat.

They still didn't take the Greeks seriously as soldiers.

The left hand squadron charged.

They were good horsemen on good horses, but they'd been out every day for ten days, and they'd been in a dozen small fights and one big one, and it was late afternoon. They hadn't watered their horses before they fouled the spring; a foolish error, or maybe the officer thought he didn't have time.

War's result often turns on things like having watered horses.

They came for us, but it was not a determined rush. They came on at a trot and no more, and they were coming uphill.

I allowed my *taxeis* to run at them for almost twenty paces.

I learned a great deal in those twenty paces.

I put my horn to my lips and blew.

The *taxeis* closed to the centre. It's easy – you just shuffle. It's also what you want to do, when half a thousand Persian horses are trotting at you. Our open line, three deep and three hundred paces across, suddenly became three solid ranks only fifty paces across, and the Persians couldn't duplicate the effort. Half of them were left with nothing but a ride across the scrubby hill, at least until they decided to swing into our rear.

Our rear rank turned around. By hoplite standards, this was pitiful: two deep, the third facing the wrong way.

I was *almost* confident that the Persian cavalry was too tired to beat us.

And again, Ka and his archers were the margin of victory. As soon as his heavy, well-aimed arrows began to knock men down, the Persians shied away. I doubt that Ka and his boys got six Persians, but they lost interest, and most of them turned uphill to get away.

Four hundred Athenian archers rose from the brush. They loosed one great flight of arrows and did five days' worth of casualties to the Persians. Where Ka took six lives, they took fifty. The Persian cavalry broke and fled.

A tired horse foundered. I saw it happen and knew I had been right. The Persian horses were too tired for this.

'Heads up!' I called. 'We're going to pursue the broken horse. Rear rank, face the front. Hello!' – the last for some Athenian boy who wasn't listening.

My heart was beating hard. I was painfully aware that the last time I'd ordered a charge against cavalry, I'd lost a lot of young men.

'Ready to move!' I called. 'Spread out as we go. Shake out. Let's go!' I called.

Of course, nowadays there are commands for all this complex tactical manoeuvre. An Arcadian has written a book. But back then, we were inventing it. Remember that my father and Brasidas' father had simply stood in a phalanx and moved forwards to the playing of flutes – sometimes a 'phalanx' that looked like a mob, with little men in the ranks, archers and slingers and men without an *aspis*.

Now we were trying to outmanoeuvre cavalry.

We didn't charge. We moved forwards at a slow jog, and as we ran, the files expanded to cover our former frontage. It was well done, but ineffectual; we couldn't catch even tired horses, and as we jogged I saw that my people were as tired as the Persians. Not enough sleep, not enough water.

The other Persian squadron should have covered the first. Instead, I saw an officer, covered in gold, turn tail and run, and most of his squadron followed him.

A clump of men stayed to cover the rout. They had bows, and they knew how to use them; nobles. Styges took an arrow that went right through his *aspis*, and ripped a piece of skin from his arm.

I could see that one of the men was Cyrus, and another was Aryanam, who I hadn't seen in years, which made the third man almost certainly Darius: my three Persian friends. I assumed that they must be in Artaphernes' bodyguard. They turned to ride away, loosing back at us, the last three men still fighting.

Ka dropped Aryanam's horse; a magnificent shot. The horse fell slowly, collapsing from a canter and spilling Aryanam on the hard ground.

Men began to run forwards to finish him and strip the corpse.

Cyrus turned his horse – one Persian against four hundred Greeks. He looked magnificent; his silk robe flew behind him like scarlet wings, and he came back, guiding his horse with his knees.

Darius turned his horse the other way.

His bow came up.

Cyrus loosed the arrow – at me. We were forty paces apart; he knew perfectly well who I was. His arrow hit my *aspis* as hard as a strong man's spear would hit, and ripped out the *antelabe*, where there are heavy bronze washers decorated with Gorgons' heads, and my left hand was full of splinters of oak from the rim.

Darius coaxed his charger to half-rear and he loosed his arrow.

One of my Athenian boys, running full out for Aryanam, took the arrow on his *aspis*. It went right through, and into his arm, and he fell to his knees. Other men stopped running, or flinched, or went to help the boy who had taken the shaft.

Aryanam rose to his feet out of the sand.

A dozen Athenian arrows fell around the Persians, but Apollo withheld his hand and they were not hit.

Cyrus dropped his strung bow into the long *gorytos-quiver* on his hip, backed his horse expertly with his knees, and reached out a hand to his friend. Aryanam took it and the horse turned, pivoting, it seemed, on the man on the ground, and in an instant he was up and mounted behind Cyrus.

Ka raised his bow.

Darius interposed his horse between us and the man getting remounted.

I tapped Ka's bow with my spear, and he shrugged.

Last Persian on the field, Cyrus turned his horse and raised an arm in salute, and hundreds of Greek hoplites shouted their admiration. He'd rescued his comrade in full view of us, under the fire of four hundred archers. We are not barbarians. We honour great courage. Even when our homes are burned and we have no water.

I am still proud that we cheered. And proud, too, that Cyrus and Aryanam and Darius were my friends. And enemies.

We won that exchange, and indeed, as you will hear, it was not unimportant. But we'd lost the spring.

Pausanias summoned the council. He publicly praised me, and Aristides, and the *thetes* class archers; perhaps the first time a Spartiate found reason to praise a lower class Athenian. The archers' officer, Leonestes, was invited to attend the meetings.

I don't mean to wax eloquent about Athenian democracy, but in a year of naval victories, no one had ever invited a master oarsmen to discuss strategy. Those Athenian archers did a great deal for the political rights of the little men.

But we'd lost the spring. That night, the twelfth in Boeotia, we had very little food, and insufficient water.

We had the usual exchanges: Adeimantus demanded that we retreat to the isthmus, and almost everyone found something nasty to say about his neighbours.

When the carping died down, Aristides raised his hand for silence.

'We need a constant water supply,' he admitted. 'The Persians may have done us a favour.'

No one else thought so, and there were catcalls.

'We haven't had enough water in four days. We need a constant water supply, and we need our supplies. There are almost three thousand more hoplites over the mountains at Oinoe in Attica, waiting to come to us, and there are two big donkey trains, afraid to cross the passes after the last massacre. I propose—'

He had to shout to make himself heard.

'I propose that we shift our ground to the left, so that we can water from the Oeroe and anchor our flanks on the acropolis of Plataea on the left and the "island" on the right. We will then control the Plataean head of the pass.' He looked at me. It was my idea, after all.

Well, it was my information, at any rate.

Pausanias shook his head. 'We cannot retreat,' he said. He was a deeply frustrated man, and he wanted his battle, and he couldn't really believe that his allies were so useless that they didn't have canteens.

Patiently, Aristides said, 'This is not retreat. We are moving sideways.'

Pausanias frowned. 'Our position here is impregnable.'

'As long as the army requires neither water nor food,' spat Adeimantus.

Pausanias looked at the Corinthian. 'You are in favour of this movement?' he asked.

Adeimantus shrugged. 'I am in favour of withdrawing to the isthmus and leaving the Athenians to make their own peace with Mardonius. Saving that, I'm in favour of moving to the left to have a source of supply. And retreat. Right now, if Mardonius attacks, we have nowhere to run.'

Pausanias looked at him. 'That is a virtue,' he said. 'I do not intend that any Greek will run.'

Adeimantus played with his beard. I disliked him; I think he was a Persian cat's-paw. But sometimes he was just another Greek politician, and that was one time.

No one wants to say, 'My contingent will fold at the first sign of a strong wind.' But he was looking for a way to say it.

I had a sudden view of our army from the other side. Their cavalry had come at us for days, and had tested each contingent. Of course, if it came to a fight, Mardonius knew just who to attack. And of course, the Corinthians and the smaller Peloponnesian cities were the worst soldiers, with the fewest canteens and the smallest food supplies, too. Inexperience magnifies error. You can quote me on that.

'I fear what will happen in the centre, if my people do not have food, water, and a little hope,' he said.

Those may not seem like strong words, but they were.

Pausanias turned away to hide his face.

Aristides decided to wrestle the bull, as we say in Plataea. 'The Persians will not attack here,' he said. 'We need to admit this. And they have found a way to wear us down. They are not Greeks. I have learned this, finally. They are not Greeks. They do not need a decisive battle. They will be fully satisfied if we collapse in the heat, and they enslave us.'

Men spat, and others muttered. The giant Spartan, Amompharetos, groaned. 'Are they cowards?' he muttered. 'Don't they want to fight? And yet I hear there are brave men amongst them.'

Aristides shook his head. 'They are a race of slaves,' he said.

I thought of Cyrus, and smiled grimly.

'I do not mean that they are cowards; merely that when ordered, they obey, and that obedience is their virtue,' Aristides said. 'They will come and skirmish every day, foul our water, deny us food, slaughter pack animals, and account these deeds of war.'

Amompharetos shook his head. 'War is when men fight hand to hand, and the better defeats the lesser,' he insisted.

I stepped forwards. 'War is when men cease to talk, and use force to accomplish their ends,' I said. 'But any force is a force of war. You speak as a Greek speaks, but these are Persians. Why would they make war like Greeks? This is how they have conquered the world. We cannot even conquer each other.'

'Why would we want to conquer?' Pausanias asked. 'I have no need of the Persian king's crown.'

'Yet in this case, we fight for our own freedom, and perhaps the freedom of Ionians and all the Greeks. Maybe even the Thebans and the men of Argos.' Aristides looked at them all in the firelight. 'We do not have to make war as they do, but we are fools if we do not appreciate *how* they make war. Mardonius does not intend to offer battle. He intends to break us with harassment and denial of food and water. We must move to a position that guarantees both.'

I stepped forwards again. 'We are not alone in having problems,'

I said. 'His cavalry is exhausted. They have taken steady casualties; they have shot most of their arrows. His army is vast and it must be difficult to feed. And we have held him fixed in place for twelve days. Do not imagine that the Persians do everything well. If we hold on long enough, Mardonius will have to attack us. Or cede us Boeotia and Thebes, and we win. Because if they abandon Thebes, they have no supplies in Greece. They must retreat all the way to Thessaly, and the war is over for the year.'

Now, I swear I hadn't planned to say those words, and I felt like Odysseus, with Athena standing whispering honeyed words in my ears.

I could tell, just looking around, that half the officers of the army had never considered why Mardonius might have to fight. Think of it one more time, friends; we were Greeks. We agreed on a date and place for a fight, we went there, and we fought. This was all new to us: strategy, and deception, and attacks on supplies. Those of us who were pirates had a much better idea of how to fight this war than the honourable gentlemen of Sparta.

Cimon stepped up after several Peloponnesians had spoken, mostly to hear themselves.

'Friends,' he said. 'Is there any man here who doubts that, given food and water, this army can stand against the Persians all summer?'

If there were men with doubts, no one mentioned them.

Cimon shrugged rhetorically. 'Then let us go where there is food and water, make our stand, and let the gods decide.'

It was the best speech of the night.

Pausanias had listened. It was, perhaps, the best reason to have Spartan commanders; they listened. They were used to listening to ephors and assemblies; they rarely lost their tempers. At some point in the debate, Pausanias changed his mind, a remarkable thing for any commander or any man, really, in a position of power.

'Very well,' he said. 'We will move tomorrow night, after the sun sets in the west. The centre will march off first; the Athenians will file off from the left and make their way to Plataea, and the right wing will be the rearguard, moving off last and covering the movement.' He looked around. 'Once the centre has set on its new positions, Adeimantus will take the Corinthians up the pass behind our new position, make contact with the supply trains, and guard them back into our new camp. Is this agreeable to all?'

Hermogenes stepped forwards into the firelight. 'The Plataeans know that ground and those trails,' he said. 'It might save time to send them.'

Pausanias shook his head. 'If you can spare some guides,' he said politely. 'But your phalanx will be too far to the left of the pass to allow you to march back and forth. The Corinthians will be right there.'

Hermogenes looked at me. Aristides looked at me.

I had no idea what either was trying to tell me. So I raised my eyebrows.

Hermogenes frowned. 'I'll send guides to you, Adeimantus,' he said.

The Corinthian bowed. 'I'll treat them like my own sons,' he said.

Amompharetos shook his head. 'I am against it. It appears we are retreating. I say no.'

Pausanias frowned. 'Your protest is noted.'

Amompharetos shook his head. 'You don't get it, do you, Pausanias? You are not a king, nor yet my superior. I say *no*. I say, let's go and get them. I want to talk about attacking.'

Adeimantus rolled his eyes. 'Zeus Soter,' he said aloud.

For the first time in my life, I agreed with Adeimantus of Corinth.

The thirteenth day dawned with the same bright, cloudless sky we'd had for the last twelve, and with the sun came the cavalry, like a plague of midges. I'd like to say it was their most determined effort yet. I know that Pausanias thought this might be the precursor to his battle, because I ran – and walked – all the way to his end of the line to obtain permission to go down the back slope and lay an ambush for the cavalry. Aristides was against it; he was set on surviving the day so that we could make our movement, and I was set on my notion that the 'little war' as we called it, the patrolling and skirmishing and attacking water carriers, needed to be prosecuted every day. It was like a good spear fight: you want to get the initiative and keep it, not let your enemy throw lightning fast blows with complex deceptions at you. If you do that, eventually he hits you.

So I left the *taxeis* with Brasidas, ran to the other end of the line, and found the Spartans' leaders all clumped around Pausanias and his seer. They were sacrificing. Pausanias insisted that he saw signs that this was the day, in bird flights and in entrails.

Teisemenos disagreed. 'If anything,' he said, 'it is tomorrow or the next day.' He smiled at me. 'What do you think, Plataean?' he asked. 'Have you made sacrifices today?'

I was embarrassed to admit I had not. I hardly ever do. It is different at sea; there just aren't enough sheep to keep killing them. I'm not in the habit.

But under the great seer's direct instruction, I took a goat, cut its throat, and let the blood flow into a bowl, opened its intestines like a priest, and read them.

Ah, I should not tell you this.

I am a pious man. And I worship my ancestor Heracles, a great hero who seldom thought his way out of a problem. But my favourite hero at Troy was Odysseus, and I confess that it came to me before that goat died that I could use the sacrifice to influence Pausanias.

So I told him what I wanted him to hear. The goat was unremarkable, as far as I could see, but I told him a fine tale of a battle two or three days hence, and of the need to meet the Persian cavalry in the field with our *psiloi*.

He tugged at his beard.

Teisemenos leaned over my hands, looking at my animal's intestines. He called for a slave and water, poured some over the liver, and then washed his hands. Then he washed mine, as if I was a great priest.

'Aristides is your teacher?' he asked.

'Yes,' I said.

'And you learned divination from Heraclitus?' the seer asked.

I agreed. 'A little, master.'

He ordered the slave to burn the corpse of my animal. 'Your reading is excellent,' he said. He turned to Pausanias. 'It is as I said; I am interested that the Plataean sees so much detail about the little men, but this is in accord with the grains of fat on the first liver. Perhaps they were the "little men".'

I felt shame then, and some confusion. Had I made it up? Or was the divination accurate, and some god had put the words in my mind?

And yet, hubris or not, I was sure I was right. I remembered the day before Marathon. We needed to brush the Persians back.

Pausanias stood there, the very image of martial splendour. His armour was completely plain, unadorned, and yet superb. His *aspis* had only the head of a bull; his helmet was almost severe in its plainness. In fact, I looked like a fop by comparison.

He didn't tug at his beard, or talk to himself. He glanced at an eagle, that rose on an updraught over Leuctra to our right.

'Zeus himself says you have the right of it,' he said, and smiled. 'You know, Arimnestos, I'd like to go off to the left with a handful of my friends and some helots and do as you say. I'm tired of sitting here, sacrificing, while you and Aristides win the laurels day after day.'

I grinned back at him. 'So go down by the Spring of Demeter with your helots and do the same.'

He looked at Euryanax. And then back at me. 'I think I will, he said. 'I long to bloody my spear, even in this little war.'

'It's not little war,' I said to the Spartans. 'It is more like hunting. Hunting men.'

Pausanias blinked when my words hit him, and his answering smile bode ill for the Persians. 'I like that, Plataean,' he said. 'Hunting men. You speak well.'

And for the first time, the word 'Plataean' didn't sound like an insult.

So, as the sun crossed the middle of the sky, I took half the archers led by Leonestes, who remembered the day before Marathon as well as I, and hundreds of the bravest of our servants and slaves, and my own men, down into the broken ground to the left.

It was ironic, in a way, that we went off to fight on the very ground where, as a boy, my brother and I had played war. How often had I pretended to be Achilles, or died as Hector, there in those folds of ground, the brush covered hills?

By the time we came off Asopus Ridge to the lower ground, there were thousands of enemy horsemen riding against the main army, and they came on in dribs and drabs from across the river, shot some arrows, threw a javelin or two, and rode away. The Saka came again; there were Persians and Paeonians and Medes.

In fact, all their good cavalry was trying to pin the Greek army in place.

Which left the poorer cavalry on the worst horses and with the lowest will to fight, prowling the flanks.

I retired well behind the fouled Spring of Gargaphia, almost four stades back, almost to where Myron's farms were below Hysiae. There was method to my madness. I didn't want the Persians on the ridge to see my movement, and I wanted my *psiloi* to gain confidence early with some easy victory.

We halted by an old mound of stone west of Hysiae and I formed all my people in a long line. I knew the little men wouldn't stay in my line, but it wanted them to have a fair start, and I lined them up on the road from Hysiae to Plataea. I took my time. I could see the dust clouds over Asopus Ridge; I knew that men were fighting there, but I didn't think that the centre would crack today. And the little men deserved some attention. They were mostly Athenian slaves, and free men too poor to serve even as archers. Some were excited to make war, and some fearful, and some clearly wanted to be elsewhere. Like all men in war.

Styges ranged the ranks, and Brasidas, while our men rested in the oak trees at the base of Cithaeron, the first shade they'd seen in days, and by a good well. Men drank, and pissed, and drank, and pissed.

I gave the same speech three times.

'Hello, lads!' I said. 'I'm Arimnestos of Plataea. We're going to walk from here to the Asopus river, and we're going to drive the Persians like cattle. Don't worry that you only have a sling. Use it. Cover each other. If the horsemen come for you, run into the rocks, or jump over a wall. Or, if it looks bad, come and get in under our spears. We'll have a little phalanx right in the centre, and there's no cavalry out there that can take us. Right? Otherwise, walk forwards, shout, and throw rocks. Remember that the Persians wear gold necklaces. Don't forget to strip their dead. And share!'

With this little appeal to greed, I ended my battlefield speech.

Like I say, I gave it three times.

Altogether, my little men and I took up almost a thousand paces in a very loose order, with the Select Men or *Epilektoi*, as we now called ourselves, in the centre. We had the Athenian archers with us, a little block to either side. We practised – once – having the archers roll in under our spears. There was a lot of cursing as the archers dumped their quivers on the ground, but we all agreed that it would work. At least once.

And then we set off to the horn call. Brasidas took Sittonax and several other men and went all the way to the left end of the line, and my sons took a horn and a coloured streamer on a spear and went to the right end of the line, and we went forwards.

It was a nightmare as long as I worried about the line being straight. It was anything but straight. It was more like a moving whip. I was ready to disown Hipponax for his stop-start movements at the right of the line, and I had no idea why he couldn't just walk forwards.

We emerged from the vines and olive groves on the slopes of Cithaeron along Myron's farm road, and there were the Lydian cavalry. The surprise was complete, and mutual.

The Athenians started to drop shafts on them.

The Lydians were not horse archers. Fine horsemen, but more given to riding people down with lances. We caught them setting fire to Myron's barns. I can't even say how many there were ... Three hundred? Five hundred? And there, again, was Artaphernes in purple, with his little troop of Persian bodyguards; *He must now*, I thought, *be satrap of Lydia like his father before him*.

My slovenly line rolled forwards to the old farm wall. I'm sure that at Brasidas' end of the line, they had no idea what was happening. But at our end, and in the centre, we all stopped at the ancient stone wall, and the slings started to snap and whoosh and crack.

And that was that. The Lydians never got formed, and never even tried a charge – over broken ground, against slingers behind a wall ... Suicide. They turned and flowed away.

Without any horn calls, the little men shrieked their joy, jumped the wall, and went to loot the corpses. Nor did they seem so little.

We moved down the ridges, and the line vanished and was never recovered. Men moved in clumps with their mates, and it all became very personal. An archer would climb over a ridge, see a cavalryman, and loose; twenty paces to his right, another enemy would throw a javelin and ride away. But even as it was deadly, it was too dispersed for the ruthless arithmetic of morale. Men might run, but they'd come back; little pockets of enemy resistance would, if they held too long, be surrounded and extinguished. I pulled the *Epilektoi* out of the line and used them to finish any of the barbarians and foreigners who made a stand, but as the afternoon wore on, it was clear that this *was* like hunting, and the *psiloi* could do it without direction. And on the other hand, the fearsome enemy cavalry seemed listless; they had orders to prowl and burn, but no plan to stand and fight, and long before the sun set, we crossed the Oeroe onto the great plain of Boeotia.

Now there was no cover.

And five stades to the Asopus river.

I halted them. We all drank water, looked at the ground; this was the ground I would occupy that night, and I wanted to see it, although, by turning my head, I could see our family farm to the left rear. I was home.

I was fighting for my life, in a war with barbarians, on the fields of my home.

And I thought that when we passed the Sanctuary of Hera, where there had once been a statue of my mother, before the Thebans smashed it.

It felt like play. And like a bad dream.

But let me say: in my head, I had made war here from childhood. I *knew* every fold in the ground. Every rock, every clump of trees.

We drank water from the Oeroe, and I was happy to see that there was plenty of flow, since the whole Greek army was planning to water here.

I watched the retreating enemy cavalry – Indians, Lydians, Bactrians, and many others I could not recognize at all. They were spread in clumps across the plain. Now, the Oeroe runs not east–west but at a sort of diagonal, and so it faces Asopus Ridge, and we had what Plataeans call Sanctuary Ridge behind us.

My point is that we now covered the flank of Asopus Ridge. We were behind the cavalry, who were trying to annoy the Athenians at the left end of the line.

I let my lads drink water, and I had a brief look under my hand, and Brasidas came, and Styges and Leukas, and Polymarchos, who was certainly doing the duty of an officer by then, roaming around, helping men over streams and pointing out targets. Any man who can train other men to have good bodies, or for the Games, can lead soldiers.

'I want to push on to the next stream bed,' I said. 'The Nesos will be empty, but my hunch is that these gentlemen,' I pointed at the clumps of retreating cavalry, 'won't be coming back to trouble us.'

Brasidas was burned red as a beet. 'I offered a drachma for a man's straw hat,' he said, and drank some water. 'He said no.' He shrugged. 'I agree. Push as far as you can. Anything we can do to make the barbarians *feel* beaten will only help us later.' He looked at distant Asopus Ridge, where the dust clouds, the rage of Ares, rose. 'If I were Pausanias, I'd say that these little men are no loss.'

I narrowed my eyes.

He made a wry face. 'But I'm a Plataean now, and I know the value of little men,' he said. 'So let's keep them alive, and hunt more barbarians.'

I couldn't tell whether he meant it or not, but Polymarchos agreed, although he suggested that we pull together more and reform the line. So we did. It was a little cooler; the hour of the day when a lazy man goes to the agora for a cup of wine.

The Plain of Boeotia was innocent of horsemen. The Lydians and the Indians had gone back over the Asopus.

We began to cover the ground towards the foot of Asopus Ridge, heading north and east. Our line was still eight hundred paces long: a net to catch game.

I can only assume that the communications among the barbarian cavalry were so poor that no one told the Medes on the right of our line that their Lydians and Bactrians were gone. We didn't quite catch them; we were too slow and too damned tired. But we scared them, and the Athenian archers dropped a dozen, and they had to run. And then we went across the dry gully of the Apotrisa stream and up the back of the ridge, almost to the point from where we'd started. The Athenian hoplites cheered us, and we found that all told, there were almost a hundred dead Mede cavalry there on the ground; we'd killed a few, the hoplites had killed a few, and the Athenian archers had done the rest. They'd wounded or killed about half as many Athenians. We'd cleared the whole of the ground between the army and Plataea, and we had not lost a single man. My *psiloi* were tired – bone-tired.

But for the first time in ten days, we owned the ground. And Pausanias had done the same off to the right: some of his helots had got over-bold and been chewed on, but for the most part, he'd pushed the barbarians off his flanks.

The army had taken casualties all along the front. The left wing was in good shape; they'd had archers, and at the end of the day, our little action had trapped a handful of Medes – small stuff, but good for morale, and as Brasidas kept saying to anyone who would listen, morale was the thing we were fighting for.

But when I walked to the right to report to Pausanias, I saw how bad the centre was. They had borne the brunt all day, and without archers or *psiloi*, on the highest ground, the farthest from water. Listen, I hold a grudge as well as the next man, but the Peloponnesians had had days of dust and blood. They were exhausted. Many were so dehydrated that they just went to sleep. They looked, and moved, like old men.

By contrast, the Spartans looked as if they were going to a party. When I came up behind their place in the line, most of them were combing their hair, while their helots fetched them water. Those same helots had spent the day scouring Long Ridge against enemy cavalry, but this somehow made them feel like men. Not that complicated. However much they hated their masters, they had been allowed to fight, and done well.

I reported to Euryanax, because Pausanias was still off on the far right.

He heard me out.

'We march at the start of the second watch,' he said. 'I'm glad you cleared the ground; my worst fear is that the bloody Corinthians sleepwalk in single file into the Persian cavalry.'

'They are in poor shape,' I said.

'Why do you think Pausanias is sending them back over the pass to get the supplies?' Euryanax said. 'There are many worthy men in the centre, but if we had to fight tomorrow, they would give way, and we would be defeated. Better that we fight without them.'

'Give them food and wine and water and they will fight,' I said.

Euryanax shrugged. 'Defeat is a worm,' he said. 'Once it crawls into the apple, it is very difficult to get it out.' He looked at the empty ridge across the river. From behind it rose the smoke of the Persian cooking fires. 'Sparta has never been defeated, so we have no worms.'

I had, in fact, been present when an Athenian army had defeated the Spartans. But there are times to tell men what you know, and times to stay silent.

'Second watch,' I said, saluting.

'Second watch,' he said.

There was little enough to eat, and drink: no wine, and little water. Most men lay down with their *aspides* by them and their spears stacked nearby; we were only going to have two hours of sleep at best.

Myron sent a dozen older Plataeans, men who should never have been in the phalanx at all, like Hilarion, to be the guides for the Corinthians. I sent Aten. He knew nothing of the local terrain, but I directed him to find me a donkey load of wine, and buy it. Two, if he could. I was determined that my lads would have wine.

The poor *psiloi*, who had walked and fought all day, had to move first, too; we needed to get what little camp gear we had clear before the phalanxes began their move. There was real fear that the barbarian cavalry would go for us in the darkness.

I didn't share it. I'm proud to say I slept like a damp log and awoke to find Gelon, my former slave, walking towards me.

'I polished your armour, you bastard,' he said.

I laughed.

He gave me a sip of wine, which was like ambrosia.

'We won't fight today,' I said. 'You wasted all that pumice.'

'Bet,' said Gelon.

'Fifty gold darics,' I said. I had a good deal more experience of war than Gelon, and I knew the drill. The barbarians were as tired as well, and, in effect, we were about to break contact. By the time Mardonius found us again, it'd be a whole new war.

Gelon shook his head. 'Fine. You're right. I take back my bet. I'd be broken by fifty darics.'

'Broken?' I laughed. 'You mean, more broken? Than owning a burned farm that's occupied by the enemy?'

We both laughed. See? The humour of the soldier. However bad it is, there's something worse, and you can always mock your own pain.

So I put on my armour. It hurt. I mean, the greatest smith of my generation made my panoply, and it fits me like a second skin. But there are always points that cut or burn: the shoulders where the bronze rests on the neck muscles; the hips; the insteps where the greaves, no matter how well made, rest; the top of your calf muscles; the left shoulder where your *aspis* rests, even with an arm piece.

But Aten was gone, so I put it all on, even the thigh pieces. Otherwise, I was going to leave them on the ground.

Gelon had even combed out my crest, which was the act of a true friend.

The moon was just rising when the Athenian phalanx stepped off. They went by file pairs from the left of the phalanx, so that the leftmost pair of files walked forwards and then turned hard to the left and walked down the western end of Asopus Ridge and headed out onto the moonlit plain, walking back almost exactly along the route my *psiloi* had taken in late afternoon to reach the ridge and trap a few Medes. The Athenian archers were long gone; they moved first, because they were terribly vulnerable at night.

My *Epilektoi* were last. We watched the Athenians file off, and then the Plataeans, and then the Megarans, and the Aeginians. The whole wing was moving, in two incredibly long files like black threads drawn across the plains.

I had my *taxeis* formed in open order, the men kneeling behind their *aspides*. They were proud, by now; proud to be last off the ridge, and aware that it was an honour.

I listened to them complain; mocking the enemy, griping about the slowness of the centre's withdrawal, mocking a Thespian who'd lost his knife in the darkness and kept moaning about it.

Soldiers.

I walked back over the ridge to watch the Corinthians and I didn't like what I saw. They weren't filing off, but moving by contingent, in clumps, and there was quite a mob of them. In fact, they had all jammed up by the Spring of Gargaphia, and I didn't feel right about leaving the ridge top. A hundred Persian cavalry would panic the lot of them.

And in fact, they looked like a rout, not a withdrawal. Already.

It was hard to see over the centre of the ridge to the Spartan end of the line. But it seemed to me that they were still there. I kept walking that way, and then hesitating. It was five stades to the Spartan end of the line; I could waste a lot of time going there, my legs hurt already, and I had a journey of my own to make.

But it certainly looked as if the Spartans were still in place on Asopus Ridge, while their Athenian allies marched away to the left and the centre fled as if pursued.

And that meant disaster.

I love to tell you, my daughter, how brave and clever I was, and I do not really love to tell you when I was foolish or weak. I never wanted to tell the tale of Lydia; and it pains me to say that I stood in total indecision atop Asopus Ridge, in the moonlight, for as much as an hour, because my legs ached, and I didn't want to walk four stades to the Spartans and four stades back.

And do you know what else I didn't want?

The responsibility.

Here's something they don't mention to you, when you want to be a hero. They don't tell you that once you start that walk, once you go over to check on the Spartans, or you run at the Persian archers – in the eyes of other men, you have accepted responsibility. Remember Eualcidas? I went back for his body. As soon as I said that I would go, every other man accepted that I would do it or die trying.

Let me try this again. If I was right, and the Spartans were still standing there, an hour after they should have marched, something terrible had happened.

And if I went and found out about it ...

I would have to help fix it.

Listen, honey. Cowardice is merely fatigue and hunger. Cowardice isn't some poor bastard who flinches at the spear because he fears death. Cowardice is when you don't want to do the thing that obviously has to be done, because your legs are tired, your sunburn hurts, and you are tired of nursemaiding. I stood there in the moonlight and I cursed like an ephebe, because I knew something was wrong, and I really wanted someone else to appear – Aristides, preferably – and fix it.

I stood by myself for so long that Brasidas came.

'Something is wrong?' he asked. 'We should march.'

I pointed off to the right. 'Doesn't it seem to you that the Lacedaemonian phalanx is still there?' I asked.

I waited, begging the gods to have reliable Brasidas tell me that I was full of old rope. It was dark; moonlight plays tricks, and I was trying to see something four stades away.

'Artemis,' he said. It was the first time I'd ever heard him take a god's name in vain.'I'm sure they are there,' he said.

Styges came trotting up. He was a hero too; he'd taken it upon himself to prowl down the front face of the ridge, to look at the crossings.

'Arimnestos?' he asked.

I reached out and slapped his shoulder.

'I could swear the Spartans are still in place,' he said. 'I'm not positive, but I'd almost swear they've moved *forwards*.'

'Fuck,' I said. What else do you say? I'm not a Spartan. 'Fetch me Olympiodorus and Perikles and Diodoros and Troilus.' The last pair were the acting *taxiarchoi* of our Ionians and our Thespians. Olympiodorus had missed the *psiloi* action in the low ground with a light wound, but I'd seen him arming in the moonlight an hour earlier.

'Styges, do you have the spirit to make a run for me?' I asked.

He nodded.

'Run down to the spring and tell me what the Corinthians are doing down there,' I said.

He shamed me by turning without a word and running. Styges had done everything I'd done the day before, and he ran as if sprinting for the laurel.

But while he ran, Brasidas fetched the other officers, and I explained as best I could why I had to leave them.

'Give me … Alexandros,' I said. 'I just want another spear at my shoulder. Brasidas, you take the command. Move west …' I trailed to a stop. I wanted to cover the Corinthians, but, it shames me to say, not enough to want to lose a single one of my men. I'd lost too many the first day. Why didn't Adeimantus have his own rearguard?

Fatigue. Anger.

'… As soon as I head off to the Spartans,' I finished.

Brasidas was impassive. Who knows what he thought of my decision?

'I don't really know the ground the way you do,' he said. And that was true. We had almost no born Plataeans; the marines all had property, but they didn't know the ground in the dark.

'You cannot miss Plataea on the height,' I said, pointing to the ruins which showed a little even in the moonlight. 'And you walked here this afternoon.'

I looked at Leukas, who had wandered Plataea often enough. 'Can you get them there?' I asked.

'Boss, I'm from *Alba*,' he said, and men laughed. A good sign. 'Sure, I'll get them there.'

Brasidas shrugged, and I realized that he was just as eager to take command in the moonlight as I was to run to the Spartans.

But likewise, I knew that if something was wrong, the one man who had no chance at all of fixing it was Brasidas, who hated many of the Spartan leaders and was, in turn, mistrusted, hated, and feared.

'Look for Hermogenes,' I said. 'Tuck in behind him on the flank of the town.'

Brasidas was too invisible in the darkness to register much reaction.

'Very well,' he said.

It struck me like a hammer. Brasidas was as tired as I was myself.

I glanced around. We had no firelight and no torch; we were the men of different cities, the last men on the top of the ridge. It was important that there be no misunderstanding.

'You all understand that Brasidas is *taxiarchos* until I return,' I said.

The Thespian, in his Bactrian scale armour, laughed aloud. 'I followed him all day yesterday,' he said. 'I'll follow him in the dark.'

They were good men. I shook hands all around, took a canteen of water, and summoned the silent Alexandros out of the ranks.

'Ready to run?' I asked.

'Oh, crap,' he said.

We both laughed.

And then we ran.

★

It wasn't a very heroic run. It wasn't like the wind, or like Pegasus. In fact, I think I stopped half a dozen times.

It must have been the end of the third watch by the time we got there, but we'd known for ten minutes that the Spartans were still standing in their ranks. About a third of their phalanx. The rest were gone.

My first thought was that all was well; it was a rearguard, watching the enemy while the main body slipped away.

But there were too damned many of them. Almost three thousand men, give or take some moonlight. Too many to lose, and too many to cover the withdrawal of as many more.

I ran on, legs burning, old wounds burning; do you know that dehydration causes all your olds wounds to hurt? Every strained tendon, every severed finger.

What joy.

Worry and fear are worse than fatigue.

I aged a year in that run.

Eventually we came up behind the Spartans. They stood neatly in ranks, with their *perioikoi* behind them, only about three hundred files wide. Even in the darkness, it was easy to spot the officers gathered at the back right of the phalanx.

I trotted up to them.

'Who are you, then?' asked a Spartiate.

I leaned over and breathed hard, while considering witty replies like, 'Where the fuck are your sentries?' and 'Why are you standing here, you idiot?'

Luckily for the league, I couldn't breathe very well. So I wheezed, and sucked in air, and hated my greaves, and by the time I was better, Amompharetos turned.

'It's the Plataean,' he said. 'So, you haven't retreated either!'

I managed a fair breath. 'By now, even my *taxeis* is gone off the ridge,' I said. 'You are the last.'

His brow furrowed. 'The last?' he said.

I nodded. 'What are you doing here?' I asked.

He shook his head. 'Pausanias is retreating,' he said. 'I do not retreat.' He crossed his arms. 'We will stand here and wait for the Persians. In the morning, they will see that we are here, and they will come, and we will fight. Finally.'

I thought of a great many answers.

I've had years to think of more.

What I said was, 'And you'll all be killed.'

He shrugged. 'Leonidas died a hero's death,' he said.

'Leonidas almost lost Greece,' I said. 'If he had withdrawn to fight another day, our naval victory at Artemisium would have stopped the Great King. Right there.'

It's hard to glare at a man in the dark.

'Leonidas died a hero,' the Spartan giant said again.

'Better that he was here right now, leading this army,' I said. 'And if he were here, he'd order you to obey and march.'

Amompharetos shook his head so his transverse crest was like a bird in flight. 'No. He would not withdraw.'

'Would you obey him, if he were here?' I asked.

There was a long pause.

'Where is Pausanias?' I asked.

A voice came out of the darkness. 'Five stades behind us. He's halted the rest of the phalanx and he's waiting.'

It was Sparthius.

'Help me convince him,' I said.

Sparthius pulled off his helmet. 'He's a stubborn brute. Amom, for the love of all the gods, stop this.'

Amompharetos turned his back and recrossed his arms.

A thousand sharp comments came to me. But, as I had all winter, I tried to get outside myself. I tried to be Amompharetos.

I was still having trouble breathing, and Alexandros wasn't doing much better.

But it gave me time to think.

I probably took twenty more breaths.

'Amompharetos,' I said, 'is it that you are more afraid of surviving failure and defeat, than you are craving victory and success? Are you afraid to turn your back for fear you will die here, retreating, and not live to see the triumph?'

Sparthius' head turned with a snap.

Amompharetos turned around. 'How dare you?' he snarled.

'All Greece waits for you, sir,' I said. 'If you die here, *we all die with you.*'

'Why are we retreating from barbarians?' he snapped.

Sparthius began, 'Because—' and I cut him off.

'It matters not,' I said, snapping out the word *not* as an order. 'The Greeks chose to retreat. Are you a king? An independent poleis? Or perhaps a friend of Xerxes?' I stepped forwards, until I was close. He was a head taller. 'The army is retreating. If you die here, I curse you for fucking it all away for your pride. Come, back up a little, and fight with the rest of us.'

He was wavering.

And Sparthius said, 'If we fail here because of you, Gorgo will never forgive you.'

The giant turned and crossed his arms. He looked out at the moonlight.

A long time passed.

Finally the big man spat.

'The phalanx will retire by files from the right!' he roared.

It was the end of the third watch or later, and I was unwilling to go back across the ridge. Dawn was an hour away, my limbs felt like lead filled them, and I elected to move with the Spartans.

Sparthius led the way, and we walked with him, spears on our shoulders and helmets on the back of our heads. I was surprised at the route he was taking; we walked almost east along the ridge and then crossed the Demeter stream.

'Pausanias liked this route the best,' he said. 'Our helots cleared it earlier.'

I tried not to be uneasy, but the route was far out of the way. All the Lacedaemonians needed to do was cross the back of the ridge and they would be in place. It was as if you were looking at a deeply bent Asian bow; the Spartans only needed to march the bowstring, but for some reason they chose to march along the U of the bent bow.

We were two or three stades into our march before I was sure that we were far off course. I waited too long before turning on Sparthius.

'Where are we going?' I said. 'That's Erythrae above us. Plataea is way over there.'

Sparthius turned. 'What?' he asked.

Only then did I realize just how bad things really were. Not only was dawn about to break, but the Spartans, the best soldiers in Greece, were ten stades out of position.

A man can walk five stades in a quarter of an hour. A fine runner can run it in the time it takes an orator to deliver a short law case; perhaps five minutes.

But for three thousand men, it's a matter of almost an hour, and the sky was getting light before we found Pausanias. He had his other two *taxeis* drawn up in a fine position, with the Tegeans beside him as well; a third of our army.

He was surprised to see me.

'You have brought my missing brother,' he said.

'Would you spare me a moment to speak privately?' I asked.

The Spartan phalanx was drawn up on a good ridge, well back between Erythrae and Hysiae. The position was a fine one, although the left, where the Tegeans were, was scrubby and flat, and the slope wasn't much. Still, the right flank was secured by the gully of the now dry, but very deep, Erythrae stream.

'How can I help you?' he asked.

'You are a long way from the army,' I said.

'I know,' he said. And then, quite simply, 'I missed my way.'

Of course he missed his way. No scouts, no guides. He went back the way he knew, towards the old camp.

'The sun is rising,' I said. I was talking to myself. 'Shall I lead you back over the hills to Plataea?'

He nodded. 'I won't pretend I'm not happy to have a guide,' he said.

And I remember saying to Alexandros, while men filled their canteens in the stream, that it would all be fine if Mardonius continued to be cautious.

Alexandros frowned. It was light enough to see a man's face. 'Cautious how?' he asked.

'He's kept all his infantry on the other bank of the Asopus,' I said, with more confidence than I felt. 'He fears us.'

Alexandros looked at the Spartan phalanx. 'This is bad,' he said.

I was just going to agree when I saw the first Persian cavalry. They were just cresting Asopus Ridge that we'd only abandoned fully an hour before, and it was like the first day all over again. The rising sun sparkled on their helmets and spear points, and kindled them with fire, and suddenly, instead of a few, there was a myriad, like a river of fire, and flowing like lava.

The whole cavalry column halted, right there, perhaps four stades away, for as long as a child would count to fifty.

I don't think I breathed.

Then, as we watched, men began to prowl along our former positions in the new sunlight. They were only eight hundred paces away; we could see them as ants crawling on a giant hillside.

And, of course, they could see us. We were on the front slope, in bronze.

If Amompharetos had marched fifteen minutes earlier, we'd have been gone.

But we were not.

I saw the scouts leave the column at a gallop, riding along the very ridge top we'd walked to reach our current position. They vanished for long minutes, and then reappeared, much closer.

I walked to Pausanias.

He was surrounded by his officers. He already knew.

I was superfluous. So I said nothing.

But I will say that they beamed like men going to a symposium. Ultimately, what the Spartans wanted was a contest. And the contest had come.

The cavalry scouts rode up, loosed a few arrows, and rode away. Most of the Spartiates jeered as they rode away.

But they were not gone for as long as it takes a man to drink a cup of wine before they were back with all the Persian cavalry.

Alexandros and I joined Euryanax's *taxeis*. I became a back ranker in the same file where I had been a file second. But because of the slope, I had an excellent view.

The horse came on, but the sheer fatigue of their horses was obvious. They were tired, and dispirited, and the Persian cavalry loosed a few arrows and then halted, almost a stade distant. There was a pause. Persians shouted insults, and the Spartans stood patiently, waiting to fight.

It was then that I saw the masses of infantry moving over the face of Asopus Ridge.

That was a dark moment, friends.

As long as it was just the Persian horse – exhausted from twelve straight days of fighting, and short on horseflesh – I was mostly unworried.

But coming down Asopus Ridge was a mass of infantry the size of our whole army, but much deeper.

The gods must laugh at men. I know now that deep in the night, Mardonius decided to ignore his seers and attack. So he attacked into our empty lines; his great army climbed the ridge that we might have occupied. But no one opposed them.

What irony. Pausanias might have had his battle.

Instead, our army was broken into two or three fragments. And Mardonius, a great general, had spotted the Spartans. And chose to isolate and destroy them first.

Most of the infantry on the great ridge turned and started for us.

Let me explain one more thing: we couldn't retreat. Not because the men around me were Spartans, although, of course, they were, and they were not much on retreat. But because of the Persian cavalry, reinforced in minutes by the Medes. They didn't waste any effort charging us; they weren't in shape for it. But if we twitched; if we retreated, they'd be on us, all around us. A cavalryman's dream.

The sun was just clearing the eastern horizon over Leuctra when Mardonius came in person. There was no missing him; he had magnificent golden armour and rode a white horse with a golden bit, and he looked like some sort of centaur god.

He rode up and down, well beyond spear cast, and gave orders, moving his men carefully.

The first *taxeis* of barbarian infantry came forwards; Persian Immortals in their high tiaras, with spears and bows. And behind them, two *taxeis* of *Sparpabara* infantry, the Persian professionals. They came up to about a hundred paces, and began to erect their great pavises, huge wicker shields, like a wall.

Pausanias and Teisemenos began to make sacrifices, looking for the omens they needed to begin the battle.

Euryanax was walking quite calmly along behind his phalanx, like a gentleman on a stroll, looking to the left and right to be sure that the Persians weren't trying to outflank them. Indeed, off to the right, I believe that the Persians pushed a lot of scrubby infantry, *psiloi* of their own. No one ever tells this story, but it looked to me as if they were badly beaten by the Spartan helots; whether they were in ambush, or simply better at throwing rocks, I cannot tell you.

But that happened first, with the Aethiopians or whomever they might have been trying to force the Spartan right. Of course, since the helots won the engagement, no Spartan ever mentions it.

Off to the left, the ground was too rough for the Tegeans to be outflanked. However, they were on the flatter ground, and as soon as the *Sparpabara* troops opposite them had their great shields set up, they began to loose arrows.

I had seen Persian archery before, but it was still a shock.

I saw the wicked flight of arrows rise like a cloud of gold-tipped smoke, and fall on the Tegeans.

Maybe fifty hoplites died or were wounded. In one flight of arrows.

The screams were like something from the slaughter of animals.

The whole Tegean phalanx flinched.

And Euryanax was beside me.

About then, we had perhaps twenty-five thousand Persians arrayed against our twelve thousand. And more against the helots. It is vital to imagine that there were twenty thousand helots – not hoplites, but every man armed with a sling or javelins and a knife; deadly in rough ground.

Probably easy meat for good Persian regulars, but of course, Mardonius put his regulars against the Spartans.

Euryanax called my name.

I stepped out of the ranks.

The Immortals were fiddling with their wicker shields, and Pausanias was on his third sheep.

I thought, for an odd moment, that Euryanax was going to ask me to run all the way to the Persians.

Instead, he shook his head. 'Pausanias is too proud to ask, but I'm not,' he said. 'Will you run to the Athenians and ask them to come and get us out of this?' He pointed, and I saw three more Persian, or perhaps Mede regiments coming up. Another twelve thousand men, give or take.

Callicrates, renowned as a great fighter, turned. We were in the same file.

'I'm sure we can take them,' he said. He gave me a big smile. 'After all, the Plataean will protect us.'

Half the phalanx laughed.

And the Immortals loosed their first arrows.

It was just like the pass above Sardis, except that I was at the back, and I wasn't running.

I raised my shield, and an arrow struck it hard enough to move my body.

A dozen Spartiates were down, and a few *perioikoi*.

Callicrates was down. The arrow had gone through his *aspis* and through his *spolas* and into his lung.

I went with Alexandros – no one needed us – and we began to haul the wounded and dead out of the phalanx. Another volley struck.

The screams to our left were steady, and horrible. The Tegeans weren't uphill of their enemy, and the archers were flaying them.

'Tegeans are going to run,' muttered Diokles. 'Fuck.'

I got my arms under Callicrates, and hauled him to the rear, uphill. He didn't scream.

He was crying.

'I didn't do anything,' he said softly. 'An arrow. Damn it. Damn it. An arrow. I never struck a blow.'

What could I say? It was through his lung, and the bright blood bubbled on his lips.

I was slightly to the rear of the Spartan phalanx, holding up his head, when there was a sound from the left.

I looked. So did Callicrates; dying, he turned to see.

He smiled. 'Ah,' he said. 'The Tegeans will charge. Gods, I love them. How I wish I were there.'

And he was gone; a fine man, the best of his generation, to an arrow, without a blow struck.

But his head was turned to the foe, and I held it up so that his dead eyes could see the Tegeans. Because they didn't break.

They did run.

But they ran at the Persians.

It's hard to tell the rest of this without confusion. I cannot even remember the order of events, and the whole of the battle is yet to happen. So I just want to take a moment to say that at the moment the Tegeans charged, the Spartans were facing a third of the enemy army, and probably the best third, too. And Pausanias, pious or indecisive or both, was sacrificing to try and get a favourable omen.

I'm going to say, without really knowing, that in the moment that the Tegeans charged, both Pausanias and Mardonius lost control of the battle.

Pausanias has never really told me, or any other man, what he had planned.

And Mardonius ...

I think he expected to bring up his wonderful archers and gradually shoot the Spartans to extinction.

I think Pausanias planned to stand and take it with his reliable infantry until the Athenians came, or until there was a favourable moment.

But the Tegeans couldn't take the casualties. No blame to them – I hope the Plataeans would have done as well. But they charged. They went at a run, all together, like the Athenians at Marathon, and the *Sparpabara* infantry shot into them and ...

Didn't break the charge.

I wasn't really watching. By then, Euryanax was pushing me away from the corpse of Callicrates, and away from Alexandros, who was already back in the ranks with his *aspis* on his arm. The Spartans had a horse; only Poseidon knows where they found it – perhaps a Persian horse.

'Get Aristides!' Euryanax said. 'By Zeus and Ares and Poseidon, get the Athenians and we can still win this. Hermes give you wings.'

When I got a leg over the horse, I was high enough to see the Tegeans clawing at the wicker shields, pulling them down and thrusting at the Persians behind them. And I could see Mardonius, off to my right, pointing something out to a man who was almost certainly Artaphernes, my enemy and my wife's enemy.

About then, at least in memory, another flight of Persian arrows came in like evil rain, and men died.

I was not hit, and neither, by Apollo's grace, was the horse.

'Go!' shouted Euryanax. He was just pushing his helmet down over his face, and he had an arrow in the face of his *aspis*, but he handed me mine. I reined back, got my horse turned, and started off up the ridge. I looked back; like Orpheus, I should not have. There were an appalling number of red cloaks on the ground, and Mardonius was just getting another regiment into his firing line by jamming his archers closer together in the space between the dry stream bed and the Immortals.

'Go!' roared Euryanax.

I was leaving Alexandros, leaving Diokles and Sparthius and Bulis and a lot of men I'd come to admire very much. But Alexandros worshipped the Spartans, and the rest of them had the contest they wanted.

And I wanted to win the battle.

I put my weight forwards, the horse responded, and we were gone.

The Spartans made their stand, for good or ill, by the precinct walls of the Temple of Elysian Demeter, on the long ridge just east of Asopus Ridge. I went over the top of the ridge and onto the track that led to the temple from Erythrae, and just as my horse's hooves raised dust from the road, I heard a great roar behind me.

I wanted to turn my horse around, but that responsibility I mentioned earlier was on my shoulders. The battle was still savable. Mardonius had made a stupid mistake, attacking the Spartans without outflanking them either east or west. I can't fathom why he rushed his attacks, unless he assumed that his archery was so superior that he didn't need to manoeuvre. It is just possible that he assumed that the rest of the Greeks were just over the crest, and not ten stades away.

I thought some of these things as I galloped along the track to Erythrae, because I had a moment to think, and because once I crossed the crest of Long Ridge, I was *alone*. There was no battle.

And still, I did not dare ride cross-country. You may think ill of me, but I thought I had all Greece on my shoulders, and to cut across the open ground at the foot of Asopus Ridge, where I could see huge mobs of barbarian infantry, seemed insanity.

Instead, I rode to Erythrae, about five stades, and turned and galloped west, due west, to Plataea. That's another ten stades, right along the clear ground at the foot of Cithaeron, and for the whole of that ride, I could see the battle laid out before me like a painting in the stoa.

Battle? I could see the victory of the Persians, and the wreck of all our hopes.

The barbarians flooded down from Asopus Ridge. Have you ever seen a big fishing boat haul ashore a huge catch, the net so full of silver fish that they can't get it aboard, so they tow it to the beach and haul it up, and suddenly you see all those fish, and then they open the net and they slide and tumble down, an avalanche of fish, flopping and slipping ... That was the barbarian army coming down from the shallow ridge of Asopus and flooding into the plain of Plataea. Right towards me. And there was no waiting Greek army.

I couldn't believe my eyes.

The barbarians were moving south and west, towards Plataea, and I couldn't see a single hoplite.

Line of sight is a funny thing, and the areas around Plataea are, as I have described, a chaos of criss-crossing ridges. So I knew that there might be large bodies of hoplites hidden from my sight, but it was ... appalling ... that I could not see a single Greek.

My horse was excellent. He ran and ran, and I flowed along with him. I might actually have enjoyed riding that horse, under other circumstances; perhaps some Persian officer's horse, an uncut stallion with beautiful manners, despite his stones. We flew. I doubt it took me a quarter of an hour from the time I left Euryanax until we came out of the Nesos Valley and climbed Sanctuary Ridge.

And there was the Greek army. Or rather, there was the centre, huddled like sheep waiting for the slaughter. They were all clumped around the Temple of Hera, drinking water, sprawled on the grass, keeping no sort of order.

Beyond them, down below the acropolis of burned Plataea, was the left wing, under Aristides. I couldn't see him, but they were formed; there were the Athenians, and there, the Plataeans and the Aeginians. The Megarans were mixed in with the centre. I saw men I knew; the Sanctuary of Hera was only a few hundred paces from the road, and there were men from the centre contingents all the way back to the road and even further back; men with *aspides* on their backs, walking towards me on the road to Attica.

I reined in by the first group of men. They were all Peloponnesians, heads down. None would meet my eye.

'The Persians are that way,' I said.

'Fuck you, mate,' said one man.

'The Spartans are dying for you,' I said, my voice thick with something very like hate. 'Turn your arse around or I'll save the Persians the effort.'

'It's all over,' whined another. 'We're done. Everyone says so.'

Men began to push past me. More and more were coming up now, hundreds of hoplites, *in armour*, leaving the field. Looking out to the north and watching the barbarians flood over the low Asopus Ridge.

'Cowards!' I said, the strongest word I could think of. 'Cowards! Stay and fight, gods damn you all!'

They put their heads down – and ran.

Towards the passes.

And I had no more time to waste on them.

I know why they ran. I know what Adeimantus said to them, may he be cursed for eternity. And I know they'd stood ten days of cavalry and dust and heat. But on that day, when the contest came, they were found wanting, and when they ran, the freedom of Greece ran away like sand through a glass. And as I rode on, I hated them more than I hated the barbarians.

Not all the Peloponnesians ran. Many of the Corinthians, and all the men of Hermione, and the Megarans, who had joined the centre and not the left when they marched, because we were an amateur army – they didn't run. They milled around the Temple of Hera.

I rode past them. I didn't see that Adeimantus would do anything to save the Spartans but talk. And I could see the Athenians; a third of the army, formed, ready to fight.

I put my horse's head at the man standing alone in front of that great phalanx.

But even as I cleared the rout, and started down Sanctuary Ridge, the fastest way to the Athenians, I began to see the last stroke of doom.

The Theban phalanx, formed in good order, was in the dead ground beyond Sanctuary Ridge. Ten thousand hoplites, with all the Boeotian cavalry, all the Thessalian cavalry, and the Lydians, infantry and cavalry. They were in the valley between Asopus Ridge and the ridges where I stood, and like the rest of the barbarians, they were moving south-west. They were the right wing, the strong right punch of Mardonius' attack, and they, alone, outnumbered all the men of our centre even if it wasn't broken, and our left.

I suppose I swore. I know that I found that I'd reined in; I was no longer riding at a gallop, but simply sitting at the edge of an olive grove. Watching the end of my world. It was like a bad dream, except that I'd close and open my eyes, and the Thebans were still there.

The worst of it was that the Theban phalanx was coming at a steep angle to the Athenians, and might actually flank them when they cleared the end of Sanctuary Ridge. Neither body could see the other. I could see both.

Listen, thugater, and all my friends. I would love to say that in that moment, I thought of how to save Greece, to win the battle.

That would be a lie.

It was too late to save the Athenians. With no centre to cover them, they were about to be buried in faithless, Medizing Greeks and Lydians.

It was not too late to fight hard and die a noble death. It was not too late to tell Aristides what he faced, so that he could act with honour. This is the highest compliment I can pay the Athenians, aristocrats and citizens too – it never crossed my mind that they would flinch. I knew they would die there, because there was no longer anything for which we should live.

So I turned my horse and went down into the fields below the acropolis of Plataea. I could see the farm where I grew to manhood.

For a moment, I could see the beehive-shaped tholos-tomb where the Hero lies.

I knew my duty. I used the last of that ride to think of Briseis.

Oddly, and with love, I knew that she would understand. I would not outlive this defeat. I would not spend my life with the mockery of Persians.

The Athenians saw me coming. Men who had been sitting in the ranks got to their feet, and I saw Hermogenes pluck up his horn, very like mine, and sound it. The whole of the Plataean phalanx emerged from an olive grove and ran to their places, where their *aspides* and spears waited for them.

It was a sight to raise your heart, if your heart wasn't dead in your chest.

I rode past them.

I rode straight to Aristides, dropped my *aspis* and then rolled off the poor beast's back.

'The Spartans are fighting for their lives,' I said. 'But never mind that. The Thebans are not two stades away, over Sanctuary Ridge, coming this way.' I pointed.

Aristides understood. He never said a word to me. 'On your feet!' he roared, no longer the politician, no longer an orator. Now the voice from his helmet was the very rage of Ares, and he dropped his *aspis* off his arm and raised his spear with both hands.

'Wheel the front to face me!' he called. 'Now!'

It is a brutal task to wheel a phalanx – that is, to make it swing like a door.

The Athenians did it as if they did such things every day. There was the product of a winter and spring of training. They did in seconds what, the summer before, they couldn't have done in an hour. They wheeled through about an eighth of a circle, so that instead of having their front face the distant Asopus, now it faced Asopus Ridge, north and east.

The Aeginians wheeled up to form on the Athenians. It was sloppy, and they had trouble getting their ranks back, but they got it done, even as the Plataeans came up. The Plataean phalanx seemed larger than I remembered, and looking at the rear ranks, I saw shields I knew from Hermione. Quite a few.

And beyond them, I saw Brasidas with the Selected Men, the *Epilektoi*.

Aristides started his speech. I hear it was brilliant. I can only say it was short, and I couldn't hear a word he said. I picked up my *aspis* and ran – ran for my own men.

I pulled my helmet down and tied the cheek plates, too, so that no one would see my face. I had decided that they didn't need to know. Let them go in bravely.

Let us end as we began. Brasidas always used to say, 'Finish as you began.' He would say it when men began to flag; he'd make them sing, or march in step.

Finish as you began.

I ran to Brasidas. I paused only to slap him on his right shoulder armour, and then I ran to the centre of my front rank.

'This is the hour!' I called. 'Now is the contest of our lives. Show them who you are.'

That was it. I remember every word.

They roared. They didn't know that the battle was lost, and neither, I realized, did Aristides.

The Athenians started forwards. I don't want to bore you with the minutiae of *tactika*, but everything – everything – in hoplite warfare is details. When we all wheeled to face the invisible Theban phalanx, we were like opening doors in a big house. We were not in line. So the Athenians' phalanx came forwards at the new angle, and the Aeginians were still sorting themselves out. It took them too long, and they fell behind, so that in the end, the front of the little Aeginian *taxeis* lagged the Athenians by forty paces or so.

Hermogenes was ready early, but he waited until the Aeginians started to march, and he lagged them by five paces or so, and I did the same, being on the right and trying to see the movement of a *taxeis* to my left, if you understand.

So we ended up moving north and west, but in an echeloned, or angled, line of phalanxes, trailing off to the right of the Athenians. And, being hoplites, we began to drift to the left, the spear side. That's what hoplites do. The shield is heavy, and you want to crawl under your mate's shield.

Against that, the very first thing we had to do was cross the spur end of Sanctuary Ridge to our front and right, and of course, it sloped down from our right to our left, and men on a slope always move downhill. So we drifted even faster to the left.

A little thing. In the midst of horror and heroism, drifting to the left . . .

Somewhere, ten stades to the east, the Spartans were fighting and dying. The sun was high in the sky. The barbarians were flooding across the plains of Plataea, and it flashed through my mind that here, in the last battle of my life, I was in the same place I'd been in the first – on the left end of the line. Except, of course, that if I looked to my right, there was *no one*. The centre were not there. They were two stades away, high on Sanctuary Ridge.

Bastards.

We – the *Epilektoi*, the Selected Men – had the hardest climb to get over the shoulder of the ridge. It wasn't steep. It was merely annoying.

When I passed the olive trees at the top, where I had sat on my horse and seen the end of Greece, I could see down into the valley on the other side, and there were the barbarians. And the Medizing Greeks. The valley of the Spring of Gargaphia was packed with them.

But the Thebans had turned their phalanx. Again, I can only guess why, but my guess is that their commander, Timagenides, saw all the hoplites gathered in the Sanctuary of Hera and assumed that was our army. So he wheeled his phalanx from its south-west course to almost due south.

And they didn't perform the wheel very well. I could see them, trailing confused hoplites like a wounded whale trails blood.

The Athenians were just slightly off angle, but it was a critical angle, and they had a little impetus from the shallow slope, and there, in the fields below the northern end of Sanctuary Ridge, the men of Athens struck the front and flank of the Theban phalanx.

The noise was incredible. There were twenty thousand men packed into a few hundred square paces, and in moments, it was chaos.

Now the sheer good fortune of our formation told. The Athenians drove the Thebans back ten paces at impact, from the advantage of ground and the advantage of the angle, and the Thebans, formed very deep, as was their wont, struggled to get their files back. They staggered, stabilized ...

And the Aeginians hit them. A small *taxeis*, but still well formed. Listen, a phalanx is most dangerous in the moment it strikes. As soon as the first impact begins, both ranks and files collapse, and you are in the hell of *othismos*, squashed flat against the man ahead by the pushing of the men behind. That is, unless someone breaks at contact.

The Aeginians, who hated the Thebans only slightly more, that hour, than they hated the Athenians beside them, plunged into the mêlée and the Theban phalanx staggered back another five paces. They were still trying to form, trying to get their depth to stabilize the front and get their best men into action. And remember that the Phocaeans and Locrians and other Medizing hoplites were there, spreading their front. And beyond them, off to my right, three big blocks of cavalry: Boeotian, Thessalian, and Lydian.

And by Ares, I wanted to kill every Theban on the plain of Plataea.

But as we stood there, I saw that the Plataeans were going to go into the Locrians and the Phocaeans. And it seemed to me that, given time, the Thebans were going to lose to the Athenians.

For the first time, a single ray of hope shone through the clouds of barbarians.

'Halt!' I said.

A lot of men looked at me as if I was insane. There was the contest. There was the battle.

But I had done this before. As long as I stood with five hundred men by the olive tree at the height of Sanctuary Ridge, I held the flank of the Plataean phalanx. Up slope from the Lydian and Boeotian cavalry, I could laugh them to scorn. They would have to *clear the ridge behind me* of eight thousand inept Corinthians and Peloponnesians before they could come at my flanks, and even as I stood there, the Megarans were getting it together. Bless 'em, they were forming ranks by the groves, and the Boeotian cavalry saw them and went forwards. The Thessalians went with the Boeotians.

Of course, the prospect of a gallant charge into a lot of unformed, badly-trained hoplites appealed to the cavalrymen more than doing their jobs and holding the flank of their great phalanx. I've known a few cavalrymen. Glory first. As much rational thought as an ephebe in a temple of Aphrodite.

But while we stood there, the battle changed. The dice were rolling. I was having trouble breathing.

Because when all that well-rested, fresh cavalry charged our broken centre, *they were wasting their spears*. Had they turned on me and the Plataeans, they would eventually have broken through us and into the flank of the Athenians' phalanx. Just a matter of fighting and numbers. And the men on Sanctuary Ridge would not have helped; eh, perhaps the Megarans would have come.

But by charging there, in the centre, the Boeotian horse brought them into the battle and wasted their own advantage. Now the cavalry was off the board for an hour, and only the Lydian horse remained: lance-armed horse I'd already beaten, about eight hundred men.

And, as I watched, I realized they were led today by their satrap, Artaphernes, son of Artaphernes. Probably with Cyrus and Aryanam close by his worthless side.

I don't think we halted there by the olive tree for five minutes. Styges says it was forever; that he was cursing me under his breath. Sittonax sat down and drank water.

I had the last Greek reserve on the whole battlefield. It probably wasn't enough to decisively affect the course of the battle, but it was enough to stop a Lydian cavalry charge once.

But at our feet, the Plataeans were locked. They were the better men; their fire burned white hot, and the men of Hermione wanted to prove they were as good as the men of Plataea. The Phocaeans were deeply divided; there were Phocaeans in our army, and they had no love for the Medes.

But there were a great many of them. The Plataeans were holding the flank for the Athenians at odds of three to one. And the Locrians were beginning to fold in on the Plataeans, collapsing their shieldless flank.

I saw Hermogenes fall, and that was the end of *tactika*. Let the Lydians charge; let Artaphernes take his revenge, or let the Megarans save us.

'We're going into the Locrians. See the man with the spider on his shield? Centre of the line strikes right there!' I called. 'Half files forwards. Close up!'

They executed like Spartans.

'Front!' I called. 'March!'

When a phalanx is closed up, even a small *taxeis* of five hundred, it doesn't move very fast. In fact, moving fast would spoil the order and cohesion that makes it so deadly. Ah, you say, but you charged at a run at Marathon. Against barbarian infantry, you win by running.

Not against Greeks.

The Locrians weren't famous as hoplites, nor the Phocaeans, but there were a great many of them. They were piling into the right files of the Plataeans, but in that moment, they were offering their flank to us.

Hermogenes died then, stabbed in the eye by a Phocaean *saurauter* as he lay, already wounded; my first real friend.

Myron died a moment later, trying to rally them as the flank began to give, as panicked men saw the crisis. And Empedocles, son of Epictetus, died too, and a dozen others, men I knew.

But the Locrians had made a stupid decision when they chose to turn the flank.

We hit them hard.

I killed my man. It was like murder – he was trying to free his spear from the press to his front, and he knew he was dead many heartbeats before my spear entered his eye. And I was done commanding; done with the weight of the world on my shoulders.

I was in the thick of the fight with a spear in my hand, and this was the contest, and I was going to die with ten men's blood on my spear. Or fifty. I had never counted, but I thought I might try, just to see, when I reached Hades, what my count was.

So I slammed my *aspis* into the armoured back of a second man, threw him forwards, widening the hole, and killed the man beyond him; careful, accurate thrusts, the way Polymarchos taught.

Styges was beside me, with Polymarchos himself behind him, and I had Sittonax behind me, and woe to anyone who faces four killers of men in the frontage of a single yard.

I'll be honest; I lost count at three.

A moment came when my spear, and that of Sittonax, and Polymarchos from off to the left, all slammed into the same man's throat in the same tempo, and we beheaded him, with spears. The Locrians could not break the flank of the Plataeans, and their spears were locked in front; they couldn't fight back, and we had our shields pinned against theirs, so they couldn't get them up, and our second and third rank spearmen were as good as their front rank men, and the collapse came very fast. They panicked; I was looking at men who died inside before my spear reaped them, because we killed our way through the three outside files the way the scythe reaps, and then they were melting, and we were still killing them, because they were also pinned in place by the Phocaeans to their right, who were still facing the men of Plataea and Hermione. It might have broken down into a mêlée, a dusty hell, but the Locrians broke too fast, and we kept our order, cleared the Locrians off the flank of the Plataeans like a sword cut, and ... And we kept moving forwards, at an angle. Order is everything; we hadn't lost ours, because the Locrians died so quickly.

And panic ...

The Locrians broke, and the Phocaeans, who hadn't really wanted to fight, began to bleed from the back ranks. Remember, in a phalanx fight, an old-fashioned phalanx has all the best men in front and all the worst at the back.

Phocaeans began to run.

The Plataeans, like their fathers at Oinoe, had come within a few steps and a few heartbeats of collapse.

But by Ares, they had not collapsed. Lysius, who had once fought for Darius as a mercenary, and Gelon, who had once fought against Plataea for Thebes, stood and refused to die, like the old killers they truly were. It is odd, funny, and sad and true, that Lysius missed Marathon because someone had to hold the citadel at Plataea, and he had held that against me and against Myron all those years. Not strongly, but it was between us, until he stood over Hermogenes' body and at last was able to show the men of his little polis what a hero he was, too.

And the men of Hermione, they were not lacking. They were on the left, and thus didn't take the casualties; they just kept pushing, kept fighting.

I wish I could speak of every man who fell, and every man who stood his ground, and pushed, or stabbed, desperate or careful. Because a phalanx does not win because of heroes. They can help, but a phalanx wins when every single man stands to his place and does his duty. And when Lysius, just fifty paces to my left in the maelstrom, sang out 'The Ravens of Apollo!' even I, in a different *taxeis*, planted my back foot and pushed. But it was the Plataean push that mattered; one last shoulder forwards and the Phocaean front rankers knew there was no one pressing in behind them, and they turned and ran themselves.

I had time. This is where battle is like a single combat. Never let the killer have time. Never let him think.

I had time.

I turned and looked at the Lydians. They were ... Arguing.

I could see a dozen men shouting at each other. They were three hundred paces away, across perfectly smooth ground, and their horses' heads pointed into our open shields. We were meat if they wanted us.

Athena was fogging their minds.

And really, it was too late to stop my *taxeis*. In some game, like polis, you can turn and wheel in combat, sliding from this opponent to that, but not in the dust and the blood. My men had crushed the

Locrians, and now, because of a very slight angle, the drift of the hill, and the luck of the gods, we were aimed at the flank of the Theban phalanx. If I did nothing, we were going to strike it about eight men deep in their formation; Brasidas, our leftmost file leader, would kill that man, and the rest of us would shear their rear ranks off like a butcher's knife takes meat off a bone.

At some point, the Lydians would charge, but by then, the whole Theban phalanx would be wrecked.

I did nothing.

We went forwards fifty paces, into the Thebans.

And the gods smiled.

Off to my left, Lysius, self-appointed polemarch, ordered the Plataeans to *halt*. And they did. So we passed across their front, perhaps ten paces in front of them. Even from my end of the line, I could see their front-rankers snatching a drink, or sinking to one knee.

We crashed into the deep, confused Thebans.

Five hundred paces behind me, the Lydians finally began to manoeuvre for their charge.

And then I was fighting.

I would have said that when we struck the flank of the Thebans, they would have run. But that didn't happen. In fact, that whole day, the hardest day of fighting I've ever known, every single thing that happened seemed to me to be at odds with what ought to have happened. The Thebans, remember, had been caught off-angle; when we struck their rear ranks, I assume they steadied because in fact, we struck them along the axis they'd expected to fight all along. And we were five hundred, and they were still ten thousand.

But we had eight thousand Athenians pushing from our left front.

And by Ares, the Furies hover close; our anger was white hot, like iron left too long in the forge, and I swear to you that every single man in our front rank killed his man at contact.

Killing Locrians was strictly war.

Killing Thebans was a holy crusade.

Our formation did not survive the second contact. The Thebans were a mob, but they were a dense mob, and, although it pains me to say it, a brave mob; Boeotian bumpkins just like me. I killed my man, and pushed in, and I hit with everything I possessed – my *aspis* punched, my spear flickered, I kicked with my hobnailed sandals, and I fought as I had never fought before, with no thought for survival.

After all, this was the end. We'd already done better than I'd imagined we would; we'd broken their right flank, and the Athenians would now, no matter what happened, defeat the Thebans.

I won't tell you I thought that. I'd kissed Briseis in my head. I was done, and there was nothing left but to leave a story of how Arimnestos the Plataean died in the fields of his fathers, killing his enemies.

I remember only one moment of that fight, like a memory of a dream. The man in front of me went down, and I don't even remember why; and I turned, as if Athena guided my hand, and plunged my spear into the unguarded neck of the man to my right, and then, rotating the spear, I slammed my *saurauter* into the neck and head of the man to my left; I stepped forwards and plunged my spear straight down into the man I'd knocked flat, killing three men in as many heartbeats. I have never fought so well, not even against the Aegyptian marines at Lade. It was like being Achilles.

And I think this was given to me as a gift.

And then ...

And then I was standing with my *aspis* sagging like a broken door, my *xiphos* in my hand, blood running down my arm and over the sticky hilt, and Styges was by me, and Sittonax. And there was nothing in front of us but the long up slope of Asopus Ridge.

The Thebans had not broken.

We had killed our way through their phalanx.

I have never known a phalanx fight to go on for so long. The Thebans formed very deep, maybe twenty men deep, filling in their rear ranks with freed slaves. And the slaves were fighting for their own freedom.

Over my right shoulder, back at the foot of Sanctuary Ridge, the Lydians had charged. But they hadn't charged us, or saved the Thebans.

They'd charged the Plataeans.

It was incredible.

We were not losing.

I had to watch for some seconds to understand that the Lydians were locked against the Plataeans, hacking overhand with their long spears.

And then I joined Styges and Sittonax and Polymarchos and the other *Lydia* marines in killing badly armed Theban slaves. We didn't have to kill many.

They began to run. The promise of freedom does not trump immediate death.

And the rest of the *Epilektoi* had either penetrated the Thebans or slid along their flank; other men began to join us. Our ranks and files were gone; this was mêlée, but not *othismos*; we were in no particular order, and men were throwing spears or fighting close, and the back of the Theban phalanx began to bend and stretch, trying to match our expansion. It was like watching a spill of oil fight a spill of vinegar; the two pools flowed. Of course there were more of them, but the more attention they gave to us, the fewer of them were facing the Athenians, and by Athena, Aristides and his front rank were as dangerous as my best. Remember that Aristides was the first true swordsman I ever faced, and I only beat him by luck; remember that he had Cimon beside him, and Cleitus, and my father-in-law Alteius, and hundreds more.

And my sons, bless them; a glance told me they were alive. And like Achilles and Hector yoked together, they cut a road for lesser men to follow.

There was a moment when it all hung in the balance. A Theban in magnificent armour burst from the back, and roared for men to join him; a knot of fighters began to form around him, and the pressure on me increased. The Thebans, incredibly, began to form a new front in combat.

Hipponax went spear to spear with the Theban. I was two men away, and Hipponax made a weight change and the Theban struck with his shield, a masterstroke, shattering the front of my son's helmet so that blood sprayed ... I got my foot over Hipponax's sprawled form. He screamed under me, and I ignored him, and as the Theban thrust with his spear, I took it on my sword, high and to the left, over my *aspis*. He expected me to cover with my *aspis*.

He should have trained with Polymarchos.

My sword cut straight along the shaft of his spear and his fingers sprayed. And in the same tempo I went forwards, hand high, and thrust into the tau of his helmet. My sword caught on his nose, and he had a moment to savour his death before the point drove into his brain, and he was dead before his limbs sagged.

He fell off my point, and the Thebans ran. I had no way of knowing, but that was their polemarch, Mardonius' friend, Timagenides, who burned Plataea, may he rot forever in the darkest corner of Hades.

I'm glad I dropped him, and gladder that he'd broken Hipponax's nose and cheekbone, but not his life or spirit.

I also didn't know that Hector's spear was in the Theban's shin, five inches deep through the greave.

I mean, I did when he fell.

Hector got my son's head up, and he was alive.

I turned. I had that sense, the way you do in a fight when you know that there's a blow coming at your head.

Behind us, the Lydians were pressing the Plataeans.

My horn was shattered at my side.

But Brasidas was not shattered, and my voice was fresh, powerful from ten days of shouting.

'Form your front!' we roared.

And faced the Lydians.

It confused our men; for long minutes, men ran to the wrong place, argued, pushed – had there been an enemy to charge us, we'd have been easy. Behind my left shoulder, eight thousand surviving Thebans streamed away. Because of the angle at which the Athenians had struck, the Aeginians had struck, and finally, we had struck, they were running due north – the road to Thebes, rather than back up the slopes of Asopus Ridge from which they'd come.

The Aeginians pursued them. Again, this was a matter of angle and initiative.

The Athenians halted. It was a little like allowing a corpse to fall off your spear. Aristides halted, and reordered his phalanx; a brilliant move because it would have been so *easy* to pursue and slaughter the beaten Thebans. Bad for Greece, but good for the Athenians. Slaughtering men while they run is very safe. Ask any cavalryman.

I had time to watch, even while I roared, bellowed, whined and whimpered at my men to reform *behind* me.

I have no idea how long it took. Styges says no time at all. It seemed to me that it took an eternity.

As soon as we had some hundreds, I waved at Brasidas and we started forwards. I wasn't on the right front any more, and we were not in anything like our original formation. We were wider, shallower, and at least a hundred men were gone.

Now that we were moving, I could see the dust all along Sanctuary Ridge. The Theban cavalry was butchering the men of Corinth. The Megarans had lost a mêlée and rallied, and were pushing against the Thessalian cavalry.

The Thessalians were looking over their shoulders, because we were starting to roll up their whole line. They were next, if the Lydians lost.

My *Epilektoi* were now headed at the *back* of the Lydians.

Everything had changed. *Everything*. At least on this flank, we were going to win.

In fact, we had won. The Thebans were running, pursued by the Aeginians and some of my men too deeply caught up in that fight to listen for orders. But if I turned my head to the right, now, I could see Aristides dressing his front rank. The Athenians were intact: eight thousand hoplites, unbeaten. Triumphant.

I could see it all.

We moved along towards the rear of the Lydians, only two hundred paces away. Men in the rear of the mêlée looked back at us.

They began to ride away.

I didn't want them to escape, to be a threat off our flank.

I've been told all my life that infantry cannot charge cavalry, and I seem to do it anyway. But my last foray had got a lot of good young men killed, and I was shy. And now that we were winning, all that false and suicidal courage fell away. I might not want to survive defeat, but I bloody well wanted to survive victory. In fact, I thought of things: of Euphonia, of Briseis.

I had a great deal to live for.

And yet, I knew that we needed this, and we needed it right away.

'Ready to run?' I called. It was what Brasidas said every morning, when we were on the beach in Hermione.

I heard men *laugh*.

'Sing the paean!' I called. We had fought twice, and not sung the paean.

And Styges, who had a beautiful voice, started the paean. And everyone caught it up. But the incredible thing is that the Athenians, who stood off to our left, now took it up and began to sing, cheering us like spectators at the Olympics, and their voices rose to the gods. I have never known a feeling like this; for ten thousand to sing for me.

I never heard a command to run at the Lydians.

And yet, we did.

We flew.

Some of them rode clear. But by Hermes, we were *fast*. It was, perhaps, the last time I ran that fast, but I covered the ground fast enough to get my spear wet, despite wounds and age, and Styges and

I killed a horse and then the man on it, and the Plataeans gave a great roar, and off to our front and right, the Thessalians broke.

Panic and rout. The Greeks started the day panicked, and settled down. The barbarians started the day in order ...

The fight with the Lydians should make a great story. After all, we were hoplites against barbarian cavalry; it's in the painting, in the Stoa. There I am, with Artaphernes son of Artaphernes at the point of my spear while Styges kills his horse; there's Brasidas in his Spartan helmet cutting down the trumpeter; the Plataeans are behind the Lydians, victorious. It is a great honour that this is one of the twelve scenes in the painting. It may have happened that way.

If I killed Artaphernes, I'm glad of it, but I have no memory of it. Although I admit that I have his cloak – a magnificent thing, dyed in Tyrian purple with gold embroidery. You've seen me wear it. I must have taken it off his corpse, because I had it on at the end of the day.

Bah. I may have put him down, or I may not have done.

But I am proud of what I did do.

I saved Cyrus. It was all Tyche – he was there, at my feet, a spear in his left shoulder, with his sabre in his right hand. And in a heartbeat, my spear flicked out and swept the spears of Styges and Polymarchos aside. A fine blow; repayment of many a guest oath. He had Aryanam wounded, behind him.

I turned to Polymarchos. He was the oldest man in our *taxeis*, and he looked grey with fatigue.

'These two are my guest-friends,' I said, in the midst of combat. 'Will you stay with them and help them live?

Polymarchos rammed his spear, *saurauter* first, deep into the earth. 'By Zeus, god of oaths, I will,' he said.

I'll run ahead of myself. As a trainer, Polymarchos was a better leech than most; he got Hector to bring Hipponax, and he began tending the two Persians and Hipponax, and men brought him other wounded. No one threatened Cyrus or Aryanam, although Darius, it proved, was face down, dead of many wounds. An hour later, some Megarans helped Polymarchos move the wounded into the shade inside the Sanctuary of Hera, and doctors came from the army.

It was then that I knew that Hermogenes was dead, for the first time, and Myron, and many others.

But I also knew that we were not done. We were winning, but we had not 'won'. Somewhere, either the Spartans were still fighting, or they were victorious, or they were defeated.

From where we stood, intermixed with the Plataeans at the end of the fight, cursing, drinking what water we had and looting the bodies, it began to look like victory. The Thessalians were reforming well down the plain, but they had chosen the road to Thebes and not Asopus Ridge. And even as officers and phylarchs shouted themselves hoarse trying to rally their men and get them formed, the Boeotian cavalry broke off their slaughter of the centre and began to retire. They were victorious, so victorious that about half of them broke through the hoplites on Sanctuary Ridge and rode off across the Plataean fields on the other side. When they caught the fleeing Theban phalanx, they beat up the pursuing Aeginians and saved the Thebans from a worse disaster than they already had. And then the Thessalians, the Thebans, and the surviving Locrians and Phocaeans reformed themselves. All together, they outnumbered the Greek left by almost two to one, but they continued to retreat.

To our front – remember, friends, we were facing north and east, towards Asopus Ridge – we could see what seemed to be another entire army. There, on our side of the ridge, there were tens of thousands of men. Up there on the ridge were the rank and file of Mardonius' myriads: Aegyptians, Aethiopians, Asians; men of a hundred countries. Most of them were ill-armed spearmen; some were bowmen.

They seemed to cover the earth.

And none of us wanted to go and fight them.

Listen, thugater, victory is almost as effective as defeat in robbing men of the will to fight. When you have faced the foe and defeated him, your whole body sags. You have done your best. No man can call you a coward. You have nothing left to prove to any man, or even to yourself, when your spear is broken and your sword sticky with the blood of other men.

The Plataeans had beaten two opponents. The Athenians had been fighting for almost half an hour in what is now remembered as one of the hottest phalanx fights ever contested by Greeks. My Myrmidons had fought twice, at odds. Beside us, the Megarans had been mauled by the Lydians, and the men of Hermione, farther down, had been slashed by the Thessalians.

But Aristides had the Athenian phalanx together.

Hermogenes was down, and Lysius was wounded. I got him into the shade with Polymarchos ... And took command of the Plataeans.

I didn't ask; the archon was dead, the polemarch was dead, and everyone knew me.

Nor did I shout. I borrowed a canteen from one man, had a drink and put him in his place, and then I moved among them, nudging Hilarion's son Aristides into his place, finding Antimenides and Gelon and putting them in the front rank.

No one told me to stuff it.

And after only a minute, Brasidas began to work with me. You would think we'd scream and rant, but yelling at tired men only makes them angry. I know. A few paces to our right, a *strategos* of Megara bellowed like a bull at his people, and they walked away up the hill and sat, bonelessly, in the shade. They voted with their feet.

And the young Athenians reformed as if they would never tire, and my marines formed the rightmost file of the *Epilektoi*, but we weren't forming as two separate *taxeis*. We formed as one body, and I built a front rank of all the most dangerous men I could find. Olympiodorus joined in.

It took time.

Men drank water, sat in their places, and waited.

And finally, my cousin Simonalkes stood up. I'd put him in the front rank, between Ajax and Achilles. He'd earned it; he was no coward.

'I guess you want us to fight again,' he said.

In this, I could see he echoed the thoughts of many men.

I walked to the front. In fact, it's probably fair to say I hobbled. I remember that my greaves hurt my feet, not because they were ill-made but because I'd had them on for fourteen straight days. There were scabs on my insteps that broke open with every step. My thighs hurt, my knees hurt, my right shoulder hurt; lack of water, enough water, makes muscle pain worse.

And every man there felt the same. These weren't slackers. Nor were they professional warriors, except a tiny handful. These were Boeotian farmers who had been made to fight and fight again.

Off to my right as I faced my Plataean friends stood the Athenians. They were silent too. There, very close to me, on the right front of their phalanx, was Aristides, who had fought in the front rank as polemarch and not been killed, a remarkable feat of arms.

Aristides told me later that he had been about to speak when I hobbled out front.

As you know, I am not one for speeches. I think most of them are silly. You remind men of their duty, and of the possibility of loot, and if you can, also remind them that very few will die, if everyone stays together.

But this was not a speech before a battle. This was a speech in the middle of a battle. Such a thing had never happened before, that I know of or anyone else.

It all came to me at once. I didn't think of it. I took one more pull from my borrowed canteen and handed it to Achilles in the front rank with my thanks, and then I looked from side to side.

'We are not done,' I said. I have a loud voice and it carries, especially when I pitch it up like a rhapsode. But they were very quiet, too, and I was surprised by the weight of their attention.

'Most of you are farmers,' I said. 'So you know what it means when a job is not done. It means more work later.' I turned, and pointed my spear at Asopus Ridge. 'If we stand here, they will either wreck the Spartans, or march away. Either way, it's all to be done again. Like propping your vines; like trimming your apple trees.'

I looked at them.

'Like ploughing,' I said.'Except ...' I went on. 'Except that as long as we have to fight *them*, we can't plough. We can't prop our grapes, or cut the new growth from our olive trees or our apples. All we'll do is fight them, and it's a waste of men and time. I say, let's do it now, and finish the job. Let's march up the ridge, break their army, and destroy them so that we do not have to fight this autumn, or next summer, or next autumn. So our sons don't have to fight Persia, and our daughters can grow to womanhood in safety. Some of us will die – now, in the hour when Nike is close. But those men will have their names honoured *forever*. And they will die knowing that they gave their lives not for some stupid conquest, not for arrogance or pride, but so that their sons and daughters could have better lives. I have been fighting the Persians for nineteen years! I'm sick of it! Let's get it done. And, by Ares, the Spartans have been fighting for *your* liberty since the sun rose. I say we go and help them out.'

A few men cheered. But what was better was the growl, the low animal sound, and then the sound of ten thousand spears clattering on ten thousand shields. It's a terrible sound; I had only heard it once before. It is the sound of a Greek army that wants blood.

Aristides came out from his corner and squeezed my left shoulder. 'Straight up the ridge?' he asked.

'And all the way to their camp,' I said.

★

We all started together. The Megarans didn't come at all; the men of Hermione and Troezen came, alone of the contingents in the centre.

We started across the plain, with the Athenians on the left, the Plataeans in the centre, and the men of the Peloponnesus on the right. Out to the left of the Athenians, a cloud of their *psiloi* and archers moved with them.

It was glorious, but it hurt my feet and legs just to walk the two stades to the base of the ridge. The back slope of Asopus Ridge was steeper than the front face, and although we started up in good order, our line was a little oblique to the slope of the hill, and our formation began to ooze away like potter's clay with too much water in it.

And then a great many things happened at once. I was on the right of the Plataeans, and I kept looking to my right to see what the Peloponnesians were doing because they were losing their formation on the slope. The barbarians above us on the ridge began to loose arrows; not many, but men went down.

I saw red off to the far right, along the crest of the long ridges that ran out from Cithaeron to Asopus Ridge. Red and bronze.

The Peloponnesians began to cheer.

Red and bronze was not a particularly disciplined column, and for long heartbeats I didn't think I was looking at Spartans. They were streaming along the high ground to my right – thousands of them. Because of the angle of the ridges I couldn't see the men they were pursuing, but there they were, and they were not beaten. They were victorious. And they were Spartans.

I couldn't know any more, but that seemed enough. My legs drew new strength, and I left my place and ran across the front of my slow-marching *taxeis* all the way to Aristides.

I pointed, but he was too far along the ridge to see anything but dust.

'The Spartans are victorious,' I said.

Ten years of age fell away from his face. He raised his voice.

'The Spartans are victorious!' he roared.

Men cried. I was there. It meant everything to us: we were not a forlorn hope; we would *not* have to do it all again. We all knew, then, that we were in a victory; that something wonderful was happening.

Fatigue leaves you. It is a remarkable thing. *Fear* leaves you. You are a giant striding over the earth, and your enemies are puny, contemptible, pitiful.

There were, I'll estimate, as many barbarians standing on Asopus Ridge that afternoon as there were men in our army – perhaps thirty-five thousand. I leave aside our *psiloi*. These enemies had not yet been engaged; they were fresh, their quivers full.

They were uphill of tired men who had fought far too long.

They broke.

We didn't kill ten of them. They wore little armour; they turned, and ran. I agree that we were coming up the face of the hill; that the Athenian *psiloi* were already on their flank; that they could see the Thebans in flight to their right, and the Persians, the cream of their army, in flight to their left, running, shattered, from the Spartans.

But they ran. They turned their backs and ran down the long slope to the Asopus river.

We plodded along behind them. We were eager to finish them, and had they stood, I think we would have beaten them in a desperate fight ... But they didn't stand.

Then we were over the top of the ridge and all we could see, all every man could see, as we started down the other side were the broken remnants of the Persian and Mede infantry; off to the east, we could see their cavalry, still formed, trying to cover the retreat and fighting with the Spartan right, where Amompharetos fought them. And before us, below us, the Vale of the Asopus was full of men, like an amphitheatre at a religious festival; more men than I have every seen gathered in one place, and all in flight, thousands and thousands, perhaps one hundred thousand men in a single glance, running down the long slope north to the river, crossing the cool water, and running up the far slope on the other side.

The Greeks gave a great shout.

And then, as we moved down the long slope to the river, the Peloponnesians began to link up with the Tegeans from the Spartan right. The two halves of our army were coming together at a shallow angle, and if we were no longer a phalanx, neither were we a mob; and as the Tegeans and the men of Troezen saw each other, someone began to sing the paean.

See? I will weep.

I have heard that women sometimes weep when the baby comes after long labour. I saw my father weep when he knew that the skill of working bronze had not left him and his god still loved him. But there were thirty thousand Greeks singing the paean – why would I not weep? Think of what we had seen and done.

We kept going. And we sang it again, so that the hillsides rang with our song, and then our feet were wet, and then we were over the Asopus, and climbing the ridge. I've heard that a regiment of the Saka made a stand and were destroyed; maybe that happened, and perhaps it is merely storytelling.

And so, after a long climb on a very gradual, low hill, we came to the point from which we could see the Persian camp.

I had seen it before, but I came to a stop. As did thousands of Greeks.

It was vast, as big as Athens. A field of tents, a forest of tent poles, and walled and ditched, with a palisade. It was like a city or a fortress.

The Spartans reached the palisade first, and there they met their match. There, the Persian infantry stood again to redeem their honour; and with the wooden walls to support them, they could ply their bows. A dozen Spartiates fell there; Bulis died, an arrow in his eye.

The Tegeans struck a different section of wall. There was no holding the army at that point; no discipline. Something went into us, and out of us, with the paean. Perhaps it was the god; perhaps Apollo or Dionysus led.

Perhaps the Tegeans wanted to prove themselves better men than the Spartans or the Athenians. They began to *scale the wall with their bare hands*.

The Plataeans came to a low spot in the walls, and there, for the first time that day, I faced Medes. They were cavalrymen, and they'd dismounted to defend the camp; professional soldiers, noblemen most of them, with bows and javelins and swords.

To our right, the Tegeans were in. A dozen insanely brave men had gone over the wall, and now dozens of them were being boosted on each other's backs and jumping over.

I was about twenty paces from the wall. It was a little higher than my chest, made of bundles of brush roped together and dropped between stakes.

I started to run.

I never thought about it.

An arrow blew through my *aspis*, showered me in splinters, and shattered against my thorax.

And I ran on.

A javelin clattered against my shield.

The army began the cheer – *eleu, eleu, eleu, eleu* ...

Three or four paces out, I threw my spear.

No idea where it went.

A pace away, and I leapt as a Mede with a crimson beard raised his sword.

I put my *aspis* against the lip of the wall like a vaulter on a vaulting horse and rolled over the top of the palisade. I landed on my feet, punched my *aspis* into redbeard, and reached for my sword.

Someone slammed a spear into my helmet. I was knocked sideways. I must have seen it coming; I moved with it, caught myself on the wall, and a shower of blows fell on the face of my shield. My helmet was turned on my head ...

I shook my head and drew my *xiphos*. It came into my hand like a friend – all those years of practice on the draw – and my helmet settled on my head and I managed to parry a javelin a little late so that the head scored my thigh going down.

Thank all the gods, none of them cut at my legs or thighs. They were desperate, and not canny close fighters, and they threw spears or shot arrows at my *aspis*, and for as long as it takes me to tell this, I was alone.

And then the men I was fighting were looking over their shoulders. Styges came over the wall, and Brasidas, off to my left, and the Medes made a desperate push to clear us off the wall. And then I was facing three men, and one had an axe. I thrust my *aspis* at him, and his mate *caught my aspis* and threw me to the ground, wrenching my left shoulder.

And Simonalkes came over the wall, and he killed redbeard, and suddenly the Medes were running and we were on them.

Simonalkes reached down and gave me his hand, and I got to my feet very slowly, but I was alive. My left shoulder hurt, but I was alive, and my ivory-hilted *xiphos* was there in the stubble of the grass.

We were in their camp.

And their camp was *incredible*.

To this day, in Athens, and even in this house, you can see the treasures we took in those hours. Goblets of gold – there's four on the sideboard. Tapestries – that one of dandelion silk thread worked on linen came from Artibazos' tent. Piles of coin; hundreds of pounds of gold and silver plate; tens of thousands of horses; enough tents to house every commoner in Attica.

And women. Thousands of women. Except that most of them

were Greeks, enslaved by the Medes and Persians, and they flung themselves on us, begging mercy and rescue.

I suppose somewhere there's a man who can rape a woman who has already been ill-used by his enemies, but I'm proud to say I didn't see any. Even the Persian women were protected; the Spartans put guards on the tents full of women.

I am an old pirate. I had never been present at the sack of a camp before, but I knew that there was a fortune to be had, and I intended that the Plataeans share it. I could see the huge tent that was Xerxes' tent, which he had left behind for Mardonius to use. It was purple, like the cloak I had taken from Artaphernes, and it stood as tall as ten men, and over eighty paces long.

You can still see it at the Theatre of Dionysus in Athens. They call it the *skene*, the tent; it's the backdrop for most of their productions.

I headed for that tent. I knew that the commanders would have the richest pickings.

I was two stades away when the Medes broke from us, and an hour before I wouldn't have said I could run two stades. But I did; I even, according to Styges, yelled that they should all follow me and be rich.

And they did.

And we were.

It was incredible, the things we found. We only made it as far as the tent of Artibazos; I could see that the Spartans, with a shorter run to make, had beaten us to Xerxes' tent. But we began to strip it, and as we already had a thousand or so Mede and barbarian prisoners, we simply made them carry our loot: silver lamps – there's one right there; a solid gold bowl big enough to bathe a baby; I sold that.

Here, look at this. I've saved this for you, my thugater, for your wedding.

Pearls.

A whole net of pearls.

Artibazos' concubine, Pharetae, surrendered to me. She had her women around her, and she was not afraid. They all had knives, and they looked like they knew how to use them.

'I am Arimnestos of Plataea,' I said in good Persian.

She bowed. 'I know of you,' she said. 'My maidens do not want to be whores and corpses. Protect us, and I will show you every treasure in this camp.'

I had Styges gather them, and then Pharetae took me from box to box, showing me spices and jewels, and we shared them all; all the big loot was taken to piles, except a little that each man might take for himself, like jewels and coins.

When we had secured the best of it, and when our servants were carrying away what we wanted immediately, mostly food and carpets for sleeping – the Persians have wonderful carpets, and their camp was crammed with food – Aristides' *hypaspist* appeared and summoned me to Xerxes' tent, where the commanders were.

I left Brasidas considering two jade necklaces. I could read his mind, and wondered which one my sister would wear.

I walked across a camp being looted to the great purple tent as big as a palace.

The tent was fully furnished and completely unlooted. The Spartans are above such things, or rather, they pretend to be above them. I could, if I were evil, name the things Sparthius took for himself and for Bulis' wife.

Never mind. Xerxes' tent was under guard. Outside were half a hundred helots; they were not shy about their looting, either, although they had to do it when their masters weren't looking. But they had a fire going and four of them were making soup. They all looked at me suspiciously.

I smiled and ignored the pile of gold coins one man had just covered with a bloody cloth.

Inside, Pausanias had Mardonius's harem: twenty beautiful women, most of them Aeolian girls, all seated comfortably on stools, safe, and, I think, happy.

Aristides was there, and Sparthius, and Euryanax.

Sparthius took my hands. 'Bulis is dead,' he said. 'But he won the laurel; he fought the Persians spear to spear. And triumphed.' Indeed, Sparthius was smiling.

Well, I'm not a Spartan, and I would have rather had Bulis there, making trouble, prodding men, laughing his great laugh, than heroically dead.

Bah.

Then Aristides embraced me. It was a long embrace. He said nothing.

Nor did I.

And Pausanias took my arm as if we were brothers. He grinned – a lopsided grin like a man who has taken a wound. 'We won,' he said.

He looked around at the dozen or so men in the huge tent. 'I invited you all so that we could share this meal,' he said.

Indeed, the middle 'room' of the palatial tent had a feast laid out: whole roast kids and lambs, covered in saffron and raisins, and great bowls brimful of red wine and white, and huge bronze platters of roast meats, and hundreds of loaves of bread; fine bread with white flour, and barley rolls made the way Lesbians make them – light as air.

And the plates were all gold or silver, as were the cups. The tables were laid for half a hundred men, and there were benches for sitting in the Persian way. Every place had a linen towel.

I kept mine.

Pausanias pointed at a Persian with a waxed beard and hennaed hair. 'My new slave tells me that this feast was set for Mardonius and his officers when they had beaten us.'

We looked at it, and my stomach grumbled so loudly that Aristides laughed. 'Hubris,' he said.

Even as he said it, a dozen helots came in bearing three bronze kettles. The kettles were full of black broth: the usual beans and pigs' blood.

I groaned.

One of the helots laughed.

And they went from place to place and poured black broth into twelve bowls of solid gold.

We went to our places: Euryanax and Sparthius, me, and Alexandros, who fought all day with the Spartans; Aristides and Cimon; Chileos of Tegea and Andronikes, his friend; Pausanias and Amompharetos; Phrynicus and Aeschylus of Athens. And when he had poured a libation to all the gods, Pausanias, the host, rose, and in his hands he had the golden bowl of Spartan black broth. He raised it and set it down by the huge beaten gold platter that held the saffroned lamb.

He looked at it for a moment. Then he smiled sadly.

'Why did the barbarians come here?' he asked. 'Did they come to steal from us our poverty?'

We all laughed. I think it's one of the best witticisms I've ever heard. And so true.

It was an odd dinner. It was like a symposium, and the subjects were heroism and war, and everyone was too tired to make any talk. I remember eating and eating. I remember draining my black broth of my own free will, and eating most of the roast kid, and some lamb, and some highly spiced Persian soup, and drinking water, glorious water. Styges came, and I heard that all our people were staying in the Persian camp; no one relished walking eight stades back to Plataea, and there hadn't been enough fighting in the camp to make it foul with carrion. Styges said he was worried about Brasidas. I pulled him down onto my bench and gave him wine, which he drank greedily, and I introduced him to Pausanias as one of the best of the Plataeans.

Nor did the Persians need their camp. When they broke, at the palisade wall, most of the barbarians ran. A few surrendered; I have heard that we took about three thousand prisoners.

The food started to wake me up. Perhaps it was the water, or the wine, but I surfaced as the shadows grew long outside. My muscles were stiff and my neck was sore, and I realized that I was eating with blood still under my nails.

Like an animal.

Pausanias was just asking how many the Persians had been, in our opinion. He was trying to understand the battle.

'Arimnestos,' he said, 'you saw both our fight and the Athenians'. Which was the hotter?'

Of course there was a bowl of rosewater. I saw it, and rose, and washed my hands.

'Pausanias, you make me feel that I am Paris, and have to give the golden apple,' I said, and they all laughed. And I was thinking of Brasidas sitting in his own darkness, and other men.

Aristides smiled. 'I fear I will prove to be Athena, and not Aphrodite,' he said.

Sparthius choked. 'I don't think we should take this thing too far,' he said, and we all laughed.

They all looked at me.

I shook my head. 'War is war, and blood is blood. When I left you, Euryanax, the Tegeans had just charged. I saw them pull down the barrier of wicker shields, and that was a great deed of arms.'

Chileos gave me a wide smile.

'But then I rode away,' I said.

Euryanax nodded. 'You weren't even over the ridge when Pausanias declared the omens favourable, and we charged. After that I was fighting.' He looked around. 'Someone killed Mardonius, though. Who was it?' he asked.

Sparthius shrugged. 'Arimnestos,' he said. He looked at me. 'Our

Arimnestos; he's from the head of the valley, and he's every bit as pig-headed as you, Plataean.'

Euryanax nodded. 'I can tell you that as soon as Mardonius went down, they collapsed. It wasn't a hot fight; all that time waiting for the great contest, and they lost it in ten spear strokes.'

Pausanias shook his head. 'Perhaps you think so,' he said. 'But the fighting went on much longer than that. Look at our losses! The Persians threw themselves at us, and dragged men down by their spears. They were *brave*.'

He looked at me. 'And on the other side?'

I sat back, drank wine, passed the bowl. 'The Athenians faced the Theban phalanx. That was quite a fight; I was in at the end.'

Aristides barked a laugh.

I raised an eyebrow.

'Arimnestos means he killed the polemarch of Thebes,' Aristides said.

Pausanias raised his cup to me. I suspect I blushed.

'It was a long fight, but I can't say how long,' I said.

'And the centre?' Pausanias asked, and Aristides and Cimon explained, and were more politic than I would have been.

Pausanias took the wine bowl when they were done. 'We won,' he said. 'But in truth, the gods gave us victory. If Mardonius had only crested the ridge behind the Spartans ...'

Aristides nodded. 'If the Thebans hadn't gone for Sanctuary Ridge,' he said.

Cimon raised a cup. 'If the Thessalian horse had charged the Plataeans instead of the poor Megarans,' he said. 'Or the Lydians had charged into Arimnestos rather than the Plataeans. All Tyche.'

I raised my cup. 'If Artibazos had made a fight for Asopus Ridge,' I said.

Pausanias stood. 'So – we won through no excellence of our own.'

Euryanax pulled him down. 'Crap, cousin,' he said. 'I'm alive because of my excellent right arm, and I wager the same is true of Cimon and Aristides, and all these fine gentlemen. We won because we were worthy to win. Here's my libation to the gods; I will never cease to praise them for this day, but by Aphrodite, brother, no long faces. We beat them.'

I drank with him, but here, on the last night of your feast, as you don the pearls I took in that camp hoping you would wear them, I say that it is a miracle that we won, and our foes, the Persians, had the victory in their hands and threw it away. At the moment that I rode away from the Spartans, Nike was fluttering all around Mardonius. And then Mardonius and his generals made every error that could be made to give us victory, and every guess they made was wrong. What can I say? War is a dangerous game; no one on all the wheel of earth had ever fought a battle on that scale – no one in Greece, and no one in Persia, either. And battles go to the army that makes the fewest mistakes.

In the end, despite it all, we made the fewest. And we fought hard.

Before the evening was over, Pausanias, a little the worse for drink, asked me if I would ride to the fleet with news of the victory.

I think I groaned. But I took Styges and we went to where the Plataeans were, all around the tent of Artibazos. I sent Alexandros to find horses.

He looked at me with his slight smile that meant that I was asking a great deal.

'You love horses,' I said. 'And Spartans.'

He laughed.

One thing we had in plenty was horses. Every one of the elite cavalry units had spare horses. I don't think Greece had ever seen so many horses – good horses, and in some cases, superb horses: big Nisaeans, and beautiful Thessalians, and pretty small Arabs that could nonetheless work all day.

It wasn't yet dark. The ravens were beginning to gather; the very ravens of Apollo that we celebrated at the Dandala. Well, Apollo's raven was on my shield, and had celebrated many a feast on the flesh of men ere that. But it is nothing that any man would stop to watch.

I found Brasidas, sitting alone in the midst of the Plataeans, and my darkest fear was not realized.

He had men all around him, but there was a distance and most of them could not bridge it. Styges could, and Achilles, and Sittonax. But the rest were too in awe of him to see how much he needed the speech of men.

I went and collapsed next to him.

'We need to ride for the ship,' I said.

He nodded. His eyes gathered focus, and suddenly he was on his feet.

'All the marines,' I said crisply. 'Alexandros is fetching horses. We ride immediately.'

Men looked up; Styges was by me, and Achilles was close. Polymarchos was nowhere to be found, because, as I have said, he spent the day and the night tending the wounded. My sons were with him. Sitalkes had been wounded days before. Ka and his helots were all looting. But Nemet thought he knew where Ka was.

I drank some looted Persian wine. I knew what I was doing; Brasidas needed to be doing something. He was blackest after battle; he had it worse than me, perhaps because he was a deeper thinker.

And I can remember drinking off a cup of wine, neat, and smiling to think that I had to ride over the mountains to Eleusis, because had I not had a mission. I would have had time to think of a hundred dead Athenians and all the men I'd left face down in the last ten days. My own and my enemies.

Best to have something to do, really.

But the touching thing, the really amazing thing that made me want to cry, was how many of the Plataeans wanted to come with us: Ajax, Achilles' brother; Antimenides, son of Alcaeus; Nicor, one of Epictetus' grandsons; dozens of men, really. Men who should have been too jubilant and exhausted to think, and they gathered around, clamouring to join me.

Styges rubbed his beard. 'Are we riding tonight?' he asked.

'We could sleep at Erythrae until the sun rises and be at the ship by noon,' I said.

Styges let out a long sigh. 'I see your logic,' he admitted. 'My bones ache.'

I laughed the superior laugh of the older man. 'Every part of me aches, young man.'

Achilles was seen to roll his eyes.

They were awake and alive, and they could make jokes.

I walked among the Plataeans, slapping backs, looking especially at men who sat alone, with their heads down. I knelt by a couple, and then found my cousin Simonalkes. He was sitting with the Athenian *taxiarchos*, Olympiodorus.

He was sitting without wine. He had a deep cut on his left thigh, neatly bandaged.

I knelt by him, although my knees protested.

'You saved my life,' I said.

Simonalkes smiled. 'I think I did, cousin.'

I reached out and took his hand. 'There it is, then,' I said.

I didn't say, there's your father's cowardice repaid; there's the Furies assuaged; there's redemption. He knew, and I knew. I had a swelling in my throat that made it difficult for me to speak, and he suddenly bent forwards, and clasped my neck the way a wrestler does. Too close.

Olympiodorus looked away, as young men do when they have no idea what they are seeing.

I held Simonalkes for a long time.

'I want you to take the phalanx of the Plataeans,' I said.

Simonalkes sat back. 'Me?' he asked.

I shrugged. 'Everyone knows you. Lysius will be well enough in a day or two. There shouldn't be any more fighting. Just see to our people. Talk to everyone. I ordered wine; see to it that everyone gets a share.'

He nodded sharply. 'I can do it,' he said.

I reached out and tapped his fist with mine. 'Corvaxae,' I said.

'Corvaxae,' Simonalkes said. It was a name that had never really been spoken between us; the name of the family we shared.

He got to his feet. 'I'll look after them,' he said.

I nodded. I walked back through all the Plataeans, stopping sometimes to say a word to a man. And when I got back to the front of the great tent, Eugenios was there with a pair of horses in his hand; Aten was unloading donkeys, and Brasidas had twenty-five men with horses. He had all the archers, and several Thespians: Eudaimon, son of Troilus, and Polycrates, who I knew a little; Antimenides and Nicanor and Aristides, son of Hilarion. I shook hands with all of them.

They rolled their cloaks, put their armour in wicker baskets on panniers, all aided by Lady Pharetae's slaves. Before the sun set on the Battle of Plataea, we were ready.

We rode out through the gap the Tegeans had made, and down the long slope to the river, where we gave all our horses water. We had pack horses; we were, perhaps, the first Greeks in history so rich in horseflesh as to use horses to carry our armour.

Then we rode up the far side and over the ridge into the gathering gloom, and along the top of Long Ridge to where the Spartans had made their stand. Helots were already burying the dead.

Mycale

The Last Battle

We rode into the ruins of Erythrae as the sun finally set, and Aten and Eugenios made a fire and we ate food that Eugenios, best of stewards, had packed from the Persian general's tent. We ate; I ate again. We drank water and a little wine, and then we collapsed. I was pretty drunk.

Styges woke us before dawn. I lay there, after he tapped the sole of my foot, willing myself to rise. The backs of my thighs were, I remember, the worst. But my neck was stiff; my right arm was like a separate being, leaden and difficult; my right shoulder hurt, front and back.

Eugenios had a small pot of hot, spiced wine. Spices were suddenly cheap. Spiced wine, usually only for feasts, was suddenly something you could have at a campfire. It gave the dark morning a festive atmosphere.

Eugenios was a quiet man, and didn't take praise especially well. But that morning I showered him in it; that spiced wine got me up. He'd fought the day before, and risen to make the fire like a slave.

We were slow breaking camp; it was hard to muster a sense of urgency. But we climbed the many switchbacks of the Oinoe road in the early morning sun, and noon found us well along the road south, with our first sight of the sea.

Perhaps we rested too often. But we did not make it to Eleusis before dark. But the road from Eleusis to our beach is broad and the moonlight was bright. We rode down to the beach, and there was the *Lydia,* drawn up stern first on the sand.

A sentry leapt for joy on seeing us, and ran, crying 'Sekla!', and then we were in the middle of all our people; there was young Kineas and old Poseidonios and hundreds more, it seemed.

Megakles said he knew that we were victorious as soon as he saw us, because of the purple cloak, which, of course, told its own story, and the horses.

It was too late to put to sea. We sat on the beach and told them our stories, and there was water aplenty, and wine.

Megakles looked extraordinarily pleased with himself, and he told me that I'd find old friends with the Greek fleet.

'Just you wait,' he said, and touched his nose.

We launched into the rising sun.

We touched at Salamis. We needed food and water for a long voyage, and we discovered, in the rising sun, that Cimon had come over the other pass from Plataea and was readying his long *Ajax* for sea just down the coast.

Salamis deserved to know of the victory, and I drove my new Arab mare over the side of the *Lydia* and swam her ashore, and then rode up and down the long beach, headland to headland, shouting news of the victory. I found Thiale, the old priestess of Artemis, and told her as much as I could in a few minutes, and she chose girls to be her runners.

I saw Euphonia. She was delighted to hear, and yet reserved; suddenly, she was old enough to not want her father's embraces instantly, and to want credit for her own achievements.

I'm not an utter fool. I sat on the rocks and listened to my daughter's adventures in keeping order among almost a thousand children.

And Thiale had a little forge; after all, she had a thousand people living in a temporary village. I went to the forge, exchanged grips with the smith, and asked him to allow me to use his anvil to take the dent out of my helmet. My apprentice turned master, Anaxsikles, had forged it well, and it hadn't let the spear blow into my brains, but I had an egg on my head and a dent a finger deep in the hardened bronze.

So, together we dismounted my horsehair crest, and my daughter took it away and washed it. The long mane was full of dust and dirt and blood, and Euphonia, for all her apparent disinterest in my adventures, was eager to clean it.

My smith's name was Leon. He was not a talkative man. But he knew his craft, and after we looked at it, he agreed with me that it would take heat to reform it, and we took out the liner – woven straw – and set it aside. Then we filled the bowl with coals from the forge fire and blew upon them until the dent shone with an angry red light, a sort of black red, the perfect heat for working bronze. We dumped the coals, burned our hands like eager smiths the world over, and then, almost effortlessly, I planished the bowl back to shape. I barely marred the finish, but under the direction of a smith probably much my junior, I kept planishing. He was right; I wanted the reworked bowl to be work-hardened and not soft, as bronze is from a fire. So I spent an hour on it, and then, when we were both satisfied with the hardness, I polished, first with pumice, and then rottenstone, and then just a cloth, until the bronze shone. And I said my prayers to Hephaestus, who is, after all, the god I most truly admire. And I felt most of the darkness lift. Craft is, I think the anodyne to war.

There was a tiny nick where the spear point had cut the metal, but no break and no hole. I enjoyed my skill, and the praise of my brother smith.

And not too far away, I saw Brasidas enfold my sister in his arms, so that when we went back to the *Lydia*, to board, Penelope was wearing that glorious necklace.

At the ship, my sister grasped my hand and nearly broke it.

'Do not let that man die,' she hissed. 'By the Furies, Arimnestos – I found you a wife; I protected your daughter; bring me back my Spartan.'

I embraced her, and she laughed, and her eyes were bright.

'I mean it,' she said. And went to look after her son.

Cimon's *Ajax* came onto the beach while we were pouring water into our Gaulish casks, and he began to take on water.

He came ashore and found me, and we embraced. Listen, thugater, there was a lot of joy that day, and for days afterwards. For me, there was the knowledge that Briseis was not yet safe, but even that could not taint the wonder of it; we'd won.

'I have orders for Xanthippus,' Cimon said. 'A different mission from yours, I suspect.' He smiled grimly.

'Am I allowed to know?' I asked.

He shrugged and looked down the beach where crowds were forming: wives coming to ask after their men. One of Cimon's slaves had a list of all the Athenian and Plataean casualties. It was a grim list, and too long. And I'd certainly done my part to make it longer.

And yet ... We won. I could regret the boys I'd lost charging the Persian cavalry, but in the end, their cavalry had been worn to uselessness by twelve days of fighting us, and every casualty mattered, and killing Masistius *had* mattered, or so I told myself. Still tell myself.

Cimon looked back at me. 'There's a rumour that the Spartans don't want to fight a naval battle now,' he said. 'They want the Persian fleet left intact.'

I understood immediately. 'To keep Athens in check,' I said.

Cimon shrugged. 'It's not Pausanias. But it is the ephors. And they have sent their own messenger, but he's to sail from Corinth.'

'Two days behind us,' I said.

Cimon nodded.

'And you bring orders for Xanthippus to fight?' I asked.

Cimon nodded.

'So we're not done,' I said.

'I told my marines last night,' Cimon said.

I blinked.

And then shrugged.

'It's like the battle,' I said quietly. 'Let's finish it.'

'That's what Aristides said,' Cimon nodded.

We had no wind at all the first hours, and the crew pulled and pulled, a nice cruising speed, and men complained of 'all these people' by which they meant an overfull complement of marines and archers. And I sat on the helmsman's bench, and the kiss of the sun seemed to burn away the pain.

On the other side of the stern, Brasidas sat, and he seemed as relaxed as I.

'There's to be another fight,' I said, after a couple of hours.

He looked at me from under my spare petasus – I'd bought a straw hat from an old woman on Salamis. 'I heard from Alexandros,' he said.

That's all, although there was a great deal of emotional content to what he said.

Sometime in mid-afternoon, a west wind arose. It was gentle at first, a light zephyr, and we raised the sails, wetting them as we set them to catch every breath of that breeze, but as afternoon wore into evening, the sack of winds was opened further, and that west wind under our stern became a full wind, and we were racing over the surface of the sea without a man touching an oar.

Being at sea on a perfect day has an element to it that is difficult to describe, as if all the perfect days are one day; as if Heraclitus' river, the one into which you cannot step in the same place twice, is in fact a pond; and everything is, in fact, the same. There was Leukas; there was Sekla; there was Megakles. We might have had the *Lydia* on the southern tack, bound for Syracusa and looking for Carthaginian prizes off Italy. We might have been crossing the Adriatic looking for Neoptolymos, or racing from Thermopylae to the fleet at Artemisium, or scouting the beaches at Phaleron.

I looked forward under the awning, at the top deck rowers: sixty men sitting as if they were passengers, chatting in the restful wind. The mainsail was set and drawing fully, without any brails.

Poseidon was wafting us over the sea.

I looked at Sekla. The dark mood that follows battle began to lift, blown away by the wind.

In its place was joy, and fear; joy that Greece was saved and the war would end.

Fear for Briseis.

Listen, thugater. I am a Hellene. All of our heroes end in tragedy, except perhaps Heracles. They fail. They die. Their loved ones die.

Only the Greeks have the saying *Count no man happy until he is dead.*

We stayed at sea all night and raised Delos in the morning. It said something about our navigation that night – sailing to Delos was no longer a matter for backslapping and congratulations, and indeed, no one even mentioned it. I felt a little like a housewife whose excellent fish stew goes unpraised.

We landed only long enough to top up our water and spread the news of victory. Delos is the home of great temples, and a clearing house of news for all of the Ionian, and they did not know yet. They knew that the two armies faced each other; they had heard of the cavalry attack on the Megarans.

I told the priest, Dion, now considerably older than when I'd last seen him, while water went aboard the two ships. I joked to him about his white hair.

He laughed at me. 'You should see yourself, old man,' he said. He brought out a woman's silver mirror he'd been given as a gift, and I looked in it.

Well. Old was perhaps harsh. There I stood, still hale, strong in my armour. But there was grey in my hair and white in my beard since the last time I'd looked in Briseis' mirror. As Boeotians say, *Winter is coming, there's frost under the barn.* I was thirty-seven years old. In fact, my thirty-eighth birthday was only a week away, at the feast of Heracles.

Well, I consoled myself that I'd just put down the polemarch of Thebes in single combat.

'I suppose I'm not as young as I once was,' I said. 'The year of Marathon.'

'Ten years ago,' he said, 'you were a fool.'

I shrugged and admitted it.

In turn, he gave me news of the fleet. 'They were here a week ago,' he said.

From him I heard that the allied fleet had stayed for almost a week at Delos, gathering Ionian allies; I heard that a number of the nearer islands had overthrown their tyrannies and sent a ship or two to the fleet. And that, further, Leotychidas had been approached by envoys from Samos, who promised that the island would change sides.

After the embassy from Samos, Leotychidas had his seer, a Corinthian named Deiphonos, make sacrifices. Dion said that Leotychidas had admitted that he was waiting for news from Boeotia; they knew that the Athenians and Spartans had marched over the mountains, and men waited, day by day, for news of the battle.

But after they received news of the cavalry fight – almost two weeks earlier, by the time I was talking to Dion – the omens of the sacrifices were strong for the fleet to move on. And Dion admitted to me that Xanthippus pressed the Spartan king hard to move.

We didn't spend the night. Cimon and I were perhaps two of the best deep water sailors in Greece. We were going to cut the chord and sail over the deep to Samos, and not coast our way around the outer rim of the sea or hop from island to island.

I poured a libation to Poseidon on the altar, and I prayed to Apollo – never my favourite god – for the safety of Briseis.

I shook hands with Cimon. 'The last time I sailed from here, your father was with us,' I said.

He laughed. 'And you left us to whore after a prize while we went and dealt with the Ionian Revolt. You took grain into Miletus and we rowed for nothing.'

'Miletus fell,' I said. 'Lade was lost.'

Most of the men with us had no idea of the darkness the word 'Lade' brought us.

But Cimon nodded. 'Now we will avenge Lade,' he said. 'And afterwards . . .'

'We will liberate Ionia?' I asked.

Cimon nodded. 'And to Hades with Sparta,' he said.

Greek unity. It lasted until the last Persian fell.

We launched into an evening. Most Greeks beach their ships at night, but my rowers, and Cimon's, knew what we were doing. Indeed, many of my rowers had seen the Outer Ocean; not a man of them hadn't been to sea at night. It was a curious ship that voyage; beside the ghosts of other men and other ships that seemed to be all about us, we flew over the sea and orders were scarcely necessary. Megakles would merely say something, and it would be done, as if the ghost of Onisandros stood amidships, ordering the oars, instead of Nikas, or the ghost of Paramanos or Stephanos was at the helm. Oars came in and out; when we landed on Delos, it might have been a ship of automata, so smoothly did we reverse ends, land, and file off the benches.

We were fifty parasangs south of Delos, and the stars were out, a vast, rich carpet of black and silver from horizon to horizon. I was curled in the stern under my purple cloak; Aten was there, and Megakles, and Sekla, and Brasidas. Most of the marines were using salt water to clean the blood and crap off their armour by the light of an oil lantern. There was wine, and a cool breeze despite our speed.

'What will we do if the war is over?' young Achilles asked.

And indeed, he'd been a marine now for three years. He'd never been much of a farmer. The *Lydia* ran down the wind, and the wine was passed.

Megakles laughed. 'I will take a round ship to Aegypt and make a fortune,' he said. He looked at Leukas.

Leukas nodded. 'I will marry Paramanos' daughter Niome, if she'll have me,' he said. 'And we'll trade.' He looked forward into the ship. 'I see a lot of likely lads who'll need work.'

Sekla smiled softly. 'I would still like to see Africa again,' he said.

Brasidas looked out over the moonlit sea. 'I will marry your sister, if you allow me,' he said.

And everyone there looked at me, and when I smiled, they took his hand, slapped his back, poured him wine.

And the ship ran on.

When the congratulations were done, Sittonax leaned forwards. He was never the best spoken, as Greek was not his language. And he was taciturn, when there were no women to impress.

But he leaned forwards and took the *mastos* of wine, and drank, and handed it on to Sekla. 'I think you are all fools,' he said kindly. 'Here, you are brothers. This is the best life any man can know. Every day, we face death. This war has forged us all. We can do *anything*. What will trade with Aegypt be, when we have warred down Persia? Look at this ship. I am no sailor, but this is the best ship I have ever seen. Why? Because every man aboard trusts every other. Storm, and battle, disease, and wine; every man aboard knows the others as he knows himself. And you would shatter this with peace? So that every man can go his own way? And starve and weep, alone, without the comrades of his youth?'

It was the longest speech I'd ever heard from Sittonax, except to induce a maiden to succumb to his charms.

Men looked at each other.

'As for me, Sittonax, I'd ask the gods nothing more than this last forever: the stars in the sky, my comrades around me, the wine. The eve of the last battle. Is this the afterlife? I ask no more.'

There was a silence.

Brasidas laughed. 'Sittonax, you are a philosopher, and all this time I thought you were a sword arm attached to a dick.'

Many of them had never heard the Spartan speak so coarsely, and they all laughed.

Brasidas poured a libation over the side. 'I am the wrong man to argue against you. That is the life that I wanted; the life I sought, until some man's spear put me in the dust.' He looked at me in the flickering lamplight. 'But I say there are other joys than battle, and other comrades than men. I say that I have made enough war for any man's life, and I will go to Plataea, and build a house, and take a wife, and learn about sheep and pigs, and be happy. And I say to you, Sittonax: you have stood at my shoulder fifty times. Come and build a house next to mine and Leukas', and we will grow old, and tell lies about what heroes we were.'

'We *are* heroes!' Sittonax growled.

'All the more reason to lie,' Leukas said. 'Only we can handle the truth, anyway.'

I remember that night, as we raced across a perfect ocean, the wind at our backs, the stars in the sky. I walked out to the ram, and pissed away my wine, and then I stood amidships, watching the sky, and looking at their faces in the lamplight.

And I thought about what it would be like to lose them, right at the end of the race.

Tragedy, thugater. I feared it.

That night I slept, and dreamed. Oddly, I dreamed of Euphonia, my first wife; I dreamed she stood by her loom, doing some fine work on a himation for me. She was speaking, but I could not hear her. I walked back and forth, trying to find her words, and I could not hear them.

That dream was with me when I awoke, and my blood ran cold.

But as the day passed, the dream shredded away like the water passing under our oars. It was another sunny day, and we still had our westerly, and no one touched a sheet all day. We were so bored that the oarsmen danced on the catwalk, and then the marines raced in armour.

The marines, who had fought for their lives at Plataea four days before.

I'm not sure that the Argonauts were as good as our people. Let Zeus strike me with lightning, but my pride was vast, and perhaps there is hubris in it. But Antimenides and Achilles ran a dead heat, hurdling the slight step at the helm deck together, and we gave them both the prize, a circle of rope.

And we laughed.

That night we were short on food, and we had raisins and sausage, and we were out of wine. But in the morning, we saw the beaches of Samos under our lee, and the beach was empty.

We landed beside Cimon, and it took less than an hour for our marines to find the remnants of fires and the palisade of a military camp. Brasidas found coals under the sand, still hot. And Styges ran to the top of a wooden watchtower on the headland, three leagues distant, with Achilles, and they returned to say that they could see ships in the Bay of Lade.

Lade.

They were in the Bay of Lade, and there was no more ill-omened place for a Greek fleet.

But the Persian fleet was nowhere to be seen. Unless it was the Persian fleet on the beaches north of Lade.

Now the Bay of Mycale is deep and wide, and Mycale is the northern shore, running with excellent beaches for eighty stades. And opposite it, on the southern shore, is another beautiful stretch of beach with the isle of Lade as an outpost and a breakwater, and at the base of the bay sits the city of Miletus, where I almost died, and where the freedom of Ionia burned.

So on a sunny day, on the beach of Samos, I relived it. The fall of Miletus, the disaster of Lade. Cimon came and we stood together as our marines came back from their searching.

'I think the fleet must be over there,' he said.

I shook my head. 'Why?' I asked.

Cimon shrugged. 'Perhaps the Persians flinched? Declined battle and ran for the mainland?' he asked.

I stood there. All the way down that beautiful west wind, I'd come in hope of a final battle, and now that I was here, I felt a great deal of dread.

But when we had our men ashore, we got our sterns off the beach and our well-rested oarsmen pulled us for the mainland, just twenty stades away.

I put Kineas aloft in a basket hauled up the mainmast. It made the *Lydia* a little harder to steer, but he was able to tell us what he saw. He saw a fleet, the hulls black and hard to make out.

We rowed.

Cimon began to fall behind. He had a fine ship and a great crew, but we were *Lydians* and we had been together a long time.

We were still five stades away when Kineas identified Xanthippus' heavy trireme, and we knew we'd found the right fleet.

And then, the waiting.

They looked as if they were formed for battle.

In fact, they were two deep, their long line angled to us, and apparently lying on their oars. As soon as Kineas said that their oars were out, I ordered him down from the mast. It was clear they were ready for battle; I assumed that some trick of the clouds kept us from seeing the Persian fleet, and I didn't want a man's weight swaying from my mainmast unless it was Ka and his arrows.

Three stades, and I could identify ships.

Two stades, and I knew which ship was Leotychidas'. I could see the Spartan king in his armour and a red cloak.

'Raise the cloak,' I said.

I'd asked Leukas to lace my new purple cloak to a halyard on the mainmast. Now, racing along the sterns of the rear division of the allied fleet, my cloak went up the mast and burst in glorious Tyrian purple.

There was a pause as if the gods drew breath, and then a long sound, floating over the water. At first it was like a wail, and then it came as a shout, and then it was a cheer.

Every sailor in that fleet knew the *Lydia*.

And the message of the imperial purple was clear.

The Spartan marines were cheering their lungs out as my rowers slowed the *Lydia* and Sekla laid us bow to stern to Leotychidas' beautiful red ship *Hyakinth*.

I jumped down onto my own ram and then up to a ladder up his stern, and then I was on the helm deck with the king of Sparta.

'Victory?' he asked. He had the same hesitation in his face that I'd had once, asking Euphonia to marry me; he hoped, but he couldn't let himself be sure.

'Total victory,' I said. 'Five days ago. Mardonius is dead, Thebes under siege, the Persian camp in our hands.'

He took both my arms, and crushed me. As I say, it was a week for close embracing.

He sighed as he released me. 'No need to fight, now. The Persians are hiding their ships in a walled camp; Tigranes, the satrap, has come down with an army to protect them.'

I looked forward for the first time. The cheering was intense. It was all around us. Even the oarsmen were cheering, and I couldn't hear anything but the voices – thousands of voices.

Over the bow, I could see the beaches of Mycale. And there was the Persian fleet – all beached. All the hulls pulled well up. They couldn't put to sea at all. Nor could we easily put fire into them, or drag one off as a trophy.

It was a fitting anticlimax; the Persians, terrified, were refusing battle. What a change!

And then, I saw that Cimon had not followed me. He'd kept going off to the left, along the rear of the fleet. Even as I watched, he was folding his oars and coming alongside Xanthippus' trireme.

Leotychidas looked out at the beaches. 'It seems a long way back to Samos for the night,' he said. 'And I really don't feel like giving bloody Pausanias all the glory.' He shrugged at me. 'Please don't repeat that.'

I haven't, until now. All of them are dead now – all the busy plotters and Spartan politicians. But I understood. Pausanias had fought the Persians grudgingly, as he was, politically, the inheritor of the Spartan strategy of conciliation. Whereas Leotychidas was the last survivor of the generations of Cleomenes and Leonidas. He believed that Persia had to be defeated. He had seen the drama from the first.

He stood on the stern of his ship, watching the shore.

I saw Xanthippus signal with a shield.

Leotychidas winced. 'What's he doing?' the Spartan king asked.

I sighed. 'I'm going to guess that he's going to attack and burn the Persian fleet,' I said.

As soon as Xanthippus' ship went forwards, the other Athenians started forwards.

Cimon's ship was moving again, going towards the distant beach, and other ships were pulling out of the allied line.

Leotychidas turned. 'There. I didn't order a thing. You are all witnesses,' he said pleasantly. 'Helmsman – lay me along the Persian ships. I'm going to tell the Ionians in their army that the Greeks have won their freedom at Plataea.'

I bowed my head. 'You are a good king,' I said.

He smiled. 'High praise from a Plataean,' he said.

'I request permission to depart. I have to beat Cimon ashore,' I smiled.

He looked forward. 'You know that we are a mere handful, with all our marines, against Tigranes. He must have sixty thousand men.'

'Carians and Ionians,' I said.

'You think they'll run?' he asked.

I shook my head. 'If my brother-in-law and my wife have anything to do with it,' I said, 'you are about to see the last battle of the Ionian Revolt.'

I'll say this once more, because really, all these tales are to help you know your parents, my thugater, as you head off to a new life. I might have been desperate to find Briseis, and I might have had every doubt about her. I might have acted like a moon-eyed boy.

I won't pretend that I was not worried about her. But she had always taken care of herself, since I had first known her. She had a power – a great power – over herself, and over others. And she knew the game better than any woman of her generation. She had been wife to the leader of the Ionian Revolt and wife, too, of the satrap of Lydia. And she had by her side the best sword in Ionia.

So ... it is not that I never gave her a thought. It is only that she was as capable of making her own way as Brasidas or Sekla. She was as far from a poor weak woman as a woman could be, and as we rowed across the back of the allied fleet that afternoon, I was, to be honest, more interested in whether she had 'influenced' the Samians and Milesians and Lesbians and Chians than I was terrified that she'd been taken or killed.

Still, I had too much time.

I had time to think that this should be the last battle.

I had time to think of where we were, on the beaches of Mycale, from whence the Persian fleet launched to crush us at Lade. Where the men of Samos changed sides.

I had time to think that I was very tired, and that I had already fought fourteen days in a row, just a week before. There was no part of my body that didn't feel pain, and the idea of putting my greaves on my calves caused me pain. Just looking at the damned things caused me pain.

Aten laid my panoply out on the deck. Then he laid out Brasidas', and Sekla's, and Leukas'.

We rowed along the back of the fleet, the purple cloak fluttering at my masthead, and men cheered.

Even as we went north, towards the left of our formation, the Athenians were already going for the beach. Cimon led the way, and he was already ashore; I'd been with him for so long I could pick him out from three stades.

'That's Gaius!' Sekla said, at my elbow.

We were just passing the ships from Troezen and Hermione.

I was procrastinating about putting on my greaves.

I followed Sekla's pointing hand and there was Gaius, standing on his amidships platform, waving madly, and by him, Daud. I had once mistaken them for brothers, and now the resemblance was deepened in middle age. Both were in fine armour.

And the next ship was Moire's *Black Raven*. He waved too.

And the next ...

The next ship was that of Dionysius of Massalia, and his helmsman was Doola.

I let out a whoop. Sekla joined me.

There was our former capture from Naxos, and there, next in line, was the brother of my heart, Archilogos of Ephesus.

I had a lump in my throat as big as a pigeon's egg. Especially when Moire flashed the signal requesting orders. I had no real idea what Xanthippus and Cimon planned, except to force a battle before the ephors could order the Spartan king not to engage.

But there was a space between the *Poseidon*, the Naxian ship, and the first Athenian ship, and Sekla turned us, with the starboard side rowers backing water, and we slid into the gap as the oars came in.

I ran forward, waving at the Naxian, Diomedes, and then forward to the bow where most of my marines were arming.

Nicanor was beaming. The boy had fought for weeks in Boeotia and now he had that glow. I wondered if he was a killer.

I knew my boys were going to be bitter to miss this action.

And I knew I was delighted that they were safe in Boeotia.

From the bow, it was clear what Xanthippus intended. The Athenians were turning in place, forming a long column, and landing on the beach to my left. To my right front was the long beach below the Temple of Mycale, who is worshipped as a sort of Zeus; much like Cithaeron, I assume.

The Persians looked to have about two hundred ships. To my front, I could see the red ships of the Red King, but of course he would be there. And beyond, a sizeable camp, but nothing like the Persian camp at the Asopus. I thought this one about a third of the size, and I could see it as if I was a bird, because it ran up the ridge behind the temple. Their army was formed behind the ships, about six stades from my ram.

It was not a small army.

'Moire is signalling,' Aten said at my hip.

I'd have given almost anything for a minute of conversation with Cimon or Xanthippus. Even as I watched, the king of Sparta rowed out of the line, heading east. But the Spartans and Peloponnesians didn't follow him.

I make this sound too scientific. My impression was that the satrapal army of Tigranes substantially outnumbered anything we could field. Two hundred allied ships with twenty marines each would make an army of four thousand hoplites. No matter how wonderful you think our hoplites were that summer, odds of ten or twenty to one were long for an armoured man facing children with fire-hardened sticks, much less the veteran satrapal troops of an experienced Persian warlord.

And my first thought was to follow the king of Sparta. I was thinking of the beaches of Cos, and despite how far they'd pulled their ships up, I was pondering a raid on their palisade. I thought it was possible that I could burn a great many hulls while they fought the Athenians.

'Sir, *Ajax* is signalling *General chase.*' Aten tugged at my chiton.

I looked up. Cimon knew my signal book; his father had written most of it, back when we were pirates.

The problem is that we had only twelve signals, and the words 'General chase' did not immediately apply.

I stood in complete indecision for perhaps two minutes. There went the king of Sparta.

There was Cimon.

The *Athenians* were provoking a land battle at huge odds while the *king of Sparta* remained in his ship, apparently challenging the Persians to come out and fight a naval action.

I had to assume that Cimon knew something I did not. He'd just met with Xanthippus. What could Xanthippus tell him?

He could say, 'The Ionians will change sides when we engage.'

It was the only solution that made sense, and in that case, we didn't need the Persians distracted by fires inside their camp. That could be what Heraclitus used to call 'counterproductive.'

We needed them focused on us, and an infantry attack on them.

And I trusted Briseis. I knew what she'd come to do. I was willing to wager on my wife.

However foolish that appeared.

'Signal *Understood.*' I ran back to the stern, the ship moving under me, where Brasidas had become, once more, a man of bronze.

'See to it that all the sailors and the oarsmen are armed. We will become a *taxeis* ashore.'

He nodded.

I'll remind you that we had the best armed and armoured oarsmen in the world, the result of five years of highly successful piracy.

'Aten! Signal *Follow me,*' I called. I turned to Sekla. 'Beach us a stade to the right of the Athenians,' I said.

'That's practically in the Persian camp,' Sekla said.

'See the stream?' I said. A small rivulet leapt and tossed its way down the mountain, a ribbon of reflected light in the brilliant sunshine, and ran down the beach almost at the foot of the Temple of Mycale.

Sekla sighed. 'Must we?' he asked.

I laughed.

I felt something I hadn't ever felt at Plataea.

'Sorry I asked,' Sekla said. 'Please don't get Doola killed, Arimnestos.'

I felt it. It is hard to explain. Some men call it the daemon. The spirit. Like a god entering into your veins, like fire in your head. I hadn't felt it since Salamis. Even then, it had been thin. In truth, it was years since the rush of combat had filled me to the brim.

I raised my arms to the gods like a young girl and sang the hymn to Heracles, and men in the oar benches took it up.

It is a uniquely Boeotian hymn; but many of our rowers knew it, and Moire's rowers, and it spread, even as Aten flashed my new *aspis* and the *Lydia* came out of the line forwards.

The *Poseidon* was already underway, and behind, Archilogos in the *Artemis*, and then Moire in the *Black Raven* and Dionysius in the *Dionysius*, and finally the *Iupiter*, with Gaius visible amidships. Six ships. A powerful squadron.

To the south, just visible in the haze, lay the islet and beaches of Lade.

I went back aft and stood as high on the swan's neck of the stern as I could and shouted for the *Poseidon*. Their marines were alert, and a young man leaned out over the bow.

'Form a line to my *left*!' I roared in my best storm-at-sea voice. I also pointed.

He nodded and shouted something and pointed to the left.

'Slow the beat,' I snapped to Megakles.

The *Lydia* slowed to a crawl.

The *Poseidon* edged to windward and began to come up on our left.

A man in armour stood on the stern of the *Poseidon,* calling to the *Artemis*.

I was confident that this one manoeuvre would be performed well, and I took a cup of apple juice from Aten and drank it off, and then a whole canteen of water, and finally a sausage of sesame seeds in honey. Delicious.

I looked at my panoply on the deck and I had a thought I'd never really had before.

What if this is the last time? I wondered.

'Aten,' I said, 'fetch me my red chiton.'

Briseis and her women had made me a chiton in the Spartan style, a *chitoniskos* of Tyrian red, with woven borders and the ravens of Apollo embroidered all around the hem. It was far too magnificent for battle, but no grown man wears a *chitoniskos* for anything else.

Brasidas smiled when he saw it come on deck, and I pulled my dirty linen chiton over my head, wiped my body, and then bathed in seawater with a sponge to be clean.

Aten was wiping my panoply. It shone like gold in the sun. Well, it ought; he was the best servant I'd ever had, and Eugenios was aboard, the most meticulous steward ever born.

I looked at the shore, and chose to wear sandals. I wrapped my legs carefully in strips of white linen, and then put my greave-straps over them – little pads of the instep that usually vanish inside the greave when you most need them – and then clipped on my greaves.

We were three stades from the beach, and my line was formed.

I stood up, and Aten put my magnificent *chitoniskos* over my head, and arranged the folds, and then he and Eugenios put on my bronze thorax, my breastplate with its hinged back, and it went on like a sausage casing over the thin wool of the *chitoniskos*.

I swung my arms.

'Perfect,' I said.

Eugenios laced on my shoulder guards, and Aten attached the cuisse, the plate of bronze that covered my right thigh.

'And the left,' I said. I rarely wore both, but that day, I expected it to be grim. And . . .

I wanted to wear it all.

I had a new *aspis*. That one – the last on the row. You can see the *aspis* I carried at Plataea; you can see where it broke and how many punctures are in the face. The Mede officer cut the rim almost all the way through, a superb blow; it lasted the rest of the day, but broke when I leapt the wall of the Persian camp. My new *aspis* was courtesy of the Persian camp: a fine shield with a bronze Gorgon's head on a bronze cover. Beautiful work. I think it was a Lydian's, or perhaps a Theban's.

It is not only magnificent, but very light.

And I took a heavy spear; the ship carried dozens. But I also took the Mede officer's javelin. I hadn't lost it in fourteen days of fighting; I was attached to it.

Brasidas grinned. 'You look like my father,' he said. 'A hoplite of the Golden Age.'

It was true. No one wore so much armour any more.

I shrugged. 'If this is the last battle,' I said, 'I want to look like a hero.'

He nodded. 'You do,' he said. 'And every Persian archer will think so, too.'

I thanked Aten and Eugenios, and my steward went off to don his own panoply, and Aten ate the rest of my honeyed almonds and sesame.

We were almost ashore.

I drank water, and watched the shore.

The Persians were coming alive to the landings going on to their left along the beach. Their whole army remained formed behind their ships, but there were men on horseback riding back and forth, and men pointing.

At us.

I remember turning to Brasidas. 'We're the Achaeans landing at Troy,' I said, joy in my heart.

Brasidas laughed. 'I don't have ten years to wait for your sister,' he said.

'She'll wait for you,' I said. 'She's Penelope!'

It was screamingly funny at the time.

I went amidships.

'Friends!' I shouted. 'I expect every man to come ashore and fight. If we win, this is the end: the end of the war. You gentlemen may find peace more expensive than you thought; best plan is to be the first to loot the Persian camp. I saw the camp at Plataea; there's enough gold there even for you bastards. Now, come and help me get it.'

I was beginning to enjoy making speeches. They roared; I wasn't surprised any more. They weren't Boeotian farmers, either, but pirates.

Know your audience.

I was the first man down the boarding ramp. I insisted we land stern first. And I ordered Sekla to stay aboard, and to take old Poseidonios and twenty other older rowers and anchor the *Lydia* a cable's length offshore.

'I am prepared to fight one more time,' Sekla said.

I shrugged. 'I'd rather you were prepared to save our skins if this goes wrong,' I said.

He shook his head.

I grabbed his shoulder. 'Sekla – you have been through it all. If my sons were here, I'd take them ashore. You can get us off the beach and through a storm with fifty rowers. Brasidas can kill Persians. Please don't make this hard.'

He saluted. That was odd; Sekla never saluted.

Then I went down the boarding ramp over the stern.

That was odd.

For a few moments, I was alone on the beach of Mycale. In all my bronze finery. I could see the Persians, beyond the little stream and the temple, perhaps three stades away. By now, it was clear they were in turmoil; their rightmost regiments, who had been facing the sea, were filing off to their right, towards me.

I was the single Greek closest to the Persian camp. Way off to my left, the Athenians were forming.

My marines came down the boarding ramp.

'Front rank,' I said. 'Just like we practise.'

Indeed, we had practised this many times, but we'd seldom actually done it. And it was an odd phalanx – most of the oarsmen had javelins, not long spears, and some had other, odder weapons: axes and tridents, useful in boarding actions; longer swords than hoplites carried; long cavalry *kopis* blades ... There was no uniformity, except that most of them had a nice white *spola* of alum-tanned leather, and almost every man had a helmet, most of them just dog-bowls like the Plataeans wore, but some Corinthians with the ear flaps cut away; some Gallic helmets too.

We looked as exotic as a Persian army, really, the more so as close examination would reveal Persian scale shirts, Carthaginian helmets, and a lot of Phoenician equipment. Our deck crew and officers had to provide most of the front rank, as we had too few marines, and I could see that Aristides, Hilarion's son, was nervous about being in the front, while his friend Nicanor glowed like a god.

The Naxians came ashore, and their oarsmen were not well-equipped, but game. I formed them deeper than the eight deep my own were formed; and then I was grinding my bronze against that of Archilogos as he leapt ashore.

'By the gods!' he said, over and over, and then he grabbed my shoulders.

'Briseis,' he said.

I nodded. 'Where is she?' I asked.

Archilogos' face worked; his cheekbones seemed to waver in the sun, and his mouth opened and closed, and he pointed his spear at the Persian camp.

'Zeus Soter!' I spat. 'She's captured?'

'No,' he said. He was afraid of my anger, and yet I was not angry. 'She went of her own will. At the invitation of the satrap.'

I almost laughed. 'Of course she did,' I said.

My wife was in the enemy camp.

I'd like to say I never feared for her. but I'm a man. I did.

For the next quarter of an hour, I greeted every friend I had in the world, except perhaps Aristides; I hugged Doola, I embraced Gaius, and I watched Daud and Sittonax reunited. And I found that, in utter mutiny, Sekla was embracing Doola on the beach.

I couldn't be angry. All I could think was that Briseis was in the Persian camp, and that the sack of a camp is a terrible thing.

Alexandros was pounding Gaius on the back; Brasidas was looking bashful, and the Persians were coming out of their camp, in long files, and forming opposite us. They were still two stades away – extreme bowshot. Brasidas had us formed: five ships' worth of marines, deck crews and oarsmen. Like me, Gaius had a trihemiola with a heavy marine complement; Moire also had the kind of crew a pirate has. Dionysius actually had even more armoured men than we did.

It was not a bad phalanx. We had more than a thousand men, even leaving men to warp our ships off the beach. And every man was a veteran.

I was just exchanging a handclasp with Dionysius when Cimon came trotting through the deep sand.

Dionysius and Cimon had threatened to kill each other, the last time they'd been together, but that seemed not to trouble them.

'Here we are again,' Cimon said.

Dionyisus nodded. 'I had to come,' he said.

Dionysius of Phocaea had been the allied navarch at Lade. He had made a good plan. He'd been a terrible navarch, a demanding tyrant at sea, but he'd been correct, too; the Greeks didn't practise enough. Later, he'd taken his men to Massalia in Gaul and made a colony there, or rather, added to an existing Greek colony, and we'd lived there for several years.

He had as much investment in the Ionian Revolt as Briseis. Or me.

And so we looked at the Persians forming opposite us and put our hands in a wheel.

No one said a thing. The four of us ... It wasn't friendship, although I admired Dionysius and Cimon was one of my oldest war-friends. And Archilogos, who had been there from the start.

We shared Lade.

'Let's win,' Cimon said. 'For all the ones who died here.'

'For all the hopes that died here,' I said.

'To make it right,' Dionysius said.

'To finish it,' Archilogos said.

And Cimon pointed to the sand to my left. 'You cut me out of the right of the line, you bastards,' he said.

'Same order as the fleet,' I pointed out. 'Where will the king of Sparta land?'

'He won't land,' Cimon said.

'Wager?' I said. 'Leotychidas has been in this thing since before we were born.'

Cimon raised his eyebrows. 'Well, I think there'll be enough Persians to go around.'

By then my brother-in-law Xanthippus had crossed the deep sand, and he came and stood with us.

'Your wife had best be right!' he said to me, in his usual accusing voice.

It would be useless for me to protest. Xanthippus was the sort of man who saw his wife as an extension of himself, which was funny, if you knew Agariste.

'By the way,' Cimon said, 'you look like Ares come to earth, you bastard.' He slapped me between the shoulder blades.

'By the way,' I said to the assembled commanders, 'my wife is in that camp. I'd like her back.'

Cimon nodded. The other men looked at the sand.

'She says she can guarantee that the Ionians will fight for us,' Xanthippus said. 'I'm taking an incredible risk—'

I thought Cimon might slap him. 'I think that the Persians may know that their Ionians aren't to be trusted,' I said. I was watching the satrapal levies form. I could see a whole regiment of Persian regulars, with spears and bows and big wicker shields, the so-called *Sparpabara*. And then, next to them in line, another of the same, and then, just forming, some Cilicians. As far as I could see, there wasn't a Greek *aspis*.

'Satrap of Lydia,' Archilogos said. 'Ionian hoplites are almost half his forces.'

Xanthippus shook his head. 'That still leaves *thirty thousand men* to face us.' He looked at my men. 'You've landed your *oarsmen*.' He shook his head.

Cimon smiled past him, at me. 'Ari, like me, has crews of fighters.' He laughed. 'We trained in the same school,' he went on.

I was watching Carians moving into the Persian line. They were, quite literally, looking over their shoulders.

'They're committed now,' I said.

'So?' Xanthippus asked.

I looked at Brasidas. He gave a sharp nod. So did Gaius.

'So we should attack,' I said boldly, but I felt the daemon. 'Now. You're formed, we're formed, and the sun is high. Why wait for them to form? Half their army is in their camp, and in one charge, like Marathon, we can go through their arrows and push them back. If we pin them against the palisade, the rest of the men can't come out.'

That was too much for Xanthippus. 'You would not wait for the Spartans?' he asked.

Cimon shook his head. 'The Spartans aren't coming.'

I flashed him a smile.

'Our line is longer than theirs *right now,*' I said. 'They are still thinking that they are facing Ionians, who will stand and wait to be shot at. Let's get 'em.'

Cimon tossed a stone at Xanthippus' feet. 'I vote with the Plataean,' he said.

Dionysius laughed. 'I agree,' he said. 'Attack.'

I understood Xanthippus' hesitation. We were badly outnumbered. But we were ashore, and short of getting back in our ships ...

'Shall I show you?' I said.

Cimon's eyes grew bright.

If this is the last time ...

'Show me?' Xanthippus said.

I turned and ran to the front of our *taxeis*.

'Listen up!' I called. 'We're going to charge the Persians at a dead run. Fast as you can, and no one eats an arrow. My wife is in that camp. I want to see every woman brought to me, untouched. Hear me, you bastards? And a fair division of loot at the end. Last man in the camp is the poorest. Ready to run?'

They started to cheer.

Xanthippus was screaming at me. I could hear my name.

If this is the last time ...

I saw Cimon sprinting for his place in his own phalanx. And Gaius, slipping into his place and raising his spear. Dionysius, the oldest man there, but I heard his roar. Sekla and Doola, Nicanor and Brasidas, Alexandros and Antimenides, Kineas and Giannis and Giorgos.

I took a moment to tie my ear flaps on my helmet. To hide my tears. Those ranks were too full. There, like the avenging Furies in a drama, were all the young men who hadn't lived to reach this day: Agios, Stephanos, Idomeneaus, Neoptolymos, Harpagos, Paramanos. And a thousand more.

'You can't do this!' Xanthippus shouted.

'Nothing fancy!' I called from the front. 'We will march forwards until I raise my spear. And then we will run like Hermes with wings on his feet. **Are you ready?**'

They roared.

Opposite us, the Persians were just setting up their big wicker shields. The *spara* is the size of a small boat, and made of thickly woven branches covered in leather. It is held up by folding props, and usually carried by the slaves of the soldiers. It is like a portable wall.

The regiment opposite me had a wall of black and white; those were their colours.

'*March!*' I bellowed.

My *taxeis* started forwards. Some of the Athenians started forwards with us, and then more, and off to the left, I heard Cimon's voice roaring the same order. Remember that we had about six thousand fighting men between us; a frontage of just six hundred paces.

Off towards Cimon, more Persians pushed out of the gate of their camp to face us, even as a horde of Athenian oarsmen, too ill-armed to fight in the phalanx, deployed to the far left where the beach ended and the mountain began.

The Persians opposite me loosed a few arrows. They were ranging shots, and I found them very useful.

A Persian master-archer with a good, heavy bow will reach out a little over two hundred paces.

That's as far as anyone needs to run in armour.

But very few Persians carry those bows; most of them have lighter bows which they loose faster. Still, they can reach out a hundred and fifty paces, easily. Of course, to do so they must loose at a high angle, so that the arrow, in the end, plummets to earth.

This creates a very small area of impact – not like an arrow shot at a flatter angle, that can hit and wound men for many paces. Archers shooting for range must successfully guess exactly where their foes will be several seconds later. Easy enough against immobile men who are densely packed. Harder if those men are marching.

As we had proven at Marathon, very difficult indeed if they run at you like wolves at a lone calf.

To my front, the Persian master-archers loosed again. Their arrows, four of them, struck almost exactly where the first flight had struck.

Even now, they'd be telling their men not to loose until we passed those arrows.

And there was shuffling in their ranks. I liked that, too. Shuffling shows nerves.

I sent Ka and his archers to the rear rank. I didn't see any use for them in this fight.

I raised my canteen and drank off as much as I could get in me. I was still in front, all alone. Xanthippus was gone; I didn't even know where he'd gone, so total was my fixation on the arrows stuck in the ground.

Another thing that's good to know. Men moving forwards have better morale then men standing still.

We were moving beautifully. It's hard to explain, but men who really *know each other* can move better than men who merely do drill. We flowed. We flowed over the ground more quickly than the Athenians could march, and we began to leave them behind.

About forty paces from the arrows.

If this is the last time ...

I had odd thoughts: different thoughts than I usually had, entering a fight. Or rather, I had thoughts.

I thought of Briseis.

I thought of Euphonia.

I thought of Penelope, and Brasidas, and I was painfully aware of him, a few files away, in the front rank of a forlorn hope.

I thought of Hector and Hipponax, and I blessed the wound that had kept Hipponax behind.

I thought of Leukas and Sekla, who wanted the war to end. To go home.

I thought, about thirty paces from the arrows, of how this was not all I was. How Calchas and Heraclitus and Euphonia and Aristides and Gorgo had made me more than this – more than a spear.

And yet, how I loved this.

About twenty paces from the arrows, I felt as if the veils were ripped away. I felt free, as if nothing could hold me, and all that was real was the two hundred paces of hard-packed sand between me and the Persians; the shallow stream, flowing over rocks across the beach. I saw it all with a kind of crystalline clarity; the Persian shield wall was sharp-edged, in black and white, and I felt as if I could see each grain of sand on the beach, I could gauge the fall of each arrow as it was launched, and I could see the dice of the gods, rolling, the Fates measuring our lives, the moment that the shears closed on the threads of our lives. The daemon had never been so strong in me.

'Sing the paean!' I called.

And we raised our voices. The paean we sang was that of Apollo, as it was his festival in Athens. We sang to the god, oarsmen and hoplites, maybe ten thousand voices raised together.

The sound echoed from the mountain. It struck the Persians; it was as if a ripple passed through their ranks.

Yes, we are coming.

As at Marathon.

As at Artemisium and Thermopylae and Salamis. And Plataea.

'Ready to run?' I sang.

We passed the little clump of arrows, and heavy-soled sandals shattered the cane shafts as we trod them into the sand.

Two hundred paces away, the Persian bows came up, and aimed at the heavens.

'Go!' I called, and I was off, a pace ahead of the pack.

And then it was the pass above Sardis again. It was just me, inside my helmet, running easily, with long, flowing strides, like a younger man; free, for a moment, from the pain of middle age. Free of thought. The veils were gone, and there was once again nothing but me and the run to the arrows.

I had forgotten. Or perhaps you can never remember, never retell.

I was ten strides into my run before I had a thought, and that thought was that if the Persians had loosed their arrows on time, they should have struck.

In fact, they overshot us, and I never saw their arrows.

And then the relentless, Pythagorean equation; I pounded forwards at my best pace, and behind me men ran like athletes, and the Persian archers reached for their next shafts and nocked them.

I looked left, over my shield, and as far as I could see, there were Greeks, and they were going forwards. And there was Xanthippus, at the head of his phalanx; whatever he thought, he too was running for the archers.

When I look back, I remember very little. I had no thoughts.

I had no doubts.

I remember being surprised when I came to the stream. The Persians were less than fifty paces away, and the stream was twenty paces broad and so shallow that it seemed to just flow flat over the sand, and I ran on, raising spray, and for the first time, an arrow struck the face of my *aspis*, and exploded, spraying me and all the men behind me with splinters of cane.

As I ran through the stream I refused to slow or look for my footing, and so I stayed half a pace ahead of the other men, or perhaps my marines honoured me by letting me stay at the pace.

At the far side of the stream was a bank, and it was perhaps a foot high.

And beyond, the *spara*.

The wicker wall stood four feet tall, and now it was hindering my enemies from shooting flat at me. And it looked like something that I could hit, running full tilt.

Off to the left, they were still singing the paean.

I remember the last three paces ...

Because I remember thinking *We have already triumphed*.

I struck the *spara aspis* first and collapsed into it, and it *moved*. Something hurt me; only later did I discover that the impact with the great wicker shield had pushed an arrow through my *aspis* and into my side; not a mortal wound, but no pinprick.

But almost simultaneous with my impact was that of Leukas, and Brasidas, and Nicanor, and Antimenides, and then the whole front rank, and we slammed into the wicker wall like the boar hurtles into the hunter's net, and we pushed it along the ground. We must have shoved it ten paces on impact, and behind it, dozens of Persians were swept from their feet as the moving edge of the great wicker shield slammed into their feet and ankles. And we were reaching over the barrier with our spears and killing them, and they, knocked flat by the skidding shields, eventually tripped the props, and the wicker shields collapsed.

They had no shields. They had javelins, and short swords, and courage, and not one of them had ever faced armoured men with big fighting shields, and we pushed them back while our rear ranks killed the men trapped under the *spara* and came on, and even flowed around the seaward end of the fight. Down there, dozens of sailors and oarsmen simply ran into the sea and plunged around the end of the Persian line, so that as I began to methodically kill the Persians in front of me, they were mobbed from the side and rear, and then we were rolling them up and pushing them north, towards the Athenians, who hit the *spara* ten paces to our left, and I saw young Perikles be the first into the wall.

And then it was just fighting. Courage and a javelin are no match for courage, skill at arms and good armour, but they were so brave that we fought long enough to exhaust us all. Despite the loss of their wicker wall and the wreck of their seaward flank, they fell back, rallied, and fought as well as the Persians had fought the Spartans at Plataea. I remember when a Persian grabbed my spear and Brasidas' and pulled them to his gut, impaling himself so that his mates could finish us; brave, and worthless. My *aspis* shot out and the rim crushed a man's face; I let go of my pretty spear and drew my sword, put my shield into another man, and raked him with the hobnails on my sandals as I stabbed at him. It was inelegant, but it stemmed the rush, and Brasidas plucked a spear from a dying Persian's hand and threw it into another, and the men facing us backed away, backed away again.

A single Persian archer drew. I saw him; I saw his target, and as he drew I raised my *aspis* to cover Brasidas. His arrow caught my rim, and his mate launched another, and I cut it from the air with my sword.

If this is the last time ...

Off to the left, there was movement, and more and more Greeks were pouring past the downed wicker shields.

The Persians bunched at our front charged us.

They used their spears two-handed now, like hunters, and they caught us spread over the sand, in no sort of order. I was by Leukas and Sekla and Brasidas, and I saw Brasidas step back to make a cut and go down. I had no idea what had hit him.

I leapt.

I was straddling his body, covering him as best I could with my shield. There were three or four on me, spears held point down in two hands, striking for my knees or for Brasidas, I know not, and I crouched as low as I could behind my *aspis* and wished I had a spear. I endured them for three or four blows as the fight flowed by me, and I knew that the chances of taking a blow from behind were mounting.

And then Sekla's hip was against mine, and his *aspis* passed inside mine, the familiar impact as a friend's shield overlaps with your own. Mine was atop his, and because of that, I could attack.

So I did.

I stepped forwards strongly on my shield foot. As I did, Brasidas, lying on his back, rifled his spear into the ankle of my opponent, perhaps the most amazing spear strike I've ever seen, and in tempo I changed my target to the next man in the line, off to my left; an overhand sword strike over his reaching spear and through his cheek to his brain, and before I could withdraw my *xiphos* the man behind him pushed at me. But I got his spearhead on my *aspis*'s face, slammed my pommel into his nose, and threw him to the ground over my outstretched left leg, and Brasidas, still prone, buried his Spartan knife in the man's neck. Only then did my blade slide free of the first of my victims, and I pushed forwards another step as the Persians gave way and Leukas locked his *aspis* to mine, and Sekla came forwards.

And then Archilogos was there, and it was not for nothing he was thought the best spear in Ionia, and he cleared a space, and Brasidas rose to his feet.

And then we killed them.

I killed, and I killed. I killed them if they stood, and I put a borrowed spear into men's unarmoured backs if they turned to run, and we pushed them back to their palisade, and those who did not climb to safety were skewered to the pilings like the skins of deer killed in spring on the flanks of Cithaeron.

I can't measure the time, but the moment came when I was trying to get my hand free of my spear, and my spear hand would not open. And Leukas was trying to give me water.

I began to come back to myself.

We were a hundred paces from the stream, or perhaps two hundred, and you could have walked the whole way on the corpses of men. The little stream ran red in the sun, and the sand was red.

It smelled like a feast day in Athens; like meat.

Leukas poured water over my hand until I could free it from my spear.

I drank the rest.

Then I pointed at the palisade. Leukas had an axe. He always had one.

'Can you make us a hole?' I asked.

*

It wasn't really my brilliant tactical sense. It was my strong desire to avoid walking the two stades to the gateway, where the Athenians were now fighting the Persian rearguard. The sun was setting; we had three more hours of daylight. And it was clear to me that we'd won.

I wanted to find Briseis.

I looked around, and I saw most of the men I loved best still standing, and I was afraid, for a moment, to look too closely. But there was Brasidas, and there Leukas, and there Sekla, and there Styges.

Leukas went to work on the palisade. His axe was dull, but it didn't matter; Styges noted that the tops of the palisades were lashed with grapevines, and when we cut those, the palisades were easy enough to push over, because they were only set in sand.

To my right, the Spartans began to land. Their ships were packed with marines – maybe forty armoured men per ship – and they came ashore very quickly. I saw the king and waved. He was grinning, and behind him, his marines were forming as fast as wine flows into a jar.

I got back my beautiful javelin, still unbroken; it's that one, of course, on the wall, with the gold and silver inlay. I picked it up while they broke the wall, and the Spartans started up the beach, heading north.

And then I was pushing my *aspis* through where Leukas had made a hole about one man wide.

I'll say, as an aside, that I assume that the Spartans never saw that we were cutting a hole in the palisade, or they had another goal. They went right past us.

I was the first Greek into the Persian camp. It was ... eerie. Not twenty paces away, an officer was talking to another on horseback, pointing at me.

An arrow hit my *aspis*.

That was the closest to terror I have come in battle in a long time. I had allowed myself to believe that the fight was over; that the contest was done, and we were going to loot the camp. Instead, I found an entire regiment of Paphlagonians and Cappadocians just inside the wall, formed and waiting, and the men opposite me, behind the two Persians, had their bows bent, and I was alone.

They were perhaps twenty paces away.

Brasidas pushed through behind me and it was too late to retreat.

One of the officers shouted as Styges came through and the archers released a storm of arrows. Perhaps there were sixty, perhaps a hundred, but they were all aimed at me.

Thank the gods, they were not Persians. They had lighter bows, and most of them missed, but a dozen struck my *aspis*, so that I looked like a hedgehog, and two or three struck my greaves. The pain was intense.

Brasidas was down.

'Come on!' I shouted, or something equally stupid.

Styges was down, too.

I was *alone*.

And then Leukas came through, and Sittonax, and Daud, and Gaius.

And the enemy infantry charged us.

All five of us.

There were two or three hundred satrapal infantry, and they roared when they charged, but really, it was the best thing for us. Better than two or three more volleys of arrows, I promise you. I got into my stance; my left shin hurt as if I had been kicked by a horse, but I could stand. I was covering Styges, who was moving, and Brasidas, who was ... not.

I couldn't spare them a glance.

Leukas got his *aspis* against mine; Sittonax was at my shoulder, Daud on my right with Gaius behind him, and two of Gaius' Latin marines pushed through – brave men, because they could see the horde rushing us and they came anyway.

And then the Asians hit us, like a storm-driven wave striking a rock. Except that we moved. They swept us back, just with the pressure of their bodies, and I was all but pinned against the broken palisade.

Sittonax was killing men with his heavy spear from behind my shield. His *aspis* was pressed into my back, and he was *strong*. Because of him, I didn't lose my feet, or fall, and I covered him. And when the rush was over, I struck.

They had no armour: no helmets; no shields.

Most of them didn't have spears – merely long knives.

For as long as they thought that they could swamp us with their bodies, they were brave. But as we started to kill them, they cringed away, and who can blame them? They were unarmed, in the face of killers, and as I was not dead at the end of the rush, I went from prey to predator, and anywhere I put the head of my little javelin, I could kill. In fact, the trick was not to thrust too far, to flick like a cat striking, so that the little head didn't go too deep. In fact, I didn't need to kill; the more men I made to bleed, the sooner they'd run. I knew this kind of fight.

But they were hundreds, and we were six. Desperate men tried to take my *aspis* by the rim, and I had to strike with my rim, with my spear, with my feet, and Sittonax was *right there* like another pair of hands.

I shuffled forwards to strike better.

Sittonax stepped up behind me, and some other man pushed through the hole in the fence. And then the whole palisade came down, and a cloud of dust and sand rose, obscuring vision, and in the haze, some brave man among them called out, and the whole horde of them were at us again.

And then Alexandros' voice roared, 'Charge!' and all our men came out of the battle haze and crashed into the Cappadocians, and they died.

I knelt in the sand and dust. For a long time, I wasn't even there. It had been so close.

Brasidas was gone. There was blood all over his head, flowing through his helmet.

Flowing blood meant he wasn't dead.

I cut his chinstrap with the little knife I kept in my greaves. The helmet didn't move.

An arrow had gone through his helmet and …

He was breathing.

His helmet was pinned to his head by the arrow. The arrow … went through the helmet, through his head.

'Don't move him,' I said.

'They're reforming,' Sekla said.

'Damn it!' I said. 'Don't die! Don't be dead!'

Leukas turned his head away.

There was nothing I could do.

Gaius said, 'Shields up!' by my side.

Arrows rattled on our shields. I was still kneeling by Brasidas.

The blood just kept pouring out of his helmet.

I felt rage, yes, and a great fatigue, as if someone had reached out from far away and taken all my daemon and replaced it with sand.

I got to my feet. It seemed to take a long time.

'Forwards,' I said.

And we went forwards. The Cappadocians broke as soon as we moved, and ran, and then we were in among their tents, and two mounted Persians beat at the fleeing men with their swords to no avail.

The nearer, a handsome man with a black beard and a magnificent robe over scale armour, reared his horse and called something. I couldn't see past him; he filled the street of tents, and my limbs were like lead.

Ka shot him. Ka's arrow took him under his ribs, and he looked startled, then horrified, and then there was nothing in his eyes as he slumped to the ground. His horse just stood there, loyal to the last, and a dozen Greeks plunged their spears into him, but he was already dead.

Later, we knew that he was Tigranes, their commander.

And then we went forwards and nothing stopped us; even funnelled by the tents, we moved from street to street, and no one stood against us.

The command tents were in the centre of the camp, just as at Plataea. And there was Tigranes' tent, or so I assumed, as it was twice the size of any other.

I was the first man to reach it, of all the Greeks. I had stopped thinking of the greater battle. I wanted to find Briseis, and I wanted to make Brasidas be alive. These were the only two thoughts I had, although I had a vague feeling that I didn't want to lose any more of my friends, either.

'Ari,' Sekla said, 'you are bleeding.'

He never called me Ari.

I went into Tigranes' tent, and killed the eunuch who came at me. He didn't have a weapon, and I'm sorry, now, but he seemed to be coming at me, and I was *there*.

Behind him, there was a great deal of blood. A dozen men were dead, all Persians in long clothes, trousers, and fine, conical helmets. And they had fought and died.

I went past them, into the next 'room' hung in carpets. A lamp of solid gold hung there, and there was a bed, a magnificent divan hung in silk.

And a corpse.

Not Briseis. Another woman, dead with a spear in her gut; a Persian.

I went past the bed hangings, and there was another 'room'. A silver bucket hung from silver chains, full of water. Behind, the side of the tent had been slashed, floor to ceiling, and hung open, and the red sunset lit the hills beyond Mycale.

I cursed.

And then I drank the water – some of it – and Sekla and Leukas drank the rest.

I went through the slit at the back. Gaius emerged at the northern end of the tent, and shook his head.

I took a deep breath. The water steadied me; someone had attacked the tent. I knew perfectly well I was the first man into the camp; so it was someone inside the camp. Someone who was willing to kill Tigranes' guards and his courtesan.

To take Briseis?

Ka pushed through the hangings, and Nemet and little Ithy and their helots. The helots – former helots, by then – had bags, and were stripping whatever they found that looked like gold or silver.

They took the bucket.

I was still trying to make my brain work.

Diomedes would have been an obvious suspect, but he was dead.

Artaphernes' son …

Dead.

Archilogos burst through the wall of the tent.

He pointed his bloody sword at the ships. 'Red King,' he grunted.

Side by side, we ran for the ships. Behind us came Ka and half a dozen archers, and all my friends. Most of the rest of my people were looting, and who can blame them? It was better than taking an Aegyptian merchantman. Every officer's tent was a palace, and we were the first in.

The ships were easy to find – perhaps a hundred paces away – and the Red King's ship would be towards the eastern end; at least, if the contingents were in the same order they'd been earlier in the year.

I ran.

Archilogos ran, and Sekla and Leukas and Alexandros and Ka.

We were so far ahead of the battle that there were women washing in the stream on the back side of the camp; they screamed when they saw us, and drew the correct conclusion.

One of them wore a kaftan. She wasn't working; she wore boots, carried a riding whip, and had her face veiled. She didn't scream, but went for a knife at her belt. Her horse was across the stream, and I knocked her flat, put my spear at her kohl-rimmed eyes, and stretched my mind to think in Persian.

'I will not harm you. I need to know if someone has run by here. Carrying a woman, or women.' Never had my camp Persian been more useful.

'Yes,' she said. 'I was just asking these women the same.'

The women had nowhere to run – we came out of their camp. Most of us had to pause, to breathe.

'I saw them from up there,' the Persian woman said. 'It is the Greek princess, and the Red King has taken her. Tigranes will kill him.'

'Tigranes is dead, and the Greeks have won,' I said.

She flinched as if she'd been struck, but then her face hardened and she shrugged. 'For now,' she said. 'Will you kill me?'

I stepped back. 'No,' I said. 'Go your own way, but there are ten thousand Greeks coming into your camp.'

She got to her feet.

'Who are you?' I asked.

She smiled. 'I am the daughter of Tigranes,' she said. 'Ataesha. And you?'

'Arimnestos of Plataea,' I said.

'Ah,' she said. 'I will remember you.' She turned, gathering the washerwomen with a few comments in Persian that amounted to *Stay and be raped if you will, but follow me if you dare.*

I took what breath I could and started to run for the beach.

To the north, I could see the Spartans up on the hillside. They had run halfway around the camp, and we had burst through it. To my left and rear, the Athenians were all around the northern gate of the camp, and there was still fighting, or a massacre; dust rose to the heavens, an offering to the gods like the smoke of sacrifices, but this was a sacrifice of blood and sweat and dust to the rage of Ares.

I looked long enough to wonder if the Athenians needed help.

Then I turned back to the ships.

Ka pointed. 'There,' he said. 'The Red King.'

He was the one with the magnificent eyesight.

'Let's go,' I said, and we were off again.

Running over deep sand, in armour.

When we reached the Red King's ships, he had his rowers aboard. His small phalanx of red marines stood with their *aspides* on their insteps, ready to fight, but resting. All along this portion of the beach, Ionian Greeks were arming, or manning their ships. There were thousands of them, and most of them had no armour.

The Red King was standing by a bundle. It was a woman-shaped bundle, wrapped in a winding sheet of white linen.

He had a spear in his hand. As we ran up, his marines snapped to attention, and put their *aspides* on their shoulders.

'And there you are,' the Red King said, and laughed. 'I knew you'd come.'

I slowed, and came to a stop.

Ka put an arrow on his string.

'Tell your monkey to throw down his bow, or I kill her. Don't come any closer, or I kill her. Everything is just as I say, or I kill her.'

I didn't answer. All I could do was heave in breath.

Ka put his bow down in the sand, the arrow still nocked on the string.

'I have wanted this. I really thought it would end differently, but then, you being you, I suppose we were always coming to this,' he said.

I continued to breathe.

'Tell all your friends to throw down your weapons, or I kill her.'

I had caught maybe thirty breaths while he raved.

I didn't think the white bundle was Briseis. It's hard to explain why; shape and size, immobility.

I didn't know what his problem with me was.

And Brasidas might speak before he died.

'No,' I said.

He turned his head. 'No? I just kill your love?'

I let out a breath. 'And then we kill you and all your people.'

He put the spear against the white bundle.

'I don't think that's Briseis,' I said.

'I promise you she is,' he said.

I took a step forwards. 'Prove it's her, and I'll negotiate. Otherwise, you are dead.'

'I doubt it,' he said.

He knelt, and pulled at a fold of the linen, and it *was* Briseis.

I got a whole pace closer to him. I was surprised; I really hadn't thought it was my wife. On the other hand, I had also decided, in the moment of grace, how to play this.

'What do you want?' I asked.

'Safe conduct. Away from your fleet.' He smiled.

He was lying. I could see it in his eyes, which were not mad. Merely … inhuman.

'You fight me, spear to spear. I kill you. Then your friends escort me out to sea, and I let her live.' He shrugged. 'You won't care.'

'And if I kill you?'

'You won't,' he said.

'You're already ruined with the Persians,' I said. 'Tigranes' daughter knows you attacked her father's tent.'

His eyes narrowed.

I could see I'd hit him. 'So ... Your plan is to kill me, one of the chiefs of the Greeks.'

'Shut up,' he said.

'And then run off to be a pirate, because the new satrap will hunt you like a dog.' I smiled. 'Good plan. I suppose you thought you'd marry Briseis over my corpse and be king of Lydia.' I had my breath back. 'Too bad you killed Tigranes' bodyguard.'

'Men like me seize the moment. We do what has to be done. We make ourselves. Ionia is done. The Persians have raped it. I can make something new. And not with you shit-smelling goat farmers.' He stood up. Briseis moved her head.

'Men like you make corpses and never count the cost,' I said. 'The best man I know is dying on the beach, and you are keeping me from him. You want to fight me hand to hand? You're an arse, not worthy of my spear. You threaten to kill my wife?' I shook my head. 'I can kill you with one spear cast, from here.'

'If I kill you, your friends escort me away,' he said.

'If you kill me, you and all your people die.' I said. 'Fuck you and your scheming.'

Ionians were coming up – dozens of them. They were listening.

And Archilogos cleared his throat. 'You are a traitor ten times,' he said. 'If you kill him, or my sister, I will kill you.'

'If he falls, I will kill you,' Leukas said.

'If he falls, I will kill you,' Alexandros said.

The Ionians began to murmur. There were hundreds of them now. They had no armour, but many of them had spears. I didn't know it at the time, but Tigranes had not trusted them, and taken their *aspides* and their armour.

The whole time we had been speaking, his marines had been shuffling, looking at each other.

'Drop your spear, and I'll let you live,' I said. 'I'm in a hurry.'

Briseis smiled ...

He turned ...

His spear went back ...

I cocked my arm to throw ...

His marine captain slammed his spear into the Red King's helmet, and he went down like a sack of sand.

I sprang forwards. I went past the fallen Red King, and there was Briseis.

'Oh, holy Aphrodite, I couldn't breathe in all that linen,' she moaned. 'Quick, husband! Take all the Ionians and attack the Persians!'

'The Persians are beaten,' I said.

'I don't care. The Athenians need to see the Ionians fight alongside them. Go!'

She was still wrapped in linen. I leaned down and kissed her. There was blood.

Then I used my armour knife to cut the bonds on her linen wrapping.

Then I stood up.

Archilogos was standing there. He grinned at his sister and then he turned. 'Men of Ionia, now is the moment of our freedom. Come!'

They growled like lions, and they followed him up the beach.

The Red King's marines went with the Ionians, except two of them: the man who'd laid the Red King low, and his file partner. They were both tall, and young, in fine armour.

The one who'd struck the blow twirled his spear and plunged it in the sand. Then he pulled off his helmet.

He looked at the Red King. 'He thought I'd let him kill my mother?' he said. And spat.

He looked at me. 'You are Arimnestos of Plataea?' he asked.

The other hoplite took off his helmet.

'I am,' I said. 'I assume you are both her sons.'

'We are,' said the younger.

The Ionians were flowing away.

'Go and fight for the freedom of Ionia,' I said. 'I won't let any harm befall your mother.'

Briseis and I walked all the way back to Brasidas. She'd been struck on the head, and she was woozy; I wanted to run. And I could barely support the weight of my arms. Alexandros and Sekla were with me; the others had gone with the Ionians, or to loot, and it was lonely.

In fact, the Persian satrapal forces didn't collapse until the Ionians struck them from behind at the northern palisade. I heard the roar as they charged, virtually unarmed, into the rear of the satrapal levies; the poor bloody Carians fought to the end, men of bronze as they were.

I reached Brasidas.

The sand around him was red and brown instead of white. Some kind hand had propped his *aspis* above him with a broken spear shaft so that the sun wasn't on him, and when I reached him, he was alive.

I fell to my knees by him.

His eyes opened.

I wanted it *not to have happened*. I cannot describe this, if you have never felt it, but I wanted it not to be true. I thought of Penelope.

'The arrow is very high in his head,' Briseis said with her infuriating calm. 'Brasidas? Are you there?'

He frowned.

'Hephaestus!' I swore.

Briseis knelt by him. She touched the arrow, and Brasidas, my Spartan friend, screamed.

I put my hand on hers.

She looked at me – that fierce, almost predatory look she wore when she was *right*. 'If he screams, it is not in his brain,' she said. 'I need a good surgeon. An Ionian surgeon with tools.'

'I don't understand,' I said.

She had hiked up her chiton, and she ran, her long legs flashing in the sun, back towards the ships.

'Briseis thinks you need a surgeon,' I said. I think I said other things of no consequence. That he should hang on. That I loved him. Other useless things. Alexandros was more practical, making shade, building a small fire.

I felt like the Spartan king in the moments that I had come over his stern.

I couldn't let myself hope.

By Zeus, I was tired. It took me minutes to remember that I had a canteen, and I drank. That cleared my head a little.

I had allowed my wife to run off into the rape of a Persian camp, and my friend was dying or already dead.

And I knelt there, virtually unable to move.

Brasidas frowned.

'Where is Briseis?' he asked, as clear as day.

'Running for a surgeon,' I said.

He didn't say anything more.

*

Briseis came back with Sekla and Leukas and a dozen of our men, and a surgeon.

He knelt by Brasidas. And grunted.

'Look at that blood,' he said in his Aetolian accent.

His slave handed him a sponge, and he used it. Some of the hot water that Alexandros had made. Want to see heroism? Boil water in the midst of battle.

And then a pair of things like the tongs a smith uses to lift red-hot metal from the fire, except that the inside edges were sharp, like scissors or cutters.

He struck like a swordsman. He put them to the helmet, and in one *snap* he cut the shaft of the arrow close to the helmet.

Brasidas screamed and his head fell forwards. His helmet fell over his eyes.

'Who cut the lace on his helmet?' the surgeon asked.

'I did,' I said.

The surgeon and his slave were holding the Spartan's shoulders.

'Try and get his helmet off,' he said.

I caught his crest. He turned his head and there was blood.

I admit it. I looked away.

'Are we killing him?' I said.

The doctor looked at me, his face as close as a lover. 'Maybe,' he said. 'If we are, it's best this way.' He nodded slightly. 'For your friend.'

I got my legs on either side of his head and caught the crest of his helmet. I was in the same position I'd been in when I finished Hipponax. And I was painfully aware of it.

And Brasidas screamed again.

'Take his helmet off,' the doctor commanded.

I gave a gentle tug.

And it came away.

An amphora's worth of blood flowed out with it, and I almost retched. His long braids were matted in blood.

Blood flowed down his cheeks, his neck.

But the arrow – the stump of the arrow – was not in his head.

The bronze point had skidded on his skull and penetrated under the scalp, riding all the way under, stretching the skin of his head, tearing it away from the skull. It looked terrible. It took me two breaths to realize that this was possibly the best outcome for which I might have hoped.

'Hold his head!' the doctor said. I pinned it with knees and hands, and the doctor pulled the arrowhead out of the other side of his scalp, and the arrow came free with a long sucking noise, and the skin of his head and face returned to shape.

Mercifully, Apollo took his wits away.

In the next hour, we moved him to the fire that Alexandros started on the beach, and Eugenios appeared, and a Persian tent was constructed. Briseis and I washed his head, and the surgeon started on other men, but he came back twice: once to pour wine on my friend's scalp, and again to order Briseis to stitch it up.

In fact, I stitched it. I'd repaired a good deal of leather, and although leather does not bleed, it seemed the better skill. I sewed the long tear at his temple. He was still out, and his breathing was shallow and not very good. I lay down by him, and Briseis lay down by me.

I awoke in darkness, and Cimon was calling for me. I slipped away from my wife.

I was alive.

The Persians had lost.

I had Briseis.

Without volition, I raised my arms to the heavens.

And Cimon threw his around me. 'We took them all,' he said. 'Every ship. Two hundred ships . . .'

'Brasidas . . .'

'I heard he was killed,' Cimon said. 'Perikles is wounded.'

'Brasidas is yet alive,' I said.

I put my purple cloak over him, and put my arms around Briseis, and went to sleep on the cold sand.

In the morning, Brasidas opened his eyes. He looked at me.

And smiled.

'My head hurts,' he said.

And that, for me, was the end of the Long War.

Plataea

Spring, 477 BCE

We have come at last to a safe port; to the end of the story, at least for now. The end of the Long War.

But I don't want to leave you on a blood-soaked beach in Asia. Really, that's no end to a tale, unless it's the *Iliad*. As Brasidas and Alexandros and Leukas and I all know, there's more to life than the point of your spear, no matter how exciting it seems.

Mycale was indeed the last battle. In the weeks afterwards, the Spartans tried hard to demand that the Ionians all leave their cities and sail west, to settle in Sicily and Magna Graecia. This is what the ephors wanted, because those aristocrats would all settle where there were Sikels, and turn them into helots. And they would, in effect, have been Spartans.

But the Spartans were behind the spirit of our age. The Ionian oarsmen were not going to be included in a great project like the resettlement of Greece in the west. And, just as Aristides had feared, the little men of Athens, the *psiloi* and the oarsmen, had felt their power.

The Athenians made a different suggestion. They wanted to keep the allies together; to admit Lesvos and Chios and Samos to the league with their powerful fleets, and to maintain the war against the Great King. And we sailed, all of us, to the Hellespont, where the bridges that bound Asia to Europe were thrown down, and we cut the cables into pieces and they went to Olympus and to Delos and to Delphi as offerings to the gods for the preservation of our liberty.

We hunted the survivors of Mardonius' army along the Chersonese, while Xanthippus laid an incompetent siege to Sestos. Moire took a Euxine grain barge stuffed with gold, not grain, one of the richest prizes I have ever seen.

And over the mountains in Sardis, the Great King dallied with the wife of one of his generals, and then his wife killed her. The satraps fell to fighting among themselves, and there was not going to be another Persian army to invade Greece.

Leotychidas, before he sailed for home, gathered all the fleet, and all the loot, and shared it as if he was Agamemnon. Actually, a good deal better than Agamemnon, and when Sestos fell and we sailed for home, we were, oarsmen, marines, and trierarchs, all as rich as Croesus.

Which was as well.

Because in Attica and Boeotia, two years of war and famine had wrecked almost everything, and only the flood of Persian gold saved our people from another bad winter. But the loot of the Persian camps paid for seed grain and stone and wood, and we spent the autumn ploughing for winter wheat and building barns and houses, and every man and woman worked, regardless of how well-born. We raised the tower I'd built over Pater's old house, and another inside the new Plataea: a tower with a large house around a central yard, with its own well. We rebuilt the smithy, with ten bays instead of three; and while there were only sheds to withstand the grim winter rain, Tiraeus and Styges and I were turning out pots and pans and water buckets and ladles, even as my neighbour the ironsmith made kitchen knives as fast as his hammer could fly.

Briseis stayed in Athens with Jocasta and with Penelope and Euphonia until I had the walls of a house built, and then they came, and it proved that Briseis, queen of Ionia, could indeed be a farm wife in Boeotia, if a rich one. Her loom poured forth textiles, with a dozen women to manage it, and with her captain-general, Eugenios, our house grew more comfortable by the day. Furnishings came from the Peloponnesus and from Ionia: a beautiful set of *kline* with ivory plaques showing the gods; I miss those. Many times Briseis and I made love on them.

People lived in Persian tents until the houses went up, and every day offered a new adventure; making our own bellows for the forges; digging our anvils out of the rubble. Clearing the rubble – how could I forget it? It seemed to go on forever, and then it was gone, and we were building.

Winter passed, and the passes opened. Penelope came, and walked with Brasidas. I offered them a shared bedroom and my sister was shocked. But they set a date, for the next spring, and Brasidas worked like a Plataean – a rich Plataean – to build her a house.

Alexandros built a farmhouse on the slopes of Cithaeron, and a barn for his horses, and a yard for his children. And he married the eldest of Epictetus' daughters, a beauty with wide eyes and a deep understanding of farming.

And Leukas asked Paramanos' daughter to marry him, and she said yes, and he took all three of our round ships to Aegypt with cargoes out of Sicily as we brought in the winter wheat and planted barley and tended our grapes. Olive groves were cleared and tended; vines pruned.

In a whole year, I never danced the *pyrriche*, nor wet my spear. I made no man my slave, nor was I a slave. I went to many weddings, however.

You were born.

Daughter of my age, child of Arimnestos and Briseis, you were born to the last autumn of our poverty – we were rich in gold and poor in food. But as you grew to wailing health, so Greece grew; our wheat was the richest harvest in twenty years, and old men said the blood of the Greeks and Persians had watered the soil.

Summer came, and the new forge was ready to open. And old Empedocles, now blind, was brought at my expense from Thebes. He blessed our forge fires, and we sang the hymns that Plataea hadn't heard in three winters, and our fires came to life. I introduced the old man to my wife, and he touched her face and smiled.

We talked, and talked, and I heard from him how unwillingly the men of Thebes had served the Medes, and I probably frowned. But he couldn't see. And in the end, I sent some bronze there to be sold, and convinced the assembly that we should trade with Thebes, as they had joined the league.

And summer passed, and they made me archon. Briseis thought it no more than my due, but I was shocked to be *archon basileus* with the black hands of a bronze smith. But I was. I signed a treaty with Athens that bound us, each to the other; and I went to Athens in the autumn to sign it, and to preside, with Aristides, over the ceremony where the treaty was ratified. There, with Aristides and Cimon, I planned my dinner. Because I missed my friends.

Sekla built a house.

Doola landed at Corinth, took a cargo of hides, and chucked you under the chin.

Leukas settled in Piraeus, which was rebuilt faster than Athens.

Aryanam recovered, and he and Cyrus took their leave with many an embrace. I had hoped they might stay, but I could not lure them while other Persians and Medes worked as slaves and every woman made a widow looked at them with hate.

'Come and see me in Sardis,' Cyrus said. 'And I will feast you for a hundred days.'

Aryanam said less, but grinned, and took my hand. 'Look,' he said. 'In the end, we're still here.'

They rode away, the first of my friends to leave me that year.

Everywhere, that summer, was the sound of the hammer and the chisel, as stone was worked and carved; statues were replaced, temples rose over ruins, and houses, piers, warehouses, barns, ships ...

And as autumn came, the grapes came in; a crop so heavy that we propped and propped again, and twice I took every man in my house out to the old farm and helped Simonalkes and his sons to get the vines off the ground.

Also in autumn, a team of Athenian architects came and began to lay out the new temples. All the members of the league had given oath not to rebuild their temples until the last Mede was driven from our soil, but the Great King was now lucky to hold on to Sardis in Asia, and Aegypt was brewing revolt, or so Sekla said.

The last course of stones went into our new house, and the hall was finished – larger even than the house I'd made to host Jocasta and Gorgo. In fact, I modelled my house on Aristides' in Athens, and I had the best stonemasons build a magnificent floor in the newest style with a pattern in mosaic; there were paintings on every wall.

But all the houses were larger, and we made the town larger, too, by moving the walls out towards Cithaeron. There was a new Temple of Hera; the Temple of Elysian Demeter was made larger, although the Thebans and the Persians had never thrown it down, and we put a small white marble building by the Tomb of the Hero, with a good house for the priest. I am proud to say that my likeness is painted there, under the altar; and the statue of Heracles is me, too. So much vanity in a man ...

But no hubris, because I gave thanks to the gods every day, and I prayed, made my sacrifices, changed my daughter's nappies and, in general, was the happiest I had ever been. And perhaps will ever be. That summer will always be golden: the smell of fresh-baked bread; the jasmine and mint of your mother's head by me on the pillow; my spear only a decoration; the heady smell of new wine and new babies; and the glorious carpet of the land of Boeotia alive with new growth.

I sent my invitations over the mountains. We laid Persian rugs from the tents of Xerxes, Mardonius, and Artibazos on our floors against the cold.

And a new year came into the world. As the snow melted, it was difficult to even find the scars of war; already Plataea was built anew. A small but rich city, nestled at the foot of Cithaeron. We held a muster of our spears, and we had almost two thousand hoplites, because we had freed virtually every slave and replaced them with our Persians and Medes and Cilicians and Thracians.

War. Some men made kings, and others slaves.

We celebrated the Anthesteria and feast of Dionysius and my ancestor Heracles. There were thirty men and women in my house, and we were nymphs and satyrs, and the laughter drove out the darkness, as it should.

And the date of my dinner drew closer.

When the first flowers blossomed, I took a handful of my friends and rode over the mountains to Attica, and fetched Leukas and my father-in-law, and Aristides and Jocasta, Phrynicus and his wife, and Aeschylus, and Archilogos and his new bride Anthea, and Briseis' two sons, as well as Cimon and his insipid Thracian wife, and we rode like a procession of kings back to Boeotia, and there was Lykon from Corinth, waiting for us on the road with a veiled lady, and Sparthius, from far-off Sparta, and Megakles and Doola from farther still, and Gaius, who wept when we embraced.

And as we rode down the pass into Boeotia, we gathered friends like the triumphal procession that, in fact, we were: Penelope from her farm; Styges from his forge, and Tiraeus; and Sekla, and Alexandros and his wife; Gelon, and Hipponax and Heliodora; Hector and Iris; Ka and Sitalkes and Polymarchos and Nemet and Moire, and Giannis, who had his own ships now, and we went to the new Temple of Hera, where the statue of Mater Hera was my mother almost to the life – sober, one hopes. And there stood Brasidas to receive his bride, and Niome to receive her groom, and Leukas and Brasidas were married, side by side, in fulfilment of promises made.

And that night, in the courtyard of our house, we lay on every *kline* from every house in Plataea. And wine flowed like the blood of heroes; we ate a whole tuna that took eight men to carry, and enough bread to have fed our phalanx at Plataea.

And the sober Spartan lady was Gorgo, and she lay between Jocasta and Briseis while they plotted the end of the dominion of someone, and shrieked with laughter, and played with you, dear thugater.

I will leave them all there. In victory. In happiness. A little drunk, and beautiful: Brasidas with his crown of ivy askew, my sister gazing into his eyes; when he made the libation to begin the dinner, Brasidas mentioned that Antigonus lay with Leonidas.

Leave us there, in the hour of bliss.

But I will say a few words more. Let us end as we began.

In the morning, my heart was too full to lie abed, nor had the wine god left me with a wooden mouth or pounding head. I kissed my wife, and rose into the dawn, and I put on my farming clothes and fetched my pretty Arab mare, intending to ride up the mountain. I did it often, when the darkness was on me, but that morning, it was not darkness, but light.

Of course, Aristides was awake before me. He had a horse as fine as mine, and we rode together, and neither of us spoke a word.

And there we stopped, by the new temple and the old beehive tomb, and we sat on the precinct wall and talked. Mostly we talked of men we had known who had not lived to see the end.

Perhaps we wept a little.

He rose. 'I want to see these trails where you hunted as a boy,' he said. 'Did you never stumble on the ghost of Actaeon, pursued by the hounds of Artemis?'

I laughed. 'I was too hungry,' I said. 'Shall I come with you?'

'No,' Aristides said, with a smile I understood.

Sometimes you need to be alone with your ghosts. I was there if he needed me.

He walked away, and for a while I could hear him moving, and it was oddly like waiting for Calchas, when he was hunting, and I was very young.

I went and poured a libation on the altar. I chopped a little firewood, for whenever the priest would come.

And I heard footsteps.

I went outside into the bright sun, and there was a man in stained leather *spolas* with a bronze helmet sitting on the back of his head, with dented greaves and a dirty chiton and a spear on his shoulder. He hung his *aspis* on the tree.

And sat ... No, he collapsed on the wall of the sanctuary.

I stepped out into the sunlight.

He was young, under the dirt. His face was burned brown and red, and his eyes were a little wild.

'Are you the priest?' he asked.

I didn't even think about it. 'At this shrine,' I said, 'every man of arms is a priest.'

He nodded. 'Do you have any wine?' he asked.

I gave him some from my canteen, and then, together, we poured a libation.

'To the dead,' he said, and his voice cracked, and he burst into tears.

I sat with him for a long time.

Epilogue

That's the end of the story. Or perhaps it isn't; perhaps I'll have a hunt this autumn, and you'll all come to hear more tales. After all, the war hardly ended there; we fought the Persians again for Asia and for Aegypt, not once but many times.

Or maybe you'd like to hear how a few of us sailed over the edge of the world, and out past Aegypt and down the coast of Africa, farther than any Greek man has ever sailed. It is a great story.

Perhaps you'd like to hear how Megakles and Cyrus and I went to India.

How we went after more tin.

Or how I conquered this place and made it my kingdom.

Listen, thugater. This may be my last piece of wisdom at your wedding feast.

No story is ever over.

The Battle of Plataea, 479 BCE

A HISTORICAL INTRODUCTION
by Aristotle Koskinas

Prologue

In August 479 BCE, in the plain near the city of Plataea, the future of Greece, and perhaps that of the entire western world, hung in the balance. Everything depended on the outcome of the clash between the mighty Persian Empire and the allied armies of the various Greek cities.

This battle was not the first, nor would it be the last between Persians and Greeks. However, it was the one which would stave off the threat of Persian occupation and ensure the independence of the Greek city-states for the years to come. In turn, this independence, and perhaps the wave of euphoria that went with winning it, would fuel a remarkable cultural bloom for the next fifty years, a period which came to be known as the Golden Age of ancient Greece.

Background

The Battle of Plataea is part of two large campaigns, known as the Persian Wars, which both took place in the first half of the 5th century BCE. As is the case with everything, these wars did not come out of the blue but were the result of events that had begun as early as the mid-6th century BCE.

It all started with Cyrus the Great, king of a small realm within the great Median Empire, who managed to defeat his overlords and establish an Empire of his own, which he expanded, by conquering Lydia and Babylonia, all within a decade (549–539 BCE). At its peak, the populous and multicultural Persian Empire boasted vast resources and stretched an impressive 6,000 kilometres from the

Mediterranean to the Hindus River and from the Red Sea to the Caspian one.

The Persian Empire respected the beliefs and customs of its subjects, as long as taxes were levied properly and no subversive activities were undertaken. The central government maintained a well-organized control over the whole realm, which was subdivided into large provinces, called satrapies. Each satrap had broad political and military authority, but was accountable to the king who closely monitored their activities. This centralized control of the land was facilitated by an excellent centralized bureaucracy, a network of well-maintained roads, and a speedy postage service which connected every part of the Empire with the capital; the Empire's military might was supplemented by an equally formidable diplomacy.

The conquest of Lydia, in 547 BCE, brought the Persians in contact with the Greeks for the first time. Their thriving cities, such as Miletus, Ephesus and more, had been established as early as the 8th century BCE by Greeks from the mainland, with which they still maintained cultural and commercial ties. As was typical with the Greeks, each city was an independent state, with its own laws, coinage, measuring standards and army. Despite their fragmentation, or perhaps, because of it, they were important centres of commerce and culture. A large part of their autonomy was maintained under the Lydians, who had exercised a rather light control over the Greeks. However, the internal divisions and antagonism between the various aristocratic factions within each city spelled problems for the Persians who found no unified ruling elite to help them rule their new subjects. So they resorted to supporting one faction in each city, appointing their leaders as tyrants in return for their cooperation. Needless to say, this caused resentment, which was later exacerbated by the heavy taxation which caused these flourishing trade centres to decline.

The Ionian revolt

Seeking to strengthen his position, the Greek tyrant of Miletus, Aristagoras, convinced the local satrap to support an invasion of the Greek island of Naxos. When the expedition ended in failure, Aristagoras, rather than face the Persian wrath, incited the other Greek cities to revolt against the Persians. His success is ample proof that sentiments in the area were ripe for a revolt; it quickly spread to all the Ionian city-states, as well as neighboring Caria and the island of Cyprus.

Knowing that help would be needed in order to stand against the mighty Persian army, the rebels turned to the mainland Greeks, but received only a token support in the form of a handful of ships from the cities of Eretria and Athens. The revolt had a few early successes, notably the destruction of the city of Sardis, but soon the situation was overturned. Internal disputes on the part of the Greeks, against the superior organization and effective diplomacy of the Persians, resulted in the defeat of the rebel forces at the naval battle of Lade, a defeat which spelled the end of the brief revolt (499–493 BCE).

The Persian expansion to the west

Having cleared up after the revolt, the Persians continued westwards, in a series of campaigns whose aim was to expand the Empire's borders into Europe. It is hard to imagine that the poor Greek soil and few resources of the entire Greek peninsula could warrant an expedition of conquest on purely financial grounds. However, the occupation of the Greek lands could be intended as a propaganda coup, against those thinking of starting or abetting a revolution against the Persian throne. The intention of drawing military levies for the Empire from the high-quality Greek infantry may also have been a consideration. At the same time, the move would secure the western border of the Empire, while opening up the way to areas far more worthy of conquest, such as Italy and Sicily, whose potential was well known.

King Darius had already lead a campaign against the Scythians, the nomadic horse archers living along the north coast of the Black Sea. Having secured their northern flank, the Persians crossed into Europe. Although their fleet was destroyed by a storm off the coast of Athos and their army was defeated by Thracian tribal warriors, the Empire was successful in subjugating the areas of Thrace and Macedonia.

The next ship-borne campaign, in 490 BCE, targeted the Greek mainland and aimed to deliver a resounding lesson to the cities of Eretria and Athens who had provided aid to the rebels. Although the islands of the Aegean were subjugated and Eretria was destroyed, the campaign ended with a resounding defeat of the Persian army in the battle of Marathon.

The Persians responded by planning another campaign against Greece, during which the battle of Plataea took place. The campaign was delayed for about a decade, due, not only to the scale of the preparations, but also to the death of King Darius which sparked a series of uprisings, which his heir, Xerxes, had to deal with.

The campaign of 480 BCE

The army put together by Xerxes, comprised of people from nearly every corner of the Empire. The Greek historian Herodotos, our main source of information on the Persian Wars, says that the army included forty-five different nations, among them Arabs and Indians, all of whom spoke their own language, carried their traditional weapons and fought in their customary manner. The army comprised of six broad ethnic groups, divided into twenty-nine different commands, representing the provinces of the vast Empire. The Greeks regarded the Persians and Medes as the most worthy opponents, as well as the heavily armoured Egyptian marines, whereas the archer riders of Skythia and Baktria were considered particularly fearsome.

The Persian army

It is hard to believe that the size of the army was as large as Herodotos claims (one million seven hundred thousand people), who gives us images of rivers and streams drunk dry by Persian horses. The main reason is not that the Persians did not have the human resources (they probably had) but rather that transferring and supplying such a vast army would require means that even the Empire did not possess at the time.

However, the expeditionary force must have been sufficiently large to ensure victory over the estimated number of opponents in a hostile territory. A modest estimate might be two hundred thousand people, including auxiliaries, plus a fleet of about one thousand warships and hundreds more transports. The warships had crews of two hundred men, plus thirty marines each, raising the total of the Persian force by another two hundred and thirty thousand people.

This huge army was lead by the High King Xerxes himself and a senior staff of six generals. The core of the invasion army consisted of the elite troop of ten thousand 'Immortals' and the divisions of the standing army, which were organized according to a decimal system of ten thousand men, further subdivided in units of one thousand, one hundred and ten men. Along the standing army of Persians and Medes, there were the levies from the different provinces of the Empire, including Ionian Greeks; these both served in the land army and contributed squadrons of triremes to the fleet.

The Persian infantry carried large pavise-like shields and spears, but their main weapon was the bow. The cavalry were noblemen who mostly used their spears and bows, although they carried swords too.

Based on descriptions of the period, it is believed that their military tactics were based on archery. The infantry would form a line of shields, under cover of which they shot arrows 'so thick that they would blot out the sun.' Their aim was to thin the lines of the enemy, causing panic if possible, and paving the way for an attack by the cavalry, who would rush into the broken enemy lines, completing their destruction.

The Persian army's main difference with the Greeks was that (with the exception of few units, such as the Immortals and the Egyptian marines) most combatants were armed much more lightly than the Greeks. Their shields were made of wicker and they wore hardly any armour, as their tactics were based on shooting arrows from a distance and rarely involved hand-to-hand combat.

It is worth noticing here that all our information about the Persian wars comes from Greek sources (Herodotos, Thucydides, Plutarch and Aeschylus), which, as can be expected, display a strong bias against the Persians. Although Herodotos praises their bravery, they are generally presented as arrogant and proud and prone to the great fault of Hubris, which, to Greeks, is the surest way to ensure one's downfall.

Perhaps these are literary inventions; what cannot be disputed is that the Persians had admirable organization and were unparalleled in logistics and military engineering. Feats such as supplying a huge host of people so far from their base, bridging the Bosporus to cross from Asia into Europe and cutting a canal for their navy to bypass the dangerous Athos peninsula are admirable even by today's standards; they certainly seemed as nothing less than science fiction for the Greeks of the time. Their diplomacy, which did not hesitate to employ propaganda or outright bribery, was something to be reckoned with, while, despite its numbers and diversity, their multicultural army maintained its discipline and cohesion. Even when retreating, at the end of both campaigns, the Persians managed to reach home in about forty-five days, in an orderly and well-organized manner.

The Greek army

This would be unimaginable for the Greeks, who had no notion of any centralized government. Instead, they were divided into approximately one thousand fiercely independent city-states, of various sizes and populations, spread throughout the Greek mainland, the islands, as well southern Italy and Sicily, and all along the coasts of Asia Minor and the Black Sea.

As mentioned before, each city, large or small, rich or poor, had its own system of government, laws, currency, even foreign policy. They were always at war with each other, usually over land borders or water rights, which maintained the able-bodied males at a constant battle readiness. Some of the larger city-states had, already by the beginning of the 5th century BCE, managed to rise above their local antagonists and attract others, forming alliances. For example the Spartans had formed the Peloponesian League, while the cities of Boeotia allied themselves into the Boeotian League, around Thebes.

It is worth noting that Thespiae and Plataea, although both in the plain of Boeotia, instead of allying themselves with the other Boeotian cities, chose instead to form an alliance with the Athenians, due to the constant aggression of the nearby city of Thebes.

Despite their differences and disputes, the Greek city states shared the same language, script and material culture, in spite of several local variations. They also had the same religion and system of values which expressed themselves mostly through the culture of the elites, in the great sporting events and offerings at certain sanctuaries of pan-Hellenic appeal.

Athens had overthrown the tyranny of the Peisistratid family and was making its first steps as a democratically governed state. This new form of government had already displayed its potential, when the Athenians had managed to defeat, in close succession, two armies, those of Chalkis and Thebes; these victories averted the threat of occupation and allowed the nascent democracy to develop. Actually, it was during their struggle against tyranny that Athenians turned to the Persian Empire seeking aid. The Persians demanded 'earth and water' in return, which the Athenian representative was quick to offer, perhaps without realizing that to the Persians the gesture meant submission. Later, the Athenian assembly cancelled their ambassador's offer, failing however to inform the Persians. Even if they had done so, it was too late – the offer had already been accepted. Consequently, when the Athenians offered help to the Ionian revolt, the Persians saw it as nothing short of treason by one of their sworn vassals.

Having been informed of the Persian intentions, the Greeks made their own preparations. The better treatment of the Ionian cities after their revolt, as well as the effective Persian diplomacy combined with the visible threat of their mighty army conspired to convince most Greek cities either to succumb to the Persians or remain neutral. Only thirty-one cities refused to accept their advances, among them Athens, Sparta and Plataea.

Their armies were made up of heavily armed infantry, called hoplites, who fought in a close formation called the phalanx. The hoplites were free citizens of the upper middle class, who could afford the cost of their arms and armour; they carried a heavy round shield and used spears and short swords. Most Greek cities had little cavalry for two reasons: first, horses were rare and expensive to maintain in the small, arid plains of southern Greece, and secondly because cavalry was practically useless against the phalanx. The phalanx was supported by bodies of light infantry called *psiloi*; with the exception of an Athenian unit of trained archers, *psiloi* usually carried javelins or simply threw stones at the enemy. They were made up of the poorer classes and sometimes included slaves.

The greatest advantage of the Greek alliance was their navy, especially the Athenian one, which began being built after 483 BCE, when the combination of silver discovered in the mines of Lavrio, near Athens, and their war against the island of Aegina, allowed a shrewd politician, Themistocles, to convince the citizen assembly that it would be wise to invest in a mighty fleet.

By defeating the Persians in Salamis, in the autumn of the previous year, the Greek fleet had prevented them from occupying and holding the Peloponnesus. King Xerxes departed with a section of the army, while Mardonius was left to winter in Greece and continue the campaign the next year. Mardonius was in command of a still powerful army, which was more than sufficient to keep the unwilling allied Greek cities of Thessaly and Macedonia under his control. He also controlled the rest of mainland Greece, including Boeotia, where Plataea was.

The Greeks on the other hand were defending the isthmus joining the Peloponnesus to the rest of Greece. Since the Persians now lacked a naval arm, they could not outflank their defenses, so the Peloponnesians felt secure and were unwilling to risk venturing north of their positions. However, their allies to the north, namely the Athenians and Plateans, whose cities had been destroyed, were urging them to advance the line of defense to include the areas of Attica and Boeotia. Understandably, the Peloponnesians were reluctant to do so, and offered instead to provide for the families of the Athenians for the duration of the war. At the same time, the Persian diplomacy was also trying to reach the Athenians. Alexander of Macedonia, acting as ambassador of Mardonius, attempted to entice them to change sides, a move which aimed at the very least to divide the Greeks, or, if the Athenians acquiesced, to acquire an ally with a body of proved combatants and a fearsome fleet in one broad coup. The Athenians indignantly refused both offers, so, while the Peloponnesians delayed sending troops to defend Athens, the Persian armies swept down and once again occupied the city, destroying what little the Athenians had just rebuilt.

The Athenians threatened to abandon the Greek alliance and settle somewhere in the western Mediterranean. Faced with the threat of losing ten thousand of the best troops the alliance had, who had the added advantage of having fought against the Persians, as well as the fleet that prevented the Persian forces from outflanking theirs at the Isthmus, the Peloponnesians had no other course of action than to advance against the Persians. The core of their army was the Spartan contingent, made up of five thousand Spartan citizens, accompanied by five thousand Spartan *perioikoi* as well as thirty-five thousand helots, approximately. Allies and former enemies coexisted with some difficulty in the Greek force, which must have numbered a total of about one hundred thousand of which thirty-eight thousand seven hundred were the hoplites.

So it was that the two armies, the Greek and the Persian one, found themselves facing each other in the scorched plain near the city of Plataea, which now lay in ruins.

The plain of Plataea

Plataea lies between the river Asopus, to the north, and the mountain of Kithairon, to the south. Its fertile plain, rich grazing land, wooded mountain slopes and ample water make it an ideal site for settlement. It is no surprise that the first signs of habitation date already from the Neolithic period. Besides its abundant resources, Plataea also straddles important routes, connecting the Peloponnesus, the island of Euboia and Athens with the north of Greece. The consequence was that Plataeans found themselves defending their land since very early in history.

The area around Plataea is called a plain and looks deceptively flat. In fact, the foothills of the mountain meet the plain forming a maze of low hillocks, spurs and gullies, small streams and other such features.

The fragmented landscape gives an impression of flatness but in fact is so complex as to create problems in the deployment of troops, especially cavalry. Countless blind spots limit visibility and therefore prevent full awareness of battle space.

Herodotos describes the site giving detailed information and descriptions; unfortunately, it is difficult to match the place names he provides with features in today's landscape and therefore the identification of where various events took place is tentative at best.

The Battle of Plataea saw the convergence of two armies in what was to be by far the largest land battle in Greece in the 5th century BCE. Several factors affected how the commanders of both armies made decisions and managed the battle.

Pausanias, the Spartan commander of the Greek alliance, had no cavalry. His aim was to lure the Persians into attacking his position at the foot of the mountain, where the broken ground was unsuitable to cavalry. He also had an overstretched supply line; the area around Plataea was destroyed, and so was Athens, meaning that his supplies had to come all the way from the Peloponnesus in mule trains. His water supply was also limited and was subject to attack by the more mobile Persian cavalry. Another problem was the size of his army; it was the first time in history that such a large number of Greeks troops had fought together. His army comprised forces who had been traditional enemies for centuries; Pausanias had to reconcile differences, encourage cooperation and maintain discipline while accommodating various demands without seeming to favour one over another – altogether an impossible task.

On the other hand, Mardonius, the Persian commander, had problems of his own. Numbers were certainly in his favour, but not so much as to make victory a foregone conclusion. His own strong cavalry was reinforced by that of his new Greek allies from Thessaly and Macedonia. Provisioning his army was easy, given that he controlled most of the Boeotian plain, while Thessaly was not far off. However, given the size of his army, provisions would eventually run out without the possibility of being resupplied from Persia, as the Greek navy controlled the sea.

A common problem which explains why the battle took more

than fifteen days to begin is the fact that both sides wanted to fight on ground that would favour their forces: the Persians would rather fight on the smooth plain to the north of the river, where their cavalry would have a free run, while the Greeks would prefer the broken ground of the foothills where horses could not go. It is perhaps no coincidence that both armies had received oracles which ensured them victory as long as they stayed on their side of the river.

The long days of waiting and baiting each other were marked by three major episodes.

In the first one, which took place after the Greeks deployed themselves at the foot of Mt. Kithairon, the Persian army tested them by attacking the section held by the Megarians, which was the most easily accessible. In this episode, the Athenians played an important part by offering support to the infantry by means of their body of archers and a company of elite hoplites. The Greeks won, and an important Persian noble, Masistius, was killed.

In the second episode, the Greeks moved their positions to the northwest, down in the plain and nearer both to the Asopus and the Persian camp. This move is interpreted as an attempt to lure the Persian army to attack them across the river. But while the ends of the line were in defensible ground, the middle was exposed to the Persian cavalry and took the brunt of their offences. Although the Greeks withstood the Persian attacks for several days, the move eventually proved a bad idea; taking the initiative, Mardonius staged an attack that intercepted and destroyed a Greek supply column. The patrols of his cavalry prevented more convoys from reaching the Greek camp.

The situation became even worse when, a little later, the Persians poisoned and blocked the spring of Gargafia, which provided the Greek troops with water; this forced Pausanias' hand.

The third episode was none other than that of the final battle, and began the night before, with Pausanias withdrawing his army to new, more defensible positions. This move, planned to take place under cover of darkness, has been discussed endlessly by both historians and military experts. No one seems to know for certain what exactly happened or why. Were the Greeks actually retreating? Was it an attempt to regroup closer to their supply lines? Or was the move a strategic retreat, aiming to lure the Persians into fighting the Greeks on ground that favoured the latter?

Whatever the thinking behind the maneuver, two facts remain

undisputed: first, complicated army maneuvers were a new concept for the Greeks, even for seasoned fighters such as the Spartans; secondly, moving thousands of troops in the middle of the night over such broken ground was a recipe for disaster. Several groups ended far from their intended positions, while the Spartans started late, because Amompharetos, commander of the division named after the Spartan village of Pitana, refused to budge, believing that falling back would bring shame to the Spartans. It was highly unusual for a Spartan commander to refuse to obey orders, but not unheard of; there had been occasions where other commanders refused to follow orders, even those of kings, based on their experience.

While some contend that the late departure of the Spartan commander was simply the result of his being a crusty old Spartan, others maintain that his delay was a brilliant ruse, planned by the Greek command, to attract Mardonius by offering him a unique chance to cut off the Spartans. Mardonius swallowed the bait, sending his Persian troops and cavalry, while, at the same time, his Boeotian allies marched against the flank of the Spartan formation. However, the latter were stopped by the Athenians, who, according to the plan, had hidden nearby with the aid of Plataeans who knew the ground, thus foiling the Persian advance.

Another theory is that the Spartans' late start was nothing more than an attempt to cover the retreat of the rest of the army; it was a flawed plan, which succeeded against all odds because of the terrain and because the more heavily armed Greeks had an advantage over their opponents at close quarters.

Still others claim that, whatever Pausanias's plan might have been, it completely disintegrated in the chaos of that night's maneuver, leading to *ad hoc* improvisations on both sides and an outcome that surprised everyone involved.

Aftermath

The end of the battle saw the Greeks victorious, the Persian commander and numerous Persian and Mede nobles dead, countless other troops slain and the Persian camp taken over by the Greeks. The Persian threat had been completely eliminated.

The Greek commanders gave prizes of bravery to several combatants and divided the booty. They buried their dead along the road from Plataea to Megara and took a solemn oath that the city of Plataea would always remain free and respected by all. In turn, the

Plataeans undertook to look after the graves of the other Greeks and offer them sacrifices once a year. Visiting more than five centuries later, Plutarch witnessed these rites performed with great solemnity and respect. Then the Greeks established a new Pan-Hellenic festival, which they called 'Eleutheria' (freedom games) that would take place in Plataea every four years, like the Olympic ones.

The Greeks decided that the cities that had sided with the Persians should be punished. Thebes was the first – eleven days after the battle, Greek forces laid siege to it. Twenty days later, the Thebans surrendered, handing over the foremost collaborators. One of them managed to escape, while the rest were transported to the isthmus, where they were executed. The worse blow for the ancient enemy of Plataea was that the Boeotian League, of which it had been a leader, was disbanded.

Part of the Persian loot was converted into statues dedicated by the Greeks to the Temple of Zeus in Olympia and the Temple of Poseidon in the isthmus, in gratitude for their victory. However, the most significant offer was the golden tripod dedicated to the east of the Temple of Apollo in Delphi. The tripod was supported by a bronze column made up of three snakes, on whose bodies were carved the names of the thirty-one cities that formed the Greek alliance. The tripod survived centuries of warfare and other disasters until, in the 4th century CE, it was taken to Constantinople by the city's founder, Emperor Constantine the Great. The city's name may have been changed to Istanbul, but the tripod is still there; recently a copy was made and placed in the archaeological site of Delphi.

The Plataean refugees returned and rebuilt their city, spending the next years in peace and relative prosperity, organizing the Eleutheria Games. However, the oaths of the Greeks were not enough to protect them during the Peloponnesian War which followed, a brutal civil conflict which pitted the Greek cities against each other, shattering old oaths, alliances and promises. In 429 BCE, exactly fifty years after the battle with the Persians, Plataea was besieged, this time by the Spartans. Most of the Plataeans once again became refugees in foreign lands, while their city was destroyed.

It is good that Arimnestos did not live to see this second destruction of his beloved city.

Author's Note

Here we are, at the end of the Long War series. I confess I hope that it is not the end, and that you will rise up and demand from Orion that I write a sequel about the voyage of our protagonists to Africa. Someone did it; the coast of Kenya was known to Greek navigators by Alexander's time. But that's another story.

I am sad to be at the end, but also exhilarated. In six books, I have told something of one of the greatest foundation stories of the west; I have mostly followed in the footsteps of Herodotos, and in fact, in almost every case, he has been my principle text and my guide. I have read dozens of secondary sources, and I have perused other contemporary Greek sources, like plays and poems by Aeschylus and Simonides. I have been to almost every location in these books; in some cases, I have stopped writing to make a specific trip.

And the place I have visited more than any other is the battlefield of Plataea. I think that Plataea is the most interesting battle of antiquity; perhaps the most complicated. The terrain is very difficult to describe, and so complex that even on the ground, or standing on the citadel of Ancient Plataea, it is never possible to see the battlefield in a single *coup d'oeil*. In many ways it reminds me of Gettysburg; which may stem from the relative movement of the two armies, or may stem more historiographically from the reality that they are the two battlefields on which I've spent the most time. (Saratoga takes a close third). But both Meade and Lee at Gettysburg had maps, and professional scouts, and a good deal of the science of measurement to enable their strategy; Pausanias and Mardonius had no maps, no charts, and nothing like military engineers or cartographers or surveyors to support their armies. I suspect that they commanded only what they could see, and that, by a process of ironies beloved of Greek tragedians, led Pausanias and Mardonius to face each other …

in what may not even have been the pivotal part of the action. I will assert here that on my second visit to the battlefield, while trying to make sense of a nineteenth century survey of the battlefield and make it work with Herodotos, it first occurred to me that the Greeks themselves might have had little or no idea how or why they won.

By the time I was done looking at the battlefield the third time, I was pretty sure that the Greeks didn't 'win.' The Persians merely 'lost.' I am now reasonably sure that when the Greek retreat collapsed on the last day, Mardonius had victory in his grasp. He'd been subtle and patient, and his excellent troops and solid planning were, in the end, simply not enough to overcome the sheer stubbornness of the Spartans and Athenians. That's the only way I can make sense of the battle, and I imagine that Persian officers for years afterwards lay on couches at Persepolis and shook their heads and wondered how on earth they'd lost to the Greeks. Honest Greeks might well have asked the same.

And my answer is that throughout history, invaders usually lose and the 'home team' usually wins. This is such a reliable indicator of military result that we might be permitted to wonder why anyone ever invades anyone. Plataea might well have come down to the simple hard reality that the Greeks were fighting for their homes. Or that may be a great simplification; certainly my portrayal of the League as wracked with dissension and distrust is not a fabrication.

I'll also note that I have fabricated a tale of a near battle by Megara. But if you read Herodotos and consider the events of the campaign, it looks very likely; look at the passes into Boeotia, and ask why Mardonius, headed for the isthmus, suddenly changes direction and falls back on his logistics head at Thebes. There are other explanations, but I think mine matches the sources and recent archaeology.

And the Battle of Mycale; Herodotos and other period sources allege it happened the same day as Plataea, but Herodotos himself suggests that this allegation is false. I assume it is; it made for a better story my way, and allowed some closure to the veterans of Lades, but it is also the way I imagine it happening. From the point of view of the Great King's hoplite levies from Samos and Lesvos, the moment they knew that Plataea was a great Greek victory, everything changed. Of course they would change sides, and of course the Persians would disintegrate, or so I see it.

And in the end we have a great symposium, with men and women on couches together. Of course, we know this happened in Etrusca;

there is serious resistance to the notion that it ever happened in Greece. I will tell you that I think that has more to do with modern attitudes than with the facts of ancient Greece. There are new articles out there on Greek art suggesting that all those women on couches might not be courtesans. What a surprise! Sometimes Greek men had dinner with their wives!

And I like ending with a party, not a battle. Just imagine what it was like, in the years after Plataea. Imagine what it must have felt like for the veterans of both genders; for what they had endured, and what they had accomplished. I think the next fifty years testifies to that; one of the greatest bursts of creativity in human history. I recommend that you read the last section with a glass of wine in hand; pour a libation for the gods, and perhaps for the heroized dead, and then drink the rest while you come to the end. For you, too have had a long journey, and I appreciate that you stayed to the end.

I'll close with thanks to my re-enacting friends, without whom these books would not have half the life they have. I have learned so much from re-enacting the period and not just reading about it that I've changed the way I write books. I owe an immense debt to all the men and women I've met and learned from, in France and Greece and the UK and Canada and the USA and Spain and Bulgaria and Italy. But most of all, I owe a debt to Giannis Kadaglou, to whom this book is dedicated, and his wife Smaro. They have entertained me, hosted me, visited, and talked; Giannis and I have walked Plataea three times, and talked a hundred times or more, live, on skype, endlessly, about helmets and about ridges and farming and anything that mattered. Without Giannis, these books would be much less alive, and I thank him.

And finally the Parthenon. I find it the most inspiring artifact in the world. These books can't include the Parthenon, because it wasn't built for many years (by Perikles, of course) but I look at it whenever I can, from the roof of the Herodion on one side of the Acropolis or from the Attalos on the other side (both great hotels in their own way). We stayed there in the days after we re-enacted the Battles of Marathon in 2011 and 2015, and I will not soon forget the sights and sounds of those trips, many of which are in this book. In the mean time, on to Marathon 2019, and the re-enactments of Salamis and Plataea in 2020 and 2021!

If you'd like to see a few of these places for yourself, look at the Pen and Sword tour website at https://1phokion.wordpress.com/ or just visit my author page on Facebook or my author site at www.hippeis.com and look in the 'agora'. I enjoy answering reader questions and I usually respond, and I almost never bite. And if you've always wanted to be a hoplite – or a Persian, or a Scythian, or a slave, or almost any ancient person – well, try re-enacting. Contact me, or visit our http://www.boarstooth.net/ website, and we'll find you a group. Maybe even ours!

Acknowledgements

Each year, since I was married in 2004, my wife and I have gone to Greece. It is from all these trips – and my oft-quoted brush with Greece and Troy and Smyrna and Ephesus from the back seat of an S-3 Viking in 1990 – that my love, even passion, for Greece, ancient and modern, was born. In this, the sixth book of my 'Long War' series, I tackle perhaps the best-known battle in the whole of the Persian Wars – indeed, one of the best-known battles of the ancient world. What I have written is heavily influenced by my trips to Greece; by days at Plataea with Giannis and many other friends from the Pen and Sword, in Piraeus and by many views out the window of an airplane taking off from Athens or landing there. My wife Sarah is always kind enough to let me have the window seat if we're passing over the Bay of Salamis. My daughter Beatrice is not always so forgiving!

Rage of Ares is a different book and I am a humbler man and probably a better historian than when I wrote the first books of this series. First and foremost, I have to acknowledge the contribution of my friends and compatriots like Nicolas Cioran, who cheerfully discussed Plataea's odd status, made kit, and continues to debate issues of leadership and character. My good friend Aurora Simmons, an expert martial artist and a superb craftsperson with almost any media (but a jeweler by profession) has quite possibly had more input on my understanding of ancient Greece than any other person besides Giannis Kadoglou, whose nearly encyclopedic knowledge of the ancient Greek world of hoplites and oarsmen continued to support me to the last page, with vase paintings produced on short notice of wedding scenes, and his own superb armour, and to whom this book is dedicated! My trainer and constant sparring partner John

Beck deserves my thanks – both for a vastly improved physique, and for helping to give me a sense of what real training for a life of violence might have been like in the ancient world; as does my massage therapist Susan Bessonette, because at age fifty-three, it is not always easy to pretend to be twenty-six in a fight. And while we're talking about fighting – Chris Duffy, perhaps the best modern martial artist I know, deserves thanks for many sparring bouts whose more exciting bits find their way into these pages, while a number of instructors – Guy Windsor, Sean Hayes, Greg Mele, Jason Smith and Sensei Robert Zimmermann have helped shape my appreciation of the combat techniques, armed and unarmed, that were available in the ancient world.

Among professional historians, I was assisted by Paul McDonnell-Staff and Paul Bardunias, by the entire brother and sisterhood of 'Roman Army talk' and the web community there, and by the staff of the Royal Ontario Museum (who possess and cheerfully shared the only surviving helmet attributable to the Battle of Marathon) as well as the staff of the Antikenmuseum Basel und Sammlung Ludwig who possess the best-preserved ancient *aspis* and provided me with superb photos to use in recreating it. I also received help from the library staff of the University of Toronto, where, when I'm rich enough, I'm a student, and from Toronto's superb Metro Reference Library. I must add to that the University of Rochester Library (my alma mater) and the Art Gallery of Ontario. Every novelist needs to live in a city where universal access to a digital library such as JSTOR is free and on his library card. Finally, the staff of the Walters Art Gallery in Baltimore, Maryland – just across the street from my mother's former apartment, conveniently – were cheerful and helpful, even when I came back to look at the same helmet for the sixth time. A helmet which I now own a faithful copy of, thanks to Manning Imperial! And now I add, at the very end, the superbly talented Jeffrey Hildebrandt of Royal Oak Armoury, Canada, who made my breastplate, and Giannis's, in time for Marathon 2015.

Excellent as professional historians are – and my version of the Persian Wars owes a great deal to many of them, not least Hans Van Wees and Victor Davis Hanson and Josho Brouwers – my greatest praise and thanks have to go to the amateur historians we call re-enactors. Giannis Kadoglou of Alexandroupolis has now spent many, many hours with me, tramping about Greece, visiting ruins from the Archaic to as recent as the Great War, from Plataea to Thrake, charming my daughter and my wife while translating everything in sight and being as delighted with the ancient town of Plataea as I was myself. I met him on a Roman army talk, and this would be a very different book without his passion for the subject and relentless desire to correct my errors, and that of his wife Smaro, whose interest in all these things and whose willingness to wear ancient Greek clothes and debate them in the New Acropolis Museum kept me focused on the details that make for good writing. We are all now fast friends and I suspect my views on much of the Greek world reflect theirs more than any other. Alongside Giannis go my other Greek friends, especially George Kafetsis and his partner Xsenia, who have theorized over wine, beer and ouzo, paced battlefields and shot bows.

But Giannis and Smaro and Giorgos and Xsenia are hardly alone, and there is – literally – a phalanx of Greek re-enactors who continue to help me. (We are recreating the world around the Battle of Marathon with about one hundred re-enactors in 2019, at Marathon – and then, as I've said elsewhere, 2020 and 2021 for the great anniversaries of Plataea and Thermopylae and Salamis and so on. Here in my part of North America, we have a group called the Plataeans – this is, trust me, not a coincidence – and we work hard on recreating the very time period and city-state so prominent in these books, from weapons, armour and combat to cooking crafts, and dance. If the reader feels that these books put flesh and blood on the bare bone of history – in as much as I've succeeded in doing that – it is due to the efforts of the men and women who re-enact with me and show me every time we're together all the things I haven't thought of – who do their own research, their own kit-building, and their own training. Thanks to all of you, Plataeans. And to all the other ancient Greek re-enactors who helped me find things, make things or build things. I'd like to mention (especially) Craig and his partner Cherilyn at Manning Imperial in Australia, and Jeffrey Hildebrandt here in Ontario, who just made me a superb new thorax for Marathon 2015.

Thanks are also due to the people of Lesvos and Athens and Plataea and Marathonas – I can't name all of you, but I was entertained, informed, and supported constantly in three trips to Greece, and the person who I can name is Aliki Hamosfakidou of Dolphin Hellas Travel for her care, interest and support through many hundreds of e-mails and some meetings. Alexandros Somoglou of Marathonas deserves special thanks, and if you ever find yourself in Molyvos

(Ancient Mythemna) on Lesvos, please visit the Sea Horse Hotel, where Dmitri and Stela run my favourite hotel in the world. Also in Greece I've received support and help from professional archaeologists and academics, and I wish particularly to thank Pauline Marneri and her son John Zervas for his translation support and of course Aristotle Koskinas and Nikos Lanser of Greece; both helped with my last Pen and Sword tour, and Aristotle wrote the Historical Note on Plataea that accompanies this volume. They are professional historians.

Bill Massey, my editor at Orion, has done his usual excellent job and it is a better book for his work. Oh, and he found a lot of other errors, too, but let's not mention them. I have had a few editors. Working with Bill is wonderful. Come on, authors – how many of you get to say that? Steve O'Gorman was the truly excellent copy-editor on this volume. We won't even talk about what he caught.

My agent, Shelley Power, contributed more directly to this book than to any other – first, as an agent, in all the usual ways, and then later, coming to Greece and taking part in all of the excitement of seeing Lesbos and Athens and taking us several times to Archaeon Gefsis, a restaurant that attempts to take the customer back to the ancient world. And then helping to plan and run the 2500th Battle of Marathon, and again the 2505th) and continuing as a re-enactor of ancient Greece. Thanks for everything, Shelley, and the agenting not the least!

Christine Szego and the staff and management of my local book-store, Bakka-Phoenix of Toronto also deserve my thanks, as I tend to walk in and spout fifteen minutes worth of plot, character, dialogue, or just news – writing can be lonely work, and it is good to have people to talk to. And they throw a great book launch.

It is odd, isn't it, that authors always save their families for last? Really, it's the done thing. So I'll do it, too, even though my wife should get mentioned at every stage – after all, she's a re-enactor, too, she had useful observations on all kinds of things we both read (Athenian textiles is what really comes to mind, though) and in addition, more than even Ms Szego, Sarah has to listen to the endless enthusiasms I develop about history while writing (the words 'Did you know' probably cause her more horror than anything else you can think of). My daughter, Beatrice, is also a re-enactor, and her ability to portray the life of a real child is amazing. My father, Kenneth Cameron, taught me most of what I know about writing, and continues to provide excellent advice – and to listen to my complaints about the process which may be the greater service. Oh, and as we enter into a world where authors do their own marketing, my wife, who knows a thing or two, is my constant guide and sounding board there. And she is also a veteran re-enactor and a brilliant researcher and questioner, and the best partner a person could ask for.

Having said all that, it's hard to say what exactly I can lay claim to, if you like this book. I had a great deal of help, and I appreciate it. Thanks. And when you find mis-spelled words, sailing directions reversed, and historical errors – why, then you'll know that I, too, had something to add. Because all the errors are solely mine.

Let me add, here at the last word … this was incredibly fun. Thanks for reading.

Toronto, July 2016

About the Author

Christian Cameron is a writer and military historian. He is a veteran of the United States Navy, where he served as both an aviator and an intelligence officer. He lives in Toronto where he is currently writing his next novel while working on a Masters in Classics.